STAR TREK™
PROMETHEUS

FIRE WITH FIRE

Also available from Titan Books

Star Trek Prometheus:
The Root of All Rage (May 2018)
In the Heart of Chaos (November 2018)

STAR TREK™
PROMETHEUS

FIRE WITH FIRE

BERND PERPLIES   CHRISTIAN HUMBERG

Based on *Star Trek* and *Star Trek: The Next Generation* created
by Gene Roddenberry, *Star Trek: Deep Space Nine* created by
Rick Berman & Michael Piller, *Star Trek: Voyager* created by
Rick Berman & Michael Piller & Jeri Taylor

TITAN BOOKS

Star Trek Prometheus: Fire with Fire
Print edition ISBN: 9781785656491
E-book edition ISBN: 9781785656507

Published by Titan Books
A division of Titan Publishing Group Ltd
144 Southwark Street, London SE1 0UP

First edition: November 2017
1 3 5 7 9 10 8 6 4 2

A CIP catalogue record for this title is available from the British Library.

Printed and bound in the United States.

Did you enjoy this book?
We love to hear from our readers. Please email us at readerfeedback@
titanemail.com or write to us at Reader Feedback at the above address.

To receive advance information, news, competitions, and exclusive offers
online, please sign up for the Titan newsletter on our website
www.titanbooks.com

To all fans worldwide,
you have kept *Star Trek* alive... since 1966

PROLOGUE
STARDATE 1966.9

U.S.S. *Valiant*, exploring the Lembatta Cluster

Space, the final frontier.

The universe was formed almost fourteen billion years ago from a single point, expanding to a diameter of more than ninety billion light years. The Milky Way, home galaxy of the United Federation of Planets, is but one of the tiny, bright specks within this black void.

The Federation was formed in 2161, a union of peace-loving races that had explored a tiny fraction of the Alpha and Beta Quadrants during the century since its founding. Still, every passing day starships and their crews pushed the boundaries further into uncharted territories on a mission to seek out new life and new civilizations, to boldly go where no one has gone before.

One such ship was the *Constitution*-class cruiser, the U.S.S. *Valiant*. She hadn't advanced to the outer frontiers of known space yet. Much to her newly promoted captain's dismay, the *Valiant* had been assigned the task of charting and cataloging the discoveries of others.

The crew members under the command of Science Officer Linda Nozawa eagerly fulfilled their duties, but Captain Jeremy Haden found that this journey did not live up to the expectations he had harbored regarding his first assignment after his promotion to command of a starship. His hope was that they would face a greater challenge once they had finished their current charting expedition in about three weeks' time.

In the meantime, he gratefully welcomed any distraction—such as the transmission from an old friend from Starfleet Academy that they had received as part of their latest data package from Starfleet Command.

Following the end of his shift, Haden returned to his cabin, dimmed the lights, and poured himself a glass of Saurian brandy. Raising his glass, he inserted the red data chip his communications officer had provided into the desk's computer console.

The display flickered to life, showing the Federation's emblem—white stars surrounded by stylized laurel branches before a blue backdrop. Then the image shifted to that of a human the same age as Haden, clad in the gold uniform of command.

"Jim Kirk," Haden said in a low voice.

James Tiberius Kirk, captain of the U.S.S. *Enterprise*, smiled, as if he'd heard Haden say his name, though of course it was a prerecorded message. Both the *Enterprise* and the *Valiant* were too far out in deep space for direct communications—with each other, or with Starfleet Command.

Haden had always envied Kirk's smile. Sometimes it seemed boyish and innocent; sometimes it was suave and charming. Haden had felt instantly comfortable in Kirk's presence when they had met during a party on Baker Beach in San Francisco as cadets.

Today, his smile expressed sincere delight and appreciation, along with a certain mischievous twinkle in his eyes. *"I heard congratulations are in order, Jerry. Captain of the* Valiant. *You really deserve that promotion. Now the easy life in the backseat is over and you get to be responsible for your own starship. Headquarters will keep you inundated with paperwork, and you'll have to be wary of any Klingon who might get the bright idea to pick a fight."* The smile fell, and his expression turned grave. *"Most important, though, is that you will be responsible for the lives of four hundred men and women."* Kirk's smile came back. *"Still, it does have its merits. You get your own yeoman—which will help with that paperwork that I mentioned—and you can lead the landing parties."* Kirk raised his left arm, showing off the gold bars on the cuff that indicated his rank. *"These three gold stripes make an impression anywhere in the galaxy."*

Haden looked down at his own cuff, where he had his own matching rank insignia.

"Still, don't expect too much of the first few months as captain. Starfleet has a habit of sending their new commanders on journeys that Zefram Cochrane definitely did not have in mind when he said we should boldly go where no man has gone before." Tilting his head Kirk chuckled and looked at his friend. *"To give you an idea, when Admiral Noguchi appointed me captain of the* Enterprise, *my assignment was to ferry a bunch of vaudevillians through the sector! Maybe you've heard of the Warp-Speed Classic Vaudeville Company of Amelia Lukarian."* He shook his head. *"You really don't want to know what a starship looks like when you have all sorts of artists and carnies running around. Anyway, I sincerely hope your first mission is different... more meaningful and—"*

A chime interrupted the message, followed by the voice of Haden's friend, first officer, and helmsman, Mark Edwards. *"Bridge to Captain."*

Placing his glass on the desk, Haden stopped the replay, and pressed a button on the table's surface. "This is Haden. What's up?"

"Captain, you might want to come to the bridge. Lieutenant Nozawa has discovered something strange."

"On my way." Haden's brandy and Kirk's message were quickly forgotten as he rose to his feet and hurried out of his quarters and into a waiting turbolift.

Where Kirk had had a vaudeville company for his first mission, Haden at least had something a bit closer to Starfleet's mission statement, as established by Cochrane, the inventor of warp drive, whom Kirk had quoted. They were cataloguing the Lembatta Cluster, an agglomeration of twenty-four ancient giant stars. Long-range sensors by other starships had found no signs of life, and the nearest spacefaring nation, the Klingon Empire, had evinced no interest in the region. What few civilizations they had encountered on the periphery of this cluster had yet to achieve space travel, and so contact with them was off-limits per Starfleet's Prime Directive.

The turbolift soon arrived at the *Valiant*'s command center. When the door hissed open, Edwards leapt out of the captain's chair to make room for his superior officer. Haden settled into his seat while Edwards relieved the ensign at the helm.

Haden looked at the viewscreen in front of the navigation console. The twenty-four celestial bodies in the cluster menacingly illuminated the nebulae that floated in space between the stars with a red glow. The red glowing dots twinkling from the viewscreen reminded Haden of the eyes of demons from some of Earth's mythologies. Adding to this impression was the fact that the *Valiant*'s sensors were frequently jammed by the red giants' radiation, leading to ghost readings. It was as if something was lurking out there that was hiding from their prying eyes.

Looking over his left shoulder at the science station, the

captain asked, "What have we found, Lieutenant?"

The petite Japanese woman dressed in the science division's blue uniform turned to face him. Smooth black hair framed her slender face that was slightly reddened with excitement. "Captain, I'm picking up a very strange radiation in Star System LC-13, which is the system directly ahead of us."

"Define 'strange' please, Lieutenant."

Nozawa shook her head. "I've never seen anything like it. It doesn't fit anywhere into the electromagnetic wave spectrum. The characteristics don't add up. I could list all the contradictions, but simply put, it's an unfamiliar energy form that doesn't match any of the physical parameters of the Lembatta Cluster."

"Are you trying to tell me that we have discovered something extraordinary?"

The scientist nodded. "I'm sure of it."

Grinning, the captain turned back to face the viewscreen. He glanced at the navigator, Peter Schwartz, who sat to Edwards's right. "Mr. Schwartz, plot a course to LC-13. Mr. Edwards, warp seven."

"Aye, Captain," both men said in unison.

"ETA?" asked Haden.

"Forty minutes," answered Schwartz.

"Very good. Drop out of warp when we reach the edge of the system, and then we all keep our eyes peeled. I want to know what caused that radiation, whether it's natural or a hostile ship."

"It's unlikely to be a ship," said Nozawa. "No propulsion system is able to emit an energy signature so strong that we could pick it up across this distance, particularly considering the background radiation in the cluster."

No known *propulsion system*, Haden thought with an

almost irrational thrill of anticipation while leaning back and crossing his legs. Aloud, he said, "We should still be careful. You never know what's waiting for us out there."

An hour later the *Valiant* assumed a standard orbit around the second planet of System LC-13, which Nozawa had pinpointed as the origin of the strange energy readings. LC-13-II was a reddish-gray planet, slightly smaller than Earth but with greater mass.

"That's weird," said Nozawa. She stood stooped over the science console, the blue glow of the sensor hood bathing her face.

Haden rose from his command chair and joined her. "What did you find out?"

Nozawa looked up. "LC-13-II is a remarkably friendly environment. There's water, vegetation, and an atmosphere that's breathable, at least for a short period of time. Still, I can't find any higher life forms down there. It's possible that there are some lower life forms in the oceans—the background radiation makes it impossible to sense the depths with any clarity. But considering the age of the primary star and the conditions on the planet's surface, I would have expected to find at least basic forms of fauna to go with the flora."

"Is it possible that your strange radiation led to the extinction of all life?"

"Possible, I suppose, but unlikely. If the radiation had biotoxic effects we wouldn't find such lush vegetation on the planet's surface."

"Right," conceded the captain. "Very peculiar." Thoughtful, he stared at the screen, where the southern continent's jagged coastline slowly passed by. "Have you been able to locate the source of the radiation?"

Nozawa nodded. "It seems to originate on the southern continent, and it's increasing by the minute. We should be right above it any moment now."

"Magnify the radiation source on the main viewer, Mr. Schwartz."

"Zooming into area," the navigator said.

The coastline jolted closer and more details of the landscape became visible. Gray waves lapped against red rocks. Several kilometers inland, Haden saw something that appeared to be the edge of a forest. Amidst the olive green plants, stony structures rose.

Edwards pointed at the viewscreen. "Jeremy, *look* at that!"

"Magnify," Haden ordered. "Mark, keep us in a geostationary orbit."

"Aye, Captain."

The silhouettes of the structures grew bigger and more distinct. Haden turned to the science officer. "Any idea what this is, Lieutenant?"

Taking a step forward, Nozawa rested her hands on the red handrail that separated the rear consoles from the command center. "They look like the remains of an ancient city. So there must have been life on LC-13-II, a civilization even." Excitedly she turned to face Haden. "Sir, with your permission I'd like to inspect those more thoroughly. This might be a xenoarcheological find of epic proportions."

"What about the radiation? Is it dangerous for us?"

"The sensors show no indication of imminent danger, sir, as long as we keep our exposure short. I recommend only an hour on the surface, and then we beam back and rest for a day to make sure there are no ill effects."

"Good idea. We'll also take Doctor Bhahani along with

us… just in case." Haden turned to Edwards.

Edwards winced from the helm control console. "Oh, no, Jeremy, don't do that to me."

Haden grinned. "I'm sorry, Mark, but someone has to run the ship, and when the captain is away that has to be the first officer. But I promise you, I'll bring you a pretty stone from the surface as a gift."

The blond man grimaced. "Well, thanks a bunch."

Several minutes later, five figures materialized on the planet's surface: Haden, Nozawa, the chief medical officer, Doctor Bhahani, and two security guards, Franco and Clarke. The captain and both security men drew their phasers, while Nozawa and Bhahani raised their tricorders. Haden scanned the area with his eyes while his science and medical officers took their readings.

They stood on the edge of a clearing within a forest consisting of tall, high trees with dark, fernlike fronds. Before them spread the ruins of a complex built with anthracite stones that reminded Haden of an Aztec temple. Most of the structures were compact, except for the central building, which had been erected in tiers and stretched up to the red and cloudless sky.

"Look at that," Haden murmured. "The ruins of a long-lost civilization."

Slowly, the landing party made their way toward the stepped pyramid.

Nozawa pointed her tricorder toward the large structure. "The source of the radiation is directly in front of us."

"Are you sure?"

"Positive."

Haden gazed at the complex. Alien symbols had been carved into the heavy stone blocks that formed the foundation. Curiously, while all the other buildings had been covered by vines and a violet ivy, the central structure was not overgrown, its surface untarnished.

The captain looked at Bhahani. "Doctor, what's your take on this?"

The medical officer shrugged. "There's only one thing I can tell you with any degree of certainty: There are absolutely no higher life forms on LC-13-II. My readings only detect several insect species living in the trees and bushes. Doctor Denning will be very interested in them, for sure."

Haden nodded. "We will inform the xenozoological department about the creepy crawlies once we return to the ship. What about the radiation?"

"It's too strong for my instruments, Captain. I recommend not exposing ourselves to it for too long."

Frowning, Haden said, "You're not helping very much, Doc."

"I'm doing as much as I can, sir," Bhahani said, "but we are faced with something completely new."

"We're Starfleet officers—we're always faced with something completely new." The captain was unable to explain why, but the doctor's response left him annoyed... much more annoyed than would be appropriate. *Go easy,* he reprimanded himself. "Well, let's take a closer look at this structure."

They walked across shattered stone slabs that probably had been used to pave the walkways between the smaller buildings. Haden wondered if it had been a temple, built to worship some god or other, or perhaps some kind of tomb.

"I don't like this, sir." Franco's eyes darted around nervously.

"What are you talking about, Franco?" asked Haden.

"I get the feeling that there's something or someone in those ruins. We're being watched."

"Nozawa?" Haden directed his gaze at the science officer. She took a sweep with her tricorder and made some adjustments. "Nothing, sir. The only higher life forms around here are us."

"It could be something our tricorders are unable to recognize," Franco said.

"What gives you the idea that someone is around here?" asked Haden.

"I have no idea, sir. I just know it."

"With all due respect to your gut feeling, that's nonsense," Nozawa snapped. "There isn't anyone around here."

Franco's face darkened. "You rely too much on your instruments, Lieutenant, and not enough on your instincts."

"We are not wild animals, Ensign," Nozawa said irritably. "We don't need to be guided by our instincts when we have data."

"That's enough! Get a grip, both of you!"

Franco glowered at him. "Yes, sir." The ensign was overanxious, not the best trait in a security guard, and he seemed inappropriately aggressive.

Then again, so was Nozawa—and Haden himself. It was wildly out of character for both of them, and he wondered if the red sky caused some kind of aggression among them.

Trying to keep a placating tone of voice, Haden said, "Just keep your eyes peeled. But keep any speculations about invisible enemies to yourself until you can give me something definite besides your gut."

The man with the red shirt nodded. "Understood, sir."

By now they had circled half of the looming stepped

structure, and were approaching the northern face of the building. Close up they realized that the rock wasn't completely dark. Thin veins of glittering ore ran through it.

"Can you tell me what this is?" Haden asked Nozawa.

She pointed her tricorder toward the inclusions. "I'm sorry, sir, the ore is not listed in the database. But it's blocking my tricorder's readings. I can't read anything inside it." Frowning, she swept the instrument from side to side, gave up, and lowered it, frustrated.

Haden shook his head. Why did he have to be surrounded by incompetents? A scared security guard, a science officer unable to take a simple reading, a doctor unable to answer a simple question…

He growled under his breath. "I should have come here *alone*."

"Captain!" shouted Clarke when they turned the corner. He pointed ahead with his free hand, phaser still gripped in the other.

At the base of the tiered building was a portal, not far ahead of them.

"I see it," Haden replied, nodding.

The portal was about four meters high and three meters wide, with the entrance barricaded by a stone slab. When they approached it, the captain realized that the slab, as well as the stone blocks around it, was covered with symbols that looked very familiar.

Pointing at the symbols, Haden asked, "Is that the Lembatta Cluster?"

Nozawa tilted her head. "It's possible. Many of the early cultures adorned their temples with constellations. Maybe this is an especially prominent star constellation in these parts."

"In any case, the question is how to open this portal. It looks unscathed, so presumably the secrets of this temple should still be in mint condition, even after all these years."

Nozawa hesitated. "Sir, I'm not sure we should advance into the building."

Haden turned to her and almost growled. "And why not? Are you scared?"

"No, Captain, but the radiation values inside these walls might be significantly higher."

"So? Do you feel any effects yet?"

Nozawa blinked. "No, sir."

"What about you?" Haden turned to Bhahani.

The doctor shook his head, looking thoughtful. "What about you?"

"How do you mean?"

"You appear to be somewhat... short-tempered, Captain. Are you all right?"

Haden made a dismissive gesture with his hand. "You're imagining things, Doctor. I'm fine."

Or did Bhahani have a point? Was he acting out of character?

Nonsense, thought Haden. *The quack doesn't know what he's talking about!*

The captain regarded his security guard. "And you, Franco? Do you also have reservations? A gut feeling or some such?"

Franco glowered at him. That was the second time he'd done so, and Haden was determined to report Franco's insubordinate behavior when they returned to the ship. "Something is there, Captain. Something is lurking in there. Something dangerous. I can *feel* it."

Haden threw his arms in the air. His people really annoyed

the hell out of him all of a sudden. "I don't believe it! What has gotten into all of you? What happened to the pioneering spirit of Starfleet? Didn't they tell us at the Academy time and again that we're supposed to explore strange new worlds? That's exactly what we're doing here!" Looking at the other security officer he asked, "Clarke, can I at least count on you?"

"Aye, sir," the stocky guard said. "Always. Let's kick a few heads in, sir."

"Well, a stone door will do for now. Come on, help me get this thing open."

"With pleasure, Captain."

Both men holstered their phasers and started inspecting the slab.

After brief hesitation, Nozawa raised her tricorder again. "I don't understand this."

Haden looked up from the slab. "What is it *now*, Lieutenant?" Haden demanded to know.

"This portal doesn't seem to have any kind of opening mechanism. It's just a huge stone slab that fits perfectly into the frame of the entrance."

"What's so remarkable about that?" asked Franco. "On Earth, every door fits perfectly into its frame. That's how it's supposed to be."

Nozawa looked at him derisively. "Once again, you haven't got a clue what you're talking about, Ensign. Judging by the buildings, a culture used to live on LC-13-II that's roughly equivalent to the Mayans or Aztecs. The buildings have been erected skillfully, but not with the technical precision that we're accustomed to. This slab in the portal has been fitted with the accuracy of approximately one millimeter—although the stone weighs several tons at least. I have no idea how the natives might have achieved that."

"We can worry about that later," Haden grumbled. "Now, I want to find out what's hidden inside this thing."

"But we haven't found an opening," Nozawa said.

Haden drew his phaser again. "We'll make our own, then."

The science officer's eyes widened. "Are you out of your mind? That's an irreplaceable scientific find!"

"Lieutenant, you're forgetting yourself!" the captain snapped at her. "What's more, you're talking nonsense. This is nothing but a door. The real treasures are behind it. Clarke." He nodded toward the security guard who also drew his weapon.

"No!" cried Nozawa.

Haden ignored her. "Fire on my mark." He *needed* to find out just what secrets LC-13-II was hiding. Since beaming down, it had become incredibly important to him.

Nozawa grabbed his arm, but Haden shook her off so violently that she staggered backward and fell over.

"Captain!" Bhahani cried disgustedly, and he ran to treat Nozawa.

"Fire!" ordered Haden.

The shimmering beams swept across the heavy stone slab. At first, the weapons had no effect on the portal. But slowly, the ore veins started to glow. Shortly thereafter, the heavy plate shattered with a deafening noise.

A strong breeze blew toward them, pushing Haden two steps backward. Red dust billowed out of the opening, enveloping all of them.

Nozawa leapt to her feet, pushing Bhahani aside. "You lunatic! What have you done? That might have been the most important discovery in the history of space travel. And you simply blasted it to dust with your phasers!" She advanced on her captain, suddenly and inexplicably carrying a club, ready to bludgeon Haden with it.

"Hey, not another step." Clarke stepped in front of Nozawa.

Without hesitation, Nozawa struck at him.

Clarke easily blocked the strike and then placed a well-aimed uppercut on the woman's chin. She staggered backward into Bhahani's arms.

"Are you out of your mind?" the doctor barked at Clarke.

"No one attacks the captain," the security guard retorted, "unless they want a smack in the face."

Suddenly, Franco started gesturing frantically. "Over there! It's coming! I knew it! We're under attack!" He started firing his phaser aimlessly. Clarke cried out in pain as his arm took a scorching hit.

Haden threw himself on the ground. *What a loser.* The thought pounded in his mind. *He deserves to die.* Furiously, he raised his revolver. *Revolver?* He briefly succumbed to confusion as to how his phaser had been replaced with an antique, but a second later it didn't matter. A weapon was a weapon.

He heard the report of the six-shooter, felt the kick in his hands as the bullets flew and struck Franco in the back.

Screaming, Nozawa freed herself from Bhahani's grip and ran toward Haden. A knife flashed in her hand. Before he could fight her off she stabbed the blade into his shoulder.

Haden gasped in agony.

"Have you all lost your minds?" the chief medical officer screamed shrilly. "Stop it, all of you, or I will have to take you all out for your own safety." With trembling hands, he struggled to adjust his phaser.

Nozawa knelt atop Haden, but he knocked her out with

a forceful blow to her temple. Growling, he flung her away. From the corner of his eye he noticed Franco and Clarke wrestling each other. Both had ripped tunics, and their faces were red and covered in sweat.

What the hell is going on here? A brief moment of clarity washed over Haden, and for just a moment, he realized how terribly wrong this all was. Was the radiation responsible for them acting like idiots? If so, why had Bhahani and Nozawa not warned him?

They want me to meet my doom! Once again, burning rage overwhelmed him. The world sank into a red mist of blood and violence. He simply wanted to kill everyone, all those who had destroyed his dream of becoming a famous Starfleet captain. Screaming, he raised the machete that was now in his palm over his head, lunging toward Bhahani.

In the sky a noise like the rush from an ocean began, and then a huge flaming body passed over their heads. Haden's eyes widened as he looked up. The others also interrupted their fighting and stared up to the skies.

It was the *Valiant* plummeting toward her doom, enveloped in a swirling, glowing mist. With a deafening thunderous roar the gigantic starship impacted on the surface, sending shockwaves across the planet's crust as if the hammer of a seething god had struck the hapless world. The ground burst open, trees snapped like matches, and the city in ruins collapsed.

What have we done? shot through Haden's mind as he was thrown into the dust. Searing heat consumed the air in his lungs while the building's heavy stone blocks dropped around the landing party. Something smashed into him with unimaginable force, and then he didn't feel anything anymore.

1

OCTOBER 29, 2385

Somewhere in the border region between the
United Federation of Planets and the Tzenkethi Coalition

A small mercenary ship floated in orbit of a gas giant, bright flashes of energy flaring through the upper atmosphere. Shrouds of mist escaped soundlessly into space, enveloping the ship's hull that vaguely resembled a mandible-bearing insect skull. The star system to which the gas giant belonged was not on any common travel routes, and was devoid of life. With its cold blue sun and six lethal worlds surrounded by a dense asteroid belt, it was not only inhospitable, but a navigational nightmare—and thus the perfect place for a clandestine meeting.

Vol-Ban paced through the ship's cockpit. "So? Where are your ever-so-trustworthy clients? I don't see anyone anywhere around here!"

Looking up from the displays of his bridge console, Rah-Ban sighed deeply, and turned around to face his twin brother. "That's because, unlike you, they aren't complete idiots. They are somewhere around here. But they'll only show if they deem it right."

Vol-Ban, pressing his fists into his waist, snorted. "Deem it right, my backside! Did they want us here or was it the other way around?"

"You're too impatient, brother. It's bad for business." As he so often did when frustration overwhelmed him, Rah-Ban reached up to massage his bony forehead that was divided into two hemispheres by a small strip of black hair.

The mercenaries were Miradorn, and they valued family bonds more than most species. He would go through hell and high water for Vol-Ban, and his brother would do likewise for him. There was no business endeavor that the twin mercenaries wouldn't tackle together.

Still, on certain days Rah-Ban wished he could jettison his partner out of the first available airlock in order to work in peace in future.

They had been doing business alongside each other for several years now, ever since winning their ship in a game at a gambling den in Sector 221-G. Traveling through space, they offered their weapons, their time, and their considerable contacts to the underworlds of various regions to anyone and everyone who wanted jobs of a dubious nature done and who were able to pay the required money. They were fast, discreet, ruthless, and didn't ask questions. They stood by the quality of their work, which was superlative.

Therefore, Rah-Ban had no intention of asking the Tzenkethi any questions. He would listen to the task they wished to hire the twins for—probably some kind of smuggling trip into Federation territory; relations between the local big powers had been rather frosty since the Typhon Pact formed—they would name their price, and negotiations would continue. Things could be pretty simple if you allowed them to be.

"Impatient?" Vol-Ban knew as much about "simple" as he knew about "waiting." "I'm not impatient. I just don't like the orange-skinned warmongers asking us to come to the middle of nowhere without showing their faces. Getting here was anything but easy. This is no way to treat professionals! Let's turn around. I don't even want their money anymore."

Rah-Ban swallowed half a dozen sharp replies. There was no point in upbraiding Vol-Ban for his almost woefully shallow definition of the Tzenkethi; they were neither warmongers nor did all of them sport orange skin. At the same time, defending the meeting point wouldn't do any good as it had been Vol-Ban himself who had navigated their ship, the *Vel-Tekk*, expertly through the treacherous star system to this destination.

Instead, he simply stated, "We're staying put."

Vol-Ban lowered his fists, his shoulders sagging. "Why?"

"Because we really need this job."

"If there *is* a job!" replied his brother, turning away from the monitor to face his brother. "Can't you see it? They are scr—"

Rah-Ban's console interrupted Vol-Ban with a shrill alarm. "A ship!" he said after glancing at his displays. "It's approaching. No, it's almost here."

"Impossible." Perplexed, Vol-Ban moved next to him, looking over his shoulder. "Was it cloaked? The sensors should have noticed it much earlier. Nobody can sneak up like that."

"They must have used the gas giant's atmosphere to their advantage." Rah-Ban stifled a curse. His fingers danced across the keys, activating scan routines, arming beam weapons, and loading torpedoes. "With all the interference around here I can't get any definitive readings."

"That's just brilliant." Vol-Ban looked back at the monitor, frowning. "We're almost blind, and we're getting visitors. Maybe we should get out of orbit in order to—"

In front of them the huge shape of a Tzenkethi Marauder emerged from the mist. Slowly the tear-shaped ship floated closer, the colors of the gas giant's yellow atmosphere reflecting on its silver hull. The Marauder silently and menacingly caught up to their much smaller ship.

Vol-Ban's eyes widened. "That thing is huge." While they had seen images of Tzenkethi ships, they had never encountered one in person before today.

"Enough gaping." Rah-Ban pushed his apprehensive feelings aside. "Let's see what they want from us." He touched the communications console, opening a hailing frequency. "This is the *Vel-Tekk* calling the Tzenkethi Marauder. We're here, you're here. Let's talk business." He waited.

The Marauder floated in space, taking up a position relative to theirs. Fleeting misty veils of the planet's upper atmosphere swirled around it, while reflections of lightning in lower layers danced on the smooth, gleaming hull.

There was no response to their hail.

The Miradorn frowned, deepening the ridge in the middle of his brow. "Tzenkethi Marauder, this is the *Vel-Tekk*. Respond!"

Again, they received no answer.

Suddenly, the Marauder turned, pointing its rear section toward their small ship.

"Hey, are they trying to impale us, or what?" Vol-Ban asked with confusion.

The proximity alarm on their console started howling. "What the..." Rah-Ban's gaze flickered toward the display. "What's that? Another ship? No! Three ships!"

"It's a trap!" Vol-Ban screamed. All color drained from his face while he started toward conn. "Shields to maximum power. Setting an escape course."

Rah-Ban didn't even listen. Without reliable sensors the *Vel-Tekk* might have been able to evade *one* ship. But three?

"That's not fair," whispered the Miradorn mercenary, staring at the main screen. "Simply not fair."

Before them, the Tzenkethi Marauder's aft section started to glow brightly. Abruptly, the tear-shaped ship darted off into the distance at full impulse power.

Less than a second later, three more vessels swooped down from a higher orbit onto the *Vel-Tekk*. Rah-Ban envisioned the pallid ship hulls as a howling pack of vengeful ghosts returning from the dead.

There were three very different ghosts. Two were elongated, featuring a tip and a narrow "belly" dotted with illuminated windows on the left and right side respectively, and two warp nacelles with red glowing heads. Ghost number three came without belly or attachment, and appeared to be an arrowhead. It featured a ship's registry that caught Rah-Ban's horrified eyes: NX-59650.

Starfleet! Two of the strange ships passed the *Vel-Tekk*, pursuing the fleeing Tzenkethi's Marauder. The arrowhead slid in front of the small mercenary ship, swerving around in order to confront Rah-Ban and his brother.

"*Fire!*" yelled Vol-Ban. "Brother, fire already!"

Rah-Ban pressed the appropriate buttons instinctively. A red beam appeared on the main screen, hitting the arrowhead's shields without inflicting any damage to them.

"Torpedoes!" demanded Vol-Ban loudly, swinging the *Vel-Tekk* around hard. "Target their phaser arrays!"

Which ones? flashed through Rah-Ban's mind. Once again, he reacted instinctively rather than deliberately; and again, his efforts didn't succeed in penetrating the enemy's shields. A fraction of a second later their ship shuddered when the counterattack hit. All the lighting on the bridge either flickered or failed, and his brother clung to conn in an attempt not to lose his footing.

Cursing, Vol-Ban changed course, but the enemy's weapons struck the *Vel-Tekk*'s shields again. Suddenly, Rah-Ban could smell smoke. The main screen failed, closely followed by weapons control on his displays.

He noticed that they were being hailed, and opened a channel. At least they were still able to communicate. Maybe their damaged ship was capable of more besides? Rah-Ban attempted to reroute the main energy, deactivated life support briefly, and then...

"This is Captain Richard Adams from the Federation starship Prometheus," a stern voice announced from the loudspeakers, echoing through the darkened bridge. *"Deactivate your shields, weapons, and engines. Surrender, and maintain your current position."*

The Prometheus! Rah-Ban had heard about her. She was a state-of-the-art battleship belonging to the United Federation of Planets. Her multivector assault mode enabled her to separate into three hull sections, which could fight independently of each other. That was why their attackers looked so strange: All three opponents were part of the same ship.

"You don't get to tell us what to do!" yelled Vol-Ban, hammering his fist onto his flickering console. His attempts to activate the warp drive in order to escape their enemy—an endeavor that bordered on madness, considering the sheer amount of asteroids in the system—failed. The impulse engines also refused to respond to his efforts. "You don't even know us!"

There! Rah-Ban almost cheered when his efforts to redistribute the ship's power bore fruit in getting the main screen back to life. He then tried to do the same for warp drive and tactical systems.

Before he could, though, he saw the blurred, distorted image on the screen, which was being transmitted by *Prometheus*. It was a warrant of apprehension for him and his brother.

"*We know that you've been undertaking illegal business deals for several months,*" the Starfleet captain said. "*Weapons deliveries to Tullinar VI, organ trafficking in the Silva sector, joint smuggling with the Pakled in the Antares territories, and now a pact with the Tzenkethi... would you like me to continue?*"

Rah-Ban's thoughts raced. Their potential employers had departed, and may even have been the ones to betray them, though that seemed unlikely. Either way, hoping to win a battle against the *Prometheus* seemed extremely bold.

That, of course, didn't stop Vol-Ban from crying out, "Brother, shoot! If we are doomed, I want to die fighting!"

The light from Rah-Ban's console keys bathed his face, as he got it working. He had regained weapons control, sensors, and shields.

"Brother," Vol-Ban urged. "Fire!"

"*We won't wait much longer, Vel-Tekk,*" the Starfleet captain said. "*Deactivate your weapons and surrender.*"

"You are an impatient idiot, Vol-Ban," Rah-Ban said, sighing as he complied.

2
OCTOBER 31, 2385

U.S.S. *Prometheus*, Bajoran Sector

All the world's a stage, and all the men and women merely players. They have their exits and their entrances. And one man in his time plays many parts, his acts being seven ages.

Pensively, Captain Richard Adams brushed the words that were written in brass letters on the bridge bulkhead with his fingers. They adorned a small plaque that was mounted next to the left turbolift door. It had been created to commemorate the launching of his ship almost twelve years ago. The words came from an ancient bard from Earth, and although Adams saw them every day upon entering the bridge, he felt they were as fresh and wise as they had been on the very first day.

"Are you ready, sir?"

The voice of his first officer jolted him from his thoughts. Slowly, he turned around.

"We're approaching our destination." As usual, when Commander Roaas smiled, the hairs on his upper lip twitched, while his cat-like eyes sparkled slightly. The Caitian was remarkably big, even for a member of his species. His auburn fur provided the feline-featured man with an almost aristocratic grace. "If you want to say a few words, now would be a good time."

Adams nodded. "Thank you, Commander."

Roaas returned to his post at the tactical station. His

hands clasped behind his back, he stood waiting for further instructions.

Adams passed the waist-high railing that separated the upper bridge section from the lower command center and went to his chair. Silently he glanced at the active stations. Everywhere, people were focusing on their work, displays were flickering, and control and confirmation signals were sounding quietly.

A stage, he thought again, allowing himself a faint smile. "Status, Commander Carson? Lieutenant Chell?"

Sarita Carson at ops quickly glanced at the displays on her half of the front console. "No reports from any of the departments," replied the young human.

"All systems functioning just fine, Captain," the Bolian at the technical station added cheerfully.

Adams nodded, pleased. "Mr. Ciarese?"

Massimo Ciarese staffed the other half of the front console, the pilot's station. The thirty-one-year-old human with his jet-black locks still appeared to be tanned and casual, even after several weeks aboard ship, as if he had only just left the Italian sun of his home on Earth. "We're right on the assigned course, sir," he said, not taking his eyes off his displays. "Warp five point five."

"How long before we reach Deep Space 9?"

"Ten minutes, thirteen seconds, Captain." Ciarese looked up, sighing contentedly. "We're almost home."

The captain nodded, satisfied. "Almost, Ensign," he repeated, turning around and settling into his chair. "Only almost."

The space station Deep Space 9 was located in the Bajoran sector. It was considerably more than a stone's throw away from Earth. Still, Adams could relate to his conn officer all too well. The *Prometheus* was returning from extensive patrol duty, and she had spent the past six months traveling along the border of the hostile Tzenkethi Coalition. Even this most remote Starfleet base seemed like a welcome piece of home.

And we need a piece of home…

Adams could have ordered slipstream propulsion to reach DS9, which would have reduced the flight time considerably. But he wanted to give his crew some time to readjust. "All right. Mr. Winter, please open a ship-wide channel. All stations, all departments."

"Aye, sir." Paul Winter at the communication station touched his controls.

Communication officers had more or less disappeared from Starfleet ships. Generally, ops or tactical officers had taken over their duties. The *Prometheus* was an exception to this rule as she frequently operated in a separated state. Furthermore, Winter was a master in his field. Nobody knew more about subspace communications than the German with Sudanese roots and a penchant for near-superhuman fitness. From the moment he joined the Academy nine years ago, he had worked in Starfleet's Communications Research Center, assisting in the Pathfinder project that had been created in order to establish communications with the Federation *Starship Voyager*, which had been stranded in the Delta Quadrant. His works about communicating with hypersubspace speeds were generally regarded as groundbreaking. Adams was lucky to have Winter, and he was confident that they would include Winter's theories in the standard curriculum at Starfleet Academy and would name lecture rooms after him.

"Channel open, Captain," Winter said.

Adams glanced at Roaas who nodded confirmation,

and then directed his attention at the main screen and deep space. He stood up again. "To all decks, this is the captain. Mr. Ciarese just confirmed that we're ten minutes away from the end of our assignment. I know that you're all longing to get there. Before we all take some time out on Deep Space 9, I would like to let you all—and I mean each and every one of you—know how proud I am of you. The *Prometheus* has proven herself under difficult circumstances, and that's due to her crew."

Suddenly he noticed that the bridge had fallen silent. From the corner of his eye he saw that his crewmembers had stalled at their stations—as the crew had done undoubtedly all over the ship—in order to listen to him. Carson had even turned to face him with a beaming smile.

"Relations between the United Federation of Planets and the alliance of races known as the Typhon Pact," continued Adams, "are anything but amicable. You are aware of that. Since the Romulans, the Breen, the Tzenkethi, the Kinshaya, and several other species have formed their alliance, we have been forced into a new cold war, and Starfleet has to perform duties along a front line instead of pursuing their research, or committing to peace. Again."

He sighed quietly. As he had done so far too often of late, he pondered the fact that Starfleet had been derailed considerably from its mission of exploration, and he wondered if they were ever going to get back on track again.

His gaze wandered again to the plaque on the bulkhead as he continued. "It had been the declared objective of our late president, Nanietta Bacco, to bring the diplomatic ice age between the Typhon Pact and the Federation to an end, and to build new bridges. The *Prometheus*'s exploration and patrol duties along the border to the Tzenkethi Coalition have played their part in making this new beginning happen. Our work here is done. It's now up to the diplomats and world leaders to nurture it to fruition. Let's hope for the best. Let's hope that our role in the next stage of history will no longer be that of warriors. Adams out."

Roaas blinked, surprised while Ensign Winter confirmed with a nod that the channel had been closed.

Adams settled back into his chair without a word. He didn't like big speeches, let alone emotive ones. And yes, maybe he did get a little ahead of himself, but the day today marked far more than just the *Prometheus*'s return home. The crew knew that as well as he did. Today, the new president of the Federation, Kellessar zh'Tarash took over office, and many were hoping that a new era would begin with her. The fact that Adams and his crew would spend this day on Deep Space 9 of all places spoke volumes, as the Federation had lived through its darkest hour during the past few weeks right here. Should he really be surprised that his choice of words reflected the general spirit of optimism?

"Our role in the next stage of history, Captain?" Roaas stood beside his superior officer, lowering his deep voice. "Are you being poetic now as well as everything else?"

"This is an order from your commanding officer," Adams whispered in the same teasing tone of voice. "Shut the hell up."

Roaas's furry nose twitched in confusion. But he followed this order to the letter.

The *Prometheus*-class had been the future of space travel. It had been a mere fifteen years since designers and engineers inside the hallowed halls of Starfleet Headquarters and the

Beta Antares Ship Yards had deemed this model to be a major quantum leap. The slender ships of the *Prometheus*-class were able to reach a top speed of warp factor 9.99, and featured state-of-the-art technology, as well as unprecedented tactical devices for the Alpha Quadrant. After all, which Starfleet ship featured not only one main battle bridge, but two smaller battle bridges as well, or could be split into three independent segments in battle situations? Which Starfleet ship boasted two engine rooms, one of which was capable of splitting into two by means of a complicated process?

"Mine," sighed Lieutenant Commander Jenna Winona Kirk, chief engineer of the *Prometheus*, lowering her tools. "Why mine, of all ships?"

"Pardon me, Commander?" Her assistant Alex Meyer looked up from the console that he was attempting to repair. "Did you say something?"

Kirk wiped the sweat from her brow with the back of her hand. "I'm just whining, Meyer. Feel free to ignore me."

The jovial man in his late thirties, who had an inexplicable passion for ancient trains from Earth, had no intention to do so. He crawled out from under his console, hit his head when trying to get up, and stood next to Kirk, rubbing the painful bump. "With all due respect, Commander, you're not whining, you're working." Dark patches showed on his yellow shirt under his armpits. "And if you ask me, you've been doing so for far too long."

"Who hasn't?" Kirk snorted. "Everyone on the ship is overworked, Lieutenant." Indignantly she brushed a strand of her dark hair from her forehead. Generally, Kirk was regarded as a sociable person. Only two things were capable of spoiling her mood: when people mentioned her not-at-all-ordinary surname, and when the machines didn't do what they were supposed to do.

"Just ten more minutes," Meyer said. "You heard the ol' man."

Kirk nodded. "I did. But, apparently, this stubborn piece of space junk didn't." Sullen, she kicked the casing of the EPS manifold in front of her. With a thud the bottom of her boot struck the metal. The manifold remained unfazed. "I've been trying to eliminate this unit's energy fluctuations for an hour!"

Meyer wiped his face and his thin beard. Kirk thought he looked tired, which put him in company with the rest of the crew. "These fluctuations are zero point zero zero three percent, Commander. There's no real cause for concern here."

"You say that *now*," Kirk grumbled. "But what if this zero zero three suddenly becomes a three without any zeroes during a battle? Maybe even a three before the point? If the secondary engine room doesn't deliver optimal results when we need them, we'll be in deep trouble. Explain *that* to the ol' man on the bridge. Adams may seem like a father figure but I can assure you, he's a tough customer. And rightly so, if you ask me. A ship at the front line should operate faultlessly, even if it's only on standby."

"It *is* operating faultlessly," said Meyer insistently. "Zero zero three is well within tolerable parameters, even more so when you're only a stone's throw away from a space station and its engineers. Don't create more work than necessary for yourself, Commander. The mission lies behind us."

"That's what you think." Kirk unfastened the tricorder from her waist, pointing it toward the permanently glowing bunch of conduits next to the manifold. "But it will only be finished once we dock at DS9, won't it? *Everything* can happen until then. And a good ship is always prepared."

And a good ship has only one erratic engine room, she added quietly. In truth, her frustration was making her do the *Prometheus* an injustice. It was a great ship, but Kirk's love for her engines was only exceeded by her pursuit of perfection. "Almost" and "as good as" simply didn't cut it for the engineer. Had that been the case she probably wouldn't have progressed past her first posting, and certainly not onto one of Starfleet's most advanced ships.

Still, it was highly frustrating having to service eight propulsion systems. She had to deal with the warp drives in both the separatable main engine and each secondary engine room, as well as three additional impulse systems in the secondary engine room, not to mention three slipstream reactors that had been added only three years ago. You could bet that at least one of her babies was causing problems for Kirk at any one time.

To make matters even worse, the temperature control in the secondary engine room was acting up, so Meyer and Kirk had to attempt their unsuccessful repairs in an environment of thirty-eight degrees.

Meyer nodded. "Very well. You're the boss, Boss." He turned around and returned to his console that was still hanging open. Tugging on his uniform collar, he tried to force some fresh air between his skin and the sheer fabric. "But once we're finished here we should pay Doctor Barai a visit in sickbay and get some treatment for dehydration. It's hotter in here than in a *jamaharon* with two hundred Nuvian concubines."

Despite her annoyance, Kirk couldn't help but laugh as she gazed at her tricorder's readings. "What kind of a twisted comparison was that? I think you've been watching too many salacious holovids, Mister."

Grunting, Meyer stuck his head out from under the console. "Risan pornography is *not* salacious, it's a recognized art form. You don't have to like it, Commander Kirk, but you have to accept it."

Kirk snorted derisively at Meyer's arch tone. "I don't have to do anything. In my family, we make our own rules."

Now Meyer laughed. "Did your famous ancestor decree that in his will?"

"He was the one who started it," the lieutenant commander replied, tucking her tricorder away again before making another attempt to optimize this ungrateful EPS manifold. "And if you don't do as you're told, *Deputy* Chief Engineer Meyer, I will continue with his legacy. Understood?"

Meyer sounded both admiring and gently teasing when he replied, "The famous method of James T. Kirk: getting your own way at all cost, and being right in the end."

"Resistance is for beginners," Kirk said dryly. Both of them snorted with laughter, and for a brief moment she actually forgot about the irritating beta engines.

3
OCTOBER 31, 2385

Deep Space 9

The new Deep Space 9 was one of the Federation's largest space stations. It was a state-of-the-art technological miracle, the result of hard work and driven optimism. The design was based on its Cardassian-built predecessor of the same name, which had been destroyed by an act of sabotage. The station of the *Frontier*-class consisted of three perpendicular ring structures surrounding a spindle-shaped core. The rings were housing docking stations for visiting ships, cargo holds, sensors, weapons, and shields. The central sphere was home to ops, housing, workplaces, and recreational facilities for the crew of several thousand people. Many light years away from Earth and the Sol sector, the new Deep Space 9 kept watch near the Bajoran wormhole, which was still a volatile hub for interstellar travel and galaxy-wide politics. Despite only having been commissioned recently, it had already contributed more to the Federation's history than its commander would have liked.

"So, this is where it happened. This is where President Bacco was assassinated."

Captain Ro Laren nodded briefly. "Believe me when I say that we weren't looking for that kind of fame. We wanted to be a symbol of hope, not one of horror." She approached the food replicator in her office, partly because she was exhausted, partly because she was eager to change the subject. "Would you also like a *raktajino*?"

Her visitor raised an eyebrow. "Klingon coffee? From a replicator? Captain, Captain… that is anything but classy."

Great, thought Ro, *a snob*. "Replicators may still fall short of the taste quality that farms and plantations yield, but you know as well as I do that you get used to them. And DS9's *raktajino* is quite good. Half of the station's crew is addicted to it. Our chief has programmed the replicators to produce a unique blend that one of the superior officers on our previous station really liked. Maybe you've heard of him? He's serving as first officer on the *Enterprise*-E these days."

The second eyebrow joined the first one. "Well, that certainly guarantees quality. Who am I to reject a coffee from Commander Worf?"

Smiling, Ro ordered two mugs of the strong Klingon brew, and returned to the desk in her office. Her guest accepted his mug, thanking her. Captain Richard Adams, who sat in the visitor's chair in front of Ro's desk, was by no means a small man. However, Ro's view of his would have been occluded if she hadn't pushed aside the mountains of reports, applications, and tactical analyses that had buried her desk. Now, in addition to a free line of sight, she had the misguided feeling that her immense workload had somehow lessened. Thomas Gray, the Irish poet of old, had been right: Ignorance *was* bliss.

Ro's unobstructed view showed her a man with dark hair, flecked with gray. He was slender and looked fairly fit. His blue eyes were alert and friendly.

"So, Captain, welcome to DS9. This is your first time in the Bajoran sector, right?"

Adams raised his mug to toast her. "That's right. I wish this would have taken place under more relaxed circumstances."

"You've got to stay optimistic, Captain," she said in a sardonic tone. She pointed at the closed office door that led to the station's operations center. "I was told that the future will begin in half an hour, and that everything will be better then."

The United Federation of Planets was in the process of ending a phase of crises that had been unrivaled for generations. Numerous wars, invasions, and assassinations had nearly brought the once strong galactic community to its knees during recent years, and they had almost caused them to forget about their goals and principles... sometimes Ro's fellow officers had forgotten even the very oath they had sworn to Starfleet.

Today, all that was supposed to become the past. Today, the galaxy was about to draw the metaphorical line under everything in order to look ahead, and not back—no matter how difficult that might prove.

"The future." Adams snorted. "Do you really believe that, Captain Ro? After the Dominion War we all believed that we would be able to go back to concentrating on exploration and research and peace. And what happened? The Borg returned. After that, our longstanding enemies formed the Typhon Pact. And then the cherry on top, Andor left the Federation, calling us traitors of our own beliefs."

"I can't blame Andor for that," Ro said quietly. For decades, the four-gendered Andorians had battled a reproductive crisis which pushed their people to the brink of extinction. Secret documents from the Federation's archives might have helped but they had been held back. The Tholians had publicized this scandal and thus destroyed a lot of trust, which is currently slowly being rebuilt, after recent medical successes.

Adams nodded. "The situation was a huge mess, the latest in a series."

Wistfully, Ro looked at the piles of work that she had pushed aside. *Who knows*, she thought with the terrifying horror of an experienced commander, *how many huge messes are lingering in that pile?* Aloud she said, "Still, today is the big day, Captain. The entire galaxy is eagerly awaiting President zh'Tarash's galactic address." Her words were an attempt to motivate herself, and that attempt failed rather dismally. "I can promise you one thing, though: there isn't a place anywhere in the galaxy looking forward to her inaugural speech more than here on DS9."

Kellessar zh'Tarash was Andorian, and she had become the new, democratically elected leader of the Federation. Ro had read the new president's resumé during the past couple of days, and she considered it ideal for this post. Zh'Tarash had lost close family members during the Borg invasion. She had opposed the social dogmas that had pushed the civilization in her homeworld to the brink of extinction. She had also had firsthand experience of Andor turning its back on the galactic league of worlds it had helped found in order to build a relationship with the antagonistic Typhon Pact.

Still, even more important was the fact that zh'Tarash felt bound by the political goals of her appraised predecessor Nanietta Bacco, the woman who had been murdered only two months ago on Deep Space 9 at the height of the crisis.

Adams sipped his *raktajino*. "The past few weeks were insane, even for us out on the Tzenkethi border. President Bacco's death almost became the final nail in the Federation's coffin. We were all shocked. Not to mention the internal problems in the wake of her death…" Adams shook his head.

"Yeah, we all saw how easily democracy can be abused,"

Ro finished his thought, "when it's timid and doesn't take care of itself. I grew up on Bajor under Cardassian rule, so I got to see how bad things can get first-hand. Luckily, the Federation didn't hit bottom the way Bajor did. We still have our ideals and we got back to embracing them. *That's* what today's about, Captain—starting a new era for the Federation and leaving the past in the past." She smiled. "Gotta stay optimistic."

Adams crossed his legs, taking a deep breath. "From your lips to the Prophets' ears, Captain." Tilting his head, he corrected himself. "Oh, I beg your pardon. You don't belong to the Bajoran religion, do you?"

"No apology needed." She waved his words aside. The times when she had opposed her people's religion with an almost fanatical fervor were long gone. Today's Ro Laren was no longer a rebel for rebellion's sake. These days she was able to acknowledge not only black and white but also many shades of gray; something she had been unable to do in her youth or early in her career. It wasn't that long ago that she never would have used "we" to describe the Federation, even though she was a Starfleet officer. "Believe me, if I was religious, I'd agree with you."

Her visitor from the U.S.S. *Prometheus* seemed sympathetic. "The craziness must have been a thousand times worse here, right?"

Ro laughed without any sign of humor. "That is an understatement. President Bacco died during the opening ceremony for the new station. The Federation News Service broadcasted images of the assassination to every corner of the galaxy. There's probably no one in the Alpha or Beta Quadrant who didn't watch it—thanks to the wormhole and Project Full Circle, it went to the Gamma and Delta Quadrant, too. Why this had to happen on *my* station..." She trailed off, grasping for words and not finding them. "I want to be honest with you, Adams. My entire crew is still suffering the aftereffects of this. I know, we're all suffering to one degree or other, but for us it's worse, because it happened on our watch. We stood right next to her when it happened. We should have been more careful."

"You *were* careful," Adams said firmly. "The images made it to the Tzenkethi border, too, Captain, and so did the after-action reports. Trust me, sometimes disasters can't be avoided, try as we might. Sometimes those opposing peace are simply stronger than us."

The Bajoran captain said nothing. She knew that Adams was right; she even agreed with him. Those were the exact words she'd used when addressing her staff whenever they felt depressed by the images of that dreadful day. *Sometimes you simply cannot win.*

Still, it was one thing to grasp this concept; it was another to accept it. "I guess the trick is not to get disheartened."

"Well said." Adams nodded, taking another sip from his *raktajino* while leaning back in his chair. "And you can tell Commander Worf from me: More beans!"

Ro burst out laughing, and her tension dissolved. "You're chipping away at his honor there, Captain."

"Absolutely not. I hold him in the highest respect as a man and as a warrior." Adams placed his mug on the desk, regarding it skeptically. "Unfortunately, his taste in coffee leaves a lot to be desired. Tell me, Captain Ro, have you ever tasted Jamaican Blue-Mountain-Coffee?"

Before she could answer, the door to her office hissed open. Major Cenn Desca, Ro's first officer, appeared. "You wanted to be informed when the festivities were about to start,

Captain," said the middle-aged Bajoran, nodding politely toward Adams as well. "I believe they are ready on Earth."

"Thank you, Cenn." Ro rose behind her desk, straightening her uniform. Looking at Adams she asked: "Care to accompany me, Captain? I thought we could both watch zh'Tarash in ops."

"In the ever-beating, proud heart of the great station Deep Space 9?" Mischief sparkled in Adams's eyes. It made him look ten years younger. "How very symbolic, Captain Ro. My first officer chided me as a poet today, but you are a true romantic."

"Don't let anyone from my crew hear that," Ro muttered under her breath. Then she and her guest started toward ops, into the future.

"If this is the future, I'm already disappointed." Indignantly, Lenissa zh'Thiin glanced over her shoulder, back at the counter where they had just placed their orders. "An embassy with integrated bar services?" The Andorian security chief of the *Prometheus* had a derogatory look on her face.

"This isn't the future, Niss," said Sarita Carson who was sitting to her right, chuckling quietly. "Technically, right now, we're in Ferengi territory. They have completely different ways—even in the field of diplomacy."

Quark's Bar, Grill, Gaming House, Holosuite Arcade, and Ferengi Embassy to Bajor was the impressively voluminous name of the multi-level establishment deep in the belly of Deep Space 9 where their small group had assembled. This highly unusual diplomatic office was run by a Ferengi, the illustrious Ambassador Quark. He was a distinctly shady character with a huge, bald skull, ears the size of toilet seats, a sly smile, and a dress-sense that zh'Thiin thought to not only severely insult the eye of any beholder, but also cause it irreversible damage. Zh'Thiin had met several Ferengi in her youth, and she had never been able to acquire a taste for their devious behavior. Ferengi always wanted to make money, and they were constantly chasing profit. They even sold their principles on occasion—a trait that the proud Andorian could not condone under any circumstances.

Zh'Thiin took a deep breath, smelling the alcohol that was lingering in the air and the odd odors of the many and varied alien species that made up Quark's clientele. She heard the technological, yet melodic droning of gambling tables, where scantily dressed women and one man tempted visitors to place horrendous amounts of money on bets, and she caught snippets of conversations in more than a dozen different languages. This was no embassy, she decided. It was not even a bar. It was unadulterated chaos.

"And you really used to be assigned here?"

Carson nodded. "Well, not here, exactly, but on the old DS9. My post was actually to the *Defiant*, a battleship that belonged to the station, but my quarters were here on the station." The lieutenant commander with the dark hair stared into space, apparently somewhat taken by her clearly pleasant memories. "Quark's used to be a welcome haven. Especially when Chief O'Brien and Doctor Bashir held one of their darts tournaments, and Quark offered prize money."

Geron Barai, chief medical officer aboard the *Prometheus*, looked up incredulously. "Prize money?" the Betazoid repeated. Barai sat across from zh'Thiin on the other side of the circular table that stood in the center of the bar. His attractive features mirrored his doubts. "Offered by a Ferengi?"

Zh'Thiin also had difficulties believing this notion. Gazing back at the counter she bent her antennae forward curiously. "Impossible. The guy just tried to sell me a glass full of greenish-yellow stuff, and didn't even know what it tasted like. He won't give away anything to anyone."

Carson laughed. "Ah, the good old Wormhole Surprise, Quark's favorite cocktail. He basically throws together anything that's past its sell-by date and needs to go, and then he calls it a specialty of the house. If I were you, I'd keep well away from that, Niss. Doctor Bashir once was bold—or stupid—enough to try a Wormhole. He was sick for three days after that... a doctor, remember!" She paused for a moment while a waiter served their drinks. Once he had placed the glasses in the middle of the small table, she continued. "You didn't listen properly, Niss, and that can be a major mistake when Quark is involved. I said that he *offered* the prize money back then. I never said that he actually *paid* it."

Zh'Thiin nodded grimly. *I knew it*, she thought. *Not a glimmer of pride in his body, but a big mouth.* "That sounds more like a Ferengi."

"Aw, c'mon." Carson touched her arm. "Don't be so hard on the good old Quark. He simply won the tournament... every time."

Jenna Kirk, the fourth member of the small party, snorted derisively. "What an impressive coincidence." She leaned back in her chair. "And you're sure that wasn't due to biased darts?"

"That depends on who you ask, Jen," Carson answered with an exaggerated innocent grin that made the chief engineer laugh.

Zh'Thiin sighed quietly, casting a glance to her left. "And what about you?" she asked the fifth member of their little bunch. "Are you already counting your cash in your mind so you can waste it on the Dabo table, or why else be so silent? Truth be told, if you weren't sat next to me, Lieutenant, I'd have assumed you'd stayed on Earth. This is your welcome party!"

Lieutenant Jassat ak Namur blinked, as if to shake away confusion, and straightened his shoulders. The red-skinned exotic-looking Renao who was taking on the conn on the bridge of the *Prometheus* seemed to wake from a daydream that must have been just as fascinating as his extraordinary appearance. Perhaps his thoughts had taken him back to the graduating ceremony in San Francisco on Earth only a few weeks ago.

"Excuse me, Commander," he said. "I'm afraid I haven't been listening."

"You mean, you've been taking forty winks," Carson teased him. "Where did you let your mind wander off to? To one of your many amorous Academy adventures, perhaps?"

Ak Namur faced the floor. "No," he answered quietly, but smiling. "No."

The lieutenant was the only Renao in the entire fleet. He had come aboard the *Prometheus* as an exchange officer years before zh'Thiin had arrived. When his tour of service had come to an end, he had requested to be allowed to attend the Academy, and Adams had sponsored him. The Renao had jet-black hair, wore golden ear and nose jewelry, and had glowing, yellow-golden eyes. Even in Quark's motley diplomats' bar he stood out like a sore thumb. When zh'Thiin looked at him, she thought of hot nights in the desert and a sky full of deep-cratered moons.

"Oh, come on, Jassat." Kirk patted the pilot's shoulder in a companionable way. Zh'Thiin knew that their friendship went back to ak Namur's days as an exchange officer. In fact,

Kirk had organized this little party. "Don't be so shy. We're glad to have you back with us. Ciarese valiantly stood in for you at conn while you were gone. But if you ask me, he took a wrong turn here and there."

Ak Namur's smile broadened. "I think, you're exaggerating," he said, and zh'Thiin noted yet again how much she liked his slight accent. "Mind you, so are the prices for drinks in this… embassy."

Chuckling with amusement, Carson looked at Quark. "I wouldn't put it past him to raise them even more sometime soon. If he destroys that computer, he will probably have to replace it."

Zh'Thiin turned around. The barkeep hammered his fist against a small console that was embedded in the wall behind his counter. He seemed fairly frustrated, and apparently it didn't help that the device promptly quit its service after the rough treatment.

"You call *this* quality workmanship?" Quark ranted. "All right, we'll try it the old-fashioned way—yelling at it!" Quark rushed around the bar and made his way between the busy tables, ignoring all the quizzical—and mocking—looks of his guests. He stopped right in the middle of the bar, looking straight up at the ceiling. "Computer, activate holoscreen!"

A soft triad rang across the bar, followed by an artificial female voice that was a bit higher pitched than the voice used for Starfleet computers. *"Activation impossible."*

Quark's fist clenched as if about to throttle the disembodied voice. "What? Computer, that screen was installed two *days* ago! It's *impossible* for it to be broken!"

"Confirmed. Holoscreen is fully functional."

Amused, Barai glanced at zh'Thiin, but the Andorian barely acknowledged his gaze. She didn't want to appear too acquainted in front of everyone else.

"Hey, Quark," a muscular Chalnoth with a thunderous bass in his voice shouted. He was clad in black clothing, and held an enormous tankard full of Romulan ale in his hand. "Switch on FNS!"

"I know, I know." The Ferengi proprietor sighed, facing his guest with an extremely undiplomatic glare. "And I guarantee you, I will get this holoscreen up and running."

"Preferably *before* the Federation News Service begins with the broadcast," another voice, which spoke with an Irish accent, shouted from a different corner of the establishment with a taunting undertone. "Otherwise, we might as well have stayed at home to watch it."

Quark groaned. His hands clutched the lapels of his garish coat as if that would provide him with much desperately needed support. Finally, he faced the caller. "If you're in such a hurry, Chief, you might as well help me. It's a technical problem, after all, isn't it, computer?"

"Negative. There is no technical problem. All systems are working within normal parameters."

The chief in question burst out laughing. Zh'Thiin sighted him: a sturdy human with curly hair, wearing a uniform with operations gold. Shaking his head, he said, "I'm afraid you're on your own with that one, Quark."

"That's Chief O'Brien," Carson whispered. "The station's engineer."

"Well, well." Curiously, Kirk looked across the room. "I've heard a lot about O'Brien. I look forward to working with him during the repair cycle."

"Pull yourself together, Jen," Carson said. "He's happily married with two kids."

"Really? Is his wife pretty?" Kirk grinned broadly.

"Keiko O'Brien is gorgeous, and also more than fifteen years older than you."

"Bah, that doesn't mean anything. You know how good facials work these days."

Carson rolled her eyes. "You're unbelievable."

"Who started it?"

Meanwhile, the crowd had begun to stir. More and more guests lost their patience with the proprietor and his lack of ability to activate the live broadcast from Earth. All of them seemed to have come here mainly for the public viewing of President zh'Tarash's speech.

Bewildered, Quark looked up to the ceiling. "No technical problem?" A series of curses in his mother tongue followed. Zh'Thiin was grateful that she didn't understand them. "Computer, how is that even possible? Either, the screen works, or it doesn't."

"The holoscreen is in perfect working order."

"So why don't you switch it on then?" The Ferengi was almost screaming now.

A completely new voice sounded from the speakers. *"Because you didn't pay the last installment."* It was male, low, and sounded smug. *"Or did you assume I would send you a brand new receiving unit, and unlock a thousand Federations channels without you fully paying me?"*

Quark sighed. "Rento."

"That's right, you skinflint," the male voice said. Quark's efforts must have opened a preprogrammed comm frequency straight to the vendor. *"Did you really think you could negotiate down the price even after you signed the contract?"*

The unrest of the guests turned into protest. Several people rose from their tables. Two Vulcans headed for the exit. A lonely Lurian at the counter stared into his tankard in disappointment.

"Rento," zh'Thiin murmured, looking at Carson. "Correct me if I'm wrong, but isn't that an Orion name?"

Her crewmate grimaced. "Yeah. Sounds like Quark has been buying from the wrong people again. The Orion Syndicate are not the most accommodating business partners. Especially if you're trying to pull a fast one on them."

"Negotiate down?" Quark's voice was cracking as he watched his guests move toward the exits in droves. "Rento, what are you thinking? I just intended to make use of the promised discount, and—"

"There was no promised discount, Quark."

"What? Of course there was. It's part of the contract, isn't it? If the delivered technology is faulty, the purchase price may be reduced by six point three seven percent."

"The technology is not faulty."

"Oh yes, it is!" Quark swallowed hard, when a table full of Bajoran laborers took to its heels in order to watch the broadcast elsewhere. "Last night, when I…"

"Just transfer the rest of the money, Quark," Rento cut him off. *"And then I will unlock your subscription, and activate your holoscreen."*

One of the leaving Bajorans put his hand on the Ferengi's shoulder. "Listen to the man, Quark. Otherwise, your establishment will be even emptier than the Badlands."

Laughter rose, mainly the derogatory kind. Someone asked for the bill here, someone else emptied their glass quickly there. Quark's had lost its fascination, for this evening at least.

Its proprietor seemed to realize that. "You will activate it immediately?" Quark asked plaintively.

"Instantly," Rento said. *"Oh, look! Zh'Tarash approaches the lectern. Oh, wait, I forgot. You can't see it. How uncouth of me."*

Quark's shoulders trembled with obvious anger. His hands tucked on his lapels as if he intended to rip them off. "That's blackmail." His words were almost drowned out by the general noises of people leaving.

"*That's market economy,*" Rento sounded unfazed. "*Hey, I think she's about to begin. I can see it on my screen. Crystal clear. What about you?*"

Barai leaned over to his crewmates, grinning broadly. "The opening act in this bar is even more entertaining than the main act. What an amazing location."

"Welcome to DS9, Doc," Carson said. She nudged zh'Thiin gently, glancing at her both conspiratorial and amused, and raised her voice. "Pay him already, Quark. We want to see the future."

The Andorian understood the hint immediately. "Fu-ture! Fu-ture! Fu-ture!" she chanted, clapping her hand on the table with every syllable.

The people waiting on the other tables joined her. The barely dressed man from the Dabo tables clapped his hands demandingly. Waiters drummed the rhythm on their tablets. Even the guests already heading for the exit stopped dead in their tracks, enthralled by the absurdity of the situation, looking at their host challengingly.

"Fu-ture! Fu-ture! Fu-ture!" they chanted.

Quark's trembling shoulders sagged. Finally, he lowered his hands, and closed his eyes. "Computer," he sighed, "voice authorization. Clear transfer Quark-Delta-Seven."

The computer voice came back. "*Authorization accepted. Transfer executed.*"

Almost immediately, a square holoscreen generated by hidden emitters appeared about one meter over the center of Quark's. It displayed the vast chamber of the Federation

Council in the Palais de la Concorde on Earth, in almost perfect three-dimensional projection. The image closed in to the woman at the lectern: President Kellessar zh'Tarash.

"About time." The Bajoran laborer nodded and returned to his table. His colleagues and many of the other guests followed suit. Several dozen eyes as well as some antennae turned toward the holoscreen.

"*Always a pleasure doing business with you,*" said Rento approvingly. The perverse delight in his voice was unmissable.

"Oh, shut up," the Ferengi snapped. He turned around, trotting back to the counter where the Lurian waved an emptied tankard in his direction.

Shaking her head, zh'Thiin looked at her crewmates. "I told you," she whispered, pointing behind her with her thumb. "This so-called future isn't half worth it so far!"

"Let's hope you're wrong, Commander," said ak Namur. The Renao folded his arms across his chest, and turned his expectant gaze upon the newly elected president.

4
NOVEMBER 1, 2385

Starbase 91

Starbase 91 had seen its best days more than fifty years earlier. Built in 2275, the *Watchtower*-class station had served as a transit point and guard post on the periphery of the Federation. Some still referred to it jokingly as the "last gas station before the unknown," even though the uncharted territories actually started many light-years further out.

Around the turn of the twenty-fourth century, the main task of the mushroom-shaped station and its more-than-two-thousand strong crew had been to monitor ship movements this side of the Klingon border, as well as keeping an eye out for ships traveling through the sector to the distant Gorn Hegemony. To this end, a constantly upgraded deep-space sensor array had been erected in close proximity to Starbase 91. It was capable of picking up warp signatures from light-years away, and analyzing them.

But then fifty years of peace had begun. The Romulans had withdrawn beyond the Neutral Zone after the *Tomed* Incident, the Klingons had gradually become allies of the Federation following the destruction of Praxis and the Khitomer Accords, and there had been no sign of the Gorn. Thus, Starbase 91 had been left to its own devices, which had led to its slow deterioration. Even when the Gorn reappeared on the galactic stage during the Dominion War and later when the Typhon Pact was founded, that process hadn't been reversed. Four years previously, plans had been drawn up for a new fleet base within the Cestus system, bordering on Gorn space. These plans had been put into motion at the urging of the then-Federation president, and Cestus III native, Nanietta Bacco. Starbase 91 had become a dilapidated station along a rarely used highway across the vastness of space.

Lieutenant Karen Adams wasn't bothered at all by any of that. The station's conduit system had its blackouts now and again, the seats in the tramway that ran along the outer edges of the upper shield section were decidedly worn, and the technological equipment wasn't just outdated, it was antiquated. But to Karen, it was all part of the starbase's charm.

Starbase 91 was Karen's first post as communications officer since graduating in the middle of her Starfleet Academy class three years previous. The dark-haired young woman was regarded as an imperturbable blithe spirit by her colleagues. She had always been fascinated by the adventurous way of life and the somewhat more robust designs of the last century. Since only a handful of starships from that era were still in service—the *Excelsior* and *Miranda* classes were about it, and they only served within the Federation's secure core areas— Karen had actively sought a transfer to a space station that was as old and as far away as possible.

She had wound up here in the middle of nowhere, where her only neighbors were the ill-tempered Klingons and the solitary Renao people. The territory of the latter was limited to a small area in space dominated by a significant cluster of red giants known as the Lembatta Cluster. Starbase 91's duties included taking astrophysical readings of the cluster and keeping a watchful eye on its red-skinned and extremely introverted inhabitants.

As a communications officer, Karen's sole participation in that aspect of Starbase 91's standing orders consisted of relaying communiqués with regard to the study of the cluster. That, and sitting in the Starlight Café in the upper part of the habitat area and marveling at the impressive stellar backdrop. Many times she had asked herself what life would be like on a world orbiting one of those red giants. But the Renao hadn't permitted anyone to cross their borders for centuries, and the Federation respected the sovereignty of non-associated planets.

Maybe the Renao will change their minds one day, Karen thought, stepping onto the turbolift that would take her to the operations center at the top of the station where she was reporting for duty during gamma shift. She sincerely hoped the Renao would do so. You didn't live next door to someone for three years without becoming curious about them.

"Good morning, everyone," Karen said to her already-present fellow crewmates in ops.

A general murmur met her greeting. "You're the only one on board saying 'good morning' just before midnight," said Lieutenant Gabriel Marceau. The colonist from New France staffed the sensor station that was adjacent to her comm console.

"I only just got up for work," Karen said. "To me, it's morning, no matter what the station computer says."

"To each their own illusions." Grinning, Marceau turned back to his instruments.

Karen didn't point out that all notions of "day" and "night" were illusory on a space station. Helping maintain that illusion, gamma shift was only half staffed during the "night." The conference table on the raised platform in the center of ops—with its eight terminals for the senior officers of the station—was empty during this shift.

The watch officer, Lieutenant Commander Agram, was a generally insular and not particularly zealous Tellarite. He was rapidly approaching his retirement, spending his final years in Starfleet working the graveyard ship of an out-of-the-way starbase. He preferred ambling around in circles for half of the shift to keep an eye on everything. Occasionally he would withdraw to an empty space in a corner. There, he would fold his hands in front of his belly, looking lost in thought. Karen imagined that in his mind he was already spending his time with a cool drink on a beach on his homeworld—or whatever Tellarites considered to be the ultimate relaxation.

All in all, the mood during gamma shift didn't quite adhere to the protocol described in the Academy's manuals, which suited Karen fine. She detested military drill, and she likely wouldn't have lasted very long on her uncle's ship, the U.S.S. *Prometheus*.

But even outside of renowned battleships, the tone within Starfleet had become sterner in recent years. Constant galactic crises such as the Dominion War, the Borg invasion, or the current conflict with the Typhon Pact were the reason that the militarists among the senior officers were increasingly calling the shots.

Lieutenant Alari, the slender, attractive Tiburonian woman who ran communications during the Beta shift, puckered up her full lips as she rose from her chair. "You're five minutes late."

Karen glanced down at the time display on the screen. "You're right. Sorry. I had breakfast with Lieutenant Cox in the *Starlight*. We obviously forgot the time."

"Cox?" Alari regarded Karen with obvious curiosity.

"From astrophysics." Placing the small gray transmission receiver in her left ear, Karen took her station.

A wicked smile appeared on Alari's face. "Haven't you spent an awful lot of time in the astrophysics lab during the past few weeks?"

Defensively, Karen raised her hands. "We're just friends."

"Sure you are." Alari giggled.

"Would you two care to let us be a part of your conversation?" Agram's rumbling voice echoed across ops.

Alari snapped to attention. "Begging your pardon, sir. It's nothing important."

"Haven't you been relieved of duty, Lieutenant Alari?"

"Yes, sir." Embarrassed, Alari brushed one of her big, strikingly shaped ears with her hand.

"Well, in that case, off you go. Get away from my ops."

"Consider me gone, sir." Alari glanced at Karen one last time. "We'll continue this conversation tomorrow. Have a quiet shift."

"Thanks. And good night to you."

"Funny, I thought it was morning for you." With a grin, Alari swiftly left ops.

Karen turned toward her communications controls. The quiet shift Alari had wished was the norm for her in any case. Very few ships crossed this sector, and the number of ships docking in the middle of the station's night was even fewer. Tonight there was one of the latter: the U.S.S. *Lakota* was on approach. The *Akira*-class cruiser made its rounds in the Lembatta Cluster, stopping by the starbase every couple of weeks. The ship would arrive in a few minutes, at which point Karen needed to supervise the docking procedure.

She called up the frequency analyses of Echelon 1, the starbase's deep-space sensor array. Its sensors were so precise that some people jokingly claimed that it could detect the hairs growing on Chancellor Martok's head on Qo'noS.

Of course, those claims tended to stay among the junior officers. The prim superior officers like Agram didn't approve of such jocularity.

Right now, there was silence in deep space. Echelon 1 read clear. Leaning back in her chair, Karen switched the surveillance back to automatic.

Marceau leaned over to her from his sensors. "Lieutenant Cox? Seriously? That guy is as stuffy as a Vulcan."

Karen rolled her eyes. "We're *just friends*. He's also interested in the Ancient Reds." The Renao referred to the Lembatta Cluster by that term. "He showed me some of his latest observations."

"Oh? And what are the celestial bodies up to? Do they see more action than the Klingons?"

"That depends. Do you remember me telling you that there's a strange radiation coming from the center of the cluster?"

"Vaguely. You said the radiation was somewhat exotic and didn't correspond to the spectrum of red giants. Weren't you going to send an information request to the Vulcan Science Academy?"

"Yup. Still need to do that."

Marceau raised his eyebrows. "It's been *months* since you told me about it."

Karen waved her hand dismissively. "Work, social engagements... You know that time flies on the station."

The lieutenant grunted. "You seem to be working on a very different starbase to me."

"Anyway, the radiation has increased again, so we were hoping to close in on its source, finally. Guess what: It's impossible. Our instruments just aren't able to pinpoint the location of the highest radiation density."

"Have you tried using Echelon?"

"Are you kidding me? This is Cox's and my private project. I know better than to ask Captain Hillenbrand to realign the array for that. I—"

A beep interrupted her. Karen faced her console.

"Oh, that's the *Lakota*. I'm sorry, Gabriel, duty calls."

He nodded, turning his attention back to his own displays.

"*Starbase 91, this is the U.S.S. Lakota*," a voice came from Karen's receiver. "*Requesting permission to dock.*"

Karen dutifully turned to Agram. "Commander, the *Lakota* is requesting docking permission."

"Mr. Fraxa?" The gray-haired Tellarite glanced questioningly at the blue-skinned, bald man at traffic control.

Fraxa checked his displays. "Dock 7 is vacant," the Bolian answered.

Agram nodded toward Karen. "Lieutenant, docking permission granted."

She opened a channel. "*Lakota*, this is Starbase 91. Docking permission granted for Dock 7."

"*Coming in for Dock 7. Thank you, starbase.*" The communications officer lowered his voice, adopting a less official tone. "*Is that you, Adams?*"

Karen glanced uncomfortably toward Agram whose eyes were still fixed on her.

"Affirmative, *Lakota*."

"*Ah, I understand, you can't talk.*" The man chortled. "*Well, this is Lieutenant Komari. Would you like to have breakfast with me again when you finish work? That was great fun last time.*"

Karen barely managed to keep a straight face. Komari wasn't a bad guy but he tended to be far too talkative, even for her liking. If she agreed to a date with him, her free morning would be out of the window. Besides, she'd rather meet up with Cox. They really needed to write this information request for the Vulcan Science Academy. "I'm sorry, *Lakota*, but that won't be possible."

"*Oh, come on, Adams. Don't be a spoi—*" His tone of voice abruptly changed. "*Understood, Starbase 91. Lakota out.*"

Agram loomed over her. "Problems, Lieutenant?"

"Erm, no, sir." Karen felt her cheeks glowing.

"It sounded like it."

"That was nothing. Just…" Her mind raced while she tried to come up with an excuse. She didn't want to get Komari in trouble. After all, she also used official frequencies for private chatter now and then. "You know, we—"

Suddenly, Marceau cried out. "What on Earth was that?" His voice expressed bafflement and anxiety, which was enough to divert Agram's attention away from Karen, to the latter's great relief.

"Report, Lieutenant," the commander said briskly.

"Sir, for a brief moment I had the feeling that…" He hesitated.

"Yes?" Agram prompted him.

"As if I had spotted something out there."

"Can you be more specific?"

"I'm sorry, sir. It all happened so fast. I briefly noticed something that might have been a particle signature from a sublight drive."

"*Might* have been?"

The slender man shrugged. "Well, the computer didn't raise the alarm. It didn't consider it a noteworthy phenomenon. Still… it looked weird to me."

Agram leaned forward. "Did we record that?"

"Yes, sir. One moment." Marceau's fingers danced over the sensor console and brought up the data. Once he got what he wanted, he pointed at the display. "There. You see? Right at this timestamp. That looks like traces of drive plasma, but they seemed to kind of evaporate instantly."

Curiously, Karen glanced at the screen and there was indeed a very brief spike. But it was tremendously weak and couldn't possibly have come from any kind of vessel. "Are you sure it's not some kind of sensor malfunction? Maybe a ghost echo from the *Lakota*'s docking maneuver?"

Marceau shook his head. "I don't think so. We only serviced the system two weeks ago. There shouldn't be any false readings."

"Could an unauthorized work drone be out there?" Agram asked.

The thought wasn't far-fetched. Sometimes, technicians snuck out for a secretive trip at night—it was a popular date spot, as the closer view of the Lembatta Cluster was spectacular.

"I'll check." Karen's fingers danced across the touch screen. "Negative, Commander. All drones and shuttles are docked."

"Sir," Marceau said, "if one of our small vessels was out there, we would see it. There isn't anything. The sensors show nothing but empty space."

Agram straightened himself. "Put it on the main screen."

The sensor officer executed the order, and a vast star field appeared on the ops main screen, the Lembatta Cluster visible in the distance. Within its depths the Ancient Reds glowed like demonic eyes, lurking beyond the stellar veil.

The Tellarite stroked his bushy beard. His small, cavernous eyes narrowed. "I can't see anything."

Everyone in ops was now interested in Marceau's glitch. Julie Butchko at tactical said, "It could be a ship using a cloaking device, sir."

"And who exactly would be flying around out there, cloaked?" Agram snapped. "Klingons? To what end? They are our allies. Romulans? I don't believe that for one minute. The Romulan Star Empire is too far away. What's more, they would have had to sneak past the listening post as well as the automatic tachyon detection grid on the periphery of the Neutral Zone, which is plain impossible."

"With all due respect, sir, it's unlikely but not impossible," Butchko said. "The Romulans deployed a completely new cloaking technology about six years ago with the *Scimitar* of former Praetor Shinzon. The ship emitted no tachyons, and left no residual anti-protons, which are the only two ways to track and locate a cloaked ship."

"Didn't a cloaked ship make it all the way to Earth three years ago?" Ensign Goldwasser chipped in from his station. "You know, the attack on the Utopia Planitia Shipyards?"

"Did Romulans do that?" Fraxa asked beside him.

"No idea. But a cloaked ship was involved, I'm sure of it."

"There!" Marceau shouted, agitated. "There's another spike." He pointed toward the display where he had frozen his readings. "That looks like drive plasma."

"It's definitely not Romulans," Agram growled. "Their cloaking devices haven't leaked drive plasma for years." He raised his voice. "Computer. Scan sector sixteen. Anything out of the ordinary there?"

"*Negative*," the female voice of the station computer responded. "*No relevant parameters exceeded.*"

The Tellarite grumbled, dissatisfied.

"Do you want me to go to yellow alert, sir?" Butchko asked.

"Are you serious?" Agram snapped. "It's the middle of the night. Do you want me to wake two thousand people because our instruments *might* show something that *could* be a ship?"

"The spike was damn small in both instances," Goldwasser added, after bringing up the sensor data on his console. "These results surely can't derive from a warbird."

"Lieutenant Adams, hail them," Agram said. "Maybe our potential visitors will identify themselves when they think that we've spotted them."

"Aye, sir." Karen opened all standard hailing frequencies. "Starbase 91 to unidentified starship. We have picked you up on our sensors, and we're watching your approach. Please identify yourself." She waited for a while before adding several other, rarely used frequencies, and repeating her transmission. "No answer, sir."

"Sir, we could have Echelon sweep the vicinity," Goldwasser said. "If anything is able to detect our timid friend, it's the sensor array."

Agram nodded. "Do it." Karen noted that the Tellarite sounded not entirely sure of himself. Karen figured he was second-guessing his decision not to wake Captain Dimitrios Charistes. But while Karen didn't always like the watch officer, she agreed with him in his initial decision. So far, they only had two minor sensor spikes to go by. It was too soon to take this beyond gamma shift.

"Reprogramming Echelon 1." Goldwasser's fingers danced across the console. "Echelon 1 ready."

"And?" Agram stared at Marceau.

"Scanning for tachyon emissions." Karen's seatmate made some adjustments. He furrowed his brow while he concentrated on his displays. "Negative, sir."

"Try residual anti-protons."

"Aye, sir."

Suddenly, Karen's receiver emitted some sounds she had

trouble identifying at first. "Sir! I've got something here!"

"Lieutenant?" Agram immediately went over to her.

"Sir, I… I believe I can hear singing." Putting her hand over her receiver, she looked at him, bewildered.

"Singing?" Agram met her gaze incredulously.

Karen touched a control. Monotonous chanting in a low voice began sounding out from the speakers in ops. It reminded Karen of Klingon ritual chants, but the language was certainly not Klingon.

"That's impossible," Fraxa said. "Sound waves don't carry across a vacuum."

"But sound waves can cause a spaceship hull to reverberate," Goldwasser said, "when the singing is loud enough, or when the ship is very small."

Marceau frowned. "But to measure for a reverberating ship's hull, we'd have to pick up reflected tracking impulses from point-blank range. That means…" His eyes widened.

"That it is right on our doorstep already," Agram finished the sentence for him. Suddenly, the phlegmatic Tellarite sprang to life. "Yellow alert. Lieutenant Butchko, raise station shields and…"

"Sir, look, on the screen!" Karen gasped. "It's decloaking." Her mouth went bone-dry while staring at the thing that was darting toward them at high velocity. "My goodness, that's a—"

A fierce impact shook the entire starbase. Energy conduits exploded all over ops, sending sparks flying in all directions. Screaming, Karen fell to the deck, pain flashing through her left shoulder on impact. Suddenly, the world around her was aflame as a roaring, raging fire storm engulfed her.

Then it went dark around Karen Adams.

5

TIME: UNKNOWN

Place: unknown

A flicker, followed by a crackling noise. Finally, an image appears. The camera shows the inside of a ruin, somewhere in a nameless desert. Bare walls made of alien stone, dilapidated. A large piece of pale cloth has been put up to keep away the brunt of the sunlight. Weapons leaning against the walls: phaser rifles, but also projectile weapons—black, shiny, and menacing.

In the center of the image, a man is sitting cross-legged. He's wearing loose clothing that covers almost his entire body. Its dark gray fabric is adorned with alien embroidery that is simple but also elegant in an exotic kind of way. His wide hood leaves his face in the shadow, but it doesn't need a vivid imagination to guess his identity, nonetheless. The deep red skin, the weak glimmer of his nose jewelry, two eyes glowing in the dark like beacons... a Renao?

"Are you listening now?" the hooded man calls into the camera. "Do we finally have your attention?"

He's clutching some kind of data display, where he's probably stored his prepared speech, but he doesn't look at it. His eyes are firmly fixed on the camera. On his audience.

He remains motionless while the camera slightly changes its angle sideways in order to present what's lying next to him in the desert sand, something crumpled-up and treated with contempt. It's a flag, light blue with white letters. A star map surrounded by a laurel wreath: the seal of the Federation. Underneath, several other flags are partly visible. A quick zoom reveals that they are from the Ferengi Alliance and the Klingon Empire.

"That was just the beginning," the hooded man promises menacingly, while the camera pans back to focus on him. "What happened on the periphery of the Lembatta Cluster may seem a tragedy to many. But rest assured it was only the tip of the iceberg. We will not rest, nor relent, until our mission has been completed."

He puts down the data display before reaching behind his back, pulling out one of the phaser rifles. Even his hands are covered with dark gloves. Placing the scratched weapon across his lap, his motions exhibit an unmistakable air of pride.

"You're asking what our goals are? The reasons behind our actions?" He snorts derisively. A quiet curse in a foreign language escapes from his lips, and then he switches back to Federation Standard, which he pronounces with a noticeable accent. "*You* are the reason! Just you. You and your blind arrogance. You and your reckless stupidity. You and your barbarism. The galaxy has turned into a place of fear and terror, and that is your fault alone. War and invasions, wherever you look. Misery and suffering. Distrust and resentment. Recent years have inflicted more scars on this universe than entire millennia before! And why?" His voice cracks with outrage. His fury is as genuine as the weapon in his hands. Genuine and palpable. "Because you allowed it to go this far. You are disrupting the harmony in space. You refuse to stay in your own territories. Any child can tell you that we all have our place within the harmony of the universal scale of all things.

Each creature has its sphere. You and all the other dominant powers in the galaxy refuse to accept this truth with stubborn naivety! You advance into places that are not yours. You harm the harmony of spheres—your own, and those you enter with your unnatural will to explore and expand. Don't you realize that your unnatural aspirations are the reason for all the misery we had to witness in recent years? Don't you understand that you are to blame for all the suffering, for all the deaths? You and your kind?"

He brandishes the phaser rifle. "You simply don't get it. Instead, you keep traveling. You strive to reach places that no human, no Klingon, no Romulan should ever set foot into. Therefore, you're a danger to the galactic harmony of spheres—and to us all." He shakes his head. "No more. We will no longer tolerate your nefarious activities, the sacrilege you're committing against the harmony of spheres, and the treason against life itself! This is not a negotiation. Discussion is of no use, for you have ceased to realize how far you have strayed, how much damage you're inflicting on yourself and other people. No, the time for words is past. The time for actions is now."

The camera zooms out a little to show the flags again. The hooded man raises his rifle, pointing it at them.

"We're ready for these actions," he announces. "Your empires need to fall, and you must be driven back into your home spheres. That's the way it should be. We are willing to be the igniting spark for the purifying conflagration that will reduce the galaxy to ashes. From these ashes, a new and better future will arise."

He gets to his feet. Shouldering his weapon, he takes two steps toward the camera. The beacons in the shadows of his face glow brighter than ever.

"Your poisonous empires and alliances need to perish," he says, and it sounds like a sacred oath. "They must burn. The slate needs to be wiped absolutely clean to make way for a new beginning."

Suddenly, he aims his rifle at the camera. The barrel points toward the audience, virtually hiding the man who might be a Renao.

"The line has been drawn," the man announces with a gravelly voice. "Remember the events from a few days ago, and you will realize that, too. Once you've done that… brace yourselves!"

The barrel of the phaser remains motionless in the center of the image as if the powerful threat requires visual underlining.

And… cut.

6
NOVEMBER 4, 2385,

Paris, Earth

The silence inside the council chamber was deafening. The oblong, windowless hall within the Palais de la Concorde where generations had held their debates and disputes on an almost daily basis seemed to hold its breath. Just like the many dozen beings that had assembled here.

They were sitting in long rows on either side of the middle aisle. The lighting that was mounted on the narrow, waist-high partitions separating these rows illuminated the horrified faces of more than one hundred and fifty eloquent representatives of various Federation worlds. They all sat shoulder to shoulder, and they all sat equally speechless.

Fleet Admiral Leonard James Akaar couldn't blame them. He occupied one of three single, shell-type seats on a marble dais that was lined with marble columns. The seats had been arranged symbolically beneath the Great Seal of the Federation. He also had difficulties finding appropriate words, although he had watched that particular holovid three times during the past few hours. It hadn't enlightened him in the slightest.

Akaar was Starfleet's commander-in-chief. The man from Capella IV was almost one hundred and twenty years old, and had been holding this post for more than four years, following a long and distinguished career in Starfleet that dated back to the late twenty-third century. While these days he spent most of his time either in his office at Fleet Headquarters in San Francisco or here at the Parisian seat of the Federation President and the Council, in his time he had seen far more than he had ever imagined possible. Not many of those things had been pleasant.

President Kellessar zh'Tarash stood at the lectern to his right. She had only been inaugurated four days ago, but she spoke with the tone of someone upon whom the burden of the presidency was weighing heavily. "One of our automated subspace relay stations near Ventax received this message approximately seventy minutes ago. It was sent all across the galaxy, into Federation, Klingon, and Cardassian space at least, and it appears to have been sent to the Typhon Pact powers as well. Whoever the sender might be, he wants to be heard. He wants our attention."

Silence. Wherever Akaar looked, he met completely stumped gazes. He knew that many of these would turn into an expression of determination soon enough. They usually did. Tragically, the Federation Council had gotten very good at dealing with horrifying messages of late.

"This message does not come without context," zh'Tarash continued. Her voice was calm and steady; her demeanor conveyed inner strength and confidence. "You know that as well as I do. I have asked Fleet Admiral Akaar to join us, so he can clarify that context for us once more. Admiral?" The Andorian woman faced him with an encouraging nod, before taking a step back from the lectern.

Akaar rose unsteadily—the shell-type seats had been designed for beings whose average height was far below that of a Capellan—and approached the lectern, straightening his crisp black and red uniform. Attentively, he waited until the president was seated. The glaring spotlight that some cruel interior decorator had embedded into the ceiling directly above the lectern began heating his head, and he could feel sweat starting to collect beneath his flowing white hair.

"Three thousand nine hundred seventy-four," said Akaar, touching a small key on the lectern's surface. Immediately, a frozen image of Starbase 91 appeared behind him at the wall, straight below the Federation emblem. "That's how many were on board Starbase 91 and the ships docked there three days ago. Remember that number. The 'beginning' mentioned in the recording you have just watched consists of almost four thousand lost lives."

A murmur rose in the chamber; the first sign of life from the council members in more than two minutes.

"And those are only the victims we know about so far. The Klingon High Council is already edgy, and I have to assume that this will not be the final toll. However, I am *not* referring to the threat that we've just heard, be it believable or not. I'm referring to the strategic value that Starbase 91 posed for us. I'm referring to the long-term concerns regarding its destruction."

Out of the corner of his eye he noticed that zh'Tarash and Admiral Markus Rohde of Starfleet Intelligence were quietly whispering to each other on the dais. Rohde probably would have been the better choice to deliver this speech.

Akaar pressed another control. The station's image was replaced by a strategic map of the region around the Lembatta Cluster. "Geographically speaking, Starbase 91 may have been remote. However, it was immensely important strategically due to its array of long-range deep-space sensors. We have lost a key observation point around near Gorn space. Admittedly, current intelligence from Cestus III is that the Gorn are keeping to themselves for the time being, unlike some of their fellow members of the Typhon Pact. Unless you have intel to the contrary, Admiral?" He looked at Rohde who shook his head silently.

The admiral continued. "What's more, they have distanced themselves from this incident and are insisting on their innocence. I tend to believe them. Still, I know I would sleep much more soundly if I could be sure that we're keeping an eye on them, and that our proverbial gates aren't left open. I'd like to be certain that our watch is still unwavering."

Akaar paused to let his words sink in with the audience. Here and there he saw nodding heads... his colleague Alynna Nechayev, for one. The admiral sat in the first row on the western side of the chamber next to a Vulcan who was clad in the ceremonial robes of an ambassador.

"I know what you're going to say." Akaar let his gaze wander from one face to the next. "The Gorn are members of the Typhon Pact, and they were renegades of this pact. Deep Space 9 fell victim to their terrorist acts only two years ago. There's now another annihilated space station near Gorn space."

Again, he paused. Words influenced thoughts, and he wanted to make the councilors think and ask difficult questions. That was the only way they could come up with a well-founded opinion. Only those who contemplated were able to comprehend.

"However, I do not believe this is the work of the Typhon Pact. I know their modus operandi, their agenda, and this is not consistent with that. I believe—and the rest of Starfleet Command agrees—that this is the work of an entirely new aggressor."

A Tellarite rose hesitantly. Akaar knew him by sight but couldn't recall his name. "Yes?" the Admiral asked.

"I'm begging your pardon, but…" The Tellarite councilor twitched his porcine nose. His cavernous eyes blinked nervously. "If this really wasn't an attack by the Pact, do you believe we're dealing with a move by the Renao?"

Nechayev rose, looking at the Tellarite. "We can't rule anything out, Delegate Kyll. The intelligence service has issued warnings for several months regarding increasing radicalization within the Lembatta Cluster. I'm sure you've studied these reports meticulously."

The biting sarcasm of the last sentence had been an open attack. Nechayev knew full well—just as Akaar and all the others did—that these reports had gone virtually unnoticed by the Federation Council.

"We shouldn't rule it out completely," Akaar said, "though it's hardly proven, either."

Nechayev faced the dais, looking Akaar right in the eyes. "That *was* a Renao in that holovid."

Turning away from Nechayev's penetrating gaze, he stared at the dais behind him. "Admiral Rohde?"

The Starfleet Intelligence head rose from his seat, facing the assembly. He did not bother to step up to the lectern, but his sonorous voice filled the chamber without the assistance of amplification. "Admiral Akaar is right, as is Admiral Nechayev. The Renao are indeed more active than they have been in a long time. More to the point, they have been more *aggressive*. We've been unable to ascertain the reason for their change in behavior… if indeed it *is* a change in behavior. The Renao are a backward species, with no technology worth mentioning, particularly not in the context of the attack on Starbase 91. The presence of this holovid doesn't change that. The Renao don't pursue any political goals beyond their own worlds and are keen on isolation, not on expansion or even a holy war. Yes, we've received reports of extremist behavior, but that's limited to small breakaway groups that don't have the resources to mount an attack such as this. Beyond that, the Renao—who are so very keen on their private 'sphere'—are unlikely to suddenly turn their attention beyond their borders." He shook his head. "No, the Renao are simply not capable of such an act of terrorism. They have shown no interest in such a thing, nor an interest in us."

Nodding in his direction, Akaar turned back to the council from the lectern. "Starfleet Command shares this opinion."

"*If* this holovid really shows us one of the perpetrators of November 1—" Rohde started.

"At least he's claiming to be one of them with certain vehemence," Nechayev put in emphatically.

A Benzite councilor two rows behind her added to the admiral's comment. "Claims of responsibility are fairly common. Every time a disaster happens, we receive dozens of alleged confessions. Most are insupportable claims of extremist idealists. Their cases should be presented to psychiatrists, not to the Federation Council."

Rohde finished his thought, ignoring the two interruptions. "—it's possible that someone wants to wave a red herring under our noses. Perhaps the Renao are merely being used as a scapegoat. This seems much more likely than so major a change in Renao society coupled with an inexplicable technology boost."

"The Federation needs to respond to this disaster," Nechayev said indignantly. Unlike Kyll, she hadn't sat back down. "Admiral, I don't believe our intelligence on the Renao—or on several other races—has been nearly as thorough as we think. We have to act *now*."

I wish that were as easy as it sounds, Akaar thought wistfully.

The heavy losses suffered during the Dominion War and the Borg invasion had diminished the fleet's strength considerably. The docks were working at full capacity to rectify that but they simply couldn't perform miracles.

To the admiral's surprise, the president appeared by his side.

"And we *will* act." Zh'Tarash placed a hand on Akaar's shoulder when he attempted to make way for her. "I suggest dispatching a ship to the periphery of the Lembatta Cluster, both to determine the exact cause of Starbase 91's destruction and to investigate once and for all whether or not the Renao are behind these tragic events. What say you?"

The unusual silence that had fallen over the council after watching the holovid ended rather abruptly. All across the chamber, delegates wanted to be heard. Akaar quickly took his seat and allowed the process to play out, tuning out the specifics in the hopes of a quick end result.

After approximately one hour, the president raised her hand and stated for the record that a resolution had been passed, which marked the end of the session.

Akaar got to his feet and remained standing while waiting for the president to leave the room. Once she departed the chamber, he went straight to the turbolift that would take him to the transporter station on the second floor of the Palais.

Within a few minutes, he materialized in Transporter Bay 5 in Starfleet Headquarters in San Francisco, the closest one to his office in that edifice.

His aide, a Vulcan lieutenant named Sendak, was waiting for him, studying the padd in his long-fingered hand. Akaar suspected that it displayed his schedule, which was about to be radically changed.

"Sendak," the admiral said as he stepped off the platform, "I need a ship."

7
NOVEMBER 4, 2385

U.S.S. *Prometheus*, docked at DS9

Captain Richard Adams was sitting in his ready room going over the personnel files of the latest additions to the *Prometheus* crew when his intercom beeped and Ensign Amanda Harris, the beta-shift communications officer, said, *"Bridge to captain."*

Without taking his eyes off the screen where he had brought up the file for a Vulcan conn officer, Lieutenant T'Shanik, the captain said, "Adams here."

"Captain, we're receiving a priority call from Starfleet Headquarters. It's Admiral Akaar."

"Akaar?" For a moment, Adams entertained the notion that the Starfleet commandant commander was calling out of friendship. Adams had served under Captain Leonard James Akaar on the U.S.S. *Wyoming* more than thirty years ago. It had been his first post after graduating from the Academy, eventually advancing to deputy security chief on the *Mediterranean*-class starship.

However, Akaar wouldn't use a priority channel for a personal call to his former protégé. "Put him through, Ensign."

"Aye, sir."

The file on the screen was replaced briefly by the Federation seal, and then by the face of the giant Capellan with his flowing white locks, sitting at his desk, fingers interlaced and a serious expression on his face.

However, that serious expression modulated to a smile. *"Dick."*

"Leonard," Adams replied, nodding.

"It is good to see you, old friend. How are you?"

"I can't complain. It's great being able to take a break after six months patrolling the Tzenkethi border. The crew really needs it."

"Did the Tzenkethi cause any trouble? Forgive me, but I haven't had a chance to take more than a quick glance at the mission report."

"No more than expected. You know the Tzenkethi, they're demanding neighbors."

His counterpart nodded sympathetically. In the early 2360s there had been a war between the Federation and the Tzenkethi Coalition. Unlike Adams, who had been serving as security chief aboard the deep-space explorer the U.S.S. *Sutherland* at the time, Akaar had been at the forefront of that conflict against the angelically beautiful, luminous figures whose culture was so contradictory to the Federation's values that diplomacy had totally failed. These days, the Tzenkethi settled for straying into Federation territory with their tear-shaped ships every once in a while, although they seemed to have become more audacious since they joined the Typhon Pact.

"How many encounters occurred?" the admiral asked.

"We saw their ships every couple of days. Sometimes I had the impression they were trying to keep us busy. But we were only drawn into more serious incidents about a dozen times, although those usually involved chasing one of their Marauders out of orbit from one of our colonies. The *Prometheus* was never really in danger. Since her upgrading after the Borg invasion three years ago she's been an even tougher nut to crack than before."

Akaar smiled. *"That was the intention."* His expression turned serious again. *"And that is one of two reasons why I'm contacting you today, Captain."*

Adams felt his body tense. The conversation had just turned official. "Is there a problem, Admiral?"

"More than that. We're heading toward a galactic crisis at warp speed. It's already all over the news here on Earth, so it won't be long before it will reach Deep Space 9. So I thought it better coming from me."

Frowning, the captain leaned forward. "What in heaven's name has happened?"

Akaar explained it to him.

Adams couldn't help but clench his fists. He felt as if the ground had been pulled out from under his feet, and he was glad to be sitting at his desk. *Starbase 91 destroyed. Four thousand deaths.* "Karen…" he croaked.

The admiral on the other side of the display paused. *"What did you say?"*

Adams refocused his attention back to the image of his old mentor. He cleared his throat. "Were there any survivors, sir?"

Akaar shook his head full of regret. *"Not as far as we know, no. The U.S.S.* Capitoline *has been there briefly in order to take initial scans before she had to continue her journey on an important mission. The station and all docked ships—one of them being the U.S.S.* Lakota—*have been destroyed completely."*

Distraught, Adams shook his head. "How am I going to explain that to her mother?"

"Whose mother, Dick?"

Adams took a deep breath. "My niece was stationed at

Starbase 91. It was her first post since graduating. She was only twenty-six."

The admiral's expression turned to one of grief. *"I'm so sorry to hear that, Dick. I had no idea."* He paused for a moment. *"There is a small chance that an escape pod was jettisoned, but the* Capitoline *didn't pick up any homing beacons. Though one could be out there with a damaged beacon."*

Akaar's words expressed a glimmer of hope, but his eyes betrayed those words. He didn't believe that for a second—and neither did Adams.

"I appreciate the thought, Leonard, but I'm not going to get my hopes up. Karen is dead, just like all the others." The captain tightened his jaw. He probably hadn't been the perfect uncle to his sister Carol's daughter. His duty in space had always come first, so at best they had all met up once a year. Still, he had always felt a special bond with Karen as she had been the only child in their family. What's more, she was the only one from his sister's family who had followed the call of the stars, just like him. *And now the stars have killed her,* he thought.

No, not the stars. A bunch of lunatics.

He straightened his back. "What is the *Prometheus*'s mission, Admiral?"

"I want you to pick up where the Capitoline *left off. Proceed at maximum speed to the scene of the disaster and find out what really happened there. We are in possession of a video with a claim of responsibility from a person who's obviously a Renao. At the same time we have reports about increasing radicalization movements in the Lembatta Cluster."*

That caught Adams's attention. "Does that mean we had a warning that something like this might happen?"

"No," said Akaar. *"Nobody could have expected such an attack.*

The station had no chance to issue an emergency call. That indicates that this attack happened with extreme speed and intensity. Renao technology shouldn't be capable of that. Starbase 91 hardly had cutting-edge technology, but they should have been able to fend off such an attack—or at least put up more of a fight than they did."

"So you think there's more to it than meets the eye?"

"Absolutely."

"The Typhon Pact?"

"We shouldn't rule anything out at this stage, and the Tholians and Gorn are both proximate to the starbase's position."

Adams nodded. While the Federation seemed to have been coming to some kind of understanding with the Romulans and the Gorn, at the very least, one never could be sure that the right hand knew what the left was doing when dealing with the members of the pact. Plus, the Tholians still maintained a hostile attitude toward the Federation.

Akaar continued. *"And that's the reason why we're sending Prometheus in particular. She's one of the fastest ships in Starfleet, and she's as powerful as a small squadron."*

"So our mission is one of investigation?"

"To begin with, yes. Your best starting point is to contact Onferin, the Renao homeworld, and question them."

"I'm a soldier, Admiral, not a diplomat. You know that."

The Capellan tilted his head. *"That is why we are sending you a diplomat. The president will be dispatching an emissary, whom you will meet on Lembatta Prime. In addition, you have Lieutenant ak Namur on board with you. I saw him at the graduation ceremony last month."*

"He rejoined us on Deep Space 9."

"He's the only Renao in Starfleet, and he's on your crew. Make use of him."

Adams wasn't sure it would be that simple. When he was

serving as an exchange officer, relations had deteriorated between the Federation and the Renao, and several of ak Namur's kin requested that he terminate his time on board. But the young man had fallen in love with deep space and had requested to attend Starfleet Academy. Adams had made that possible—but it had cost the Renao dearly. He had been forced to turn his back on everything the Renao people deemed sacred. It would likely be difficult for ak Namur to return to his old home in a situation like this.

He's a Starfleet officer now, Adams thought. *He has to face this challenge just like the rest of us.*

"Is there a problem, Captain?" Akaar had apparently noticed Adams's hesitation.

"No, Admiral. No problem. You can count on us."

"That's what I wanted to hear."

"Is there anything else I should know?"

"We're sending everything we have on the Renao in general and this attack in particular."

"All right." Adams glanced at the chronometer that was mounted on the wall next to the door. "It's 2100 ship's time. I will recall all personnel and speed up our final repair work. We should be ready to depart when alpha shift begins tomorrow morning."

"Excellent." Akaar sat up at his desk. *"That will be all, Captain."* His hand moved toward the control panel on his desk to sign off. *"Oh, and Dick… take care of yourself and your crew."*

"I will," Adams promised.

"Good. Akaar out."

"Thank you, Commander, for the guided tour on your ship," said Miles O'Brien, the chief of operations from Deep

Space 9, as they approached the lock he and his assistant Nog had used an hour earlier to come aboard. "I've always wanted to climb aboard a *Prometheus*-class starship. It's always a privilege to visit the first ship of its kind. And the multivector assault mode is a damn fine piece of technology. I'd love to see it in action, and the same goes for your slipstream drive."

Commander Roaas tilted his furry head. His whiskers twitched almost imperceptibly. The Caitian was proud to serve aboard the *Prometheus*, and he always appreciated appraisal by specialists. "I don't know whether you'd really want that, Chief. Usually, we're in fairly precarious situations when we have to separate the *Prometheus*."

O'Brien scratched the back of his head. "Yeah, you're probably right."

"I would also like to express my gratitude," Nog piped up. "It was very kind of you to make time for us."

Roaas looked at O'Brien's deputy. Nog was a Ferengi—a species that wasn't particularly renowned for selflessness and honorable service. Roaas wondered which personal experiences had brought Nog to Starfleet. "You have helped us out with parts and personnel during these past few days in order to put this ship back in immaculate condition. Commander Kirk was extremely pleased with your crew's work. It seemed only fair to give you the grand tour."

"Oh, on the subject of Kirk…" O'Brien hesitated as if he was embarrassed to ask this question. "Is she… I mean, is she a member of *the* Kirk family?"

"Why didn't you ask her yourself when we were in the engine room?" said Roaas.

"Well, I didn't want to be pushy. I'm sure people probably ask her that all the time."

Roaas couldn't help but grinning. "Actually, you might have a point there."

"So? Is she related to James T. Kirk? You know, we used to have a Jamie Samantha Kirk on the station, she was a granddaughter of Kirk's brother... if I'm not wrong."

"In which case those two ladies might indeed be related. Commander Kirk is his brother's great-granddaughter."

"Ha, I knew she bore a resemblance to him."

"If you say so." For Roaas, human women looked completely different from human men. As far as he was concerned, Jenna Kirk might as well have been Captain Adams's daughter.

O'Brien's expression became pensive. "I wonder if there's ever been a Kirk in Starfleet who wasn't related to the captain of the NCC-1701."

"I'm afraid I can't help you there," said Roaas.

The combadge fastened to his uniform jacket beeped, and the captain's sonorous voice said, *"Adams to Roaas."*

The Caitian said, "Please, excuse me for a moment." He tapped his chest. "Roaas here."

"Commander, please join me in my ready room immediately."

"I have just finished a guided tour for Chief O'Brien and Lieutenant Commander Nog. I'm on my way."

"Very well. Adams Out."

Terminating the connection, he faced his guests. "I'm very sorry, but I've got to leave you now. Duty calls." He approached the lock, touching the control on the wall to open it.

"No problem at all," O'Brien replied, waving his hand dismissively. "We've taken up enough of your time. It was a pleasure to meet you, Commander."

"The pleasure has been all mine." Roaas nodded

farewell. "Chief, Commander."

While both engineers left for DS9, Roaas headed toward the turbolift to go up to deck one where the captain's ready room was located. He approached the door and buzzed in.

"Come," Adams's voice came through the door, which prompted the door to hiss open. He entered the room, and the door closed behind him.

"Captain."

Adams stood by the window on the other side of the room, staring out toward the cold, distant stars on the other side of the pane. The light was dimmed and there was no indication Adams had been working on anything immediate.

The captain greeted his first officer without turning around. "I'm glad you're here, Roaas." His voice was filled with gloom, which caught Roaas's attention immediately. Adams seemed slumped, as if a heavy burden weighed on his shoulders.

"Are you all right, Captain?" he asked, approaching him.

Adams didn't answer for a while. He kept staring out of the window. A portion of the new Deep Space 9 was visible, behind it the vanishing shape of a Rigelian freighter, heading toward a seemingly empty point in space. A moment later, space seemed to explode into an enormous blue vortex with a center, glowing in gold. The freighter headed into the wormhole, which collapsed almost immediately upon the freighter entering it.

"I've seen this at least a dozen times in the past few days," Adams said into the silence. "But I've never actually appreciated it. The beauty of the wormhole, I mean. Are we now so apathetic due to all these galactic crises that we don't even perceive the wonders surrounding us? Do we just look at them, and our spirit of research remains dormant?" He faced Roaas. It seemed to the Caitian as if the wrinkles in his old friend's face had sharpened.

"What's happened, Captain?" he asked quietly.

"We've got a new mission."

That didn't bode well. After the required repairs had been finished, the *Prometheus* was meant to head to Risa for a well-deserved week's shore leave. "What is it?"

Adams stared out of the window again. "Some lunatics have blown up Starbase 91. The U.S.S. *Lakota* was docked there, and has also been destroyed. Almost four thousand are dead. Starfleet has received a video with a claim of responsibility from a group of radicals. They claim that this attack is their way of declaring war on the entire galaxy. They're not just after the Federation, they're also coming for the Klingons, the Ferengi, and heaven knows who else. Supposedly, the Renao are behind it."

Roaas's ears twitched. "That doesn't make sense."

"No, it doesn't. The Renao aren't advanced enough for such an attack, and they're also isolationists. Galactic politics have never interested them so far."

"The Typhon Pact?" Roaas asked.

"We can't rule that out, although we have official condemnations of this act already, one of them from the Gorn. We've been tasked with heading there, and finding out what happened. We're also supposed to contact the government on Onferin in order to find out their stance on this incident. A special envoy has already been dispatched."

Roaas nodded. "I see. When are we going to depart?"

"Tomorrow at 0800."

"I'll get everything ready."

"Thanks, Roaas."

The Caitian took that as a hint to withdraw and return to

work but he hesitated. Something about Adams's demeanor deeply irritated him. The loss of a starbase and a starship was tragic, without the shadow of a doubt. But usually, that kind of news didn't affect Adams that way. Roaas hadn't seen his friend this distraught since the destruction of the U.S.S. *Red Cloud*. The heavy cruiser of the *Akira*-class had been under the command of Adams's wife, Rhea Kadani, and it had been part of the fleet consisting of forty ships that defended the planet Vulcan against the Borg during those horrendous days in 2381, just like the *Prometheus*.

Only four ships had survived that battle. The *Red Cloud* hadn't been one of them.

Suddenly it dawned on Roaas: The captain's niece, his sister's only child, had been serving on the starbase. She had to be one of the four thousand victims. A wave of compassion swept over Roaas. The Caitians were a people to whom their family, their clan, meant everything. Roaas could empathize very well what Adams must have been going through in that moment.

"Captain," he said quietly. "Your niece?" He let the words linger in the air.

Adams stiffened almost imperceptibly. "Initial reports state that there have been no survivors."

Roaas put his hand on the other man's shoulder. "I feel for you. We'll find the perpetrators. And they will pay for that."

The captain glanced at his first officer, nodding quietly.

The intercom beeped, and Harris's voice said, *"Bridge to captain."*

Roaas lowered his hand, and Adams straightened as he walked over to his desk. "Yes?"

"Captain, we… are receiving an official communiqué from the president of the Federation. She is talking to the press in the

Palais de la Concorde. Apparently... there's been a terrorist attack. Starbase 91 has been completely wiped out."

Roaas saw his captain drawing a deep breath. "I know, Ensign," he said.

As of that moment, the whole entire galaxy knew.

8
NOVEMBER 5, 2385

Tika System, Klingon Empire

Tika IV was not a beautiful world by any stretch of the imagination. Several broad ice and stone rings orbited around the dirt-brown gas giant that consisted of helium and hydrogen. A solitary, tiny space station drifted in orbit. It had been abandoned and left to discover its own destiny in the vacuum long ago. Now it was adrift and it ended up a little closer to the planet every year. The gas mining company it had once belonged to had ceased to exist ages ago.

Silent space, silent night. If it hadn't been for the gas giant's small moon that was dotted with deep craters and rough boulders, the entire Tika system would have fallen into oblivion. With this moon, however, it boasted at least one valuable waypoint.

Those who only knew this moon from afar called it Tika IV-B, and all they cared about was its profitability; those, who actually set up camp here, called it *qung*—the Hole.

K'mpoch had never known a more beautiful place in his life. The muscular worker with his shoulder-length brown hair and the scarred chest had grown up on one of the worlds on the periphery of the Klingon Empire, where the youth indulged in bloodwine and brawling so they didn't have to contemplate more useful pastimes. When he was barely old enough to find a space port by himself, K'mpoch had hidden in the bay of a smelly freighter, his mind set on fleeing toward the future. He had no aim, no plan—he just wanted to get away.

His way led him into some of the most disgusting areas of the Empire, including one penal colony. Then he wound up at the Hole.

He had been blind drunk when he signed up, and he truly couldn't remember anything about it. One night, after he had just left the penal colony behind, he had been roaming around some bars and dives looking for arguments and alcohol, and he had found both in abundance. Next thing he knew, he woke up with a huge gap in his memory on a transport ship among a bunch of guys who were even more dumb and rugged than he was. In his pocket, he found his first wages and a five-year contract with his signature on it.

Since then, K'mpoch had been working underground. The Hole—that insignificant looking piece of rock in orbit around Tika IV—boasted rich dilithium reserves, and K'mpoch now belonged to a two-hundred-strong workforce prospecting for crystal treasures deep underground. They hauled the stuff to the surface that fueled the empire's space ships. They were living in plain barracks, far away from any civilization, protected from the void of space only by a vaguely glimmering energy field high above their heads, but they fulfilled an honorable duty.

At least, that's what they told themselves whenever the Hole stretched their patience.

"*DenIb Qatlh!*" cursed Rotal, furiously punching his gloved fist onto the controls of their small and old *yolok*, their mining vehicle.

"Is it still not starting? How many times do I have to inform the main office before someone moves their ridges down here to fix it?"

K'mpoch stifled a cynical grin. He didn't see any point in increasing his foreman's fury. "Try again," he suggested, just like he had done many times during the past few days. "Right hand on the drive control, left hand on the steering controls, and then take it slow and steady."

Rotal glared at him as if he intended to rip his head off, before spitting into his throat. "You reckon?" he growled, every syllable dripping with sarcasm.

They were both wedged into the driver cabin. Behind them, on the long truck bed, lay several tools waiting for their daily usage. When K'mpoch looked through the small cabin window and beyond the open vehicle hangar doors, he could spot the blocks made from perma-concrete and transparent aluminum in the twilight. He and his boss had only left them a few minutes ago to start their work. The early shift was settling down to rest there now. Artificial light illuminated the plain facades. Their mine was located on the dark side of the moon. Even during daytime, it was black as night here.

"Come on," said K'mpoch, ignoring Rotal's tone of voice, and nodded toward the *yolok's* console. Patience was a virtue, not a weakness. That was one of the things the Hole had taught him. "Just like yesterday, wait 'til it's warmed up slightly, and then…"

Rotal hit his helping hand aside. "Are *you* the foreman now?" he snapped at his passenger. Rotal was almost eight years younger than K'mpoch, but he had never heard about the concept of respecting his elders. "You think you know better than me?"

K'mpoch waved his hand dismissively. "I just want to get into the mine, boss."

"And I want new vehicles. And if I don't get what I want, why should you be so lucky?"

K'mpoch kept quiet. He wasn't looking for a fight, not this early in the day. He'd rather save his energy for the mine and its dilithium veins.

"Well?" Rotal followed up aggressively, grinning menacingly when his passenger didn't reply. Several of his teeth were blackened from decay, and his breath reeked. "That's what I thought. You have a big mouth but don't know anything."

Silently, K'mpoch counted to ten. It wasn't worth getting agitated. Rotal was a stubborn idiot, and he would never change.

The idiot reached out with his left hand, touching the small comm device below the cabin roof. Immediately, it sprang to a colorful life, and random noises crackled inside the transport's cabin. "Yolok II calling main office. Base, respond."

No response. The crackling seemed to increase as if even the radio was conspiring against Rotal.

"Yolok II to base," the foreman repeated. "Damnit, are you still sleeping it off over there? What's going on with you? I'm sitting here in a broken-down vehicle, *again*!"

Nothing. If anyone in the main office was able to hear him, they obviously didn't care about his accusing tone of voice. K'mpoch found it increasingly difficult to stifle a grin.

The moon didn't have any atmosphere at all, apart from the artificial one inside the dome. There was no greenery, no water, and no life. But there were ample mineral resources; in fact, the moon was so rich in these resources that beaming posed an incalculable risk due to their radiation. Every last piece of equipment needed to be transported by "worm"—or *yolok* as the workers called their small plated-wheel mining vehicles in their native Klingon language—into the mines.

The same applied to the workers, of course. Around the beginning and end of each shift, the dirt roads between the mines and the accommodation area became very busy. Minor collisions were commonplace, and it showed on the *yoloks*.

"Kahless give me strength," Rotal grumbled, making another futile attempt at starting the old transporter. "I'm surrounded by idiots..." He glared at the comm device. "Yolok II to the *pujwI'* sitting in the main office and is apparently a few worms short of a full plate of *gagh*... respond, damnit! Come in!"

K'mpoch shook his head. "Let's just take another car."

"We will," his seatmate growled. "But before I heave all that stuff from this truck bed to another, I want to let the idiots up there know how much they're getting on my nerves! Yolok II to..."

A piercing howl interrupted his call. It came from the hidden loudspeakers of the comm system, and only lasted a few seconds. As soon as it ended, a loud alarm siren sounded.

K'mpoch looked at Rotal quizzically. "What's that all about?"

"I tell you, what it's about," the foreman answered angrily, "our *pujwI'* up there fell asleep on the wrong console."

Lights came on in the barracks. Apparently, the alarm was not only audible via the radio. K'mpoch reached for the door's opening mechanism. "Hang on," he muttered.

"What?"

K'mpoch opened the door. There it was—the sirens were wailing loudly across the entire complex. The sound rose and fell, and it seemed to come from all directions at the same time.

"What is going on?" Rotal took his hands off the controls. "Nobody mentioned anything about a drill."

It wasn't a drill. K'mpoch didn't know why he was so sure, but he was. He had an extremely uneasy feeling. "Let's go and have a look," he said, and was already halfway outside the cabin.

"Bah." His foreman shook his fist, before following him. "Look at what, exactly? The idiots who are scared by a drill?"

K'mpoch quickly crossed the hangar. Before stepping outside, he hesitated in the doorway, scanning the area with his eyes. People had appeared by the windows and doors of the barracks—tired men from the earlier shift. They seemed puzzled. K'mpoch looked left toward where the administration building marked the perimeter of the complex. It was brightly lit. Did his eyes deceive him, or did he notice hectic movements behind the main office's windows?

"We're under attack," he murmured, more amazed than concerned.

"Nonsense," Rotal growled, suddenly standing next to him. But K'mpoch sensed doubt in his voice. "Why should anyone attack us? This is merely a zit on the spotted ass of the empire. Where's the honor in that, you fool?"

K'mpoch shrugged, looking up to the energy dome and the distant stars of the Tika system. "Not everyone is looking for honor…"

Nothing was out there. No aggressor anywhere. No noticeable danger—just quiet, silent space.

"And anyway," added Rotal. "If we were to have visitors, that *pujwI'* should have mentioned something ages ag—"

He didn't get a chance to finish his sentence. A low voice added to the wailing of the sirens, shouting from the loudspeakers all over the complex. "*Attention! Attention! Intruder alert. To arms! I repeat: Intruder alert. To arms!*"

But it was already too late. A fraction of a second later, the energy dome high above K'mpoch's head glowed bright red. It was the last thing that the Klingon saw in his life.

9

NOVEMBER 5, 2385

Council Chambers, Qo'noS

The Klingon Empire's multi-level government building stood right in the pulsating center of the First City, as the proud—but not necessarily creative—warriors had named their capital many generations ago. It was dozens of meters high, reaching up to the overcast night sky. It served as a symbol of Klingon strength and steadfastness. Columns lined the entrance area, where the Empire's emblem was displayed in impressive size on the dark façade, illuminated day and night by hidden lanterns.

Alexander Rozhenko hurried up the steps toward the building's main entrance, tightly wrapping his cloak around his body to keep warm. He was the son of two public Klingon figures. His mother had been Ambassador K'Ehleyr, a human-Klingon hybrid, and his father was Worf, son of Mogh. He'd spent the best part of his childhood and adolescence aboard various starships, at diplomatic receptions, and in the care of the Rozhenkos, his father's foster parents.

His mother's violent death was one of the reasons why he had lost his way early in life. Approximately ten years ago, he had finally developed an interest in Klingon culture, although he was permanently at odds with it. After initial difficulties, he had finally found his place in the Klingon military, not least because his father and Chancellor Martok, then a general, had put in a good word for him, followed by a second career in the diplomatic corps, also owing to his father's status and contacts. Rozhenko had been working for almost six years as Federation Ambassador in the Klingon Empire, a job previously held by each of his parents at different times. He served as liaison between the Klingons and the United Federation of Planets, and he had realized a long time ago that he was predestined for this post. It was the perfect place for a person who straddled both nations, yet had no real place in either of them.

Not that the middle of the night in the High Council is a good place for anyone. Sighing, he entered the government building. His hair, bound into a ponytail, was dripping with water. An attaché, who had apparently been expecting him, scurried toward him in the entrance hall. Larger-than-life statues of various warriors and politicians lined the plain stone walls. Braziers burned in between them, chasing the night shadows away. The smell of smoke and sweat lingered in the air.

"Ambassador," the pale attaché greeted him with nervously fluttering hands. A tiny mustache blemished his upper lip. Judging by his slenderness, he was of Munjeb III origin, one of many worlds under the Klingon flag. "My name is Korrt, sir. The chancellor himself has ordered me to take you to him right away. The council is already assembling in the Great Hall."

"Is this about Tika IV-B?" Rozhenko asked. He allowed Korrt to guide him, although he would have found the way blindfolded.

"I'm afraid I don't have access to that kind of information, sir." Korrt glanced around furtively as they climbed up the steps to the Great Hall. The wide door was already open, two armed warriors standing guard on either side. Beyond the doorway, Rozhenko spotted the first council members. They were engrossed in conversation, gesticulating furiously, and they were evidently enraged.

"If you'd like to enter?"

Rozhenko ignored Korrt's slight bow at the gate to bid him farewell, and went into the Great Hall. As always he found it elating to enter this room. Nowhere else, not aboard a Bird of Prey, and not even in any of the monasteries did he feel closer to his Klingon heritage than here. The hall was the core of the ancient government building. It was rectangular with a high ceiling. Visitors walked across the shiny marble floor to a dais, where they had to climb up two steps. Various artificial light sources discreetly illuminated the throne of the esteemed chancellor. It was the only piece of furniture in the entire room. A circular, cast-iron chandelier hung above it from the ceiling. The emblem of the Empire was mounted on the otherwise bare wall behind the chair.

Rozhenko let his eyes wander. Everyone was present. The High Council was comprised of more than two dozen representatives of the Empire's most powerful families. They oversaw the welfare of their people. As usual, the chancellor presided, and he was already seated in his chair.

Martok, the one-eyed veteran and leader of the Klingons for more than ten years, sat there with his fingers interlaced in his lap. He wore the ceremonial robe of his office. Rozhenko had served under him in the Klingon Defense Force and knew how little the old man with the wild mane of hair and the bushy eyebrows thought of such symbols of status and grandeur.

"Ambassador," shouted Martok when he noticed the latecomer, beckoning him closer. "Come. Here, to my side."

The chancellor is asking me to join him? Surprised, Rozhenko followed the request. He usually addressed the council in his role as ambassador from the floor or he stayed in the background to observe. This was something different.

He greeted Martok with a nod.

But Martok was already looking the other way at the council. "Silence!" He had to stomp his foot three times before they finally grew silent. "We shall begin!"

"Is it really true, Chancellor?" a giant with a gray beard shouted. Rozhenko couldn't bring his name to mind. A deep scar ran across his right check—a mark of honor. "Did these red-skinned demons back up their words with deeds? Is this a repeat of what happened at Starbase 91?"

Murmurs rose in the hall. Clenching their fists, the delegates exchanged looks and uttered curses. Composure and being Klingon were two concepts very seldom related—except where Martok was concerned.

The chancellor rose from his seat. "I convened this session in order to inform you all of the latest developments. Our mining facility on Tika IV has been the target of a malicious, unprovoked attack by unknown forces, and…"

"Unknown?" the gray-bearded man cut him short and snorted derisively. "Let's not be fooled! We all know who's behind that nefarious act, don't we? This Renao fanatic announced it; it was too bold a statement to miss!"

"The Federation has its doubts about that," Martok replied loudly. He stared at the man with the gray beard, threateningly. "There is no evidence save for that holomessage, to which you're obviously referring, Grotek."

Grotek spat. "The Federation is a bunch of quixotic weaklings. The day when I will listen to what Earth and the Federation lackeys have to say will definitely be my final day."

"Chancellor, I must agree with the son of Braktal," Britok

said. The muscular representative of the House of Konjah glanced at Grotek, nodding. He wore his Defense Force armor, his hand resting casually at his hip, poised to pull out his disruptor. "What evidence does President zh'Tarash need if a confession isn't enough for her? Does she need to witness the atrocities of these red-skinned cowards first hand before she's prepared to believe it?"

"Well, she won't have to wait long," Grotek stated, and everyone around them murmured approvingly. "Remember the flags in the dirt in front of the Renao. If we don't act now, these *petaQpu* will target their next objective soon. They're attacking out of nowhere, Chancellor! They deceive us with half an eternity of inaction, and when they finally show their true colors they don't even have enough honor for a fair fight face to face! In the name of the Klingon people I demand revenge!"

"Listen to Grotek!" Britok demanded. He no longer addressed the chancellor; instead facing the council. "Do we really want to stand idly by until they have made a decision on Earth? Are we turning into Starfleet's lapdogs? If so, we should cancel the Khitomer Accords that bind us to be the Federation's allies, immediately!"

At this moment it dawned on Alexander why Martok had summoned him. "The Lembatta Cluster is part of Federation territory," he said loudly and firmly. Silence fell over the council. More than twenty pairs of eyes stared at him, clearly annoyed at his unsolicited contribution to the discussion. "It wouldn't be a good idea if you hastily dispatched an invasion fleet to that region. Such an act might be misinterpreted."

"Bah!" Britok took a step toward the dais where Martok and Alexander stood. "Let Earth be afraid. If they're failing to notice our true motives, it's because they're slow-witted. Let zh'Tarash believe that we're coming for her. It's imperative that we act *now*!"

"Zh'Tarash is no fool," Martok took control again, his deep bass carrying through the hall. "But it seems to me that you are, Britok."

The man from the House of Konjah squared his shoulders, and his eyes widened. His accusatory gaze was fixed on the chancellor. "How *dare* you?"

Alexander shook his head. "No, how dare *you*? As a member of this esteemed assembly, you should be aware of the current shape the Defense Force fleet is in. You should also know how little is truly known about the circumstances surrounding the tragedies at Starbase 91 and Tika IV-B. And you should know that more than loud noises and rash actions are required in order to respond to provocations."

"Spoken like a true Federation lapdog," Britok growled. "Once again, the son of Worf shows his true colors."

"The son of Worf is still 'Ambassador Rozhenko' to you," he snarled with an icy voice, his glare fixed on the man in uniform. "What's more, I'm also the son of Ambassador K'Ehleyr. Your house has a lot to thank her for if my memory serves. You would be well advised to remember that... son of Graak."

That had hit home. Alexander noticed that Britok's face had drained of color. It was widely known throughout the First City that the House of Konjah owed most of its wealth—and the social status coming with it—to an export deal with the Pakleds that the late ambassador had arranged for Britok's father. The family all too willingly profited from this deal but they preferred not to mention this agreement openly. The Pakleds were by no stretch of the imagination the sort of business partners who would earn a high-ranking and renowned Klingon honor.

Alexander didn't allow Britok to come up with a verbal counterstrike. "Let me speak to my superiors in the Federation *before* you embark on a campaign against Onferin with what little the Defense Force can muster right now." Slowly, he shifted his gaze from one furious face to the next. "I can understand your fury. What's more, I share it. And I share your concern. But I also know that President zh'Tarash is not your enemy; she's your ally. The best course of action in response to the incident on Tika IV-B is by means of dialogue."

"Which I have already initiated," Martok said. He had settled back into his chair but he didn't seem placid at all. "I was told that the Federation will dispatch a ship to the Lembatta Cluster. Its mission is to shed a light on Starbase 91's demise—and to get to the bottom of the holomessage."

"*One* ship?" Grotek glanced around incredulously. "Why not a runabout? Or a shuttle?"

"The ship they are sending is the U.S.S. *Prometheus*, under the command of Captain Adams," said Martok.

Grotek fell silent. He was obviously familiar with this name—and he was aware of the firepower that this ship had at her disposal.

"I intend to follow the Federation's suit," the chancellor continued. "We will also send a ship to provide backup for Captain Adams and assess the situation." He stroked his shaggy beard. "And if we find out that the Renao are behind these attacks…"

The chancellor left his sentence unfinished. No further words were needed to clarify the meaning—even Martok's composure had its limits.

"I will go along for this mission," Alexander said suddenly, surprising himself as well as everyone else. "As liaison between the two factions. I will act as the direct link between us and the *Prometheus*."

Martok simply nodded. Rozhenko couldn't help but feel that the old strategist had expected him to volunteer.

I'll never question why he's asking me to attend the High Council again, the young ambassador thought. *The answer will invariably be that he wants something from me.*

"Which ship will it be?" Britok faced his head of government. He still felt depleted from the virtual blow that Rozhenko had dealt him. "We *must* act, Chancellor. But there is, as far as I know, only one ship near that region, and it's in orbit around Korinar, is it not?"

Martok sighed quietly. "I'm afraid so."

10
NOVEMBER 5, 2385

Korinar

The Chic Inn was anything but that. The rundown, distinctly unhygienic dive in an alley of a nameless settlement that had formed around the small space port had nothing in common with exotic elegance.

Dirty tables had been placed around a small and filthy stage in the taproom of the one-story building. Small spotlights cycled through a color-changing sequence every couple of seconds, illuminating two scantily dressed Orion dancers who went about their job with a distinct lack of enthusiasm. Music that was only bearable if you had consumed a considerable amount of alcohol continuously blared from a hidden loudspeaker in the low ceiling. A bald Cardassian with tattoos on his upper arms loitered behind a long counter by the right wall, watching the dancers while less than three steps away smugglers sealed deals under his ridged nose. Near the back wall, a handful of scruffy figures had gathered around a Dom-jot gambling table that had definitely seen better days, much like them. The air was smoke-filled and so thick you could have cut it with a knife. The stench of sweat and fermentation assaulted unsuspecting nostrils.

Especially near the floor.

Kromm pushed himself up from the stone-tiled floor with his hands, coughed up blood, which he spat out, and looked up. "Is that all you've got?" the young, strong Klingon snarled, the bloodied corners of his mouth twitching.

The Chalnoth was big. *Very* big. He wore a fishnet muscle shirt showing off his broad shoulders and muscular build. His pants were greasy, his belt had been cobbled together from leather and small bones, and his disheveled dark hair seemed to form some kind of corona around his incredibly ugly head.

"*Terik* no touch with hand!" he growled, baring the formidable tusks in his mouth. Menacingly, he shook the fist at Kromm that just seconds ago had swept him off his feet with ease. "Never touch *terik*. Rules are rules, Klingon!"

"And just who's making the rules these days, hmm?" Kromm staggered when he made it back to his feet. Not taking his eyes off his opponent, he dusted himself down. "You?"

The brute from the planet Chalna nodded firmly, taking a step toward Kromm. "Me," he stated belligerently.

The corners of Kromm's mouth twitched again. Two could play the aggression game—especially on an evening like this when he was spurred on by bloodwine. "You," he repeated, only slurring his words ever so slightly, "and whose army? Eh?"

That was precisely what the Chic's clientele had been waiting to hear. Kromm had barely evaded the hideous giant's second hit when the music stopped. When he returned the punch and almost broke his knuckles on his opponent's remarkably hard abs, they were already surrounded by a crowd consisting of far more than just Dom-jot players. The giant threw his head back and laughed. One of the Orion dancers had already grabbed a data pad, taking bets on the outcome of the brawl that was about to ensue.

"*My* rules, Klingon!" the Chalnoth shouted. "On Korinar only my rules!"

We'll see about that, thought Kromm, swinging for him again.

The Korinar system was located deep in the Beta Quadrant on the periphery of the Klingon Empire, and it was both small and insignificant. If a band of Tholians hadn't attacked this system several years ago, chances were that nobody would have heard of it outside its borders that were hardly ever crossed. Korinar III was the only Class-M planet in this system, and it had once been a settlement of Klingon idealists who wished to bring their lives back to the basics of Kahless's day. After several decades, however, little remained of that idealism. These days it was only the criminal riff-raff from nearby border worlds, or the odd space traveler who had strayed from moral and interstellar paths who found their way to Korinar's streets… or Korinar's dives.

Kromm ducked away from the Chalnoth's huge hands before lunging at him. He threw himself against his opponent but failed to knock him down. Instead, he felt the forceful impact of a knee.

He muttered, *"ghay'cha'*," gasping as the air was forced out of his lungs.

The gawping onlookers cheered. Kromm could hear them through the rushing of his own blood in his ears. The noise was giving him a headache—or was his bleeding chin the cause?

"My Korinar!" the Chalnoth cried gleefully. "My Korinar!"

That was enough. Kromm dropped backward as efficiently and forcefully as his drunken state permitted, brought up his right knee and kicked the stalwart loudmouth between the legs. He grimaced as his backside hit the ground hard.

Still, he had hit the bull's-eye. Kromm heard groaning from the crowd. He blinked and when his focus returned, the giant had doubled over, looming over him. His ugly face was pale, and his mouth formed a silent O. He rolled his eyes.

Uh oh.

Kromm rolled sideways, bumping against the legs of several onlookers. The Chalnoth dropped to his knees, emitting a surprisingly high-pitched wail, before falling flat on his monstrous face in exactly the same spot where Kromm had been lying only seconds earlier.

The crowd erupted. Klingons with enormous potbellies who probably weren't able to recognize honor if it bit them on the nose, demanded their winnings at the top of their voices. Frustrated, a shady looking Edosian sporting a broad scar on the left side of his face, walked to the exit, pushing everyone who got in his way aside. The smugglers at the counter gave each other a high five—they had evidently bet on the drunkard from Qo'noS.

Kromm didn't let his audience wait for long. As soon as the Chalnoth had hit the floor, the Klingon clambered to his feet again. He would have immediately fallen again if the crowd hadn't supported him, but he was certain of victory. With a triumphant grin on his lips he growled, lifted his foot with his heavy boot, and had every intention of placing it on his opponent's back.

But the giant whirled around. Before Kromm realized what was happening, the revolting monster was on his back in front of him, grabbing his foot with both hands and turning it abruptly. Bones cracked; the sound drowning out even the groaning of the spectators. Kromm felt as if someone was inserting red-hot blades into his ankle. His immediate reaction was to stare incredulously. Then fury kicked in, eliminating the agony along with any rational thinking.

"Prepare to meet your makers!" the Klingon hissed, white foam spraying from his trembling lips. He screamed furiously, and the sound echoed around the bar. Clenching his fists, Kromm pushed himself off the ground with his uninjured leg and pounced onto the sneering Chalnoth.

What had begun as a simple fight over a game of Dom-jot had turned into a fight to the death. Kromm was in a state of blood frenzy, fueled by alcohol. There was no logical reasoning with him; all he could think of was defending his honor. The fraudulent giant had taken him for an idiot once too often. Now he would pay for that, even if it was the last thing Kromm did.

The crowd jeered when the mismatched opponents went at each other's throats. Everyone backed away when the Klingon and the Chalnoth rolled over the floor. Dimly through his bloodlust, Kromm could hear new bets being formed in the crowd.

He clasped his hands around the Chalnoth's neck, squeezing tightly, and his opponent started wheezing. The giant tried to hit him and kick him but Kromm was relentless, ignoring his agony. All he needed to overcome his pain was the furious glint in his victim's eyes.

Suddenly, the Chalnoth's head shot forward, and he bit Kromm.

It was like an explosion at Kromm's neck. He roared when his opponent's enormous tusks sank into his flesh. Reflexively, he lost his grip of the giant's neck. Instead, he used his bony forehead as a weapon and head-butted him.

At that moment, someone fired a disruptor in the taproom, and its noise was even louder than the crowd, echoing across the taproom.

Instantly, silence fell. The entire bar, it seemed, held its breath for a brief, perplexed moment. Three dozen heads turned, looking from the fight at the Dom-jot table to the Chic's entrance.

The woman in the doorway was as lovely as sin. Long, dark hair flowed down her back, framing her thin face. Her cranial ridges were small, but not too small, and her curved eyebrows were almost divine. She wore the uniform of the Imperial fleet... and held a disruptor in her raised right hand.

"I'm glad I finally got your attention," she said. Everyone in the bar stared at her, but her brown eyes were fixed on Kromm. Every syllable of her words expressed disgust and fury. "I need to talk to you... *Captain*."

She deliberately spat the last word out like an insult. Kromm sighed deeply, hit the Chalnoth between the eyes one last time—which rendered him unconscious—and scrambled to his feet.

"Commander," he shouted, dusting his uniform off with one hand, needing the other hand to support himself on the gambling table. "What do you want? Did you miss me?"

The crowd stared at him. *Captain? This guy?*

Grinning, Kromm raised his hand and wiped the blood from the corner of his mouth. He didn't care what they thought, and it didn't do any harm to be underestimated.

Commander L'emka still stood in the Chic's doorway. Furiously she glared at her commanding officer, still aiming at the bar's ceiling with her disruptor.

"Aww, c'mon," Kromm slurred. Spreading his arms he staggered toward her. "What's wrong with a little fun? Would you rather I died of boredom in that rattrap up there? I'm not like you, Commander."

L'emka lowered her weapon. Jutting her chin out, she took one step forward. "No, sir," she replied, sounding even more scornful than the unconscious Chalnoth had done earlier. "That you are not. And the former flagship of our fleet is not a 'rattrap', either."

The music resumed. The Cardassian behind the counter had obviously decided that the brief moment of shock was over. From the corner of his eye Kromm noticed the Orion women taking to the stage again, while the other guests of the establishment returned to their filthy tables.

"Former flagship," he repeated under his breath, before letting out a loud belch. The I.K.S. *Bortas* was past her prime. The war was over. Why open up old wounds? "What the hell are you doing here, anyway?" he snarled at L'emka, coming to halt in front of her. He blinked until he got rid of his double-vision. "Is your communicator broken?"

The commander reached out with her left hand for Kromm's wrist. At first he wondered whether she intended to attempt to restrain him, but then she ripped his communicator from his wrist.

"No, not mine," she growled, presenting his obviously destroyed device.

Kromm's eyebrows remained arched. "Mhm, collateral damage."

"Indeed." She sighed. "Captain, you *must* be available at all times. Always. How often must I tell you…"

He raised his hand defensively. "It was destroyed during an honorable fight!"

L'emka's expression said more than a thousand words. Most of all it said how little the Chic had to do with honor in her eyes. "Could you at least accompany me?" she asked a little too forcefully for his liking.

"To the ship?" Kromm grimaced. "Over my dead body. It may have escaped your attention that our bloodwine supplies are desperately low, and if I have to listen to one of Nuk's mind-numbingly boring stories ever again I swear I'll go berserk."

"You have an urgent call, sir," L'emka said reproachfully. "On the ship. We would have put it through to you but…" Again, she held up the useless remains of his communicator.

Kromm hesitated. Usually, the fleet only contacted him to make sure that he hadn't drowned in a wine barrel yet. There was nothing urgent about these calls. Nobody put pressure on a son of the House of DachoH, which was one of the wealthiest and most influential houses on the homeworld.

"A call? Who from?" he asked skeptically.

L'emka told him. Captain Kromm instantly sobered up.

11
NOVEMBER 5, 2385

I.K.S. *Bortas*, in orbit around Korinar

The I.K.S. *Bortas* was a ship of the *Vor'cha*-class. She orbited around Korinar like a lazy bird of prey would hover above its victim when it wasn't particularly interested in it. Behind the flat, bifurcated bridge module with the huge primary disruptor weapon at the front of the ship followed a massive neck that flared out into broad wings with their red-glowing warp nacelles. The attack cruiser had twenty-six decks and was capable of a maximum speed of warp 9.6. Powerful disruptor cannons were mounted in both the ship's bow and aft sections, and it also had a considerable supply of torpedoes and a cloaking device at its disposal.

Songs should have been sung about this ship; it was a ship for heroes.

Alas, at present it was anything but heroic. Squaring his shoulders, Captain Kromm brushed his hair back to smooth it out after having been disheveled by the brawl, before limping into his small ready room. Dim light from circular lighting sources illuminated the weapons and trophies mounted on the walls. They were supposed to emphasize the commanding officer's strength and dignity. Everyone aboard knew that Kromm didn't earn most of these merits. The majority of his trophies originated from other members of his famous House.

Kromm cleared his voice while sitting down on his hard chair. Expectantly he looked at the comm console on the wall across the room where the Empire's emblem was displayed.

"I'm ready, Klarn," he shouted, knowing that his communications officer on the bridge would open the communication frequency.

Two heartbeats later the emblem disappeared from Kromm's monitor and was replaced by Chancellor Martok's face.

"*Qapla'*," Kromm offered the traditional greeting of warriors, beating his right fist against his chest. Wincing he realized that his ribs were still hurting from his fight with the Chalnoth.

Martok's healthy eye glared at him, impatiently. "*Captain Kromm. How good of you to make it, finally.*"

"Begging your pardon, Chancellor, but I had urgent business to attend to on the planet's surface."

"*On Korinar.*" The corners of Martok's mouth upturned slightly, but it wasn't a friendly smile. "*How are the prices for bloodwine down there? Urgent?*"

Kromm gulped. "Chancellor, I…"

But Martok waved his hand dismissively. "*I'm not calling to reprimand you, Captain. Scolding a hero of the Ning'tao would be improper; even I know that, believe me.*"

Kromm wanted to protest but Martok simply continued.

"*And we both know that you weren't transferred to the Bortas because you were expected to perform galactic masterpieces. So, please, spare me your pack of lies, Kromm. Let's just say that certain truths best remain unspoken.*"

Kromm jutted his chin. Chancellor or not, he was rapidly losing his patience with this conversation. "Then what *will* be spoken of in this call?" he asked brusquely.

"*Desperation*," Martok answered quietly. He looked down for a moment. "*Trust me, Kromm, it was born from pure desperation.*"

The hot-headed warrior remained silent for the next few minutes—while his amazement increased steadily. Martok told him about the tragedies near the Lembatta Cluster, about the fate of Starbase 91 and the dastardly attack on the dilithium mines in the Tika system. With every passing minute, Kromm's anger intensified. Only when Martok finished did the captain realize that he was clenching his fists.

"Do you want me to go to Onferin?" he asked, hardly able to believe his luck. "Should I let these cowardly red-skins know that they have made a poor choice in enemy?"

Martok didn't share his enthusiasm, that much was obvious. "*I want you to fly to the edge of the Lembatta Cluster,*" he replied. "*You will meet up with a Federation ship and…*"

"Chancellor!" Interrupting the head of the Klingon High Council in this manner was unthinkable, yet Kromm couldn't help himself. What he'd just heard was tantamount to a sacrilege that seemed to outweigh his own inappropriate behavior. "The Federation? With all due respect, sir, these bigmouths haven't got a clue when it comes to taking drastic measures. Just look at them! Do we really want to allow them to water down our justified anger with their Federation diplomacy?"

Martok sighed, but it sounded stern and not suffering. His gaze was fixed on Kromm. "*We don't want anything, Captain. I want. And last I checked I was still the leader of our glorious empire. Which makes me your commander, or would you care to dispute that?*"

Kromm didn't say anything. He felt reprimanded—but he also felt that he was right. He *was* a hero from the

Ning'tao, damnit, and not a stupid boy. Didn't that count for anything anymore?

"*Captain Kromm?*" Martok prompted him.

Finally, he nodded. "You're the leader of the empire. It... it's my honor to serve you and the empire."

Martok's eye glinted again. "*Glad to hear it,*" the old Klingon growled, pointedly straightening his ceremonial robe. "*The* Prometheus *is waiting for you near the debris of Starbase 91. If my files are correct you should be able to make that journey within four days. Therefore, you're my closest ship, Kromm—whether you and I like it or not.*"

"Four days," he promised without checking. He had no idea how far they had to travel but he didn't want to give Martok any more ammunition. "We will not let you down."

"*I hope not, son of Kaath,*" his chancellor stated. The little reference about Kromm's successful father who led the House of DachoH, stung. "*In fact, I sincerely hope not.*"

Kromm gulped once again. "If that would be all, sir..."

"*You're dismissed, Captain. Set course for Starbase 91, or rather what's left of it. And I suggest you find it in yourself to resist the temptations of your... urgent business. At least this once.*"

Kromm briefly closed his eyes. Otherwise, shame, anger, and his sense of honor might have induced him to say things that he would probably regret later.

"*Oh, one more thing,*" Martok said, and Kromm opened his eyes again. "*I'm placing a diplomat by your side—the Federation's ambassador to us, Alexander Rozhenko. He will serve as a liaison between you and the* Prometheus. *The ambassador has already departed on the U.S.S.* Aventine, *which will meet up with you.*"

A watchdog! Worse still... one selected from the bunch of diplomats that knew much more about desks and office hours than the realities of battles. Marvelous!

Don't think about the ambassador, Kromm chided himself. *And ignore Starfleet and their weaklings. This is a chance like you hadn't thought possible for years. The Renao—use them to prove yourself to Martok. Take advantage of their wrath!*

"The *Bortas* will serve the empire honorably, Chancellor." His voice quivered with anticipation, frustration, and bloodwine.

Martok nodded. "Qapla', *Captain!*"

And he signed off.

12
NOVEMBER 5, 2385

U.S.S. *Prometheus*, en route to the Lembatta Cluster

Crouching, Lenissa zh'Thiin circled around her opponent. Her antennae were bent forward intently, while she watched the man's every move. She was poised to react should he attack. At the same time, she was anxious to find a gap in his defense. Both her hands were raised, ready to fight. To her crewmates from Earth she would probably resemble a boxer from their homeworld, but Lenissa didn't fight with bare hands; instead, she held an *Ushaan-tor* in each hand respectively. The flat, semicircular blade with the handle on one side and a jagged edge on the other side was Andor's traditional tool in the ice mines. It could be found in almost every household, especially in rural areas. Children used it as a toy.

At the same time, the *Ushaan-tor* had a ritual connotation because it was used during *Ushaan* duels, when two rivals fought for life and honor following a complex code and while being chained together.

Both blades in Lenissa's hands were blunt, just like the blades in the hands of the Caitian first officer Roaas. Lenissa and Roaas were in a secluded part of the sports facility on the *Prometheus*. Next door, several men and women built up their strength and endurance on multifunctional pieces of sports equipment. Lenissa and Roaas, on the other side, practiced their fighting skills with exotic weapons.

Roaas attempted a lunge. The blade in his left hand swung around in a shimmering arc, coming down on Lenissa from above. With lightning reflexes, she blocked the hit with her own weapon. Within the blink of an eye, she also parried the Caitian's low attack. She slightly twisted the second blade, catching the edges of their *Ushaan-tors*. Whirling around past Roaas's arm, she attempted to thrust her first weapon into his side. But the Caitian also turned away from her, and she hit thin air instead. The momentum of their movements separated them, and they took their respective stances again about three steps apart.

"Very good counter," he praised her reluctantly, "just a little slow." His tail swayed behind him like a snake that was dancing to a hypnotic flute.

"You'll get tired eventually, old man," Lenissa taunted.

"Your words merely show how little you know about us Caitians," he replied, his whiskers twitching in amusement. "The steppes on Ferasa are hot and vast."

"I seem to recall that the Caitians stopped being nomads and hunting for their nourishment centuries ago. Doesn't your species consist predominantly of vegetarians these days?"

"We're not running across the wilderness in search of food," Roaas said, "we consider it relaxation."

Lenissa smiled knowingly. "Let's see how relaxing you find this." With an outcry, she sprang into action.

When the Andorian woman had joined the *Prometheus* as chief of security six months earlier, she had realized soon after that she had found a soulmate in the older Caitian. He was a warrior, just like her, and his extensive knowledge about combat styles and weapons of various cultures had quickly fascinated Lenissa. She had enjoyed fairly comprehensive combat training during her time at Starfleet and hadn't realized how many gaps she still had in her knowledge. Roaas not only helped her close these gaps, he also taught her a Caitian method of motion meditation that helped her find her inner balance in times of turmoil.

Today, he wasn't the teacher—she was. Roaas was familiar with the usual *Ushaan-tor* combat style, of course. But when Lenissa wasn't involved in ritual duels she preferred the technique with two blades, and that was how they pitted themselves against each other at this moment.

The Andorian used a quick succession of hits to chase her opponent across the training area. Much to her dismay, Roaas parried her every move, although he wielded the *Ushaan-tors* for the first time today.

"You're pretty good with these blades," she admitted, gasping.

"Perhaps I should've mentioned…" Abruptly, Roaas crouched down, whirling around with one leg stretched out, and swept her feet out from under her. She hit the gym mat hard and wanted to roll sideways but the older Caitian suddenly knelt on top of her, pinning her upper arms to the floor. The tip of his right blade stopped approximately one centimeter away from her throat.

"… that Caitians are masters in dual-wielding. It's in our genetic code." He flexed his furry fingers with the retractable claws suggestively.

Then he rose to his feet, taking both *Ushaan-tors* into his left hand and offering Lenissa his right hand to help her up. She didn't really need his help but she appreciated the gesture.

"You also made one mistake, Lenissa," Roaas continued.

"Which is?" she asked. Her sports tunic had slightly rolled

up when she fell to the ground, and she straightened it with one hand.

"You tried too hard to win against me, and to finish the fight quickly. That made you neglect your defense. Being overeager never helped anyone. A fighter always needs to be in control. It's essential that you remain patient, waiting for the right moment to attack—and you obviously need to be aware when this moment has come."

"True," said Lenissa, "patience is not my forté. Someone who waits is simply too scared to act. You need to be offensive if you want to keep the upper hand."

"That might be the case when fighting against weaker opponents. But when faced with an equal or even superior enemy you can only win if you're cautious." Roaas went back to the center of the gym mat to pick up his blades. "One more round?"

Lenissa grinned. "Absolutely."

Half an hour later they went their separate ways. Lenissa returned to her quarters. As senior officer she enjoyed the luxury of a single cabin, albeit one of negligible size. When she entered, the computer automatically switched on the lights. Immediately, she dimmed them. As far as she was concerned, it was now time to start the cozy part of the evening.

She got undressed, tossing her sweaty clothes into the recycler. When she was done, she walked across her quarters and went into the small sanitary area. The pulse vibrations of her sonic shower made her skin prickle and relaxed her muscles. Sighing, she washed down the dried sweat and the burdens of the day.

All in all she led a good life aboard the *Prometheus*, and

she had settled in fairly quickly after being transferred here. Richard Adams was a strict but fair captain, and she had found a remarkably empathic mentor in the first officer. Her subordinates in the security department didn't give her much reason for complaint, either. Most of them were very professional and efficient in their work.

Despite all that she still felt a permanent, uneasy tension.

I guess I'm my own worst enemy, she mused. Even as a child, everyone had stated that she had a pretty adverse combination of traits… she wanted to be a perfectionist, while at the same time she had no patience. Lenissa always wanted to be the best and strived to exceed the high expectations that everybody placed on her. But she lacked the necessary calmness to work her way up. Still, her drive got her to graduate from the Academy with the highest grades in her class—and helped her become one of the youngest superior officers in Starfleet. *I must never give anything less than my best*, she frequently urged herself. She had to prove to the other senior officers—not just Adams and Roaas, but also Carson and Kirk—that she was worthy of her post, and she had to prove it every day.

Clean but not really relaxed, Lenissa stepped out of the sonic shower. Before leaving the sanitary area she scrutinized herself in the mirror. Her reflection lifted her spirits considerably. Her body didn't show any signs of aging. Her muscles were lithe, her blue skin firm, and there wasn't a wrinkle in her face. Lenissa knew that vanity was unbecoming of a Starfleet officer. *But everyone has their little weaknesses*, she thought, stroking her flat belly with satisfaction.

She went to her wardrobe next to her bunk, choosing comfortable pants and a top similar to a kimono to go with them. Both were white like the snow-covered wastelands on her homeworld of Andor. Finally, she strolled to the replicator.

"A portion of cooked *Dreaak*, and a bowl of *Honar*," she ordered. "And a pitcher of citrus-flavored water."

A shimmer announced the arrival of the ordered items in the output compartment.

No sooner had Lenissa sat down with her meal at the small table near the door when her doorbell sounded. Her antennae bent forward expectantly. "Come."

The door hissed open and Geron Barai entered. Just like Lenissa he wore casual clothing—brown pants and a blue and brown top. The Betazoid doctor's gaze wandered from Lenissa to her dinner.

"Bad time, Niss?"

"Not at all," she replied. "I'm just having dinner. Sit down. Can I offer you something?"

"No, thanks, I've just eaten in the Starboard 8," the doctor said, referring to the club run by a Bolian named Moba. Alpha shift tended to gather there in the evening during their spare time. Lenissa herself was among them, enjoying the company of her crewmates. The only exceptions were the evenings that she trained with Roaas or met up with Geron. "But I guess I'll have a glass of citrus-flavored water," he continued, settling on a chair across the table.

She poured a glass for him, and he took a sip. His near-black eyes were fixed on her. Lenissa was fairly certain that he didn't use his telepathic talent, but she could almost hear his thoughts. She didn't need a vivid imagination to do so, though. There was only one reason why they got together in his or her quarters every couple of nights. Outwardly, they maintained the illusion of just being friends, but in truth they had—as Carson had once put it—a "friendship with benefits."

Yet another problem Lenissa had been battling since childhood… She was unable to commit herself. Almost every one of her people had returned to Andor in recent years. They did so to find a companion, to bring children into the world, or to undertake other practical efforts to overcome the terrible reproduction crisis that the Andorians had endured for so many decades. Lenissa, on the other hand, had traveled deeper into space, further away from her home, her parents, her *Chi* and her *Zhi*, and her former friends. There had been several attempts to involve her in the attempt to save her people but she had fled. She didn't want anything to do with all of that ever again.

With that in mind she had limited her love life to simple and straightforward flings. Unbridled fun and no commitments was Lenissa's motto. With her looks it had never been difficult for her to find willing partners—neither at the Academy nor on the ships where she had served. Even aboard the *Prometheus* it had taken less than a month before she had won the Betazoid ship's doctor over. His manner of dealing with sexual matters was pleasantly relaxed, and his looks made Lenissa's antennae quiver in anticipation. The dark eyes, the boyish smile and his hands… Some cultures said that a doctor's hands were able to work miracles. *And they're not wrong*.

A broad grin spread on Geron's face. "Maybe we should talk later," he said.

Lenissa blinked, confused, realizing that she had been lost in thought for a while.

"What?"

"I did ask you what your day has been like." His voice lowered, taking a conspiratorial tone. "But you seem to have skipped our usual preliminary banter."

Emitting a sound of pretended indignation, she threw her napkin at him. "And just who gave you permission to eavesdrop?"

Geron laughed. "Trust me, I don't have to put much effort into sensing your feelings. You're almost screaming them at the world. You're lucky that Vulcans' telepathy is touch-induced; otherwise, Senok and T'Sai would be staring at the ground in severe embarrassment right now, no matter where they were on board."

Lenissa's face started glowing. "You're forgetting the new Vulcan woman."

"T'Shanik."

"Oh, right. Isn't she at conn right now?"

"Yeah, she's on beta shift. Although she won't have much to do while we're in the slipstream to Lembatta Prime, I guess." Geron placed his forearms on the table, leaning closer to her. "So... would you like to answer my question, Lieutenant Commander, or should we postpone our conversation to later?"

For the duration of several heartbeats they looked each other deep in the eyes. Then, Lenissa seized Geron by the collar, dragging him onto his feet as she stood up. The glass of citrus-flavored water toppled, leaving a puddle on the tray. She didn't care.

"I guess we're talking later," Geron stated, desire creeping into his voice.

"Talking is for politicians," she said. Her antennae vibrated when she pulled his sweater over his head. "I prefer to act."

"Very good." He untied the knot of the fabric belt that held her kimono-like top, pushing her toward the bed. "Me too."

Half an hour later they were lying side by side on Lenissa's bed. The thin shimmering blanket covered their naked bodies halfway. Lenissa's head rested on Geron's shoulder, and he had put his arm around her. Her antennae swayed slightly while she was drawing imaginary circles on his chest.

She knew what she was doing was dangerous. For her, having sex with the doctor was nothing more than a selfish act of satisfaction of a sexual desire. So far, so good. She had ample experience with short, heated periods of passion that didn't involve feelings. These displays of affection afterwards, however, usually led to some kind of bond between two partners.

Counselor Courmont would probably have interpreted the fact that Lenissa was still lying here, rather than getting up, sending Geron away and continuing her interrupted dinner, as a sign that she still nurtured an underlying desire for a feeling of security and stability.

Not that Lenissa would ever have revealed this affair to the counselor. She would rather confide in the *Prometheus*'s Emergency Medical Hologram—and the EMH was a considerable pain in the backside.

"What's preying on your mind?" Geron asked quietly.

She hated it when he asked her that question. It always proved to her that to him, her feelings were like an open book. His words also proved to her that there was indeed something preying on her mind, although she refused to acknowledge that. "Nothing," she answered curtly.

Geron shrugged slightly. "Okay."

Now, *that* was something she appreciated in him, and it was probably the main reason why Lenissa allowed herself to be carried away to such dangerous moments as lying in his arms. Geron could have scrutinized her mind with ease, digging up everything that she was hiding deep within herself. But he didn't. Occasionally, he invited her to talk. He probably couldn't help himself—he was a doctor. Whenever she declined or reacted reluctantly, he would drop the subject.

Geron attempted to change the subject. "Am I now allowed to ask how your day was?"

"Exhausting," Lenissa murmured and sighed. "I had to work through an entire padd full of information from Starfleet Intelligence on the situation in the Lembatta Cluster. Afterward, I had to attend a security meeting with the commander. Then training. Finally, you…"

"Shouldn't I have come today?"

Lenissa looked up to him. "Of course you should have," she reassured him. "It's not my body that's tired. It's my mind."

"I know what you're saying. My mind is racing as well."

"How so?"

"I have committed myself to a refresher course in Renao physiology and psychology. Since Jassat left the ship four years ago, my knowledge has become somewhat rusty."

"You went through all that effort for Jassat?" Lenissa asked, amazed.

"No," Geron replied, shaking his head. "I'm trying to understand the Renao's mentality as a people. The Renao have always been somewhat radical, but the attack on Starbase 91 simply doesn't add up."

"Do you know more now?"

"Unfortunately, no. Despite all our previous encounters we know woefully little about this species."

"Yes, I had the same feeling while sifting through the SI files. After I finished I had more questions than answers."

"It seems we're heading toward the unknown."

"Yeah, so it would seem."

They fell silent again. Lenissa felt Geron's hand gently

stroking her bare back. It was probably an automatic gesture, and she had unwittingly enjoyed it up until this moment. But now it made her feel uneasy. *Damn, what's going on with us?* They were lying here like a couple. If it carried on like this Geron would probably want to sleep over soon. *Two mugs of hot katheka for breakfast and a kiss on the cheek before we begin our duty. Is that what we're heading for?*

Almost abruptly, Lenissa let go of him, rolling around and sitting up on the edge of the bed. "We should call it a day," she murmured. "It's late, and we're facing an important assignment tomorrow."

Geron remained silent behind her back for a moment. She sensed that he wanted to object but swallowed his words. "You're probably right." The thin blanket rustled as he pushed it aside and got up. While he got dressed, Lenissa picked up her top, putting it back on. When she stood up, tying the knot of her belt, he was already putting his shoes on. He smoothed his dark-brown hair with his fingers, eyeing her with a side-glance from the other side of the bed. "Will I see you tomorrow?"

"That depends what the day brings," she replied, wrapping her arms around her body. "I'll be in touch."

"Alright." Gentle, like water that patiently wears down rock, his eyes bored into her mind. She knew that he was seeing through her. You can't fool a Betazoid. "Good night, Niss," he said quietly.

"Good night," she said.

He left.

Lenissa zh'Thiin was now alone in her dimmed cabin. *Honar* in citrus-flavored water swam on the surface of her small table next to her. There were tears in her eyes that she didn't want to cry. *This is going too far,* she thought. *I must finish with him.*

Squinting, she took deep breaths to fight back the feelings that were surging up within her. After that, she stepped away from her bed. Spreading her legs slightly she stood in the center of her quarters. With calm, flowing movements she began the meditation technique that Roaas had taught her. Whether it would help her find her inner balance today, Lenissa didn't dare to predict.

13
NOVEMBER 5, 2385

U.S.S. *Prometheus*, en route to the Lembatta Cluster

"Is there something wrong with your uniform, Lieutenant?" The Bolian proprietor of Starboard 8 looked quizzically at Jassat ak Namur from his side of the curved counter.

Jassat realized with irritation that his right hand rested on his black-and-gray top on his chest as if he had been fiddling with it. Quickly, he removed his hand. "No, nothing," he said, maybe a little too quickly to sound believable.

In truth, the uniform that he had received only days earlier when he had come aboard the U.S.S. *Prometheus* as freshly graduated Lieutenant from Starfleet Academy felt stiff and scratchy—as if it hadn't been worn-in properly yet.

Jassat ak Namur knew that this notion was utter nonsense. The uniform for Starfleet members came from a replicator and was custom-made. It consisted of several layers of synthetic fabric, and the innermost layer was usually adapted to the needs of the specific species in order to avoid skin irritations and guarantee maximum comfort.

It wasn't the uniform that made Jassat feel uneasy. The reason was deep within him.

The barkeep leaned across the counter. He seemed to be in a talkative mood. At the moment he could afford to be. Although half of the tables in the club, which could accommodate approximately fifty guests, were taken, everyone seemed to be sufficiently catered to.

"I think, we haven't met yet," the Bolian said. "My name is Moba. I've been on this ship for almost two years. And you? Have you come aboard during the change of crew on Deep Space 9?"

Jassat nodded. "I'm Jassat ak Namur. I've just graduated from the Academy."

"And you got a place on the *Prometheus* right away?" Moba sounded impressed. "You're one lucky guy."

"That didn't have much to do with luck," Jassat replied. "I served for a year as an exchange officer on the *Prometheus* before I enrolled."

"Oh, I see. Let me guess: first contact with the Federation, cultural exchange and suddenly you got itchy feet and didn't want anything more than to see the galaxy." The blue-skinned man in the fashionable gray and violet suit of a civilian grinned broadly.

"Yes, something like that," Jassat said.

Although he had no intention of saying anything else, his counterpart said, "Before you go on—what would you like to drink, Jassat? Or would you prefer to be called ak Namur? Or should I call you Lieutenant?"

"Jassat will be fine. I'll have..." He hesitated. He hadn't been in the Starboard 8 for four years. Back then, a Tellarite by the name of Gaav had run the club. He had been the most ill-tempered bartender you could possibly imagine. "You used to have this juice here. It was green and very refreshing. Slightly sour. Commander Kirk and I used to drink it."

Moba waggled one finger. "Say no more! I know exactly what you mean. One moment." He turned around, facing the impressive mixing device that was mounted on the wall behind the counter. Today's food replicators were able to synthesize almost every food or drink that was reasonably well known throughout the Federation. But just like every member of Starfleet, Jassat knew that even the most sophisticated technology could not even come close to real, biological ingredients. The machine hummed and gurgled while Moba fiddled around with it.

While he waited, Jassat took a good look around the Starboard 8. He had walked through the ship's corridors deep in thought earlier, and hadn't noticed where his steps had unwittingly led him, before Moba started talking to him. Nobody in the club belonged to Jassat's immediate social circle. He did recognize the faces of several people in here but they belonged to different departments. Quite a few engineers were around, and the *Prometheus*'s science officer, a Benzite called Mendon, sat on a table in a far away corner, talking to a Grazerite whom Jassat didn't know. In fact, many new faces had been added to the crew in the past few years. The *Prometheus* had changed.

Jassat knew that transfers and promotions were part of a Starfleet officer's career, but that didn't make it any easier for him. At least the senior officers hadn't changed. Adams, Roaas, Carson, Kirk, and Barai had all been aboard during Jassat's time as exchange officer. That was at least some consolation.

Moba turned back to Jassat, placing a glass with a cold mint-green liquid under his nose. "Q'babi-juice," the Bolian said. "Jenna's favorite drink. I bet that's what you were talking about, my friend." He nodded encouragingly. "Go on, try it."

Jassat sipped carefully. His lips parted in a little smile, and he nodded. "You're right. That's exactly what I was talking about."

"Excellent." Moba rubbed his hand. His glance wandered through the club. Once he was satisfied that no one needed his services, he leaned across the counter once more. "Tell me, Jassat, I don't want to seem overly curious, but may I ask which species you belong to? I've been serving on two space stations and six ships—including a *Galaxy*-class and a *Sovereign*-class, no less. They are huge, accommodating some thousand crew members. But I don't think I've ever seen anyone quite like you."

"I…" Jassat hesitated. The *Prometheus* didn't receive any current news while she was in slipstream. The entertainment displays on the far side of the counter still showed the Federation news from the previous day. They dealt with the end of Andor's reproduction crisis, the initial days of the new Federation president, trade issues with the Ferengi, and the Federation's partnership with the Cardassian Union, which had suffered since news had emerged that the former Federation president, Nanietta Bacco, had been murdered two months ago by members of the True Way, a Cardassian group of extremists.

And there was news about an attack on a space station near the Lembatta Cluster. His people, little known to or noticed by the galactic society, had claimed responsibility for this atrocity.

"It's alright." Moba shrugged his rounded shoulders. "You don't have to tell me if it makes you feel uncomfortable."

Jassat shook his head. "No, you might as well know, since it's no secret. I'm Renao."

The Bolian looked at him pensively for a moment. "Hmm, never heard of them," he said. Then he furrowed his bifurcated brow. "Hang on." His gaze flickered to the screen that was mounted only a few meters away on the wall, where some expert from Earth gave his view on the latest events. Jassat couldn't understand him as the voices in the Starboard 8 drowned him out, but the image of a *Watchtower*-class space station behind the man said enough.

"Oh," Moba said. "Now I understand your concern. But don't worry. There's an old Bolian saying: Don't judge a woman by her mother. What I'm trying to say is this—it's not your fault if your people go on the rampage." Sympathetically, he lowered his voice. "Is that what's bothering you? What's happening with your people?"

"Among other things," admitted Jassat. "But I have visited the Home Spheres only twice within the last five years. My view is that of an outsider. I know that will change just as soon as we reach the Lembatta Cluster. But everything that is happening there still feels distant and strange."

"Is that why you look as if you feel uneasy in your uniform?" the curious barkeeper asked.

"Hey, Moba!" one of the engineers shouted from his table. "Do we have to throw our glasses on the floor to get you to come by?" He and his three comrades waved their empty glasses.

"We'll talk again in a minute," Moba promised before hurrying around the counter to serve the thirsty men.

Is that why I feel uneasy in my uniform? Jassat repeated the barkeep's question in his mind. How could he explain that to the other man? Or to himself?

Jassat belonged to a civilization where everyone and everything had its specific place within the numerous spheres of life. If you were born into a certain neighborhood of a city, that neighborhood was your home. You stayed loyal to it, and in return, it offered security. Of course, the Renao knew that they needed to refresh their gene pool to ensure a healthy development of their species. To that end, the ritualized exchange of members from neighboring spheres was permitted. Even so, by the time an inhabitant of the basalt deserts on the northern continent of Onferin wound up three light-years away on the coast of the Narad Sea on Lhoeel, he would have had to pass at least four sphere borders. Very few Renao achieved that feat during their lifespan.

This way of life had been maintained for centuries, so every Renao had an ingrained desire for stability. It had only been during the past few decades that Jassat's species had increasingly utilized faster-than-light travel. They had established first contact with the United Federation of Planets. All these events had led to the beginning of a breakdown of internal dogmas. Bold young people such as Jassat had served as exchange officers aboard Starfleet vessels after an association agreement between the sphere of the Renao and the Federation had been agreed to.

During his time aboard the *Prometheus,* Jassat had crossed more spheres than any Renao in the history of his people. The only reason he could bear these relentless changes was his environment's consistency aboard the ship. The rooms and corridors of the *Prometheus* had become his sphere. He belonged here just like his superior officers, friends, and crewmates did—especially Jenna Kirk, Sarita Carson, and Captain Adams, who had taken him under his wing.

Suddenly, everything had changed. The political situation had deteriorated, and the Renao had recalled their officers to their respective Home Spheres. But Jassat didn't want to go back. He wanted to see the stars—but most of all he didn't want to leave his new home. In order to stay aboard the *Prometheus*, he needed to graduate from Starfleet Academy to endorse the commission he had attained within the Renao fleet. For four years, he had fought a battle to accept San Francisco on the planet Earth as his new sphere. It hadn't been easy because part of a cadet's life was traveling to different worlds, and training flights aboard other vessels. His comrades had provided Jassat with the stability that he so desperately required. During his four-year tenure, there had been little to no fluctuation, which was gratifying.

He had struggled through and graduated. And now, he was back here. But the *Prometheus* suddenly felt different. He had read that she had been modernized after the Borg invasion of 2381. Several corridors and rooms had undergone changes; most of all the main engine room where the modern slipstream reactor glowed next to the warp drive's matter-antimatter reaction chamber. What bothered Jassat even more were the changes in his personal environment. He had grown used to his fellow cadets as they were the only constant feature during his life at the Academy. Maybe he had grown too used to them. Now, they were all gone and strewn across dozens of ships throughout Federation space. His former comrades had carried on living their own lives during the past few years. Lieutenant Garrett Moss, who had been the alpha-shift communications officer several years ago, had left the *Prometheus*, and had been replaced by Paul Winter. Sarita Carson seemed to have found a new best friend—this Andorian security chief. And Adams… He had only seen him briefly during a short welcoming ceremony when the "newcomers" had come aboard. The captain had smiled and said that he was happy to have Jassat in his crew. Then again, he had said that to everyone.

"I'm sorry, that took a bit longer than I thought." Moba reappeared on the other side of the counter. "Now, where were we? Ah, I remember—your uniform. So, where's the itch... metaphorically speaking?"

Before Jassat could reply, his combadge beeped. *"Adams to ak Namur."*

"One moment, please," Jassat said, turning around and tapping the small device on his chest. "Ak Namur here, Captain."

"Please report to my ready room immediately, Lieutenant."

Jassat's heartbeat increased. It seemed as if the captain had read his thoughts. "Understood, sir. I'm on my way." He signed off and turned back to the Bolian barkeep. "I'm sorry, I must leave."

"Of course. No problem. What did my so-called father always say? When duty calls, don't wear ear-defenders. Just tell me what's troubling you another night. I'm always here."

Jassat had no idea what the Bolian bartender's father's saying actually meant, but he didn't really care all that much at present. He was already making his way to the exit.

Richard Adams wasn't looking forward to this conversation. He valued Jassat ak Namur. The young Renao had turned out to be dutiful, modest, and inquisitive. These were traits of a true Starfleet officer. But ak Namur was part of a civilization that unexpectedly had declared war on the entire galaxy, and the *Prometheus* was on her way to find out the extent of the threat and to react appropriately. Considering the nature of this journey, Adams couldn't avoid this encounter. He needed to know whether his protégé was ready for this mission.

His doorbell chimed, and Adams asked his visitor to enter. Ak Namur hesitantly walked into the room. "You wanted to see me, Captain?"

"Yes, come in, Mr. ak Namur." Adams sat behind his desk,

beckoning the young Renao to come closer. At that moment the intercom beeped and the voice of Lieutenant Commander Senok, the watch commander for beta shift, sounded over the speakers. *"Captain, we're almost on the outer edge of the Lembatta Cluster. Leaving slipstream now."*

"Understood," Adams replied. "Wait for my orders before continuing our journey."

"Aye, sir."

Adams signed off. He felt the ship trembling slightly when it dropped from slipstream into normal space. Jassat ak Namur held his breath, gazing at the window behind Adams's back. The captain swiveled around on his chair and got up. Stepping to the window he took in the view of the panorama before his eyes. A huge nebula filled the emptiness of space before them. It looked like the menacingly steaming aura of a monstrous lurking cosmic life form that was staring at them with two dozen glowing red eyes. Adams had read that the Lembatta Cluster was called *'eng mIgh* in Klingon, which translated roughly into "Cloud of Evil." It wasn't particularly scientific, but the captain understood why someone would come up with that name. "Impressive view," he said.

Ak Namur drew closer and stood next to him. "Yes," he simply said.

The Renao with his crimson skin, jet-black hair, and glowing yellow eyes also resembled an unsaintly figure from Earth's mythology. This appearance was, of course, misleading. Jassat ak Namur couldn't hurt a fly. But was this frame of mind similarly exotic among his people as his excitement of discovery was?

Adams tried to begin this delicate conversation with small talk. "I can hardly imagine what it must be like, living in the light of these dying stars."

The lieutenant's expression showed a hint of wistfulness, but his demeanor also displayed an obvious tension. "The sky on Onferin, where I was born, is always red. In the early hours of the morning it turns into a pale pink, around noon it glows bright red, and when bad weather is coming, it's like coagulated blood. This light seems to bring out all kinds of passion—even dark ones, apparently."

"Yes, from where we are standing it certainly looks that way," Adams said. "What's your stance on all that, Jassat?" He used his visitor's first name deliberately to create a more intimate atmosphere. He also wanted to express that he wasn't speaking as captain to his subordinate, but instead as a father figure to his protégé.

Ak Namur shook his head. "I don't understand it, Captain. I really don't. It's true that our people value the harmony of spheres above all else. According to our faith, everything in the universe has its place. This place was assigned by a cosmic order, and that's where we belong. This faith has been deeply rooted since the early days of our culture, and it has always been ruling our way of thinking and acting."

"I remember that Starfleet's philosophy to explore the entire galaxy had been one of the reasons leading to the deterioration in relations between the Federation and the Home Spheres," Adams said. "Peaceful as our mission might be, to some Renao leaders it came across like an outrage." He remembered the words of the radical man in the video message to the Federation Council. *The galaxy has turned into a place of fear and terror, and that is your fault alone. War and invasions, wherever you look. Misery and suffering. Distrust and resentment. And why? Because you allowed it to go this far. Your unnatural desire to expand is tipping the balance in space. Your striving for new worlds and new civilizations, your attempts to build bridges in places where nature didn't intend them to be let you forget where your natural spheres are.*

"All that is true," said ak Namur. "But the harmony of spheres applied to the generation of our fathers. The young Renao know that this faith is obsolete. They know that a universe full of wonders awaits those who have the courage to overcome their fears and go forth. Well, at least they knew that a couple of years ago." The young man fell silent for a while. He seemed to be so unsettled that Adams regretted not leaving him behind on Deep Space 9 when he found out where their mission was taking them. He should have left him there, no matter how useful Admiral Akaar deemed the Renao officer to be.

"But even if they reverted to the old traditions and mindsets, the radicals' actions still don't make any sense," ak Namur continued finally. "My people are not stupid, Captain. They may not agree with the Federation's way of life, or indeed that of the other superpowers in the galaxy, but they do know that they can't do anything about it. A small nation such as ours that occupies not even ten planets will never be able to fight against the combined forces of the Klingons and the Federation, not to mention the Typhon Pact powers. The attack on Starbase 91 therefore seems completely pointless. It's an act of violence that won't achieve anything. I can't rule out that some lunatics on the inner planets dream of a fight against the rest of the universe. You will find fanatics in every civilization. But there's a vast difference between dreaming and acting. Acting would require these people to leave their Home Spheres. And those who espouse that view would shy away from this step, because in order to achieve their goal they would have to become what they loathe most—a disturbing factor to the harmony of spheres, a sphere defiler."

Adams looked at ak Namur pensively. "Thank you, Jassat. It's good to get that perspective. But allow me one last question." He fixed the young man questioningly with his eyes, adopting a more official tone of voice. "Do you feel ready, Lieutenant, to meet your people as a Starfleet officer, and to do everything that's required of you in that position, in order to preserve peace?"

Ak Namur seemed uncertain for a moment. Obviously, he had asked himself the same question. He straightened himself, nodding. "Yes, Captain. I do wish that my return to the Home Spheres could happen under more amicable circumstances, but I will do my best to help you find out who murdered so many innocent people. The perpetrators should receive their just punishment, whether they are Renao or not."

"Very well." Adams smiled slightly at the young man. "I didn't expect anything less from you." He put a hand on ak Namur's shoulder. "Come on. Let's go to the bridge and set course for your homeworld."

Ak Namur nodded and smiled back. "Yes, sir."

They crossed the room when the intercom on Adams's desk beeped again. *"Bridge to Captain Adams,"* said the voice with the slight New Zealand accent, belonging to beta shift's communications officer.

Adams activated his combadge. "Adams here."

"Sir, we have received a priority message from Starfleet Headquarters."

Adams's stomach turned. *Please, let it be a message that the special envoy is late,* he prayed to the universe, though he had a suspicion that it was much worse news than that. He gazed at ak Namur. "Go on ahead. I'll join you in a minute."

"Yes, sir." The young Renao left the room.

As soon as the door had closed behind him, Adams sat down behind his desk. "Patch it through, Ensign Harris."

Admiral Akaar's image confirmed the captain's premonition a few seconds later. As usual, Starfleet's commander-in-chief sat behind his desk in his office. *"I'm afraid there has been another attack by the group that calls itself Purifying Flame. The Klingons have lost a moon in the Tika system not far from the Lembatta Cluster in an attack that is very similar to the one on Starbase 91. According to our information there have been no survivors."*

Adams briefly closed his eyes, shaking his head. This was a nightmare.

Akaar continued impassively. *"There was another claim of responsibility, but this was sent specifically to the High Council on Qo'noS."* The white-haired Capellan laughed without humor. *"To say that the Klingons are angered would be the understatement of the century. They are seething. Some voices are already demanding a raid on the Renao's Home Spheres. Fortunately, reason is still prevailing, so that will not happen, but Chancellor Martok has dispatched a ship to investigate the matter. It's an old* Vor'cha*-class battle cruiser commanded by an overzealous warrior by the name of Kromm. If he was on his own I'd send you reinforcements, just in case. But according to the Palais, Ambassador Rozhenko is accompanying him. Still, I wanted to warn you. Don't leave the field to the Klingons, Captain; otherwise, we'll be heading straight toward the next galactic crisis."* Akaar leaned toward the screen. *"Look after yourself, Dick. Akaar out."*

14
NOVEMBER 6, 2385

I.K.S. *Bortas*

"Haven't you got better things to do, Lieutenant?" Sighing, Rooth wiped his face with his callused hand. "Do you really have to waste my time with *this*?"

The eyes of the Klingon standing on the other side of the desk widened. "Sir, I assure you… this issue is anything but a waste of time. This *jeghpu'wI'* has sabotaged my console, without a shadow of a doubt!"

The office of the ship's security department was deep inside the ship's belly, several hundred steps away from the I.K.S. *Bortas*'s command center. Lieutenant Commander Rooth was in charge. But you didn't have to be a security chief to realize one thing—Lieutenant Klarn was an idiot. He had just been ranting and raving all the way from the bridge to this office.

"And why should he do that, hmm?" Rooth asked, bringing up the related personnel file on his computer screen with a distinct lack of enthusiasm. "*Bekk* Raspin has been in the Klingon Defense Force for just over six months, and he has never given us any reason to suspect him of sabotage." *And why should he start with your station of all places?* he added to himself. Klarn's communications console on the bridge was by no means the ship's centerpiece.

"Are you not listening?" Lieutenant Klarn clenched

his fists, and his shoulders trembled aggressively. "He's a *jeghpu'wI'*—enough said!"

"That merely means that he comes from one of our conquered worlds," Rooth stated. "From Rantal. It also says that his people are inferior. That's all."

"Oh, really?" Leaning forward, Klarn rested his fists on Rooth's desk and glared at him. The light from the small overhead lights reflected from his uniform's metal shoulder plates. "Why, do you think, isn't there anyone else from Rantal in the entire force, eh? Why, do you think, did the military leaders give *jeghpu'wI'* a wide berth for centuries, and preferred to go down honorably in battle rather than having an inferior being on the bridges of their ships—talented or not?"

Rooth sat back in his chair, folding his hands in front of his chest. "Enlighten me," he said mockingly.

"Because they're animals!" Klarn shouted. "These *jeghpu'wI'* don't deserve our trust. They don't know honor, nor do they know anything about victory. Do we really want to go down in history as the ship that tolerated an inferior being on its bridge? Do you really want to live with that disgrace, son of K'mpath?"

Rooth sighed again. He sympathized with Klarn, which was the worst part in all of this. This was by no means the first time that he'd heard stories such as this one. The gray-haired Rooth was more than sixty years old, and he had been aboard the *Bortas* longer than any other member of her crew. He had already served under Chancellor Gowron, before and during the war. In his youth he would also have fought tooth and nail—with a *bat'leth* if necessary—to make sure that both the ship's reputation and his own weren't tainted by the presence of an inferior being in the crew.

But over the years, Rooth had modified his views. Time had honed his eye for essential facts. Since he had personally met the great Emperor Kahless, clone of the original historical figure, Rooth had shed the extremely martial aspects of his personality. He had turned to the lore and wisdom of Kahless the Unforgettable. Now, more than two decades after this fateful encounter, Rooth had found his inner self. His mind was alert, his body fortified by experience and reason.

"Now we're getting to the bottom of this," he said, looking at Klarn. "This isn't about sabotage, and not about things that *Bekk* Raspin has allegedly done. This is about you and your so-called disgrace."

The lieutenant straightened himself, squaring his shoulders. But his expression showed anything but respect. "My console," he snarled, and his bushy eyebrows almost met above his nose, "has been damaged. And this... this *bekk* was the only one who could have touched it unnoticed."

He had all but spat out the rank. *Bekks* were the lowest ranking members in the Defense Force. Almost no one of the officer class looked upon them favorably; and certainly not if a *bekk* was also *jeghpu'wI'*.

"Material fatigue, Lieutenant," Rooth said, rising behind his desk in an attempt to end this conversation sooner. "Everything will break eventually. Perhaps you should go and see a technician rather than security."

"Is that your answer?" Klarn exploded. "You..."

Rooth raised his hand, gesturing toward the door. "Dismissed, Lieutenant," he said quietly, but firmly.

Klarn blinked incredulously. Finally, he regained control over himself. His fists were still clenched.

"This isn't over yet," he said with a snarl.

The security chief nodded, unfazed. "I will let Chief

Engineer Nuk know that you're on your way to see him." He stepped toward the door that opened promptly. The plain, dimly lit corridor came into sight. "Now."

Another few seconds passed before Klarn finally tore himself away. Silently and visibly dissatisfied he stomped out of the room. Rooth watched him until he disappeared around a corner toward the engine room.

Back at his desk, Rooth touched a button, opening an internal channel. "Rooth to engine room."

"Nuk," was his old friend's short and prompt reply.

"You're getting a visitor, old man," Rooth said. "A furious visitor, no less."

"I can't wait," the chief engineer replied, and he sounded almost cheerful. Nuk was of the House of Kruge, a family famous for building ships. The crew had deemed him eccentric, and he got on far better with his engines than he did with living beings. He was happiest when he could spend his time with technology. Rooth, as his longstanding crewmate, thought that those traits made Nuk the perfect engineer. *"He can take it out on the stubborn propulsion system."*

Rooth grinned. "Is it still causing problems?"

"Not for much longer," Nuk answered with a suggestive tone in his voice, before signing off.

Short and sweet as always. Rooth's grin broadened. Silently, the security chief looked at his monitor.

"Computer, where is Commander L'emka?"

Schematics of the I.K.S. *Bortas* appeared on the small monitor. A pulsating red circle showed the first officer's location. She was in her quarters, just like Rooth had hoped.

A few minutes later the old warrior stood in front of the young officer's door. He had to ring twice before she opened.

As soon as the door opened, she snapped, *"nuqneH?"* Her

apparel was scanty and soaked in sweat. The scents of candle wax and incense wafted around the air in her small dimly lit cabin.

The corners of Rooth's mouth twitched when he noticed her body odor. L'emka's sweat smelled like harvested grain on the farm worlds where she came from. He smelled vastness and strength... and more. "Am I interrupting anything?" the old warrior asked roguishly.

L'emka brushed her long dark hair back with one hand. "Combat training. Once again, Commander, what do you want?"

"Klarn," said Rooth.

L'emka lowered her hand first, followed by her head. A low groan escaped from her throat. "Not again..."

"I'm afraid so."

She stepped aside, inviting him into her quarters. Rooth entered the room. He had never been in the first officer's cabin before—at least not since L'emka had been living there—and he was surprised to see what she had done with it. The walls of the small, windowless room had been decorated with sharp blades. A *bat'leth* was mounted on one wall; the blade of a *tjtiq* reflected the flickering candlelight from another. He saw an artistic handmade tapestry telling stories of daily farming routine and harvesting cycles in many illustrations. A narrow cot with a shoulder-high privacy shield was on the back wall next to the door that led to the sanitary area. Rooth didn't see a replicator; L'emka usually ate with her subordinates in the mess.

"What's he done this time?"

Rooth shook his head. "Nothing. He just... ponders too much for my liking. And that leads to rather silly ideas." He told her about the communication officer's visit.

"Xenophobia on a Klingon bridge." L'emka snorted amused but there was no joy in her eyes. "Now there's a surprise."

"Klarn has got too much time on his hands," Rooth said. "Just like the rest of us. That sometimes allows unpleasantries to surface that the crew would be less susceptible to under different circumstances. When are we finally meeting up with the *Prometheus*?"

"In three days," the young commander replied. "The flight doesn't get any shorter just because people are constantly asking about it."

"See?" Rooth growled, nodding. "We're all bored."

"Most of all we have a task to fulfill!" L'emka pointed out. She sat down on the floor cross-legged, starting to wipe clean the blood-stained *d'k tahg* that was laying there. Yet again the security chief wondered what exactly she had been up to when he interrupted her. "Martok wants us—us of all people—to shed a light upon Tika IV-B's fate. Martok himself! The crew would be well advised to prepare for this mission rather than wasting time with useless trifles."

"The crew is not used to being important," Rooth replied dryly. Affectionately, he stroked the outer cabin wall. "This ship… it's seen some great times. During the civil war it was even the late Chancellor Gowron's flagship before almost being destroyed during the attack on Cardassia Prime. And today?" This time, he was the one who snorted. "Today, we have a callow youth, the idiot son of a noble family on our bridge. Hero of the *Ning'tao*, my ass. Kromm wasn't even aboard when that ship achieved its heroic feat."

"Kromm is a high-born drunkard," L'emka said derisively. "He was well infused with bloodwine when he spoke to Martok yesterday."

Rooth turned around, facing her. "He's a Klingon!" he stated, raising his voice. "And he's young. Of course he's drinking. Of course he's loudmouthed and hotheaded. That's not the problem, Commander."

"Then what is?" She looked up at him, fury in her eyes. L'emka had worked her way up the ranks from being a lowly *bekk*, receiving a battlefield commission in the waning days of the Dominion War. The young farmer's daughter was grounded, purposeful, and thorough. No wonder that she thought that Captain Kromm, who had to be the most dubious command partner they could have lumbered her with, was weighing her formerly promising career down—though her low-born status probably had something to do with her being assigned to such an idiot. With every sentence, her voice raised a bit more. "Where *is* the problem, Security Chief? Mh? Where does the *Bortas* fall short if not with her commander? What is it that drives idiots such as Klarn and our 'Captain Bloodwine'?"

The old warrior nodded appreciatively. She had never spoken this openly to him. L'emka's patience had obviously worn very thin. Rooth wondered what would happen if it ran out.

"The problem is the past eight turns," he answered quietly. "Command gave Kromm this ship back then to get rid of him. They wanted to give him a post befitting his social standing, and one that wouldn't pose a disgrace for his House. But the generals know Kromm all too well. They consider him to be just as unfit as you do, Commander."

L'emka wanted to protest but Rooth waved his hand dismissively. They both knew that he was right. Why lie?

"That's the reason why they don't assign the *Bortas* any important missions," he continued. "They parked Kromm on this ship on the edge of their field of vision, along with this ship. We've been out of the loop for eight turns, Commander. *That's* the problem. We've been watching for far too long while others accumulated glory. The empire doesn't expect anything from us. So we're not used to making a difference anymore, to get involved. We have weakened, and we're idle." *And instead of finding worthy opponents, we're getting agitated over a harmless Rantal.*

The first officer remained silent, and that told Rooth more than a thousand confirmations. L'emka put the now gleaming *d'k tahg* aside. Leaning forward, she blew out one of the three candles that were burning in front of her in copper bowls, spreading their scent throughout the room.

"We've been given a chance," she said finally. Her voice was quiet and a little defiant. "This joint mission with the Federation is our opportunity to prove ourselves. We can show everyone that the *Bortas* still has life in her yet. This ship can be more than its commander who's resting on other people's laurels." Her hand reached for the *d'k tahg.* "We must and we will prove that to our people, Rooth. With or without Kromm."

The old warrior grinned. "With," he said calmly. "For now, let us say, 'with,' Commander. Agreed?"

Her hand slid back to her lap. For now, L'emka and he were in agreement. "I'll talk to Klarn," she promised. "Again."

He nodded gratefully. "And I with Nuk. We'll see if the old fool isn't able to produce a bit more steam for his turbine if I ask nicely."

"Steam? Turbine?" Laughing, L'emka rose from the floor and escorted her visitor to the door. "Commander Rooth, you really have been out of the loop for too long. Didn't you know that the Defense Force has upgraded their ships with warp engines?"

Rooth raised his bushy eyebrows. "All this newfangled nonsense!" he jokingly complained. "Whatever next, mh? Women on the bridge?"

Rooth could still feel the friendly thump that she landed on him for this remark after he had returned to his security office. Satisfied, he grinned.

15
NOVEMBER 6, 2385

I.K.S. *Bortas*

The U.S.S. *Aventine* was a *Vesta*-class starship and probably the most modern one in Starfleet. Her quantum slipstream drive and the Mark XII phaser banks aroused Captain Kromm's envy, but he instantly took a dislike to the only passenger aboard.

"Ambassador, Captain," Kromm greeted Alexander Rozhenko and Captain Ezri Dax just as soon as they had materialized in the I.K.S. *Bortas*'s transporter room. "Welcome aboard."

Rozhenko wore dark, simple clothes. His black hooded coat covered the dark overall with the broad belt. His face was inscrutable when he nodded at Kromm, and he seemed almost indifferent.

The woman by his side was one and a half heads shorter than him, and she wore the uniform of a Starfleet captain. "Thank you for seeing us right away, Captain," she said. "The Federation insisted that you and the ambassador embark on your journey immediately."

"The Federation is not alone," said Kromm. He made two steps toward the transporter platform, beckoning Rozhenko to come down. "The High Council is also very interested in hunting down the wretched villains of Tika IV-B. The Renao will curse the day when they raised their hand against the

Klingon Empire... that much I can guarantee."

"Maybe it wasn't..." Dax started.

But Rozhenko was faster. "Maybe it wasn't the Renao," the ambassador said calmly but firmly. "One of the mission objectives is to establish their guilt or innocence. Don't forget that, Captain Kromm. So far the evidence is very ambiguous. There are many questions around, but precious little certainty."

Dax nodded. "The Federation wants all hints and theories looked into with an open mind. I'm sure that Captain Adams agrees with that notion."

"Evidence." Looking at Dax, Kromm waved his hand dismissively. "You're a Trill, Captain. You belong to a species where mortal host beings enter into lifelong symbioses with seemingly immortal intelligence forms, which are handed on to another mortal host once the previous one perishes. Bearing that in mind, you probably have lived through several fascinating lives so far. Why do you of all people approach me with a ridiculously dull-witted, deeply human presumption of innocence? The Renao confessed!"

"*One* Renao," she reminded him. Her light blue eyes held his gaze. Her tone of voice was courteous, but reserved and firm. "And even that is only an assumption. And may I add that 'innocent until proven otherwise' is not just inherently human, Captain Kromm, but also universally ethical."

Kromm was amazed. The looks of the small Trill with her shoulder-length black hair and dainty figure didn't appeal to him. But apparently, that unspectacular appearance concealed a very forceful temper. No wonder that she had been at loggerheads earlier this year with the corrupt Federation government preceding Kellessar zh'Tarash. Dax clearly had honor in her bones!

"We're looking for answers, not prejudgments." Rozhenko stepped off the platform to stand next to Kromm. His gaze expressed gratitude when he faced Captain Dax one last time. "Safe travels, Captain. And please let your first officer know that the next round of Fizzbin will be mine to win!"

The young woman smiled cordially. "I'm sure he won't like to hear that, Ambassador. Sam Bowers is capable of many things, but not of losing. Not even in a game of cards."

"All the more reason." Rozhenko nodded. "Take care."

"Godspeed, Ambassador," Dax said. "Captain."

"*Qapla'!*" replied Kromm, squaring his shoulders while watching the Trill woman disappear in the transporter's red swirl. One second later she was gone, back on her own ship that had rendezvoused with the *Bortas*.

Kromm turned to his guest, sizing him up briefly. Rozhenko seemed small to him. The dark clothing wasn't able to conceal the slender shoulders. His beardless face's features were too soft for Kromm's liking... almost effeminate.

"As I said, Ambassador, welcome aboard the *Bortas*. We will resume course to the Lembatta Cluster immediately." Kromm pointed to a *bekk* with a full beard, who stood silently behind the transporter console. "Should Brukk show you to your quarters? Or would you like to accompany me to the bridge and meet my staff?"

The ambassador shook his head. "Thank you, Captain, but I'm familiar with the *Vor'cha*-class, and I can find my way around the ship with ease—I will go to my cabin to study some more reports before we meet up with the *Prometheus*. Unless—do you play Fizzbin, by any chance?"

"Fizzbin?" Kromm laughed, half incredulously, half appalled. "No. A child's game is unworthy of a warrior."

"To each their own," Rozhenko replied with an indulgent

smile that Kromm desperately wanted to punch. "Open your mind, Captain. Otherwise, you might miss out on something." With these words he nodded respectfully, turned, and left the transporter room.

16
NOVEMBER 7, 2385

U.S.S. *Prometheus*, Lembatta Prime

"Standard orbit, Lieutenant ak Namur."

"Aye, Captain, standard orbit."

From his place in the command chair on the *Prometheus* bridge, Richard Adams watched Lieutenant ak Namur entering commands into the conn in front of him. On the main screen the red glowing spheres of the Lembatta Cluster changed their positions, and the yellow-green globe in the center of the display grew consistently, before it transformed into a concave horizon on the left side of the ship.

The flight from one end of the Federation to the other hadn't even taken a day with the *Prometheus*'s slipstream drive. Once they arrived at the outer reaches of the Lembatta Cluster, the stellar density forced them to slow down to conventional warp. A flight at higher speed would have been too risky. So they reached Lembatta Prime, one of the Federation's worlds in the outer regions of the cluster, around lunchtime on the third day after their departure from Deep Space 9. If they had been limited to traditional warp drive for the entire journey, it would have taken weeks to get there.

Below, the planet's surface slowly slid past. Adams sat up straight in his chair. He looked left toward his communications officer. "Mr. Winter, announce our arrival to flight control."

"Yes, sir."

While waiting for the officer to complete the formalities required by protocol for arriving starships in orbit around a Federation planet, the captain directed his attention back to the world that filled one half of the bridge's main screen. Just before their arrival in the system he had read up about Lembatta Prime in his ready room. The planet was smaller than Earth, but due to its mass it had almost the same gravity. It orbited its sun—a red giant within the cluster—just within the habitable zone, but the heat on its surface was unpleasant. Vast areas on this world consisted of deserts, which explained the planet's yellow color. The green parts were oceans, so colored by oxygen-producing algae. These algae were also the world's most valuable export as they contained enzymes that were incredibly useful for medical research.

The planet had been colonized by the Federation roughly eighty years ago. Since then, the inhabitants had spread along the coastlines. Today, Lembatta Prime had approximately twenty million inhabitants, including a small percentage of Renao. They had settled here during the years when there had been political rapprochement between the Federation and the Home Spheres. The way Adams had understood it, the sun dominated the cultural and religious lives of these people. Important holidays took place on the days before and after a total eclipse of the sun. As Lembatta Prime boasted three moons, that was rather a frequent occurrence.

Winter interrupted Adams's thoughts. "Captain, we're being hailed by the planetary government."

Adams rose from his chair and stood on the top of the three steps that led down to the control pit. "On screen."

The image changed, and a woman of approximately fifty years appeared. She was clad in a robe of flowing fabrics in various hues of blue. A bronze brooch adorned her chest.

Her skin was tanned, and the dark hair was braided into a sophisticated style. Relief was visible in the woman's eyes, and her voice mirrored that emotion.

"Prometheus, I'm Governor Elenor Sarin. I'm glad you're here."

"Madam Governor, my name is Captain Richard Adams. We came as quickly as possible."

"Your arrival has already been announced. If I can assist you in any way, shape, or form, please let me know."

"Thank you very much. How is the situation on Lembatta Prime, if you don't mind me asking?"

"So far, there haven't been any incidents. But everyone is naturally very worried. We all heard about the explosion on the starbase, and the threat from the Purifying Flame has been all over the local news. Since we are direct neighbors of the Renao Home Spheres, many fear that we might be one of the terrorists' next targets. We don't have a fleet at our disposal for our defense, and the ambassador arrived in a scarcely armed courier vessel."

"The special envoy is already here?"

"Yes, he arrived this morning. As far as I know he's in his hotel in Sun City." She hesitated, glancing at someone who was outside the field of sight. *"I stand corrected, Captain. I have just been informed that he is already on his way to meet the Renao representative in their embassy."*

"Very well. We will meet the special envoy there. And I assure you, Madam Governor, that we will do everything in our power to protect Lembatta Prime from a terrorist attack."

"Thank you, Captain. We appreciate that. Sarin out."

Adams looked at his communications officer. "Mr. Winter, contact the embassy and announce our arrival."

Winter acknowledged that order.

"Commander Roaas, Commander zh'Thiin, Lieutenant ak

Namur," the captain said, "you're with me."

"Sir, do you think it's wise for me to come along?" ak Namur asked hesitantly. "You know that I don't have the best standing with my people. I have left the Home Spheres. I don't belong to them anymore."

"You're a Starfleet officer," Adams said. "I expect the embassy staff to treat you with the same respect as the rest of us. Besides, you may be able to provide us with valuable insight into the behavior of our hosts."

"Understood, sir." The young Renao left his console, joining the Caitian and the Andorian.

Adams faced his second officer. "Commander Carson, you have the bridge."

"Aye, sir." Carson left her place at ops while replacement crew took the conn, ops, and tactical stations.

"Oh, and Carson," Adams said, already on his way to the turbolift where the others waited for him.

"Yes, Captain?"

"Keep your eyes peeled for anything out of the ordinary. The terrorists might have cloaking technology at their disposal."

"I'll have Commanders Mendon and Kirk recalibrate the sensors to search for suspicious radiation and propulsion residue."

"Excellent. Do it." Adams knew that Carson had served on the U.S.S. *Defiant*, which was the only Starfleet starship with a cloaking device. If any of them knew how to detect cloaked enemies, it was her.

The captain stepped into the lift with the rest of the away team, and shortly after that they beamed down to the planet's surface, materializing in the embassy's courtyard.

The first thing Adams noticed was an extraordinary

pattern of entangled gold rings that had been embedded into a floor of polished, light gray stones. Dark red columns lined the circular yard. Beyond, the embassy buildings extended into the distance. Three people stood in the shade of the columns, clearly expecting the visitors. They stepped out into the open when they saw the newcomers.

Adams didn't know the first two men. Both were clearly Renao, as they had the same red skin color as ak Namur. Their faces also sported the familiar gold jewelry that was attached to the skin, and their eyes glowed noticeably. The men wore black robes, adorned with gold ribbons.

The third man was considerably older than his companions. He also wore a robe but it was white and gray. A bronze-colored pin was attached to his collar—a small triangle, its tip pointing toward a specific point within a circle. This was the IDIC symbol showing its bearer to be an advocate of the philosophy of Infinite Diversity in Infinite Combinations. The man's iron-gray hair was cropped short and it didn't cover his pointy, elegantly curved ears.

When Adams recognized his counterpart, his eyebrows rose. "Ambassador Spock!"

Spock was one of the most renowned figures within the Federation—and beyond. He bowed his head. "Welcome to Lembatta Prime, Captain Adams."

Jassat ak Namur stared in awe at the famous half-Vulcan. He had never met him personally before but he did know all about the exceptional role that Spock had played in the history of the Federation. His career was textbook material at the Academy: first officer of the legendary U.S.S. *Enterprise* under James Tiberius Kirk; driving force behind the reconciliation process between the Klingons and the Federation after the moon Praxis had exploded; the Federation's longstanding ambassador in the Romulan Star Empire, attempting for years to reunite Vulcans and Romulans. Hardly any event of galactic consequence over the past one hundred and twenty years had taken place without the involvement of this serene man, who was driven by logic and empathy in equal measure.

And now he was here to put Jassat's people to the test and to find out whether the Renao were all fanatic serial killers.

Somehow, Jassat felt both honored and uneasy.

Spock introduced the dignitaries by his side. "These are the ambassadors Himad ak Genos and his deputy Seresh ak Momad."

"Pleasure to meet you," Adams replied. He pointed to his colleagues. "My first officer, Commander Roaas, my security chief, Lieutenant Commander Lenissa zh'Thiin, and my conn officer, Lieutenant Jassat ak Namur."

"Captain," said ak Genos, drawing a circle with his right hand in the air in front of his chest—a gesture of greeting. "Commanders." He studied Jassat. "And you must be the Renao serving in Starfleet."

"Yes, Mr. Ambassador," Jassat said.

Ak Genos faced Adams. "I hope he doesn't put our people to shame."

"Mr. ak Namur is an exemplary officer," Adams said, to Jassat's relief. "I have the utmost confidence in his abilities and his knowledge. That's the reason why I have asked him to accompany me here."

"I'm pleased to hear that." The ambassador's voice didn't betray anything, but Jassat had the feeling that his demeanor slightly stiffened.

He just realized that a renegade and sphere refugee is supposed to assess him and his people for Starfleet. The young Renao could easily imagine that the ambassador might not be delighted about that.

Ak Genos made an inviting gesture. "Please, follow us into my conference room. We can take counsel about the events of the past few days."

It struck Jassat that the ambassador didn't use a universal translator. What's more, he spoke Federation Standard remarkably accent-free. He must have had close contact to the outworlders during the years of rapprochement between the Federation and the Home Spheres.

The group left the courtyard behind, walking through a broad corridor that led deeper into the building. They went past circular passages twice. Bilingual signs on the wall announced that they were walking from one embassy department into another. Many of the Renao they encountered were clad in similar ankle-length robes to the ambassador and his deputy; some wore pants and jackets pertaining to the colonist's fashion on Lembatta Prime. The majority of employees were men. They only saw two women. Both were clad in elegant dresses made from flowing fabrics. *Things haven't changed much during the past few years,* Jassat thought.

Although the Renao made an effort not to stare, Jassat felt the double-takes that the mixed away team attracted. The population on Lembatta Prime was primarily human; it was rare for the embassy staff to encounter an Andorian or a Caitian. Lenissa held her head high with pride, while Roaas seemed filled with determination.

Jassat also garnered attention from his fellow Renao; some curious, many disapproving. Even to those who worked and lived voluntarily outside of the Home Spheres, a Renao committing himself to deep space was at best a suspect sphere defiler.

"You got here fast," Adams said to Spock in front of Jassat while they walked along the corridors. "Were you in the vicinity?"

"No, I came from Vulcan," replied the ambassador. "But I made the journey aboard the U.S.S. *Bohr.*"

"The *Bohr*…" The captain searched his memory. "*Merian*-class, right?"

"That is correct," Spock said. "Like all ships belonging to that class she has been equipped recently with a quantum slipstream drive."

Adams sighed quietly. "At this rate the warp era will be over soon."

"That is not entirely impossible," the ambassador agreed. "Especially where the Federation is concerned. And no matter how carefully Starfleet will conceal this technology from the eyes of others, it will eventually become accessible to other nations as well. That may not be a detrimental development since it would bring the people of the galaxy closer together."

"The only question is whether they are ready for it," Adams mumbled.

Most of the space in the conference room was filled with a sickle-shaped table. The pointed ends almost touched each other. Comfortable chairs had been arranged around the table. Jassat noted that they had been manufactured on Earth. A large panorama painting hung on the room's back wall. It depicted a rough and rocky landscape, covered with rusty dust, below a red sun. In the background huge structures that looked like beehives towered over the landscape. The image radiated somber beauty. *Onferin*, the young Renao realized, and a touch of sadness washed over him.

"Our home," Ambassador ak Genos explained to Captain Adams. "The Bhorau Desert on Onferin at dawn. In the background you can see a bunch of Griklak-hives, dwellings of giant insects native to Onferin. They are virtually extinct these days but thousands of years ago they were the predominant life form on Onferin. Our ancestors built their first cities in abandoned Griklak-hives because they offered ample space and at the same time excellent protection against a hostile environment. That's how the concept of Home Spheres came about."

"That's very interesting, Ambassador," said Adams. "But if it's all the same to you, let's talk about the present, not about the past."

"Of course, please, be seated."

They settled down around the table. Spock as mediator took the seat between Adams and ak Genos. Jassat found a seat next to Lenissa right on the far end. That was fine by him. Coming back home had caused an emotional rollercoaster within him. Happiness mixed with sadness, curiosity with fear. So he was grateful to take a back seat, watching, but not actually speaking.

"Ambassador," Spock began, "I assume you have been just as well informed about the events of the past few days as we have. I will therefore spare myself the trouble of playing the Starfleet recordings taken around the field of debris, or the video from the Purifying Flame claiming responsibility."

"Of course. We know what happened on the borders of the Home Spheres," ak Genos replied. "And we strongly condemn such terrorist acts. But the Renao people have nothing to do with these attacks. Yes, it's true, we do not condone the Federation's philosophy to expand uninhibited further and further into space. How often has your unrestrained desire for expansion caused millions of deaths throughout the galaxy? And yet, our protests have always been peaceful. We only took appropriate diplomatic steps such as severing contact with you and concentrating on our inner matters. Violent murder of thousands of people is not what we desire."

"What about the Klingons?" Adams asked. "There has been an attack on the Klingons as well. A dilithium mine has been blown up, and there has been another video claiming responsibility. And Tika, just like Starbase 91, is in close proximity to the Lembatta Cluster. Do you think that's coincidence?"

"On the contrary, Captain," the ambassador replied. "I'm convinced that this was arranged very deliberately, and that it was carried out by an unknown power, which quite clearly is keen to commit atrocities, laying the blame on the doorsteps of others. Maybe we should take another look at the videos after all. You will soon realize that nobody can deduce any solid facts from these transmissions. Is the man beneath the cloth really a Renao, or has he donned a disguise? Does he really say what he appears to be saying, or has the audio track been tampered with?"

"Our experts have already thoroughly looked into that line of questioning," Spock said. "I can assure you, Ambassador, no alterations have been made to this recording."

"And I can assure you: that man in front of the camera represents neither the government nor the people of the Home Spheres! It's much more likely that he is a sphere defiler—much like the lieutenant—who doesn't live within the Lembatta Cluster anymore, and hasn't done so for quite a while. There, far away from home, he has joined the Typhon Pact. You must have noticed that the attacks were directed against the Federation and the Klingons—the so-called Khitomer Powers. Why didn't they attack targets in the Gorn Hegemony? To we Renao, the Gorn are as guilty of violating the universal harmony as the Federation or the Klingon Empire."

Jassat knew that wasn't strictly true. The Gorn Hegemony was a comparably small power bloc in the framework of the Alpha Quadrant. Contrary to Federation, Klingons, and Romulans, the Gorn's intention to expand in space was fairly limited. If radical movements existed in the Home Spheres, they would certainly turn on the Gorn last of all. But he kept his objections to himself. Voicing them seemed inappropriate in this situation. He would inform Captain Adams later.

Just like he would inform him that something wasn't quite right. Jassat couldn't tell with absolute certainty, but he sensed that the ambassador was keeping something from his visitors. His voice and his demeanor expressed righteous anger about the accusations made against the Renao. But his purple eyes flickered in a way that he perceived to be great nervousness. Again, Jassat could not confront the ambassador openly about it. The scandal would have been far too great. Still, he was deeply concerned about the implications of the ambassador's behavior. Clearly, there was much more rotten in the Lembatta Cluster than ak Genos let on.

The conversation among Spock, Adams and both Renao diplomats was fairly short and unproductive. Ak Genos insisted that this was a conspiracy against the Renao, and he reminded them of the biggest sticking point the Federation also had: his people didn't even have the technology available to commit such atrocities.

In the end they went their separate ways peacefully, but dissatisfied.

"If you come across any helpful insights, no matter what kind," Spock said when they parted, "the Federation would regard it as an important sign for a peaceful future coexistence if you were to inform us."

"That goes without saying," ak Genos said. "In exchange we would appreciate receiving any new findings from your investigations. If enemies of the Renao have slipped into the Lembatta Cluster and settled here, we need to take measures against them."

"We will keep you posted." Adams looked at the Vulcan special envoy. "Are you prepared to accompany us to the *Prometheus*, Ambassador?"

Spock nodded gracefully. "Indeed. My luggage can be retrieved from the hotel residence."

"All right." The captain touched his combadge on his chest. "Adams to *Prometheus*. Five to beam up."

A shimmering veil of light engulfed them, and several seconds later they arrived back on board.

"That wasn't very productive," Adams stated when they stepped off the transporter platform.

"That was not to be expected," Spock replied. "This conversation was merely our first attempt. It will reach its conclusion at a later date."

"And what are we going to do next?" the captain asked.

Spock expressively raised one of his eyebrows. "I suggest we take a closer look at the scene of the crime."

17
NOVEMBER 9, 2385

U.S.S. *Prometheus*, on the periphery of the Lembatta Cluster

Starbase 91's expanse of rubble covered almost one point five million kilometers in space, spreading further by approximately one kilometer per second. Not much was left of the large *Watchtower*-class space station. It had been literally blown to pieces that had been scattered all over the void. Richard Adams felt a huge lump in his throat staring at the few pieces of wreckage visible on the bridge's main screen. Shimmering dust and radiation spikes on sensor displays of the science station were the only indications of what had happened here.

So this is Karen's grave. What a place to die. And what a way to die. Suddenly and without so much as a chance of survival. He knew that his emotions were overwhelming him, but despite being annoyed about it, he didn't deny himself that moment. He wanted to grieve for Karen. *On the other hand, this might not be the right moment,* he mused, knowing that he was on the bridge surrounded by his officers. What's more, Spock stood next to him.

If Adams had shared his grief with the half-Vulcan, he might have pointed out logically and analytically that Karen had been lucky in a way. Death is always part of a Starfleet officer's life. Space is a dangerous place, where not only do hostile species try to end your life, but technical problems, unusual cosmic phenomena, or dangerous conditions during away missions on planets might kill you—not to mention the unforgiving vacuum of space itself. There were thousands of different ways to lose your life, and most of them were far more unpleasant than being torn apart by a huge explosion. Karen probably hadn't experienced any pain. In fact, she had died in a place that she had chosen as her home, surrounded by colleagues she valued. Except for a natural death at an advanced age surrounded by loving family members this had probably been the next best thing for her.

Adams didn't share his feelings with Spock or anyone else present, though. Instead, he fought back his grief. Later, in his quarters, he would drain a bottle of Andorian ale in memory of his niece. Right now, work was waiting for him.

"Mr. ak Namur, please take us to the center of the detonation," Adams said. "One quarter impulse."

"Aye, sir."

The stars on the periphery of the screen began moving as the *Prometheus* gathered speed.

Adams turned to his science officer. "Lieutenant Commander Mendon, carry out a broadband scan of the area. I want to know what happened here."

"Understood, Captain." The blue-skinned Benzite stood at the back of the bridge at the science station. He turned toward his console, entering input. White steam rose from the respirator's mouthpiece that was fastened on his uniform tunic. Benzites didn't necessarily require respirators in order to breathe in oxygen-nitrogen atmospheres anymore, but Mendon belonged to a minority. Their genetic code couldn't be altered without severe health risks, and therefore, they were still dependent on respirators.

Adams gazed at Spock, whose face looked as if it had been

carved from stone, which probably conveyed his dismay far better than any emotional outburst could have done.

"According to the available data, the explosion must have been of significant proportions," the ambassador said quietly. "One would assume such scale is the result of a reactor core breach."

"The residual radiation confirms this assessment," Mendon said behind them. "There has been an uncontrolled matter-antimatter reaction."

"That can't be all." Adams stepped forward to the upper edge of the few stairs leading down to the control pit. "Something must have caused the breach. Something coming from the outside."

Mendon typed more commands, studying the results. "No energy residue pertaining to weapons fire. I'll check the area for particle residue of known explosives." After a while he continued. "No signs of anicium, tricobalt, ultricium or any similar compounds. Hang on! I'm picking up minute amounts of trilithium."

"Trilithium?" Adams looked at Spock quizzically. "Don't the Romulans use some kind of trilithium isotope in their plasma torpedoes?"

"That is correct, Captain. I would also point out that no plasma torpedo would be capable of causing such vast destruction of a starbase as swiftly as we see here."

"Trilithium is also used as a conventional explosive," Roaas said from the tactical console. "However, you'd need several tons of that stuff in order to destroy a station of this size."

"Sir!" Sarita Carson turned away from the ops console, looking at Adams. "What if the trilithium had been combined with other components to increase its explosive power? I'm thinking protomatter and tekasite."

Spock raised an eyebrow. "A remarkable combination. I would enquire as to what led you to this possibility."

"I used to serve on Deep Space 9 during the Dominion War. When the conflict started to get out of hand, a changeling attempted to turn Bajor's sun into a supernova by flying one of the station's runabouts into it. He had a bomb consisting of trilithium, tekasite, and protomatter on board. We were able to stop him with the *Defiant*, but if we'd failed, the entire Bajoran system with everything in it would have been annihilated."

"Mind you, I'd rule out the Dominion as perpetrators," said Adams. "They haven't demonstrated any tendencies to set up a foothold in the Alpha Quadrant in recent years."

"Although those incidents hadn't been made public back then," Roaas said, "I'd wager that the intelligence services of all major powers of the quadrant are aware of this explosive mixture. It's possible that this information has been leaked to any number of more dubious factions."

"The volatile and dangerous nature of protomatter has been known for more than a century," said Spock. "It contains a power of creative potential; however, it is also capable of devastation."

Adams turned to regard Spock, as it sounded as if he spoke from experience. Then he recalled that the ambassador did, from his days as a Starfleet officer. "Project Genesis. Protomatter was used during the attempt to fill uninhabitable worlds with life, wasn't it?"

"You remember correctly, Captain," Spock replied. "The danger lies in the fact that protomatter triggers an extreme transformation of matter with its cascade effect wherever it hits. That way, life can come into being, and a dead star can be reignited, as Professor Gideon Seyetik demonstrated in 2370 with the star Epsilon 119. However, a thorough analysis of the local conditions is required, as well as a precise usage of protomatter. Otherwise, the transformation that happens is uncontrolled and extremely destructive."

"That would explain the force of the explosion here," Roaas said.

"But there's a problem, Captain," Mendon said. The baleen-like extensions around the Benzite's mouth twitched briefly, a sign of dissatisfaction. "Once protomatter has reacted it's no longer traceable. It is completely transformed."

"That is not entirely correct," Spock objected. "It is true that the protomatter itself will be completely transformed, but its influence can still be proven indirectly by the matter that has been created. If we could bring some pieces of debris aboard, we could analyze them in the laboratory."

Adams nodded. "Very good. Let's get that underway. But first of all, we should substantiate Commander Carson's theory by finding tekasite."

"I'm already on it, Captain." Mendon turned back to his console.

"What do we know about this compound?" the captain asked.

Spock tilted his head slowly. "The substance itself is not highly explosive but it can be used as an excellent enhancer for other explosives. That could be the reason why the changeling chose to use it for his attack on Bajor's sun. Tekasite is also very rare. Should we be able to find traces of it, we might have the means to track the perpetrators."

"Sir, there are definitely traces of tekasite in the debris field," Mendon said excitedly.

Adams, Roaas, and Spock exchanged knowing glances. "So there we have two of the three substances required to build an extremely dangerous bomb. I don't think that's coincidence." He turned his attention to the fore. "Mr. ak Namur, take us into transporter range for some of the bigger pieces of debris. We'll bring them aboard for examination."

Spock raised an eyebrow. "I recommend that you have personnel in EV suits bring the wreckage to the shuttlebay. The transporter might alter the subatomic structure, making it difficult to recognize the traces of protomatter transformation. Even the traction of a tractor beam might have a deleterious effect."

"A spacewalk?" Adams glanced at the Vulcan skeptically. Spacewalks were awkward, dangerous, and generally unnecessary when you had transporters and tractor beams. But Spock's recommendation had pointed out the problems with the usual methods.

The captain glanced at his science officer questioningly.

"Sir, I agree with Ambassador Spock," said Mendon. "If we want to be sure not to contaminate any of the pieces of wreckage with energy we need to bring them aboard manually."

"Very well." Adams went to his command chair, opening a channel to the engine room. "Adams to Commander Kirk."

"*Kirk here, Captain,*" the chief engineer's voice came from the loudspeaker.

"Prepare the shuttlebay to receive wreckage from the debris field."

"*Understood, Captain. I'm on my way.*"

He turned to Roaas. "Assemble a salvage team. They should start work immediately."

"Aye, sir." The first officer rose and left the bridge.

"Maybe we'll even find out how the culprits went about it," Lenissa zh'Thiin said, leaving her place at the environmental controls to the right of Adams in order to take Roaas's place at tactical. "I really can't believe that someone would be able to smuggle such dangerous substances aboard a space station and into a dilithium mine."

"The Bajoran bomb was constructed on Deep Space 9," Carson said. "Mind you, the changeling looked like Doctor Bashir. He had security clearances that simple maintenance technicians or mine workers wouldn't possess."

Jassat ak Namur turned around on his seat. "Captain, that is another piece of evidence supporting the notion that the Renao are *not* responsible. Tekasite is known in the Home Spheres, and there are two or three places within the Lembatta Cluster with natural deposits. We also might have a handful of scientists capable of synthesizing trilithium. But the handling of protomatter is well out of our technological league."

Adams nodded. "Thank you, Mr. ak Namur. Your assessment has been noted."

"Sir!" Mendon said suddenly in response to several beeps from his console. "The computer has discovered something amidst the wreckage that shouldn't be there."

"On screen," Adams ordered.

The science officer tapped a command into his console, and a moment later the overview of the debris field changed. Zooming into a specific part of the area, a deformed piece of wreckage became visible. It was black, curved, and looked as if its surface had once been smooth.

Adams squinted. "How big is that chunk of debris?"

"Approximately one meter, Captain," Mendon said.

"Composition?"

Mendon called the sensor readings up on the screen. Even these preliminary readings indicated clearly that this piece of wreckage could not have been a part of the space station.

"Anyone got any idea what that might be?"

"I do, sir," zh'Thiin said quietly. The Andorian woman's antennae that protruded from her white hair twitched forward like annoyed snakes. "I bet one month of holodeck time that fragment out there is a piece of hull from a Romulan *Scorpion* attack fighter."

A cold shiver ran down Adams's back. If his security chief was right, this crisis had just taken a turn for the worse. "Ensign Winter, relay the order to the salvage team to bring that piece of wreckage aboard. I want it scrutinized."

"Aye, sir."

I bet these are the remains of a Scorpion *attack fighter*, thought Lenissa zh'Thiin again as she stood in the shuttlebay on deck eight with Roaas, Kirk, and Spock half an hour later. The *Prometheus* shuttles had been shifted to the rear of the bay. An engineer in an EV suit had hauled the metal piece aboard, and now Kirk and Lenissa checked it with their tricorders. Roaas and Spock were watching them.

"I'm picking up radiation residue from an impulse engine," Kirk announced, staring at the displays on the device in her hand. "These are without doubt the remains of a ship. Judging by the construction materials, it's of Romulan origin."

"I knew it," Lenissa said in a strained voice. "And I'm picking up the weak tachyon radiation that would be typical of a cloaking device."

Spock raised an eyebrow. "This new evidence is alarming. A *Scorpion* attack fighter with a cloaking device would explain why the station did not notice their attacker's approach. As it was also destroyed, we cannot rule out the possibility of a suicide mission."

"You mean, the pilot had a bomb aboard and flew his cloaked fighter with full impulse speed into the station?" Roaas asked.

"Considering the information that is now available to us, that would be a plausible scenario," the ambassador replied. "It would explain Starbase 91's sudden end. The pilot had no need to deactivate the cloaking device in order to hit the station. The crew had no warning whatsoever. And a bomb consisting of trilithium, protomatter, and tekasite need not be particularly large to destroy an unprotected space station. The bomb that the changeling used during the Dominion War fitted into a runabout."

"But one thing doesn't quite make sense," Lenissa said. "The Romulans are pretty far away from here, and the *Scorpion*-class is a short-range attack fighter without warp drive. That means the culprit was not alone. It's impossible that he could have covered the distance from the Romulan Star Empire to the Lembatta Cluster. There must have been a mothership somewhere."

Kirk frowned. "Starbase 91 was a listening post. They had a powerful deep-space sensor array at their disposal, and they should have been able to locate ship movements beyond the border to the Klingon Empire. They would never have missed a mothership, no matter how far out it had been parked."

"Unless it was also cloaked," Lenissa said. "We know that the Romulans have state-of-the-art cloaking devices that can shift their Warbirds out-of-phase. Even a sensor array wouldn't be able to detect such a ship."

"If all that is true, if the Romulans are truly behind this, that raises some unpleasant questions." Roaas's ears twitched, while his tail whipped from side to side. "Why are they attacking a space station and a mining moon when both are a long way away from their own borders? Are they acting on their own initiative or do they have orders from the Typhon Pact? And what do the Renao have to do with it? Is the video claiming responsibility merely a distraction, a red herring for us? I find it hard to believe that they would have sided with the Typhon Pact."

"It might also be interesting to know why the pilot—if he really is Romulan—committed suicide destroying the station," Lenissa added. "The Romulans abandoned that tactic two centuries ago, during the war between Earth and Romulus. Let's be honest: if the Romulans really made the effort to fly a cloaked Warbird past all our sensor grids and patrols across Federation territory, why didn't they make good use of it? A volley of heavy plasma torpedoes would have wiped out Starbase 91 just as effectively."

"Under those circumstances the station would have been able to send a distress signal," Spock said. "It would have then been widely known that elements of the Romulan Star Empire had attacked a Federation station. That would have led to diplomatic implications, a situation of which the current Praetor of Romulus would not want. Gell Kamemor has already publicly aligned herself with a de-escalation of the current situation for months." The Vulcan studied the piece of wreckage pensively for a few moments. "Clearly, this matter requires further investigation."

Lenissa didn't like the sound of any of this. President Bacco had done everything in her power during her past months to extend a peace offering toward the Typhon Pact. There had been talks giving cause for hope that the cold war, currently prevailing in space, might come to an end. The dawn of a new era in the peaceful exploration of the galaxy was meant to be Bacco's legacy. Had all her efforts been in vain? Had her legacy already lost all value a few weeks after her death?

Spock squared his shoulders, pressing his hands against each other in front of his stomach. "Of paramount import at present is to *not* jump to conclusions. We have claims of responsibility from an allegedly radical Renao movement, we have traces of an extremely dangerous explosive, and we have wreckage from a Romulan attack fighter. This does combine to form a coherent picture, and wild speculation could dangerously place the blame on the wrong party. Such false blame would have fatal consequences."

Fatal is the right word, Lenissa thought grimly while images of hostile fleets flying toward each other, firing their weapons relentlessly, flashed through her mind.

"I'm picking up an approaching vessel," Sarita Carson reported from the ops console.

Adams, sitting in his command chair awaiting the results from the team in the shuttlebay, looked up. "What kind of vessel?"

"A Klingon *Vor'cha*-class attack cruiser."

"On screen," Adams ordered.

The image changed, and the olive-green starship appeared on the main screen.

"We are being hailed," Ensign Winter reported from the comm station.

Adams rose from his chair. "Open channel."

The image changed again, and the constricted bridge of a Klingon ship, illuminated in dim red light, came into view. A Klingon, wearing a gray-brown leather cassock over his standard-issue armor, stood in the center of it. He had shoulder-length, thick hair, and a thin long beard.

"I'm Kromm, captain of the attack cruiser Bortas," he announced in a tone of voice tantamount to a challenge. *"We're here to investigate an attack by Renao extremists on the Klingon Empire, and to hunt down those who are guilty of this crime."*

"Captain Adams of the U.S.S. *Prometheus*," Adams replied with a steady gaze. "We are also investigating an attack on the Federation that might have had its roots in the Lembatta Cluster. I suggest coordinating our efforts, Captain. We were told that Ambassador Rozhenko is with you."

"That's right," the Klingon said.

"Very good. Ambassador Spock is accompanying us on this mission. Why don't you come aboard, and we can discuss our results so far. Afterwards, the diplomats can decide how we should proceed."

The notion that politicians should have the final say seemed to invoke disgust in Kromm. Nonetheless, he nodded.

"Agreed, Captain. We will beam aboard your ship." Without another word he cut off the transmission.

"Delightful conversationalists," Sarita Carson murmured.

Adams activated the intercom. "Bridge to transporter room."

"Kowalski here."

"Prepare to beam a Klingon delegation aboard."

"Aye, sir."

The captain changed frequencies. "Bridge to Commander Roaas."

"Yes, Captain?" the first officer's voice answered.

"Meet me along with Commander zh'Thiin and Ambassador Spock in the transporter room," Adams ordered. "We have visitors."

"Visitors, sir?"

"The Klingons are here."

18
NOVEMBER 9, 2385

U.S.S. *Prometheus*, on the periphery of the Lembatta Cluster

"Bah!" Kromm had entered the U.S.S. *Prometheus's* conference room no more than fifteen minutes ago and he had already hammered his fist on the table for the third time. "You can't be serious. I know your file, Adams! You're not a coward!"

The long table stood alongside the windows in the room. The temperature in the room had been adjusted to suit humans. Eight people sat around the table for this discussion. Next to Kromm sat L'emka, who just emitted a strained sigh, and Chief Engineer Nuk. The latter appeared to be asleep. His eyes were closed and he breathed steadily and calmly. Across from the table sat the ambassadors, Rozhenko and Spock, along with Commander Roaas and the security chief, Lenissa zh'Thiin.

The Andorian's gaze seemed fixed onto the windows and the space beyond them, where floating debris of the former Federation station 91 was visible. Members of Starfleet wearing heavy EV suits with small thrusters and even smaller spotlights floated among the remains of the tragedy that had happened here, trying to secure any available evidence.

At the head of the table sat Captain Richard Adams. Above the center of the table hovered a star chart of the cluster; a three-dimensional holographic projection consisting of air and blue light, slowly revolving around its axis. Adams had concentrated on this projection... until Kromm's outburst.

"You might be right there, Captain," the human said, crossing his arms in front of his chest. "But I also know your file. And I see the way you're conducting yourself here. Therefore…"

"Conducting?" Kromm laughed. Incredulously, he stared at Commander L'emka who quite clearly didn't share his indignation. Quickly he looked back at Adams. "Are you insinuating that I'm just playing a role? Captain, your ever-so-noble Federation is not the only victim of these dishonorable Romulans! Have you already forgotten? Qo'noS also has reason to grieve—and to be furious. That's why Martok sent the *Bortas* in the first place!"

"So far, it's still debatable who the perpetrators are and…" Commander Roaas began.

"The hell it is!" Kromm interrupted the Caitian loudly. "You found the evidence yourself, damnit! What else do you need?"

"Certainty," Adams replied before Roaas, who clearly had difficulty remaining patient, could say anything. "And most of all we need respect, Captain. Generally, no one is to be interrupted while sitting at this table. I would appreciate it if you could also adhere to a tradition that is well-established aboard this ship."

Kromm snorted. That was typical for Starfleet! Did the Federation prefer to turn a blind eye to the truth because they were so peace-loving? It was no wonder that the formerly strong league of worlds had slipped from crisis to crisis during recent years. On Earth, they obviously preferred to sit back and do nothing instead of getting their hands dirty.

"The Romulan senate is a scheming, paranoid collection of warmongers," the Klingon snarled. "All Romulans are. I know that species better than you do, Adams. I know what they're capable of."

"And I know them far better than you do." Ambassador Spock, his hands calmly folded on the table, faced Kromm with a steady gaze from his brown eyes and spoke in a quiet voice. "Considerably better than you, I suspect. Your description does not correspond with my experiences."

Kromm had never before met the one-hundred-and-fifty-year-old Vulcan—a living legend in his own right. He had heard and read a lot about him, though, especially about the many years that Spock had spent in the Romulan underground. They said that Spock had pursued an absurd dream there: the reconciliation of Romulans and Vulcans. Both peoples were vastly different, but according to biology and genetics they must have been brothers eons ago. Kromm thought it spoke volumes that Spock's dream still hadn't come true. It proved that even great personalities of his caliber could become obsessed with completely unrealistic goals. Even legends grew old.

Kromm turned on him, although he found himself instinctively keeping his temper in check while speaking to such a legendary figure. "Well, in that case, let us *do* something, instead of sitting here and asking questions that have long since been answered. The Typhon Pact made no pretense of the fact that they are hostile toward you and us. What happened here and on Tika IV-B is testament to that." His gaze wandered to Rozhenko. "These attacks may be out of character for the Renao as you so eloquently keep pointing out, but I can guarantee you, the Romulans would carry them out just as swiftly as a *taj* would end up in a chest!"

"A precise analysis of the *Scorpion* wreckage is yet to come," L'emka interjected rudely. "So far, Captain Adams's team was only able to conduct a superficial..."

"You know the Pact, all of you!" Kromm screamed. The longer he sat at this table, the less he believed his eyes and ears. "You know what they are capable of, Captain! Remember Deep Space 9! Think of all the conflicts that the Breen have caused you in the past. And the Tzenkethi, the Gorn, and the Kinshaya. What more do you need? How much more obvious does Gell Kamemor have to be, before you finally realize that she is your enemy? Does Earth have to be in flames first?"

Adams rose, walking to the window. "Praetor Kamemor is a dedicated friend of the Federation. She's a woman of reason and vision. She worked together with our late President Bacco on a lasting peace between us and the Romulan Star Empire. It wouldn't make any sense whatsoever for Romulus to ruin this work and their mutual legacy now."

"And yet you're looking at debris out there." Kromm also got up because the discussion seemed to be coming to an end. In his eyes it had done so long ago. "The universe is not logical, Captain Adams. Yesterday's friend might be today's liar." At this point he couldn't help but shoot a warning glance toward the insolent L'emka. "Therefore, I suggest we take this new evidence and use it for a joint raid on Romulus's borders. We should let the treacherous *petaQ* within their senate know that they have picked on the wrong opponent."

"Expensive," someone suddenly grumbled to the right of him.

Slowly, Kromm turned around. The gray-haired Nuk still had his eyes closed, and his huge calloused hands were neatly folded on his impressive stomach, but apparently he had followed the conversation closely.

"What?" Kromm asked incredulously.

"War," grumbled the quirky engineer into his disheveled beard, before giving off a relaxed sigh. He seemed to be so calm that it bordered on uninterested. "War costs."

"Your engineer puts his finger on a very important point

there," Alexander Rozhenko said. The hint of a smile played around the corners of his mouth. Kromm would have loved to punch it out of his face, right there and then. "War costs. If we attack Romulus—be it for a good reason or not—Romulus will strike back. And the Federation and its allies—one of them being the Klingon Empire—will be involved in the next interstellar conflict."

"Which we simply can't afford," finished Roaas. He seemed to have calmed down, judging by the tone of his voice and his impersonal expression. "Dominion War, Borg invasion, the Typhon Pact… Our shipyards are operating at full capacity, but the strength of our fleet is still not back to the level it had been before the war. And I'm sure I don't have to discuss the lack of qualified staff officers with you, do I?"

Kromm sat down again, very slowly and without taking his eyes off the Caitian. "What is that supposed to mean, Commander?" he snarled aggressively. The dig hadn't eluded him. If this walking piece of fur wanted trouble, he could have it.

"That's enough!" Adams swung around from the window. His disapproving expression matched the tone of his voice. He went back to the table, pointing at the holographic star chart. "We will give every detail, every trace, and every theory of this case the attention it deserves, have I made myself clear? No exceptions, no short cuts, no excuses. We will draw our conclusions, and they will be *well-founded* conclusions, based on facts, and not on prejudice. And most of all they will not be based on dubious confessions."

"Captain!" Once again, Kromm hammered his fist on the table. Nuk winced, startled, opening his eyes. "The Renao *did* confess."

Adams raised his hands defensively. "Don't worry, Kromm. Onferin is still on the list of places that I intend to visit during this mission. But before we head to the Renao homeworld we should ensure that our crime scene out here doesn't conceal any more secrets from us. All in good time. Violence doesn't solve any problems, Captain—knowledge does. I'm sure Chancellor Martok would agree with me there."

"The chancellor demands answers, Captain, and he wants them soon."

"As do we," Adams replied. "And I have a hunch that we will find some of them on Lembatta Prime. We should take advantage of that opportunity before moving on. To do otherwise would be inefficient to say the least."

Kromm struggled. On the one hand, he deemed Adams's strategy too hesitant. On the other hand, he wanted to honor the High Council in the way it deserved, investigating the case thoroughly so not to miss any enemies of the empire against whom they could take vengeance.

So he finally yielded. "Very well. We shall do it your way, Adams. For now! If this only costs us time without leading to success, we will continue our conversation—with clearer words. Is that understood?"

Roaas glowered at him. "Threats are uncalled for, Captain Kromm!"

But Adams waved his hand dismissively. "Don't worry, Commander. Kromm and I understand each other."

With these words, the meeting ended. Kromm left, and he was not particularly satisfied.

Adams stared after the Klingons until the conference room door hissed shut behind them. He took a deep breath. *That went worse than expected.* Kromm was likely to be a bigger problem than anticipated. He lacked vision, and tried to make up for it with pride and volume. Adams didn't have any doubts that he could soothe his ruffled feathers again should the circumstances require him to do so but he wasn't all too keen on the notion.

"Captain?"

Spock's voice jolted him out of his thoughts. The old ambassador had drawn close to stand next to him without him noticing. Clasping his hands behind his back, Spock looked at Adams with an impassionate expression. It seemed as if he hadn't witnessed the argument with Kromm.

"Ambassador," Adams said, facing him. From the corner of his eye he noticed zh'Thiin and Roaas standing by the windows, whispering to each other. "What can I do for you?"

The half-Vulcan raised one eyebrow. "I believe I can do something for *you*, Captain Adams. I am finding these modified *Scorpion* attack fighters to be increasingly troublesome. With your permission, I wish to renew some of my contacts on Romulus. Perhaps with their aid, I may uncover more information without alerting the praetor and the senate. Would your Ensign Winter be able to open a secure subspace frequency so I may reach Romulus?"

Adams nodded. A touch of relief flooded over him, as this was an actual productive course of action, as opposed to what Kromm had been suggesting. "Of course, Ambassador. If anyone can do that it'll be Ensign Winter. They call him the subspace magician here on board."

Spock raised his eyebrow again. "Remarkable. I was not aware that the habit of promoting extraordinarily talented officers to the level of miracle workers still existed within Starfleet."

The captain chuckled. "The universe is a dangerous place,

Ambassador. Simple spacefarers like us have a tendency to feel more secure when we can rely on witnessing a miracle now and then."

The Starboard 8 was almost empty. The majority of alpha shift was already sound asleep in their cabins after having been relieved from duty and it would take another two hours before the personnel from beta shift would populate the corridors. But that wasn't the only reason why Jassat ak Namur was faced with empty tables when he entered the small club on deck eight of the *Prometheus* that was one of the crew's favorite recreation centers.

It's the view. They're staying away because of the view.

Outside the three rectangular viewports that took up the majority of Starboard 8's exterior wall drifted the debris of Starbase 91 through the empty void of space. Beyond the rubble, the cluster nebula lurked menacingly with its dark red glowing in front of a black backdrop. This view would certainly not lift the spirits of Starfleet officers after work. Not under these circumstances.

"Lieutenant."

The bartender's friendly shout distracted Jassat from the debris. Squinting, the young Renao looked to the right toward the underlit white counter. Behind the counter stood the Bolian. A lonely engineer sat in front of the counter on a stool that was upholstered with dark fabric. He stared into a glass filled with a dark amber drink. The screen at the other end of the counter displayed a political talk show on the topic of the "Renao Crises." According to the text overlay, that was the name given to this matter. The sound had been muted.

"Are you trying to take root on the threshold?" the

bartender shouted. He grinned broadly. "Come in, Mr. ak Namur. Make yourself at home."

Home. Visually, that might be the case—the *Prometheus* was home to Jassat, by now probably even more than the cluster out there. For years he had yearned to return to this ship, and to be among these officers again. For years, he had dreamed about sitting in the Starboard 8 again.

But now? Empty chairs at empty tables? And the uneasy feeling that this home was no more than an illusion.

Hesitantly, Jassat went to the counter. The engineer briefly looked up. Was he imagining things, or did this man's expression show skepticism? Skepticism… and maybe even a silent accusation?

Word about the disaster in the Tika system had long since gotten around the crew. The second video of the alleged Renao claiming responsibility was being played on the news nets around the clock. Jassat couldn't blame his crewmates if they regarded him with mistrust. He didn't know most of them, and they didn't know him. Still, it hurt him considerably.

Again, Captain Adams's question echoed through his mind. *Do you feel ready, Lieutenant, to meet your people?* Adams had wanted to know whether he was prepared to defend the Federation's values against the Renao, who might be deluded, and might look upon him as a traitor. A stranger. Jassat had affirmed that question. But what about the Federation citizens, who were looking at him as if he was an alien? What about people like this engineer and his accusing gaze? The man by the counter was by no means the only one, as the previous days aboard the *Prometheus* had proven to Jassat. Wherever he looked, he was met with mistrust. Not necessarily on the bridge but on the lower decks. Almost everywhere, he noticed questioning gazes, frowns, and whispers behind his back. Shipmates fell silent when he came around a corridor corner. Near the engine room, some ensign had even snapped at him, calling him a "murderer." Jenna Kirk who had witnessed the incident by chance, had given the man a proper dressing down so that he took to his heels just as soon as he had been dismissed. But Jassat was worried... what's more, he *knew* that wasn't the end of it. That was how it always began, and that was never where it ended. Mistrust generated fear, and fear led to violence.

"What's your poison?" The bartender rubbed his hands together. "The usual?" The dedicated gesture and the broad smile chased Jassat's worries away, at least for the moment.

"The usual?" The Renao was amazed and amused in equal measures. "I only ever ordered a Q'babi juice once here."

Moba raised an admonitory finger. "But you said that you used to drink that juice way back when. Oh yes, I do remember such little details. Especially, if they come from the only Renao who ever happened to stroll into my small club. Besides, apart from you and Commander Kirk, nobody asks for Q'babi juice. Most people think it's too sweet. But what did my cousin on Rigel V always say? 'Tartly or sweet, all good things are neat!'"

"In that case—the same as always," Jassat mumbled, a little perplexed but generally grateful.

Since he'd been back on the *Prometheus* one feeling had gradually grown stronger: a premonition that everything was wrong all of a sudden. He felt exactly what Thomas Wolfe, an ancient author from Earth, had written: "You Can't Go Home Again." During his time at the Academy, Jassat had thought about the *Prometheus* and his goal to serve aboard her again almost every day. To be in his chosen Home Sphere. Now that he had reached that goal and his dream had come true, he felt increasingly like a stranger.

"Our conversation four days ago was interrupted," Moba chatted while pouring Jassat's favorite drink, "and I never got a chance to ask you what you've been up to these past couple of years."

"I spent the better part of the past few years in lecture rooms," replied Jassat dryly.

Laughing, the Bolian placed Jassat's glass in front of him on the counter. "Don't give me that! I've heard thousands of stories about the Academy. There's always something going on there. You have completed an education and become a Starfleet officer. That must have been some adventure in itself."

To what end?

Jassat took a sip from his drink, and suddenly he was glad that he didn't have to answer straight away. When he had decided to join Starfleet, diplomatic relations between his people and the Federation had already been far from ideal. The Renao had gradually turned their backs on the rest of the quadrant. Old trade agreements had been terminated, former alliances had fallen into oblivion. Jassat had never quite understood the reasons, but in those days he hadn't cared much either. He was no politician, and in all honesty, he couldn't understand his people's isolationism—not then, and not now.

Especially because it led to absurdities—many people close to him took offense to his career choice. Some even called him a traitor... not to his face, but behind closed doors. Kumaah, Moadas, and Evykk had been his best friends. They had been through thick and thin with him since their childhood days. But they abandoned him as soon as he decided to pursue his dream of a life in Starfleet, away from the Home Spheres. During his four years at the Academy, contact had been sporadic, and finally broken off altogether. Jassat regretted that, but he suspected his friends' only regret was that Jassat had done what he did.

"So?" Moba smiled, inviting and genuine. "Let's hear it."

Jassat took his glass. "Forgive me, but I'm not in the mood for stories today. Some other time, Moba. Thank you for the juice." With that he turned around, walking toward the windows on the other side of the room. The bartender with his admirable permanent optimism and the inexhaustible supply of questionable aphorisms meant well, but that didn't alter reality.

Silently, he stared into space while the minutes passed by. The "Cloud of Evil" was clearly visible beyond all the debris. It completed the picture, Jassat mused, as if it had been created just for him: at the front floated the destroyed remains of one Home Sphere, before the backdrop of the impenetrable nebula, which contained the other one. Both were a mystery to him. He didn't feel at home in either of them anymore. They both had become unfamiliar… or maybe he had become unfamiliar. This sensation hurt him more than he could possibly put into words.

Jassat sipped his juice. The thick liquid trickled down his throat. He remembered the time before attending the Academy when everything seemed to be much easier. When he had been able to sit next to Jenna and the others in Starboard 8 without having to worry about skeptical looks. The juice still tasted the same. A taste could also be a home, Jassat pondered, but not one that was sufficient.

"You seem to be deep in thought, Lieutenant."

The quiet voice was right beside him, but Jassat hadn't realized that he had company. Surprised, he turned around.

His surprise increased when he recognized Spock by his side. The diplomat wore a simple robe made of rough fabric. "Am... Ambassador." Jassat gulped. "I beg your pardon, what did you say?"

"That you seem to be deep in thought. And apparently, these thoughts are not pleasant."

Jassat was amazed. One of the most famous personalities in the Federation concerned himself with his innermost thoughts? That was... absurd, surely?

"I venture that you experience a sensation of being uprooted," the half-Vulcan said, turning his gaze toward the red cluster beyond the debris. "So close to the Home Sphere and yet, metaphorically speaking, further away than ever. More unfamiliar. And you feel prejudged—here as much as over there."

The young Renao swallowed. With a few short sentences this old ambassador had summarized him even more precisely than he himself had managed after days of brooding. "Yes," he said quietly.

Spock steepled his fingers. "Are you, by any chance, familiar with the events that occurred one hundred and nineteen years ago between my former ship, the *Enterprise*, and the Romulan flagship *Algeron*?"

Jassat wracked his brain. "I'm afraid my history seminars have furnished me with too much knowledge, instead of..."

The man next to him nodded understandingly. "The *Enterprise* encountered Romulans for the first time since the Earth-Romulan War ended. Several outposts along the Neutral Zone had been destroyed by an unknown attacker. When we followed the distress call, we discovered the Romulan ship. My predominantly human crewmates found out on that day that there's an undeniably close relation between my people and the Romulan people."

Now it was Jassat's turn to nod as he began to remember. This remarkable mission had been the subject of seminars, of course. But why did Spock tell him about that now?

The ambassador answered that question immediately. "The crew suspected me of treason because the hostile Romulans looked like me. They no longer regarded me as their partner; instead, they thought I had allied with the enemy. They became skeptical and scared and…"

"Dismissive," the Renao finished the sentence. Spock's hint of a smile told him that the Vulcan had expected that. "Ambassador, I had no idea."

Spock made a dismissive gesture. "It *was* a long time ago, Lieutenant. But history is repeating itself, regrettable as that may be. Premature judgment is passed far quicker than well-founded judgment. That aspect of what is sometimes referred to rather ethnocentrically as human nature has not changed, unfortunately. Emotional species have a tendency to project the deeds and opinions of one person onto entire peoples." He fell silent for a while, dwelling on his thoughts. "These are uncertain times, Lieutenant. Times that will leave scars on all of us. Wherever fear reigns, ideals end up being sacrificed. That was the case a century ago, and I would surmise that it will be the same today."

Jassat had the urge to swallow again. He remembered the talk show, the looks from his colleagues, the whispering. One question was on the tip of his tongue, and he was almost ashamed to ask it. He couldn't keep it to himself any longer, though, because it had been nagging him for too long. "And what if it's true?" he blurted out. "What if these atrocities have really been committed by Renao? I couldn't possibly imagine an explanation for that, Ambassador, but I also saw those videos!"

Spock gazed intently at Jassat. "*If* it is true, we will attempt to understand their reasons. Lieutenant, we are never just a crowd, never a generality. Each one of us—be they Vulcan, human, or Renao—decide for themselves, and thus everyone is responsible for their actions individually." His tone of voice was calm and friendly as before, but in his eyes stood sobriety and compassion. "It is simple—one might even say simplistic—to look at the atrocities of individuals and extend suspicion to an entire nation. But there is only one standard we can truly apply—our personal standard."

Jassat lowered his head. He didn't have an answer to that, but at the same time he felt that he had never before wanted to say as much as he did in this particular moment. And he was grateful.

"Stay true to yourself," he heard Spock say. "You owe it to your Home Spheres. Both of them."

When Jassat looked up again, the Vulcan had already departed. Jassat noticed the door to Starboard 8 closing behind him. He also realized that the engineer had left in the meantime.

"Another one?" Moba shouted from his counter, happily waving an empty glass around. His smile was broad and warm. "For the good old sense of home?"

Jassat ak Namur nodded, walking over to the counter. "To home."

19
NOVEMBER 10, 2385

Ki Baratan, Romulus

Dark storm clouds hung above the Romulan capital city. Thunder rolled. Above the Apnex Sea nearby, where Ki Baratan's founders had once settled, lightning brightened the dark skies.

Thokal pulled his cloak's hood deeper over his face, walking faster. The city's streets quickly emptied, especially the area where Thokal was heading.

The Chalandru neighborhood was old, older than most other neighborhoods in the city, and it showed. It was full of multistory buildings with blind glass window panes and dirty façades. Abandoned small stores with poorly covered windows and doors probably housed entire populations of *Nhaidhs* and other vermin that bred in there. The resident holoemitters probably hadn't projected their three-dimensional adverts onto the perma-concrete sidewalks for longer than anyone could remember.

There wasn't a location in this coastal metropolis where you could feel further away from the government district with its huge palaces made from rodinium, stone, and transparent aluminum, and the impressive state hall where the senate sat. This was the very last location where you would expect to meet a member of this elitist circle.

That was precisely the reason why Thokal lived here, and

had done so for decades. The old Romulan with his white hair, bulging forehead, and paunch had settled down here shortly after his arrival in Ki Baratan. Back then, Chalandru hadn't been this dilapidated, but its future had been easily predictable. Thokal had seized the opportunity and had bought a three-story, narrow house in a side alley. Since then he had hardly spent a night elsewhere—although his duty had sometimes forced him to do so. But these days were also long past.

The Romulan hadn't set foot in his old office in the city center for years. He didn't have any intention of doing so, either. Quite the contrary—he sometimes thought that there wasn't anyone in the whole of Ki Baratan who enjoyed his retirement more than he did. Not a day went by when Thokal didn't thank the gods of *Vorta Vor* that he wouldn't have to deal with diplomats, rulers, and the never-changing scheming in the government district ever again.

Thokal was happy. And he intended to stay happy. With a grateful sigh he walked up the four steps leading to his front door. He took off his hood to allow the scanner that was embedded in the wall to read his wrinkled face and his iris, before comparing the scan with the databanks in the house computer. The door recognized him and opened.

Ignoring the wailing sirens that seemed to draw closer from parallel streets, Thokal entered his home. He was an experienced inhabitant of Chalandru and as such was well used to those kinds of background noises. They were part of the everyday routine and just as normal as the adolescents lurking at every corner or the derelicts inside the former parking lot near the transit station.

He closed the door and set his luggage down.

Silence. Finally, silence.

"Computer, dim the window panes," he said into the void. The house technology, which boasted quite remarkable features, followed that order instantly. Within a few fractions of a second the house's windows were impenetrable for both prying eyes and any spy drones that might be nearby. Of course, nobody would be able to realize that from the outside.

"Light."

Two old-fashioned floor lamps in the room's rear corners switched on, illuminating the entrance area with a discreet but warm light. Thokal looked at his cramped bookshelves reaching all the way up to the ceiling, his comfortable wing chair, and the small table where he had been writing his memoirs, although he knew they would never be published. Everything seemed fine and the way it had been prior to his departure. Everything seemed as usual.

Reassured, the old Romulan took his coat off, hanging it on the hook on the inside of the door. He groaned while taking off his boots, and heard the pouring rain that had just started outside. He hadn't come home a second too early.

It was then that he noticed the difference.

"I'm growing old," he mumbled a little surprised and a little annoyed. When he was younger, he would have noticed the blue book in the middle shelf immediately, and not half a minute later. "Old and blind."

The shelves lined the entire right wall of the room. They were testament to his many interests, but they also mirrored his almost archaic fondness for non-digital reading. First editions of appraised lyricists stood next to polemic pamphlets of ancient theologians, political treatises were next to escapist fiction, upscale erotica hid behind standard works of historians. No one else would have found their way around this mixture of genres, but Thokal knew exactly where he'd find which volume, which information and which adventure. Just like he knew that the thriller *The Raptor's Stroke of Wing* had never been published in a blue cover.

The small book in the middle shelf was a computer-created fake, and usually was white in color.

If it presented itself in blue, the house computer wanted to relay a message to its owner inconspicuously.

The book hadn't been blue for months. An uneasy feeling crept up on Thokal. He put on his slippers, switched the lighting off in the room and stepped out into the hall. Several steps later he stood atop the cellar stairs.

"Light," he ordered again, and a circular overhead lamp illuminated the square room beneath his house.

Thokal went down the stairway and looked around. The shelves down here were considerably less beautiful. They lined the walls, holding various belongings of Thokal's life: memorabilia from strange worlds that he had once visited, imported animal food that his also imported pet hadn't been able to eat all of—and that he didn't have the heart to dispose of—models, tools, etc.

He went to the back wall. To the inexperienced eye it might not have seemed special, but he knew that it reached half a meter too far into the room. Grunting, the old Romulan pulled a blue toolbox from the middle shelf, which lowered into the cellar floor immediately.

This technology wasn't any less old-fashioned than the hardcover books upstairs on the ground floor. But Thokal liked this little gadget and preferred it to all holoscreens and energy fields. It had more style. And of course, since it was a physical mechanism, it was undetectable by scans.

Behind the shelf that disappeared into the ground, a small column with an almost even surface came into view:

the house computer's core in a black casing. A small display was embedded at eye level, showing the emblem of the Tal Shiar—the Romulan intelligence service, and Thokal's former employer. Below the display was a small, flat console. Thokal waited until the floor above the shelf had closed again, before approaching the column.

"Sound shielding," he ordered the computer. "Lock doors and windows."

"*Affirmative*," the computer answered. Thokal had programmed the computer to acknowledge orders vocally only if the entire building was sealed and tap-proof.

"Source of message?"

"*You have received an encoded message from the Federation starship* Prometheus. *The message is one day, six hours, and twenty-eight minutes old.*"

Prometheus? Thokal furrowed his bulging brow. He knew the name, but only from statistics and reports. It was difficult to imagine that a Starfleet crew would contact him—especially not by these means.

"That's impossible," he mumbled. "This channel is secret, and only the reunification movement knows about it." He raised his voice. "Computer. Who is the sender of this message?"

"*Unknown. Code does not permit identification or the extraction of any information regarding its contents.*"

Again the Romulan hesitated. If the computer was unable to decipher the incoming transmission, how should he?

Thokal raised his eyebrows. "Computer, is the encoding based on a password?"

"*Affirmative*," the artificial voice answered. "*In order to access the message, a question must be answered.*"

"Provide the question."

The voice coming from the comm system changed. *"Is M'rek culprit or investigator?"*

Thokal recognized that voice instantly and relaxed. "Both, old friend," he replied, thinking again about *The Raptor's Stroke of Wing*. "You know that as well as I do."

The Tal Shiar emblem disappeared from the computer display. Instead, the face of a man whom Thokal had known for decades, and whom he valued as one of his closest friends, came into view. Together they had fought for the reunion of Romulans and Vulcans—a goal that hadn't been accomplished yet, but neither of them intended to give up on. Judging by the background, Spock sat in a starship cabin, and he was calm as always.

"Greetings, Thokal. I hope this message finds you well."

"What do you want, Spock?" Thokal murmured, although he was talking to a recording.

"The circumstances force me to ask you for a favor. I assume you still have contacts in the Tal Shiar?"

Thokal snorted. "What do you think?" He might have been retired but that didn't mean that he had broken with old habits... habits that had become second nature for him. Not a day went by when the former data analyst didn't use his secret access to the servers in Tal Shiar's central office in order to browse the latest reports at his leisure. Of course, no one in the central office was aware of this encroachment, and they never would be because Thokal had taken precautions on his last day at work before retiring.

Spock told him in a few words about the events on the periphery of the Lembatta Cluster. Thokal was aware of most of this information already but mainly from the government news sources, as he hadn't been able to access the secret service's files during his short vacation. There was, however, one detail that he hadn't heard of so far, and it amazed him deeply.

"*There is evidence amidst the starbase wreckage of a Romulan attack fighter. A Renao has confessed to the atrocities, which contradicts the origin of the vessel we found the remains of. Thus far our investigation has only resulted in illogical conclusions. What I require from you, Thokal, is information about this attack fighter. We must know if the Typhon Pact in general and/or the empire in particular are truly behind this attack. Or has Romulus provided the Renao with military equipment? I'm relying on your information-gathering skills.*" He nodded. "*You have my gratitude, Thokal. Spock out.*"

That was the end of the message. The emblem returned to the monitor, along with a blinking icon that indicated a data package that had been attached to the transmission. Thokal assumed it was all the information Spock had with regard to the Romulan wreckage found in the debris of Starbase 91.

Thokal shook his head. "I was only away for a few days..." he mumbled. Sighing deeply, he began his task.

20
NOVEMBER 10, 2385

Cestus System

The Sphere is everything.

Mossam ak Foral's dark red hands flew all over the helm controls, adjusting his course here, confirming the course corrections there.

He didn't find it difficult to believe this core statement of his culture. Here, far from home and surrounded by strange stars, he understood it better than ever. And this understanding increased his motivation even more.

"Remaining flight time?" an agitated and impatient voice came from the communications system and seemed to fill ak Foral's small cockpit. *"We're here, aren't we? So, where's the target?"*

He did not object to his companion's tone, for he shared his passion. He called up the flight status on his console monitor immediately. "Soon," whispered ak Foral when he saw it. The flames within him flared higher than ever. "On the other side of the planet." After this short statement, he resumed the agreed radio silence.

Cestus III was an ocher-colored globe in a black void. The Class-M planet was on the periphery of Federation territory, close to the border of the Gorn Hegemony. The last President of the Federation, Nanietta Bacco, had been born here, and had served as the world's planetary governor for many years before becoming president. He had been told during their briefing that the most popular sport there was baseball… whatever that was supposed to be.

Yet all of that was of no interest to ak Foral. It was not that Cestus III was important, but what was located behind it. The closer he drew, the more he was convinced that he was in the right place. Finally, he could do what he had been born for and fulfill his destiny. He looked at the ship's displays and sensed the other object in the cockpit. This object was a square, three-piece container taking up the entire co-pilot's seat in the two-seater spacecraft. This gave ak Foral's mission, and that of his companion in the second attack fighter, which also had a "present" installed, their meaning.

The Sphere is everything, he thought again, sensing the blood in his veins, and the beating of his heart. Was that elation? *The Sphere is everything.*

Ak Foral turned his head so he could look out of the cockpit's broad, concave porthole. The second attack fighter was only a few dozen meters away from him but as invisible as ak Foral's own slender spacecraft. Even the target's sensors wouldn't detect them. The target would never spot them until it was too late.

Both attack fighters darted through space toward the planet, before circling it. Ak Foral knew that the long journey would come to an end soon, and new determination rose within him. Again, he looked at the displays of his weapon systems. Everything seemed perfect, and everything had been fully charged.

Satisfied, he looked up—and for a brief moment he caught his breath. He had previously seen the target location on holorecordings, but they were no comparison to what was before his eyes now. And of course they hadn't conveyed the emotion that washed over ak Foral as he approached.

We're here. This realization was bigger than anything he had ever felt. It filled him completely, and made his inner flames rise. *Finally.*

The fleet base in high orbit around Cestus III was a metallic gray kraken in the night of space. It was the central haven for all Starfleet spaceships doing their patrol duty at the borders to the Gorn Hegemony. Tired crews could rest here, and countless engineers worked tirelessly to repair docked ships. The Unified Federation of Planets had built this complex three years ago at no expense spared. For ak Foral one thing was clear: this base was a stepping stone for further advancement into space, so they could cross even more sphere borders. It was a tool of doom.

Ak Foral looked at his readings. Currently, not all docking berths were taken. He only saw six ships at the station's docking arms. Its elongated centerpiece housed the base's administration, as well as recreational facilities and crew quarters.

He took his hands off the console. For a brief moment he closed his eyes, drew a deep breath and basked in the emotions of the moment. Ak Foral listened to his inner flame, enjoyed its blaze, and also enjoyed the certainty.

Finally. Finally, everything made sense.

When he opened his eyes again, he saw the weapons display. Silent alarm signals had started to blink. The left disruptor bank was close to overloading; ak Foral sighed with elation when he increased the values with a push of a button. Then he turned back to the helm. The small *Scorpion*-class vessel was exactly on course, heading toward the center of the spacedock. The Federation station grew steadily in the viewscreen as he approached.

Above the course readings, the countdown sprang to life as it had been programmed to begin at this distance. Ak Foral watched the displays and knew that his partner in the second ship saw them as well.

Ten, nine, eight…

"Align right disruptor bank," he told the board computer just as the alarm signals on the left one turned dark red. "Zero in on foremost docking arm."

The console confirmed the order.

Four.

Ak Foral looked through the viewscreen at the huge repair station that steadily grew.

Three.

He reached behind his seat, touching the object on the second seat. The meaning of his life. His blessing.

Two.

He closed his eyes, thinking about home… about glowing sphere buildings below the three moons of Onferin. About the vastness of the desert and the salt of the large ocean. About the flapping wings of *Kranaals*. Gratitude washed over him, a never before felt sense of humility because he could serve his home. What the elders had said was true: The Sphere *was* everything.

One.

"Fire," whispered Mossam ak Foral blissfully, and the black, cold night turned into a burning day.

21
NOVEMBER 11, 2385

Federation Council, Paris, Earth

"When will you finally be prepared to admit that we're at war?"

The Klingon Ambassador to the Federation, K'mtok, was a giant of a man. With his broad shoulders and his formal robe that he wore over his military armor he was quite an impressive view. He was pacing up and down in front of the Federation Council. He clenched his gloved right hand to a fist, menacingly shaking it toward a screen that was embedded into the wall behind him. They had just watched the latest video of the Purifying Flame, claiming responsibility for the destruction of the base in orbit of Cestus III.

K'mtok had been the first to raise his voice after they had watched the transmission. Most of the other council members were still far too shocked about the news that the terrorists had struck again after such a short time. But Kellessar zh'Tarash, who was presiding over this special session, stood behind the lectern at the front side of the room, knowing that this calm wouldn't last long. Once the assembled dignitaries had overcome their horror, their fury would be rekindled. The president didn't want to contemplate the consequences. *I haven't even been in office for two weeks*, she thought angrily. *And already more Federation citizens have perished than during the entire term of office of most of my predecessors.*

"The Renao's actions exceed an act of simple terror," K'mtok continued with his harsh voice. He bared his well-visible fangs, glaring around. "A starbase, a mining colony, and now the Cestus III station. Thousands of dead, and nine of your starships. How long will you sit by and watch death and destruction before you finally *do* something?"

The question wasn't entirely unreasonable, even if the president didn't like the fact that K'mtok was the one asking it. The first incident had been a terrible isolated case. The second one had given her antennae the creeps. But the third one demonstrated clearly that this was more than just a spontaneous act of violence from this so-called Purifying Flame. The way things looked, these fanatics wouldn't just go away. They seemed to be serious about attacking all power blocs in the Alpha Quadrant.

"If the Romulans or the Gorn were behind these attacks," K'mtok snarled, "the Federation would have had long since deployed their forces. And they would be right to do so, because atrocities of this scale amount to nothing less than a declaration of war. But when it comes to the Renao, they're acting like confused *chuSwI'* that can't find their way to their subterranean burrows. What's the matter? Are you scared to do what must be done?"

"And what, do you think, must be done?" asked council member Cort Enaren from Betazed.

"It's about time you deployed ships to the Lembatta Cluster!" shouted K'mtok. "And I don't mean just the *Prometheus*. Deploy an entire fleet—and put those Renao in their place! Declare a blockade against these Renao Home Spheres. Eliminate their military. Occupy their planet. By Kahless, prevent them from executing a fourth attack that might be even worse than everything we've seen so far!" The

Klingon ambassador turned to Admiral Akaar, threateningly stabbing in his direction with his index finger. "If you won't do it, we will."

"Ambassador K'mtok!" Zh'Tarash straightened behind her lectern. "Less of your threatening gestures." Her antennae bent forward belligerently. "The Lembatta Cluster may be an independent region in space but it's still located within Federation borders. We will not allow a Klingon invasion force to cross into our space in order to wage a war against a nation that hasn't even been proven guilty yet."

"And how long will it take for this evidence to become available?" the Klingon argued heatedly. "How many of my and your people need to die, before you're convinced that the Renao are guilty? The High Council demands action from the Federation! Preferably right now, before more Klingon worlds go up in flames!"

"The crews of the *Prometheus* and the *Bortas* are doing everything in their power to shed light on the reasons behind these attacks, and to hunt down and arrest the culprits," said the president. "We are expecting a detailed report soon."

"That's not enough," seethed K'mtok. "You can collect evidence and question witnesses when there's been *one* murder. Being faced with thousands of murders demands military action, a sign of strength. The Renao need to know that crimes against the Federation and the Klingon Empire will be punished with an iron fist. To quote an ancient Earth idiom, you must fight fire with fire!"

"There's another aphorism, as well," mumbled Admiral Markus Rohde, sitting near zh'Tarash in the first row. "Fighting fire with fire will leave nothing but ashes."

The Klingon ambassador ignored him.

Altoun Djinian, the human council member from Cestus

III, spoke up. "With all due respect, *Zha* President, I have to agree with the ambassador. The destruction of our base was a devastating tragedy. According to the latest information, almost twenty thousand people were killed in the attack—not just station personnel, but also civilians on the planet, hit by debris. The U.S.S. *Solaris* crashed into a resort. Fortunately, it was the off season, but the location has been completely annihilated and seven hundred people died. That must not happen again under any circumstances!"

"Not to mention the fact that our security situation in that region doesn't improve at all," the porcine-faced delegate Kyll of Tellar grumbled. "So far, we lost nine patrol ships in the vicinity of the Gorn. The Federation's outer flank has been exposed."

Zh'Tarash quizzically looked at Starfleet's commander. "Admiral Akaar, how quickly can you deploy ships to the borders of the Lembatta Cluster? Although I don't even want to contemplate the invasion of any planets, it's essential that this part of space is closely monitored."

The tall Capellan rose from his chair near the lectern. "*Zha* President, I'm mustering as many ships as I can possibly afford to. As you know our resources are precariously limited. The U.S.S. *Bougainville* and *Iron Horse* are the ships closest to that region. The *Bougainville* has already been recalled from its cartography mission, and has been diverted to Cestus III. The *Iron Horse* will patrol around the Cluster. Additionally, I have ordered the U.S.S. *Capitoline* to head over there as assistance for the *Iron Horse*. Any other ships will take at least five or six days to get there."

K'mtok looked at Akaar with a suggestive grin. "If you need assistance, the High Council has deployed six ships to Korinar. They will arrive in three days."

"For now, we'd like your forces to remain on standby at the border, Ambassador," Akaar said. "We'll inform you if we need the assistance of the Klingon Defense Force."

"Be wary, Admiral," the ambassador said. "If anything else happens, if these extremists attack just *one more* Klingon world, we will hold the Federation personally responsible for not carrying out their security duties. And then, you should let us take matters into our own hands, or the Renao will be the least of the Federation's problems. That, I promise."

K'mtok's words had the desired effect. There was uproar in the Federation Council's assembly hall. Each council member voiced their opinions how to react to this crisis in general and the Klingon's threatening behavior in particular. Kellessar zh'Tarash sighed inwardly. Her antennae lowered slightly.

Some days she wished she hadn't gone into politics at all.

Lembatta Prime

"Leave the talking to me from now on." While Ambassador Rozhenko said those words to Captain Kromm under his breath, Adams had excellent hearing, and Spock, who walked by his side, had the legendary ears of a Vulcan. Both men exchanged a quick glance behind the Klingons' backs, and Adams noticed the smallest hint of an amused glint in his companion's eyes.

As a cadet I never thought it possible that Vulcans might have a sense of humor, he mused. *But in time you learn that nothing is set in stone within the universe. Even a species that is renowned for not having emotions and for following logic consists of individuals. And each one of them needs to find their own balance of reason and emotion.*

Spock apparently leaned toward a philosophy of balance

in his advanced age—rationality that didn't completely ignore the heart. The young Klingon captain on the other hand let his emotions run away with him, that much Adams had already determined. Kromm was a man harboring a lot of rage and a thirst for action. Why, Adams didn't know. He assumed that this was due to misplaced pride. Klingons had the tendency to overrate their personal pride, which rarely ended well for them, or their environment.

All things considered, Adams wasn't surprised that the more moderate Rozhenko reprimanded Kromm, while they all followed a lackey through the Renao embassy's corridors. He was taking them to Himad ak Genos. Upon their arrival, Kromm had snubbed their welcoming committee harshly. The diplomat was obviously concerned that the conflict might escalate if they gave Kromm free rein.

The Klingon captain's answer consisted of a reluctant growl. "Just tell these red-skins that this is not a courtesy call. If they don't acquiesce, the *Bortas* will teach them some humility."

"I'm sure that won't be necessary," the son of Worf replied quietly and impatiently.

Behind the four men, Lenissa zh'Thiin and the gray-haired Klingon security chief Rooth followed. They were both escorts and advisors. Adams had already noticed that the veteran Rooth was much calmer than his captain. He seemed almost relaxed while he surveyed his environment.

Zh'Thiin, on the other hand, was like a coiled spring. The neatly curved antennae on her head swung back and forth. They seemed to be sweeping their environment for possible dangers.

Ambassador ak Genos was expecting them in his conference room just like last time. His deputy Seresh ak

Momad was also present. After a brief welcome, which consisted of a grim growl in Kromm's case, Spock and Rozhenko came straight to the point.

"The attack on Starbase 91 was extremely well prepared," said Spock. "The aggressors had a cloaked spacecraft at their disposal and access to dangerous substances. This was not a spontaneous act of angry young men and women. Behind this attack is a dangerously well-organized movement that plans far in advance. We need to find this movement and prevent further attacks. To that end, we require your assistance."

"I already told you during our last meeting that you are looking in the wrong place. The Renao nation has nothing to do with this act of terrorism."

"*Acts* of terrorism," Kromm growled quietly. "Let's not forget Tika IV."

"Correct," Spock conceded. "The so-called Purifying Flame has claimed responsibility for two attacks already. Apparently, this group's members are Renao. We are aware of the fact that the entire Renao nation is not guilty of these crimes. However, the current evidence suggests that an underground movement exists in your Home Spheres that you are probably unaware of."

"That's impossible," said ak Genos. "And even if that was true, they wouldn't have access to ships with cloaking devices. Such a technology is unknown in our world—and we haven't had any commercial relations with outworlders for decades."

"Forgive me for saying this, but you can't know that for certain," Rozhenko said. "Your word alone that your Home Spheres don't pose an immediate danger to the galactic peace is not sufficient. We require assurance."

The Klingons' presence seemed to unsettle ak Genos. That didn't surprise Adams, all things considered. Even the calm Rooth had an undertone of threat. They were doing the old Earth game of "good cop, bad cop," and the Renao ambassador obviously had no idea how far the "bad cops" were prepared to go.

"What do you want from me?" ak Genos asked.

"We want you to clear the *Prometheus* and the *Bortas* to enter your Home Spheres." Adams, being the senior officer of this operation, took over. "We require freedom of movement for the away teams who need to land on planets within the cluster in order to investigate. We will gladly cooperate with the administrative and security forces on your worlds but we will object to any kind of obstruction as far as our work is concerned."

The ambassador gasped. "You really expect us to allow two battleships to enter our realm? That we will allow armed landing parties on our worlds? That's… I will never be able to get that past the Council of the Spheres."

Kromm growled menacingly but Rozhenko gestured for him to back off.

"Do you follow the news from the Klingon Empire, Ambassador?" Rozhenko asked. "Because if you don't, I suggest you start doing so. The Klingon High Council has been very agitated since the attack on Tika IV. Some have suggested a full-scale invasion of the Lembatta Cluster in order to end this threat to the empire. These voices have become increasingly louder. Some ships are already waiting only a few light-years outside Federation space, ready to strike. If we are forbidden from continuing our investigation within your borders, nothing will be able to keep that war fleet away from the cluster. So I have to beg you to cooperate, Ambassador. Prove that you have nothing to hide, and that you are genuinely interested in keeping the peace in the quadrant."

Spock added, "Should we indeed find extremists on your worlds, then this will not lead to a condemnation of the entire Renao nation. All we will do—in cooperation with your people—is avert further danger and bring the offenders to justice. We will not occupy the cluster, and as soon as the crisis has been resolved, we will withdraw all personnel from the Home Spheres. On this you have my word and that of the Federation Council."

Ambassador ak Genos exchanged a silent glance with his deputy. The other man nodded slightly, although his face showed an expression as if he had just been forced to eat live *gagh*.

The ambassador held out his arms in a gesture of resignation, lowering his eyes. "I acknowledge the special circumstances, and will ensure that the council accepts your demands. Expect your entry clearance shortly."

"Please ensure that the bureaucratic barriers will be quickly overcome," Rozhenko said. "The sooner we can give our governments a situation report from within the cluster, the easier the voices of reason will find it to prevail in this precarious situation."

Ak Genos's lips were a tight thin line when he nodded. "I understand. It will not take long. Now, if you will excuse me, I must begin the process."

Spock tilted his head. "Farewell, Ambassador. And thank you for your cooperation. I hope when we meet again it will be under more pleasant circumstances."

Upon their return to the ship, Adams found yet another priority message from Akaar at Starfleet Command. This time the news was even worse: there had been an attack on the fleet base at Cestus III. The base and six Starfleet vessels had been destroyed, with thousands of lives lost, including civilians on the planet.

"The most frustrating thing is," Akaar said with a sepulchral voice, *"that we would not have been able to prevent this attack, even if we had received your preliminary report regarding Starbase 91 earlier. These new Romulan cloaking devices are extremely difficult to penetrate without a specialized sensor array."*

"The S.C.E. should get on that ASAP," Adams muttered, referring to the Starfleet Corps of Engineers.

"Even so, the warp sensor grid on the system's periphery didn't trigger an alarm. The attackers must have dropped out of warp well outside of the system, in the same manner as Romulan ships did back during the Earth-Romulan War. Small ships approached their targets at sublight speed, thus deceiving the warp sensor grids that the Vulcans had provided for the coalition. But that should be impossible today. The detection grids reach deep into empty space, so an approach with sublight speed should take weeks in order to remain undetectable. If that's the case, then the terrorists have planned these attacks very far in advance." Akaar sighed. *"We're deploying ships to the Gorn border to ease the burden. Additionally, we will unfold a network of patrols around the Lembatta Cluster. This doesn't alter your mission, Captain, I merely wish to inform you that you can count on rapid assistance, should it be necessary. In addition, the Klingons have been put on high alert. They're amassing a fleet on their side of the border at Korinar. For now, they've promised to remain on their side of the border until they are called for help, but the more time passes, the less likely that they will stand by."*

The admiral leaned forward, his voice almost pleading. *"Please hurry with your investigation, Dick. The mood here is rapidly getting worse. Akaar out."* The Capellan's image disappeared and was replaced by the Federation's seal.

Adams stared at the monitor on his desk with a grim face. "I'm doing my best, Leonard."

He sincerely hoped it would be enough.

22
NOVEMBER 12, 2385

Ki Baratan, Romulus

The city center of Ki Baratan was the political heart of the entire Romulan Star Empire. It beat every day with all its might. Between dusk and dawn the venerable old buildings made of stone, the modern office palaces, and the lush, well-groomed parks were bustling. But the air didn't smell of the fustiness of century-old conferences, strict protocols, or the evil spirit of some of the active senate members. Instead, it smelled of the nearby Apnex Sea, of vastness and opportunities.

Thokal liked this smell. Climbing the broad stone stairs to the Admiral Valdore Building's entrance, he also pondered that he was growing too old for these games. The retired data analyst panted before he'd even walked up half of the stairs. The cold wind gusting against him as if it intended to blow him away didn't make his undertaking any easier, either.

The Valdore was located on the outskirts of the government district. The rectangular building boasted eight floors, wide windows, high columns, and an impressive mosaic made of colorful glass, gold, and flat stones with patterns above the entrance that measured almost five meters in diameter. The mosaic depicted the emblem of the Star Empire, a proud warbird with its wide wings spread, clutching the twin worlds Romulus and Remus in its talons. Thokal had always considered this image both elating and depressing.

Atop the stone stairs was a small courtyard, lined with larger-than-life statues of famous senators. Numerous hidden cameras and just as many heavily armed uhlans, who were anything but hidden, safeguarded the yard. At the far end, next to the wide entrance gate that was flanked by two uhlans, the gatekeeper of the Valdore—a living anachronism from pre-technological times long gone—waited for him at his checkpoint.

"What can I do for you?" asked the young Romulan when Thokal arrived. He didn't sound as if he really cared for an answer.

Thokal rested both hands on the small sill outside the checkpoint window while he struggled to catch his breath. The long walk from the transit station, the relentless gusts of wind, and the stairs all took their toll on him, much more than he had expected.

The young man at the checkpoint became impatient. "Do you have an appointment or a permit?" he urged brusquely. "I don't have all day, you know!"

"Me... neither." Thokal was still breathing heavily. Leaning forward, he placed his wrinkled face in front of the small scanner of the identification console to the right of the window. "Identification for access," he ordered the device.

The scanner reacted immediately. Blue light shone on the face of the old Romulan, scanning and taking in every pore, ever little facial hair on his face. Shortly after, the scan was finished. Thokal stood up, waiting for a moment.

"You're not in the system," the young gatekeeper said in a bored tone. "Do you have an appointment?"

"Uhm, not quite."

Thokal's thoughts raced. Today of all days! The old analyst had been expecting one of the subroutines in the security network to detect the program he'd inserted to give him access to the building some day. But why did today have to be that day?

"I'm sorry, but under the circumstances I can't let you pass. This building is not open to unauthorized individuals. If you could leave the premises, please…"

Three government employees left the building with brisk steps, crossing the yard. One of the well-dressed men looked at Thokal quizzically, which made the old Romulan hesitate briefly. But then they passed him and were descending the stairs.

"I said, you should leave the premises," the gatekeeper repeated, slightly louder this time. With his index finger he pointed in the direction where the three officials were heading. "Understood?"

"My apologies," Thokal mumbled as he turned on his heel, rushing after the three men as fast as his legs permitted. The men had already a considerable lead, and they had almost reached the bottom of the stairs. He had to try, though.

"Maldaro?" he shouted. "Maldaro, is that you?"

The three stopped. Confused, they turned around.

Even without his Tal Shiar background, Thokal would have been able to read the recognition in the face of the official on the left side. Maldaro was of medium age and fairly muscular. He carried a datapad tucked under his right arm, and he seemed to be in the hurry, just like his companions.

"Maldaro." Thokal smiled at him almost genuinely. "What a wonderful coincidence to meet you. Would you have a moment for me?"

The younger man's expression could hardly conceal the skepticism. He nodded, nonetheless. "You go ahead," he said to his two colleagues. "I'll catch up with you at the transporter station." The two men headed off, both looking rather confused.

Maldaro took out the datapad before clasping his hands behind his back. Reluctantly, he glared at Thokal. "What do you want, Thokal? And what are you doing here, anyway? I thought you were sitting somewhere in the park feeding the vermin!"

"Trust me, you don't want to know what I want," Thokal answered, panting. In the meantime, he had also reached the bottom of the stairs. Again, he needed a moment to recover his breath. "And what I'm doing here could mean the end of your career if anyone found a reason to link you to me."

Maldaro squinted. "In that case, I'd better call security."

"I wouldn't do that if I were you," Thokal whispered as Maldaro raised his hand to beckon an uhlan. "Unless…"

He didn't have to finish his sentence. Maldaro's face revealed that the younger ministry official had understood him perfectly well.

Maldaro looked around frantically but the terrible weather had fortunately chased away any possible unwanted listeners.

"What do you want, old man?" he snarled, lowering his hand. "And more to the point… what do you want from *me*?"

"I'm calling in my favor," Thokal answered.

"You did that ages ago. With interest."

Thokal tilted his head slightly. "Oh, really?" he feigned ignorance. "I should know that, don't you think?"

"Thokal, I can't…"

"Oh yes, you can. And you will, Maldaro. Otherwise, I will not only forget the favors you did me in the past, I'll also forget that I promised to keep quiet. Do you want your family to see those recordings?"

Maldaro winced, as if he'd been hit. "You said you'd destroy them! Thokal, you promised me!"

The old man squinted in feigned astonishment. "I did? Well, that would have been pretty foolish of me, don't you agree? Such wonderful leverage is worth more than money—especially since you never know when you might need it again."

Silence. Maldaro was quite obviously seething, but he didn't do anything.

Cornering a man like that here on Romulus—especially in Ki Baratan's government quarter—could easily end your life. But Thokal knew Maldaro: despite his impressive figure he was a coward and far too gutless to order a murder, let alone commit one.

The old agent left the young official to stew for a few more seconds. Finally, he nodded. "So?"

"I'm listening," Maldaro growled and his broad shoulders sagged.

Thokal explained briefly what he expected. And with every word, the color drained a little more from Maldaro's face.

Basically, it was the same everywhere in the government district, thought Thokal, grinning to himself. You just needed to know the right people, and all doors would open for you. Not to mention that you could claim any back office you wanted.

The old data analyst had been sitting in this small room on the third floor of the Valdore for three hours now, and hadn't been disturbed yet, just like Maldaro had promised. During this time he had actually managed to hack into the central computer of the military logistics department—a feat he hadn't been able to accomplish from his cellar back in Chalandru.

It's good to know people in high places, thought the old Romulan. *And even better that I still have leverage against them.*

Thokal's Tal Shiar education had been decades ago but he'd never forgotten one phrase his teachers had used: In order to reach a goal, all means were allowed.

Satisfied, he watched columns of data scrolling past on his monitor. Now and then, he would save some of the data on an isolinear rod that he had brought along for the purpose. This particular model was undetectable to the scanners at the building's exit. Most of the time, though, he just let the computer do its work. And he waited.

After another half an hour, he found something. Quickly Thokal stopped the data stream. Frowning, he skeptically stared at the monitor display. Those details surely weren't right. Or were they?

He had found inventory sheets from five years earlier, a time when the Romulan Star Empire had been riddled with chaos. The rebel Shinzon—a clone of Starfleet captain Jean-Luc Picard of the U.S.S. *Enterprise*-E—had killed the entire senate here in Ki Baratan, and then was killed himself, laying the foundation for a civil war the likes of which this empire had never seen before. Two independent factions had emerged from the power vacuum that Shinzon had left behind: the suddenly shrunken and weakened Star Empire, and the new Imperial Romulan State, led by Commander Donatra. The latter had conquered several agriculturally important worlds with strength in numbers and by sheer force, effectively depriving the Star Empire of essential food suppliers. Without the humanitarian help of galactic neighbors such as the Federation, Romulus's population would certainly have starved.

A lot had happened since those days. The Imperial State no longer existed, and unity had been restored. The senate had been re-filled, and the praetorship was in the hands of the moderate Gell Kamemor.

Not all questions raised during that chaotic era of schism had been answered, though. In fact, not all of them had been asked. Questions like: "Why do these inventory lists contain discrepancies?"

Thokal rubbed his chin as he always did when he sensed a discovery. He compared the listings of ordnance just before the fall of the Imperial State with the files listing the military equipment that had been reintegrated into the Romulan Star Empire. He saw gaps, not very obvious ones, but they existed nonetheless.

There was a handful of *Scorpion* attack fighters missing. And several freight units of trilithium for military usage.

All of this material had been stationed in bases on Achernar Prime, Thokal realized, *and then they simply vanished without a trace*.

At least the files created that impression. Obviously, that fact had gone unnoticed during the excitement of domestic reunification. One discrepancy more or less in the files—who cared when the Romulan family was reunited?

Or had anyone deliberately taken precautions to prevent these facts from surfacing? If so... who? And for what reason?

Thokal didn't know what exactly he had uncovered. But a lifetime of analyzing intelligence data told him that this *was* a discovery of some magnitude. Especially since Spock specifically wanted to know if Romulus had provided the Renao with military equipment, including specifically *Scorpion* fighters.

"It would almost appear they have, old friend," Thokal mumbled in the empty room. He saved the classified files of the Romulan Defense Ministry on his isolinear rod, before stashing it in his pocket. "But I need to be certain."

When Captain Adams entered the ⟨...⟩d on deck nine, he was met with sheer chaos.

An area on the left side of the room had been cleared the day before, so Science Officer Mendon and his team of engineers and scientists had enough room to study the remains of the *Scorpion* spacecraft and the debris of Starbase 91, which had been transferred here from the shuttlebay. Now he saw all the finds scattered all over the deck. A handful of officers in blue or gold uniforms walked among the debris, some with tricorders, and others with padds in their hands. Next to the multitude of charred components stood a mobile computer console. Three small displays showed various analyses that Adams couldn't make heads nor tails of.

"Ah, Captain." Mendon walked toward Adams. "I'm glad you could come right away."

"You said it was urgent."

"That it is. And most of all, it's enlightening. If you'd like to follow me?"

Without waiting for a response, the Benzite headed toward the mobile workstation and its displays. The cargo bay's lighting reflected off his moist and shiny bald head.

Adams knew his science officer's enthusiasm for his work, and didn't need a second invitation. He gave Mendon's

...oined the Benzite, trying to focus ...t on what he was studying. The debris ...ries of his niece, and he knew that he mustn't ...t to distract him if he wanted to finish this mission ...ently and expediently.

"I'm listening, Mr. Mendon," said the captain.

"You see this, sir?" The Benzite pointed to one of the displays. Adams saw an endless column of numbers and terms. Mendon pointed at a second display where a simulation of a *Scorpion* attack fighter slowly revolved around its axis. "And here? Isn't that unbelievable?"

"Definitely," said Adams. "And if I had brought Commander Kirk along, I might have a clue what you're talking about. Could you possibly convey your report in Federation Standard instead of gestures? With as few technical terms as possible?"

The Benzite looked up. Taken aback, he squinted and took a deep breath from his respirator. "Oh, I'm ever so sorry, Captain. I probably went ahead of myself, which isn't useful at all. Let me rephrase this into what you consider to be simple terms: this *Scorpion* attack fighter does not originate from Romulus. In fact, I daresay that this attack fighter has never been within the Star Empire's borders."

Isn't that lucky, Adams thought, but he resisted the urge to speak out loud. "But… this type of spacecraft is definitely Romulan. The *Scorpion*s have been manufactured since…"

Mendon waved his hand dismissively and interrupted the captain, something Adams might have taken offense to had he not been aware of the diligent and zealous nature of Benzites—especially this Benzite. "Be that as it may, look at the details on this monitor? At first glance everything seems to be in order. The hull's alloy is the same as that of the Romulan model. The same applies to the design of the lateral fin, and to a piece of the cockpit pane we found. But if you look closer, everything collapses like a house of cards. The quality of the workmanship doesn't meet the required Imperial standards. Electronic components are obviously of inferior quality. Just look at this and ask yourself: is this really a *Scorpion* spacecraft?"

Adams hesitated. Indeed, the longer he looked at the animation on the small display, the more differences he noticed. The ship's shape, the size, the material composition—everything suggested "*Scorpion*"… the details, however, showed countless inconsistencies.

"This isn't a Romulan attack fighter," the captain said. "This is… a copy…"

"Precisely," Mendon confirmed. "A modified and—if I may say so—fairly amateurishly modified copy of a *Scorpion*. This isn't the real thing."

Adams leaned forward as if he were able to make more sense of the data columns that way. But he had seen and heard enough. He didn't like any of it.

"If this ship didn't come from Romulan stock," he said menacingly quiet, "then the Renao are top of our list of suspects again. Wouldn't you agree?"

"I wish I knew, sir," the Benzite said. "I can tell you one thing though; the ship flying the attack against Starbase 91 was not built to last past its first mission. It was supposed to fulfill *one* purpose, and I'd wager that its destruction was part of the plan."

Nodding, Adams sighed, dreading how Kromm would react to this information.

24
NOVEMBER 12, 2385

I.K.S. *Bortas*, en route to Onferin

Kromm realized that his mouth was hanging open, and he closed it quickly. Did he hear that correctly? Or did the bloodwine play tricks on him?

"Computer, repeat message," he said in his silent ready room.

Councilor Grotek reappeared on the screen of his comm console. The gray-haired warrior with the long scar in his face stood in a room illuminated by torches. Behind him, Kromm spotted stone walls and a segment of a window with a view to the First City's skyline. Grotek was calling from his home on Qo'noS.

"*Qapla', Captain Kromm,*" the old man started. "*I hope this message finds you well. Especially your livers.*"

Kromm growled quietly. What did these council members take him for?

"*You should be aware that the High Council does not expect miracles from you. They do not even expect you to act. Why should they? After all, the hero of the Ning'tao hardly needs to prove himself through actions.*"

Furiously, Kromm hammered his fist on his chair's armrest.

The old warrior finally came to the point. "*But you should know that we wouldn't reject any actions from you. Martok*" sometimes is his own worst enemy, and is often overly sympathetic to the Federation. There are members of the High Council who think that this is a time for action."

He leaned forward, and Kromm felt as if Grotek's eyes bored into his. There was no escape from this glare. "*The Renao pose a threat to the Klingon Empire, and they are a disgrace for the galaxy. Qo'noS would be… quite satisfied if they were finally able to reap what they sowed.*"

Again, the old man paused to emphasize the sincerity of his words.

"*You are already in Renao space, captain of the* Bortas. *You have the Empire's former flagship at your disposal. You…*" Grotek grinned. "*Well, I hope you're hungry.*"

Another pause. Kromm growled again, but this time it was not from annoyance, but rather because he felt the hunger the old warrior was talking about. It was the hunger for honor, for blood, for justice. And Grotek's message only increased it.

"*If that's the case, Captain,*" Grotek continued, "*you should know that much of the High Council shares this hunger. Not Martok—and even if he did, he would probably not voice that opinion. The Federation's leash can be appallingly short.*" He snorted derisively. "*But many of us also feel this hunger. As far as these dishonorable Renao are concerned, you can count on the Council supporting any solution for this problem, Kromm— even if it wasn't quite suitable for the diplomatic mission you were originally assigned. Do you understand, Captain?*"

Kromm nodded. He was alone in his ready room as usual. Now he wished both his entire crew, and his family back on Qo'noS could see him. Him and his hunger.

Grotek tilted his gray-haired head. "*If so, show us. Surprise us. With honor. Qapla', son of Kaath!*"

"*Qapla'!*" Kromm replied to the traditional salute of honor, before he realized that Grotek couldn't even hear it.

The prerecorded message was finished, and the Empire's emblem was back on the display. Kromm looked up.

"Kromm to bridge."

"L'emka here, sir."

"Commander, I'm on my way to you. Is Ambassador Rozhenko with you?"

"No. The ambassador has gone to bed in his quarters. We don't expect him back for another four hours."

"Very good," Kromm mumbled, clenching his fist.

25
NOVEMBER 13, 2385

U.S.S. *Prometheus*, near Onferin

The orange-and-red-glowing primary star of star system LC-4—the inhabitants called it Aoul—greeted them with a thunderous roar. This noise was accompanied by a slow, rhythmic pulse, similar to a heartbeat. Lenissa felt as if the star was a living being, an awe-inspiring guardian who was asleep but might wake from its slumber at any time if the crews of the two tiny starships sneaking into its vicinity didn't tread very carefully.

The sound came from a program that transformed a star's spectral readings into an acoustic profile. This analyzing tool reached back to the early stages of astrophysics, but Lenissa had learned during a visit to the Starboard 8 that the so-called "star music" was high in demand on Benzar. So it wasn't a surprise that Mendon used it when scanning the star as they approached. The *Prometheus* had just crossed the outer system borders.

Visually, the giant star was on the main viewer. Its evaporating outer gas layers, which formed a nebula in space, made it look even larger than its already considerable size. The star's radiation caused disturbances that took the form of the occasional white flash, but their intensity and volume increased as they approached Aoul. Roaas had already given the order to activate the shields to prevent unnecessary exposure for the crew. Sickbay prepared to prime the away teams to ensure they wouldn't suffer from radiation during their visits to Onferin.

Lenissa was certain that she wasn't the only one who wondered how there could be life in a region of space as brutal as this.

"Mr. Mendon," said Captain Adams, "please switch off that noise."

"Yes, sir," the Benzite science officer said, sounding somewhat disappointed.

The roar subsided and was replaced by the soothing and reassuring humming and beeping of the ship's systems.

"Captain, two Renao patrol ships are approaching," Sarita Carson at ops reported.

"Ah, the welcoming committee," said Adams as Lenissa turned around just far enough to see the small crescent-shaped ships. With their broad propulsion section in the center of the ship they reminded her vaguely of the ancient *Intrepid*-class of the 2150s. The only difference was that they only had one warp nacelle. The ships were dark gray in color, and their propulsion glowed red like the central star of their home. Lenissa thought they looked more like space pirates rather than official government vessels.

"Open hailing frequencies," the captain ordered, rising from his chair. "Patch in the *Bortas* as well. I want Kromm to listen in." Ambassador Rozhenko had—somehow—gotten Kromm to agree that Adams would be their voice, and that the Klingons would remain in the background.

"Frequencies open," Winter confirmed.

"This is Captain Richard Adams from the U.S.S. *Prometheus*. We're here, along with the I.K.S. *Bortas*, on behalf of the United Federation of Planets and the Klingon Empire.

Our presence has been authorized by the government of the Home Spheres. We are on course to Onferin."

The image on the screen didn't change but a moment later a crackling voice with a strong accent came from the comm system. *"This is system patrol Aoul-5. Follow us, and don't deviate from course. Any violation will be punished immediately."*

Silently, Adams gave Winter a sign to interrupt their connection. "Commander Roaas, is there anything aboard the Renao ships that we should be worried about?"

The first officer looked up from his tactical console. "Negative, sir. These ships are outdated. Their propulsion can probably muster warp five at best; their impulse drive seems to be considerably less efficient than ours. If I read their energy patterns correctly, their on-board weapons are similar to the phasers that Starfleet used approximately one hundred years ago. The ships also seem to have missile rockets at their disposal, but their projectiles are far too slow to reach us. Our phasers could intercept them with ease."

"Very well, thank you. I thought so but wanted to be sure. Re-open frequency, Ensign."

Winter nodded. "Yes, sir."

Adams raised his voice. "System patrol Aoul-5. Understood. Lead the way; we'll stay right behind you. Adams out."

Two hours later, they reached the orbit around Onferin. The planet itself was a gray and purple globe surrounded by a dense atmosphere, which prevented them from actually seeing the surface. Mendon wasn't able to bring geographical details on screen even with his sensors.

"Remarkable," he stated from the science station at the

back of the bridge. "The atmosphere is concentrated with highly reactive molecules. These probably prevent LC-4's severe radiation from reaching the surface. Additionally, the magnetosphere is strong enough to divert the relatively weak stream of particles coming from the primary star. Solar winds of cooling stars such as red giants mainly consist of neutral atoms and molecules such as carbon monoxide, silicates and similar compounds, which are comparatively harmless. I never thought I'd say this, but the living conditions on Onferin shouldn't be much worse than, say, in the desert around Las Vegas on Earth."

Paul Winter glanced over his shoulder. "How do you know Las Vegas?"

"We did a survival training exercise there when I was at the Academy," Mendon said.

"Maybe Mr. ak Namur should tell us something about his homeworld," Adams said. "If anyone knows the conditions there, it's him."

Jassat ak Namur turned around after putting his station on standby. Since they had arrived at their standard orbit he could afford to let the computer handle things as long as that status remained. "I'm sorry, but I wouldn't know what to tell you, Captain. There's so much to say, but at the same time I know so little of what has happened there in recent years. It's correct that Onferin is a harsh world. Huge oceans cover more than half of the planet, and they are brimming with various life forms. Purple-colored algae produce the majority of our oxygen. At the same time, they serve as food for the fish, which then become food for the larger creatures of the sea. The lands are dominated by stone deserts. Enormous canyons run through these deserts, and at their bottom, impenetrable jungles lie in eternal twilight. Most of Onferin's flora and fauna will try to kill you given half the chance."

"Sounds like a delightful holiday resort," Carson commented dryly.

"For adventurers and game hunters, definitely," ak Namur replied. "But you might like our cities. Captain, you saw the painting in ak Genos's conference room in the embassy on Lembatta Prime?"

Adams nodded. "The Griklak hives on the legendary world Iad."

"Exactly. Our architecture is based on those to the present day. I don't want to spoil your first impression by saying too much, but the city spheres on Onferin are a most astounding view for anyone seeing them for the first time."

"Captain," Mendon said. "I'd like to visit these cities. Those excursions could be extremely informative."

Adams raised a hand. "I really do appreciate your zeal, Commander, but for now we're only sending diplomatic and investigatory away teams, not scientific ones. I'd like to get an overview of the situation before risking my crew's lives."

"I understand, Captain." The Benzite seemed disappointed.

"Sir, we are being hailed from the planet."

Nodding, Adams faced the main screen. "Open channel."

The planet's image was replaced by a red-skinned Renao with black hair. Judging by his striking golden facial jewelry and his noble-looking black and golden robe, he was a representative of the planetary government. He made a circular gesture with his right hand in front of his chest. *"Greetings, Captain. I am Councilor Shamar ak Mousal. I preside over the ministers' council of Onferin, and I'm president of Renao's Home Spheres. As supreme representative of my people, I bid you welcome."*

"Thank you, Councilor," Adams replied. "I assume Ambassador ak Genos has informed you about the purpose of our visit."

"He did indeed. And the council has agreed to authorize your being on Onferin. Right now, it is night in the city sphere Auroun, but tomorrow morning—in seven hours of your time—we will be glad to welcome you in the council to talk about the next steps. Please refrain from sending members of your crew down to the planet's surface before that time. I would also like to advise you not to use your transporter technology. Ionized particles in Onferin's atmosphere will disrupt your transporter focus. You will probably have information to that effect in your database from the time when the Federation and the Home Spheres still had commercial relations, but I'd like to point that issue out nonetheless. You would be well advised to use your shuttlecraft. Of course, I can always send a transfer ship to pick you up."

Adams shook his head. "That's very kind of you, but that won't be necessary. We will use our own shuttles."

"As you wish. I will send you the coordinates for the landing platforms at the minister's council. I will see you tomorrow."

Again, ak Mousal performed the circular gesture but this time counterclockwise. Then the connection was terminated.

Adams nodded, looking at Lenissa and the others. "All right, we've got seven hours to find out as much as possible about Onferin and the Renao. Mr. Winter, inform Ambassador Spock that I'd like to meet him in the conference room in thirty minutes. Invite the Klingons as well. All others—get to work. I'll be in my ready room."

Adams turned toward his ready room and added, "Mr. ak Namur, come with me please? I have a special assignment for you."

"Yes, Captain."

The young Renao rose from his console.

Curiously, Lenissa watched him and the captain leave, wondering what special mission was in store for Jassat.

26
NOVEMBER 14, 2385

Onferin

Six people headed to the planet's surface the next morning in one of the *Prometheus*'s shuttles: two from *Prometheus*, Adams and a security guard, Ensign Elisa Flores; the two ambassadors, Spock and Rozhenko; and from the *Bortas*, Commander L'emka and her bodyguard, a huge Klingon called Grakk.

Captain Kromm had refused to join the talks. "I've lost all interest in standing next to you silently, while you negotiate with these red-skins," he'd snarled. "Besides, someone with command authority needs to stay with the ships if this turns out to be some kind of ambush. So you take Commander L'emka—she's used to standing around silently."

Kromm's decision had come to Adams as something of a relief. The ill-tempered Klingon was more than likely to make their talks more difficult. His second in command on the other hand was an extremely competent officer and remarkably moderate character, based on her service record and his brief interactions so far. Adams wondered how much of a future she truly had in the Klingon Defense Force. Intelligent women were something the patriarchal Klingon society didn't always take well to. *Maybe I could talk her into signing up on the* Prometheus *once this is over*, he thought with amusement. *Even Jean-Luc Picard might be envious if I had a*

Klingon woman of her caliber among my crew. The commander of the U.S.S. *Enterprise*-E still was one of the very few captains within Starfleet to have a Klingon among their staff, that being his first officer, Commander Worf—who was also Ambassador Rozhenko's father.

The shuttle entered the lower layers of the atmosphere, the shields protecting them from the considerable turbulence.

Several minutes later they emerged from the dense clouds, and the travelers were greeted with an unusual view. Right in front of and below them on the rocky coastline that bordered on the purple shimmering ocean rose a city. The outskirts were characterized by hydroponic gardens that were cultivated under large glass domes. At the shoreline were extensive port facilities, and offshore, they saw countless little trawlers. All this was testament to the fact that the Renao made their living from capturing sea-animals and cultivating the oceans. To the east they spotted an industrial estate with high warehouses that were connected by a suspended transport monorail system.

The city center was a vast complex consisting of three connected arcologies. Three egg-shaped buildings reached to the sky. Their tops were sloping as if someone had cracked the eggs open with their knife. Inside, they revealed gigantic light shafts. Hundreds of small flying vessels swarmed around the impressive trio of buildings like insects did with their home hive, which this city very much resembled.

"Their spacefaring vessels may not be very impressive," L'emka said, breaking the amazed silence in the passenger cabin, "but they know how to build houses."

"This is not unexpected," Spock said. "The Renao ascribe an enormous ideological value to home and hearth. It is only logical that they have devoted so much of their efforts to making their home as livable as possible. The inevitable corollary is a neglect of transportation." He pointed toward a single elevated monorail way that disappeared toward the east in the mountains.

Flores, sitting at the flight controls in the cockpit, swerved to the left, heading straight toward the arcology closest to the coastline. Upon their approach, Adams noticed that there were windows all over the outer walls of these constructs. He also saw galleries on dozens of levels around the egg-shaped colossus, where Auroun citizens sauntered, and the small insect-like transport vessels landed.

They approached a landing platform protruding from a wall in the upper third of the arcology. Gently, Flores touched the shuttle down.

A reception party of six uniformed officers awaited them after Adams had opened the hatch and they emerged. The officers' expressions were stony, but the captain hadn't expected anything else. They were soldiers first and foremost, and neither the Federation nor the Klingons were very welcome here, as much as the president of the Home Spheres said they were.

"Please follow me," the leader of the group said. He must have been a high-ranking officer if the medals on his chest were anything to go by.

They climbed into an open vehicle with wheels and left the platform. Warm wind engulfed them, and the smell of saltwater and seaweed reached Adams's nostrils. Some screeching sea birds circled above their heads in the hazy sky, which was tinted in an orange glow by the sun. The numerous flying vessels around them sounded like a swarm of excited fruitbats.

Through a circular entrance that was also guarded

by soldiers, they delved into the inner core of the city. Their journey took them down a straight tunnel that was illuminated by dimmed red light. Several corridors branched off, and they saw signs and marks with symbols. To the left and the right of the lanes, shoulders had been marked where men and women in formal clothing purposefully strode from one corridor to the next. Adams assumed them to be government employees.

After approximately fifty meters their transport stopped. Before them, the tunnel opened into a circular hall with a high ceiling. An exotic crystal sculpture towered in the center, illuminated by colorful spotlights on the floor. Several corridors branched off this hall as well, but Adams's attention was drawn toward a glorious double portal. Outside, more men in uniform stood guard. Adams leaned towards Spock, who sat next to him.

"Apparently, we're approaching the heart of the Home Spheres."

"Indeed," the Vulcan replied.

They left their vehicle, and the officer marched toward one of the guardians. He uttered a short command in the Renao language. The universal translator translated it with a short delay. "Open the portal."

The man obeyed. Without a sound the heavy portal swung open. Their guide made an inviting gesture. "The councilors await you."

Expectantly, Adams walked though the portal with his companions. Flores and Grakk stopped at the doorway. Behind the door was a large, circular chamber. The floor was tiled with a stone similar to marble. Rows of seats lined the walls. Spectators or companions of the council members probably sat there. A large crescent-shaped table stood in the center of the room, similar to the table in the ambassador's conference room on Lembatta Prime. The difference was that this was timber. For a world with little vegetation such as Onferin that was quite the luxury.

The ceiling was adorned with an intricate painting. The captain recognized a stylized image of the Lembatta Cluster. Seven planets surrounded by overlapping circles were very prominent in the image, but even more noticeable was a sparkling star in the center of the cluster.

To Adams's surprise, only two men were present in the room. One of them was Councilor Shamar ak Mousal. The man next to him had silver hair and wore similar clothing to ak Mousal, so the captain assumed him to be a representative from another planet of the Home Spheres.

"Captain Adams," ak Mousal said, approaching with his colleague in tow. He performed the circular gesture in front of his chest.

"Councilor ak Mousal," replied Adams, mimicking the gesture somewhat clumsily. "May I introduce my companions: Ambassadors Spock and Rozhenko, who will be speaking on behalf of the Federation, and Commander L'emka, first officer on the I.K.S. *Bortas*, representing the Klingon Empire."

The councilor welcomed Adams's comrades before pointing to his companion. "This is Councilor ak Bradul, my defense minister. We're expecting the other councilors momentarily."

"You shouldn't have come here, Captain," the older Renao said with a scowl. "Your presence is disturbing the harmony of the spheres."

"My apologies, Councilor ak Bradul, but that can't be helped," Adams replied. "There have been three attacks on targets within the Federation and the Klingon Empire, and

Renao have openly claimed responsibility for those attacks. That situation is too precarious to make allowances for cultural sensitivities, I'm afraid. Our own harmony has been even more greatly disturbed. We need to put out this fire before it can become a conflagration. And the only chance to do that is right here."

"The Onferin government condemns what has happened strongly," ak Mousal stated firmly. "Please believe me when I say that we had nothing to do with these attacks. Those are quite obviously delusional extremists, and we offer you our unconditional support in your fight against them."

Adams acknowledged these words with a mixture of skepticism and relief. "That's good to know, thank you very much, Councilor."

He had expected further excuses the likes of which he had heard from Ambassador ak Genos. The councilor on the other hand seemed to be absolutely aware of the gravity of the situation. Perhaps ak Genos had told him about the Klingon threat to invade the Lembatta Cluster with a full fleet if their investigations didn't make any progress soon.

And perhaps he also knew that certain truths concerning his society couldn't remain hidden once the away teams began taking a long look at Onferin.

Ak Mousal's eyes sparkled meaningfully. "Believe me, Captain; we all want to resolve this situation as soon as possible. The sooner we find the culprits, the sooner you will leave us again, and the harmony of the spheres will be restored."

He's pretty straightforward for a politician, Adams thought. *Perhaps we might avoid the next war just in time, after all.*

The councilor pointed at the stone table. "Come, please be seated. We will need to talk about many details as soon as the others arrive."

Ak Bradul clapped his hands loudly, and an orderly appeared from an alcove behind the benches along the wall. "Four chairs and drinks for our guests."

The man nodded and disappeared hastily.

Spock spoke up while they strolled into the center of the room. "Councilor, may I express my admiration for the painting on your ceiling? I expect that it represents the Home Spheres."

"That is correct," ak Mousal said. "These are the seven Home Spheres of the Renao. On the periphery is Onferin— the world we have been calling our home since the transfer ten thousand years ago. The other spheres are Lhoeel and Yssab, Xhehenem and Catoumni, Acina and the innermost world is called Bharatrum."

Spock nodded slowly. "If I understand our records about your Home Spheres correctly, all those worlds have only been colonized during the last one hundred years, since your people achieved faster-than-light travel."

"That is correct. Lhoeel was the first world to be colonized exactly eighty-two of your Federation years ago; and our colony on Bharatrum is only about ten years old."

"I am somewhat surprised by the urge to expand shown by a nation whose philosophy is rooted deeply in the principle that every part has its firm place within the universe." Spock raised an eyebrow. "On the surface, it appears illogical that you would engage in an act, that of colonizing other worlds, that would seem to fit the definition of what you call sphere defiling."

Ak Mousal smiled tightly at him. "Under normal circumstances you would be correct, Ambassador. But you don't know the historical background to our philosophy. According to history, the entire Lembatta Cluster is our Home

Sphere, thus we are expanding within its natural borders." The Renao politician raised his hand, pointing at the celestial body in the center of the painting. "Do you see that world there?"

"Of course."

"That is Iad. According to legend, this is the home of the Renao nation, while at the same time being the heart of the Lembatta Cluster. There are no records about this world. Our knowledge of Iad is based on ancient stories that have been handed down from generation to generation. These claim that our nation originates from that world, and that our people lived there until ten thousand years ago, when the transfer took place. The circumstances of this transfer have been lost to history. All we know is that it happened."

"How do you know?" L'emka asked.

"Well, there are no archaeological findings on Onferin older than ten thousand years. Additionally, our biologists have determined that an evolutional development of a species such as ours is not possible on this world. We simply *cannot* originate from here."

"But you're sure that you come from Iad?" the Klingon woman asked.

"Yes. All knowledge about our ancient home might have been lost throughout the millennia, but the name always stayed with us." Ak Mousal hesitated, and then raised his hands in a gesture that might have been the equivalent to a human shrug. "Or at least it's the name that has been associated with our Sphere of Origin throughout the centuries."

Spock tilted his head. "What do you mean?"

The supreme representative of the Renao sighed. "Naturally, we visited the center of the Lembatta Cluster just as soon as our technology permitted it. There is no planet anywhere in there that might have spawned life, and we haven't found one anywhere within the Home Spheres. Iad doesn't exist, Ambassador. It's merely an idea—and our point of origin remains a mystery."

27
NOVEMBER 14, 2385

Onferin

Aoul was a gigantic red-glowing speck in the hazy sky. The scattered light illuminated the stone desert. It shone on the bright sand, into the deep canyons and on the remains of the Griklak hive that rose up almost defiantly from the vast wasteland. It was the silent relic of a long-lost civilization.

Jassat ak Namur stood in civilian clothing by the window of the Kranaal, a small transport aircraft, looking down on the hive. For a brief moment, he almost believed that its breathtaking sight could make him forget all his worries.

"One last sweep of the complex," the voice of the Kranaal pilot came through the lieutenant's earpiece, drowning out the humming of the insect-like wings on the roof. "Afterward, we will land. Please have your entrance passes ready."

The handful of Renao who shared the solar-powered Kranaal's passenger cabin with him, murmured approvingly. Red arms were being stretched out, red fingers pointed down toward the historical building. Massoa—which was the name of the complex—was half an hour's flight away from Auroun's borders. It was a warm morning, a perfect day to go to one of the most popular excursion destinations on the entire northern continent. Although they were still dozens of meters in the air he could already spot the many Kranaals on the airfield behind the gigantic hive. He could also see numerous groups of Renao walking to and from the structure. They reminded him of San Francisco and his first weeks at the Starfleet Academy. Back then, he had also spent every minute of his spare time exploring the sights in the area: the Golden Gate Bridge, Alcatraz, the view from Upper Lombard Street. Obviously, on Onferin there weren't any tourists from other worlds like there were on Earth, but in both places the natives never seemed to lose interest in the history of their planet.

Jassat understood them all too well.

"The hive of the Massoa complex was one of the earliest Renao dwellings on this planet." The pilot audibly wasn't all too interested in the lines that he was rattling out. His passengers probably knew all those facts anyway. "Inside, the first members of our species settled down, before building their own hives in its image near the coast several generations…"

Jassat blocked out the voice, staring at the almost egg-shaped large object. The Kranaal slowly descended on its eastern side. The outer walls of the former insect hive bore the marks of sharp desert winds. The remains of five significantly smaller buildings in the sand surrounded the central structure. Some of them were right beside the large sphere, others stood several dozen meters further away. As the Kranaal descended, Jassat watched the visitors of the complex, milling about in the ruins. Just like him, most of them wore traditional clothing made from dark colored fabric with red adornments, and the facial jewelry typical for their species.

Visually, I will not stand out at all, the lieutenant thought, and was pleased.

Finally, the little transporter touched down on the airfield, and the fluttering wings that were fastened to the roof came to a standstill. *Let's hope it will be enough.*

Ever since he had started exploring Onferin on his own, he felt as if he was being watched. Jassat knew that he was imagining things, but he couldn't shake off the feeling. It was an absurd belief that the inhabitants of the Lembatta Cluster would react hostilely toward him and regard him as a stranger, especially now that he had swapped his Starfleet uniform for traditional garments and colors to blend in.

In his heart of hearts he knew the reason for his paranoia… It was based on the looks he had been given aboard the *Prometheus* since the incident at Starbase 91. It was based on the comments that he had received from his friends when he had announced that he intended to join Starfleet. And it was based on the fear not to belong anywhere, and to be exiled— even here, deep in the heart of his old, beloved home.

The cabin door slid open. The Kranaal's passengers exited, and stood in the warm desert air. Jassat followed suit. From the ground, the Griklak hive was even more impressive than it had been from the air. It was a giant in the middle of nowhere, silent and yet full of significance. It bore witness to the age of this world, to the will to survive of former Renao generations, to the myths of times gone by, and to the pride for the future. It filled Jassat with a deep awe that he hadn't felt in a long time. If the Sphere was everything, structures like the one of Massoa were the origin of everything. The nucleus. Home of all homes, and almost as important as Iad.

"Enjoy your stay," the pilot said, but he was already eyeing the people waiting for their transport back to town on the edge of the airfield. He seemed to be even less interested in them than he had been in the visitors he had just dropped off. "If you want to go back, just return here. The Kranaals leave every hour on the hour."

The visitors walked across the airfield toward the outer

ruins, Jassat among them. Adams had ordered him to mingle with the locals in order to get a taste for the general mood among the common Renao. The captain hoped to gain impressions and information about Onferin and its inhabitants that the politicians and diplomats couldn't or wouldn't give him.

Because Onferin harbored secrets. Jassat sensed that much.

Minutes passed, then hours. Silently, the *Prometheus* conn officer meandered about the ruins. Although he had come to study the locals, he couldn't deny the magic of Massoa. Every stone, every grain of sand, each desert wind, and every sunray from the distant, warm sun told of a time before time, and of the cradle of Jassat's own heritage. No matter what uniform he wore, he was Renao. Nothing would change that.

A merchant stood by the entrance to the main building, offering *leys* in clay jugs. Jassat bought one and enjoyed the taste of the sticky and salty drink. *Leys* was made of the blood of *Ganarro* caterpillars. The burrowing animals that were as tall as a Renao lived in the sand of the vast deserts in the east. *Leys* was a delicacy but virtually unknown outside of Renao space.

Like so many things from here, Jassat pondered and the thought made him sad. *Like almost everything.*

But then he stepped inside the main building, and everything changed.

Massoa's middle hive was like an overgrown termite hill on Earth. The lieutenant saw traces of generations past immortalized everywhere: caves that had been carved into the hive, broad sidewalks, and the remains of small bridges. A light shone from a circular hole at the upper end of the bell-mouthed Griklak relic, illuminating the hive sufficiently to prevent visitors from stumbling on the uneven stairs, or falling over their own feet. Jassat had noticed that some of them had brought small flashlights. Carrying these, they even dared to venture into the dark caves, their ancestors' living areas or into the subterranean narrow tunnels.

Then a voice that was both familiar and strange at the same time called to him. "Jass? Jass, is… is that really you?"

He turned and saw Evykk ak Busal. She didn't carry a lamp. Her smile beamed far brighter than any artificial light could ever do in any case.

"It *is* really you! Jass, I can't believe it!"

She was dressed in similar clothes to the bored Kranaal pilot. They were tailored from a stony gray fabric with embroidered ornaments. Jassat gawked at her for several heartbeats before he realized that she was one of Massoa's staff.

"Ev?" he uttered finally. Squinting, he almost believed he was dreaming.

The young woman laughed that laugh that Jassat remembered so well. They hadn't seen each other for years, not even via subspace communication. And time had changed his old friend: Evykk had always been pretty, but now she was breathtaking. Her dark skin, the gold on the bridge of her nose, the purple sparkling eyes and the strong physique made her look like a person who was in control of herself and her life.

And she wasn't suited to Massoa at all.

Ev spread her arms and walked toward Jassat. With her hand she performed the traditional circular gesture before putting both hands on his shoulders. This silent greeting was among the most heartfelt within the Renao culture. Her eyes bored into his as if she could see right into his soul, and her smile was like Aoul's beams reflecting from the glass façade of their mutual Home Sphere that was far away in Konuhbi.

"What *are* you doing here? I thought you were on a ship."

"Ev," Jassat repeated as if it would become more true if he said it often enough. "Evykk. Little Evykk from Konuhbi."

"Hey, less of the 'little'." Her tone was half disapproving, half mischievous. "That was a long time ago."

"What are you doing here?"

She laughed again. "I asked first." Finally, she shook her head and pointed at herself. "I can't help but feeling that you've spent too much time in the sun. I've never known you to be so slow off the mark. Just look at me and you will know everything you need to know. I'm working here. Would you like a guided tour through the subterranean tunnel system? If so, you found your guide. And I guarantee you: the descent is a little arduous, but it's worth it."

Jassat looked at her clothes again. "You're a tour guide?"

"We all have to fulfill a purpose, don't we?"

"But what about Konuhbi? The sphere?"

"You of all people ask that question?" She smirked, and that smirk was even more reproachful than her earlier glance. "We all serve our home, Jass. Even—and perhaps especially—if we tend to our roots. I'm here because I want to learn. Understand who we are and how we became what we are. And I'm not staying long. The exchange program with Konuhbi only lasts for a few weeks. Afterward, I'll return to the good old sphere with my new experiences."

Jassat was flabbergasted. But most of all, he was happy, this chance encounter with an old friend burning away the paranoia and loneliness that had been tormenting him since he reported back aboard *Prometheus* at Deep Space 9. "Evykk," he muttered under his breath, but then he started laughing as well.

"You're repeating yourself. Is that what you learn at the Federation school that you so desperately wanted to attend? Talking in circles?" Then she smiled. "I'm only joking. I know that you've been in the sun for too long." She interrupted herself as another female visitor—a Renao of medium age with dark hair and a toddler by her side—approached her, asking for a guided tour through the tunnels. Ev nodded. "All right, Jass. Duty calls. Nice seeing you again—even if you weren't very talkative. Hey, if you find your speech again some time today—Moadas and I live in the southern arcology in Auroun. Second level, apartment 27, right next to the hydroponic gardens. Come by tonight and we can catch up. I'd like that, and I'm sure he would as well."

Again, he squinted blankly. "Moadas… is here as well?"

Evykk shook her head, smirking. "Jass, Jass, Jass. You should really stay in the shade until sundown, okay? All this light is too much for you."

She performed the circular hand-movement that indicated a farewell, then she escorted the woman and her child to the tunnel entrance where a group with more visitors already waited. Jassat gazed after her until she had disappeared into the darkness below Massoa.

"Come on; tell us—what's the status of the Federation's defense?" Moadas ak Lavoor laughed, as he filled his glass again. His movements were already erratic, and his humor left a lot to be desired. "Do you already have your own starship to conquer foreign worlds?"

Jassat ak Namur took a sip from his glass, wondering not for the first time tonight why he had come here. The encounter with Evykk had been very cordial; but seeing Moadas again had turned out to be much more difficult.

For almost two hours, the three of them sat in the small worker's flat, which the two staff members of Massoa shared. His old friend from Konuhbi enjoyed *bri*—a strong alcoholic drink—with so much fervor that it would have brought honor to a Klingon with a barrel of bloodwine. Moadas was already slurring his speech, and his green eyes were glazed over. Small bubbles of saliva had appeared in the corners of his mouth. Unlike Evykk he hadn't changed. She wore black and red casual clothes, while he was still clad in the tour guide garments. His attire seemed strangely out of place within the walls of this small home that was situated in a rather rundown area of the arcology, since it conveyed some kind of importance that neither his behavior, nor the view from the window, seemed to live up to. The southern arcology was the only one in Auroun without an ocean view, and level two didn't allow a distant view either. All Jassat saw when he looked out the window front was the façade of the western arcology and the sand between the two buildings.

"Leave him alone, Moa." Ev shook her head. She took the bottle of *bri* that stood on the stone table in order to fill Jassat's glass again, but he waved her off. "Jass did not come here so you can wind him up or argue about politics with him. He's here for old times' sake, isn't that right, Jass?"

"He's here because he knows where he belongs," Moadas uttered before Jass could answer the question. It sounded like an objection. "Because he's a proud Renao and not the Federation's servant."

"Can't I be both?" Jassat asked, sharper than he intended. It was the first time he had spoken for some minutes. He felt as if he was picking up on a conversation that he'd put an end to years ago with conviction, and he decidedly disliked that feeling.

His old friend shook his head so insistently that his nose jewelry almost shifted out of place. "Just how do you think that would be possible, hmm? How should you have a place and not fill it? Where's the harmony in that?"

"Then again, you're here and not in Konuhbi either." Evykk smiled.

Moadas put his glass down. "That's different, and you both know it. Massoa also belongs to the great order of things. Tarra, or whatever the name of the world is where Jass's new masters reside, doesn't. Not for us."

"It's Terra, and if you were able to think a little further than the brim of your *bri* bottle, you'd recognize its beauty, as well as its significance and that of the Federation."

Moadas glared at him, as if Jassat had slapped him in the face. One second went by in utter silence, then another… and then the drunken man threw his head back and laughed.

"And just which significance would that be, hmm?" asked Moadas. "Is it significant to forget your roots? To leave your sphere in order to disturb those of other beings severely?"

"The Federation doesn't disturb, it…"

"Oh, yeah?" Moadas raised his dark eyebrows. His eyes glowed belligerently. "Not everyone sees it that way, old friend."

Evykk sighed. "Moa, please. Enough."

But Jassat frowned. "Not everyone?" he followed up on his words. "What do you mean, Moa? *Who* do you mean?"

Moadas waved dismissively. His red hands grabbed the *bri* again. "Forget it. Ev is right: drink and be welcome, Jass. You may be a fool now but you used to be part of our world. That does form a bond. Once you have drunk enough, you'll return to your spaceship anyway so you can disturb other spheres."

Jassat swallowed, clenching his fists. He rested them on the stone table. "A fool? I'm Renao, just like you are. I come from Konuhbi, just like you do. It's not that I *used to be* from this world, I *am* from this world!"

"Jass," Evykk said quietly. "Don't. Just leave it. Let's talk about something else."

But he had no intention to do that. Moadas's insults had opened a valve, and now the fury that he had bottled up for so long boiled over.

His friend also had no interest in making peace. "You're not like me, spaceman," Moadas growled derisively. "Nothing like us at all."

"Are you the one to make that kind of decision these days? Is it up to you to decide who belongs to Onferin and who doesn't?"

"Your deeds decide that!" Moadas shouted. He hit the table with the palm of his hand, and Evykk winced. "You turn up as if nothing happened, Jass. But we both know that your ship is waiting in orbit. You didn't come alone." Reproachfully he looked at Evykk, his finger pointing at Jassat. "This is not a touching homecoming, don't you see that? Not a reunion for old times' sake, and not a late realization. Jass is here because his Federation is here—and just like them, he doesn't belong here at all. Not if he represents what they stand for."

"For a breach of galactic harmony," Jassat said what was obviously on the tip of Moadas's tongue. He thought about the terrorist videos claiming responsibility, and how similar they sounded to what Moadas was saying now. "Is that what you mean? And to whom were you referring when you said that not everyone saw it my way?"

Moadas flared. He reached under his clothing, pulling

out a rectangular document, which he dropped on the table. "That's what I mean."

The lieutenant picked up the document. It was some kind of flyer—printed paper made from dried and industrially bleached algae. A symbol of a flame was visible on the upper half of the page with some small printed text underneath. Jassat didn't have a lot of time to study the content, as Ev snatched the page off the table before he could get more than a glance.

"Don't, Moa," she said quietly. "Not him."

"Why not?" the drunken man snapped at her. His voice was mocking, and an aggressive fire burned in his eyes. "He claims to be one of us. Let him prove it. Let him defend the order as well, for the spheres."

Lowering her eyes, she shook her head without a word.

"What is that?" the lieutenant asked his childhood friend. "This Son of the Ancient Reds. Who is that supposed to be, Moa? And what kind of work are you really doing out there in Massoa?" He pointed at the sheet that Evykk clutched in her clenched fist. He'd only been able to read a few phrases on the flyer before she took it away, but what he did see greatly bothered him. "Are you there to distribute propaganda to the masses? To represent the views of the Purifying Flame?"

Moadas rose, his eyes fixed on his guest. "We are tour guides, spaceman. Nothing else. We offer orientation to those who seek it. We show them a direction."

"Into violence?"

"Into order."

The lieutenant studied his hosts silently. Dozens of questions went through his mind, and he didn't like any of them.

Finally, Evykk ak Busal also stood up. "I think, you'd

better go now, Jass," she said, still averting her eyes. "It was nice seeing you again, but…" She didn't finish her sentence. Her silence said more than words ever could.

Jassat went to the front door. In the doorway, he looked back one last time. "You're wrong," he said. "If you really sympathize with the views of these terrorists, you're damn wrong. Talk to me! Let me help—you and all the others suffering from the poison that the Purifying Flame is spreading. That's what we're here for!"

Evykk's eyes welled up with tears of helplessness, shame, and melancholy.

"You've already done more than enough, spaceman," Moadas stated. He glared at Evykk, and it sounded like a threat. "Get lost. Once and for all."

Jassat turned on his heel and departed. His heart was unbearably heavy, and his thoughts raced. He knew that he had to act, but the decision to reach for his combadge, hidden in the pocket of his outfit, was the hardest he had ever made.

In the eyes of Lieutenant Klarn of the I.K.S. *Bortas*, the day had started miserably, but it had just taken a turn for the better. Purposefully, the Klingon entered the second level of the southern arcology.

"This way," he told the other three members of this strangely mixed away team. "This Caitian said it is somewhere over there. Apparently, their Renao-pet is waiting for us outside the front door."

"His name is…" started Ensign Simanek of the *Prometheus* security detail.

But Klarn waved him off. "His name doesn't matter to me.

He's Renao. That says more than enough."

Again, he asked himself why Captain Kromm had agreed to mixed away teams working on Onferin. A team purely consisting of Klingons would have been much more efficient searching the harbor near Auroun. But no, he and *Bekk* Ruut had to drag two members of Starfleet security around all day for this task. So far, Ensign Simanek and Lieutenant Jansen had been fairly bearable—at least they didn't get in the way all the time, or asked their captain for permission every time they wanted to turn a corner. But still, they were a nuisance.

"On my ship," the Klingon communications officer continued, "a man from a nation of terrorists wouldn't be allowed to continue his service, that much is certain."

Unexpectedly, Jansen nodded. "Hear, hear," he mumbled approvingly.

Surprised, Klarn glanced at the ginger-haired Norwegian and laughed. Maybe there was hope for these Federation lackeys after all.

The team of four walked along the arcology's corridor silently; Klarn was two steps ahead of the others. The Renao did indeed wait outside the small home. He looked downcast and insecure—the perfect Starfleet officer. The closer the away team came, the more his shoulders sagged.

"Are they still in there?" Klarn quietly asked the lieutenant from the *Prometheus* who still wore civilian clothing. Ruut, Jansen, and Simanek stood next to the front door, waiting. "Both of them?"

Jassat ak Namur nodded. "Only a few minutes have passed since I left them. I kept my eyes glued to their quarters. If they didn't use a transporter, they're still in there."

Klarn grunted, satisfied. "If we can't use transporters, the locals can't either. And besides, didn't they say that your species is technologically deficient?" He pulled the disruptor from his hip.

"Listen," the Renao started again. The weapon seemed to scare him. "Those are… were friends of mine. And I'm not exactly sure about their involvement with the Purifying Flame. It didn't seem to me as if they're part of the organization. At least not of the inner circle. They… Lieutenant, they're probably just followers. They distribute propaganda material out there in Massoa, that's all we know." He looked at Simanek and Jansen. "Do you really need weapons under those circumstances?"

Klarn shook his head. "We're here because you deemed them suspicious, Lieutenant ak Namur. Suspicious enough to inform Commander Roaas. He gave us the order to come here because we happened to be the closest away team. So I suggest you let us do our work. Keep your regrets and your doubts to yourself."

"But isn't it enough if those two simply…"

"Be *silent*." Klarn looked at him sternly. "You said those two might be a lead to the terrorists. That is all that matters. If the consequences of your own suspicion frighten you, *Lieutenant*, I recommend you leave."

Ak Namur stared at him silently. Klarn sensed that the Renao's mind was working overtime, and that his sense of duty battled against emotions.

"We're dealing with it, Lieutenant," said Simanek with calm determination. "You go. The cavalry is here."

That seemed to calm the Renao slightly, and he turned around and left. He still seemed downcast but that didn't matter to Klarn.

"There's a good pet," the Klingon leader of the away team growled and grinned satisfied. He checked his disruptor's settings before looking at his team. Ruut had also drawn his weapon. "All ready? We're going in. I don't think we will come across much resistance."

Simanek and the other human exchanged glances.

Klarn didn't miss this silent exchange. Frustrated, he sighed. "Are you also going to bother me with moral qualms?"

Simanek shook his head. "You know something, Lieutenant? I think we need a quick break. I feel an urgent call of nature that can't be postponed… if you know what I mean. Don't wait for us with the arrest."

"Are you insane?" Ruut snapped. "Are you an officer or a child?"

Klarn stopped him with a wave of his hand. He understood what the Starfleet officers were truly saying. "It might be for the best if no members of Starfleet are present for this." Klarn was all too aware what would happen in that case: ak Busal and ak Lavoor would be handed over to the local authorities, and then be questioned—maybe in the presence of a representative from the *Prometheus*, but primarily by their own people. The Federation always made a point of being friendly to the locals, didn't they? That was the core of their pathetic inefficiency: they were too soft.

"I had friends on Starbase 91," Simanek said. "I believe they deserve justice. Just like we all do. And if we want to prevent further casualties, we can't waste any more time… for example with insufficient interrogations."

"You deal with the two suspects," Jansen agreed. "Simanek and I will plead ignorance if anyone asks. But I'm sure that won't happen any time soon. By the time Roaas realizes that ak Namur's childhood friends have disappeared, you might have extracted all relevant information from them so we can put a stop to these bastards. In that case, nobody will ask any questions about the 'how'."

With these words, he and the ensign turned, and went back the way they had come.

Ruut went to stand next to Klarn. "Can you believe that?" the Klingon security officer asked, dumbfounded.

"Starfleet officers with sense." The lieutenant grinned approvingly. "Don't tell the captain. He might swap ships."

Sometimes, the end justifies the means, Klarn thought. *Wasn't that an idiom from Earth? If so, it was definitely time that Captain Adams's colleagues remembered it.* The Klingon nodded toward Ruut. Raising his disruptor, he kicked down the door to Moadas ak Lavoor's quarters, in a great mood all of a sudden.

28
NOVEMBER 14, 2385

Konuhbi, Onferin

"Adams expects the impossible from us," Jenna Kirk said as they left the shipyard behind. "We're supposed to find a needle in a haystack—and preferably within twenty-four hours."

While Lenissa zh'Thiin agreed with the human chief engineer, she did not say so out loud, as she would never be so disrespectful as to criticize the captain out loud. Jenna Kirk had known Adams for ten years, so perhaps she might be able to afford a somewhat informal approach, but Lenissa preferred to err on the side of respecting the chain of command.

Besides Lenissa and Kirk, their team consisted of two Klingons: an engineer named Mokbar, who had scarily sharpened teeth, and a mountain of a security officer called Grakk. While Mokbar showed genuine interest in working with both Starfleet officers on their task, Grakk merely marched behind them in silence with a grumpy face. Lenissa assumed that he didn't like being ordered around by two women who together hardly weighed as much as he did alone.

Looking back at the shipyard, Jenna Kirk sighed before turning her attention to their small vessel where their pilot, Keeper ak Bahail—a member of Auroun's security forces—waited. "What's next?"

"Hang on." Lenissa pulled her padd out, bringing up a table with target objects that had been assigned to their group. "A chemical plant in the south of Konuhbi."

"Great. As if we haven't seen enough of those this afternoon already."

Since lunchtime they had been on their way to check plants and factories in the industrial city of Konuhbi. Captain Adams and Ambassadors Spock and Rozhenko had wrested permission from the council of spheres to check on shipyards and factories that were theoretically able to build attack fighters of the *Scorpion*-class or to handle dangerous substances such as protomatter. The analysts of the *Prometheus* and the *Bortas* had identified quite a few targets after a few orbits of the planet. Since then, ten away teams with four members each had been deployed to investigate them.

Lenissa, Kirk, Mokbar, and Grakk had been assigned to the city of Konuhbi, two hours' flight north of the capital city Auroun. As this was the most important industrial city of the planet, where the bigger of the two shipyards on Onferin was located, the *Prometheus*'s chief engineer had taken over this mission personally. Lenissa couldn't help but feeling that Jenna Kirk regretted this decision already.

Following the list that Commander Roaas had provided, they had investigated four different chemical plants thus far. They swept the grounds of each location with their tricorders, which had been modified by Commander Mendon to be particularly sensitive to the substances for which they were searching. They also couldn't rule out the possibility that prohibited experiments were being carried out in shielded rooms. Even the combined personnel from the *Prometheus* and the *Bortas* was insufficient to turn over every stone on a planet such as Onferin.

We'll need to be extremely lucky to find anything, Lenissa thought. *That's if there is even anything to find on Onferin, and the culprits aren't in one of the other six inhabited or seventeen uninhabited systems in the cluster.*

"You know, at least the shipyard was kind of interesting," Kirk continued irritably. "Fair enough, the people there looked at us as if we were lepers, and I don't think I've encountered that much silence since the day I told my first boyfriend that I'm…" She hesitated and glanced at her Klingon companions. "Oh well, it doesn't matter. But I would be lying if I said that I hadn't been curious about the Renao's technological achievements. And now? Yet another chemical plant." She snorted unenthusiastically.

A siren wailed behind them, indicating a shift change. Lenissa saw small figures that had just been bustling about in the nearest of the three enormous dry docks, putting down their tools to hand over to their relief so they could continue to work on the crescent-shaped patrol ship being built there.

For a brief moment, she wished her shift would also end. Ever since they had reached the Lembatta Cluster, free time had been a rare commodity. She longed for some passionate moments with Geron to relieve some of the pressure that had been building up inside her, since she was surrounded by ill-tempered Klingons, inscrutable Renao, and an army of silent dead souls. *Mission before pleasure,* she thought.

"Come on, Commander," said the young Andorian woman. "The sooner we work through that list, the sooner we can return to the ship."

"You're right there," Jenna said.

They climbed aboard the Kranaal, a flying vessel that Kirk had called an "oversized dragonfly," whatever that meant.

Their pilot started the takeoff sequence. "Where to?"

he asked. He seemed just as discontented as Grakk about receiving orders from women.

Lenissa told him their destination.

She thought briefly that Klingons and Renao should really get along just fine. Both societies were ruled by morose men who had little use for women. *Some of that attitude is still prominent in Jassat as well,* she mused. *He's not a man for festivities either. But at least he respects the fact that women hold command posts within Starfleet. In that respect, he had certainly benefited from his time at the Academy.*

Ak Bahail swerved the Kranaal to the left, flying them across the industrial estate. In approximately one kilometer's distance, the egg-shaped arcology of Konuhbi towered. The thousands of Renao working in the surrounding plants and at the shipyard lived there. The arcology was neither as glamorous nor as large as the Auroun complex. There were hardly any gardens, and the outside galleries looked untended. Apparently, even the Renao had class distinctions that were reflected in their living conditions.

"Do you know what's strange, Lenissa?" Jenna Kirk unexpectedly blurted out into the almost silent cabin, where only the Kranaal's flapping rotor wings and the occasional beeping of cockpit instruments were audible.

Lenissa turned away from the window and looked over to the other woman. "What?"

"They were building another ship in the back of the shipyard. This square thing that looked like the old *Antares*-class freighters."

"Yes, so?"

"I took a few scans with my tricorders. Professional curiosity, you know. And I realized that the drive seems to be completely different from the one they're using in these patrol ships we saw."

Lenissa felt her antennae bending forward curiously. "What do you mean?"

"Well, there's a matter-antimatter reactor like the one we know from our ships, only much more primitive. Yet they seem to lack the technology to produce a warp bubble." Kirk frowned.

"That ship was still under construction," Lenissa said. "Isn't it possible that the warp nacelles—or wherever the Renao put their warp field generator coils—hadn't been implemented yet?"

"I don't think so. I couldn't see any nozzles for warp nacelles, and the hull had been completely sealed already. They would have needed to beam the coils aboard to be able to implement them. But the Renao don't have transporter technology."

"Maybe it's a transport designed to stay within the system so it doesn't need a warp drive?"

"Yes, maybe..." The chief engineer looked to be deep in thought. "Or maybe these guys have developed a very unusual drive technology in recent years."

Shortly after their discussion they landed outside a plant's exterior wall. Next to the front gate the company name CEMOUDAN was written in large letters. The wall had been built from dark brown stones, and was covered in graffiti. Apparently, even on Onferin, young people liked to go on a rampage with spray paint. One or two of the efforts even displayed a modicum of artistic talent. Most, however, were simply scribbled letterings or simple symbols.

Mokbar was staring at the graffiti as they exited the Kranaal. He pointed at one scrawling. "Commander Kirk, look."

On the corner of the wall near the opening to a small alley was a demand written in Federation Standard: "Down with all sphere defilers! Long live the Harmony of the Spheres!" A red flame had been painted next to it.

Lenissa lifted her tricorder and recorded it.

"The flame," she addressed their pilot, "what does it stand for? The Purifying Flame, perhaps?"

Ak Bahail raised both hands as a gesture of ignorance. "I have no idea."

Lenissa's antennae stretched into his direction. "Do you really have no idea, or are you just not telling us?"

"What's that supposed to mean?" The glow in his yellow eyes intensified.

"That you haven't been particularly helpful, although this is meant to be a joint operation among the Federation, the Klingon Empire, and the government of the Home Spheres. I get it, you don't want us on your world, but we won't go away, unless we find out who's responsible for the attacks against us. So you can either continue to sit around pouting— in which case we'll stay even longer—or you can lift your red ass from that pilot seat, and help us so we can go home as soon as possible. Because, trust me, we're not enjoying this, either."

Ak Bahail glared at her for a few seconds. Finally, he snorted. "All right. Yes, the symbol seems to represent the Purifying Flame. They have been turning up for a few weeks now. That's all I know, really. I mean, I've heard rumors about them—that they believe the lore of harmony to be universal, applying to space as a whole. It's their duty to reestablish order in the galaxy, to save it from disruption by sphere defilers—like you all. I've heard that the movement started in the depths of the cluster." He leaned back in his seat, crossing his arms before his chest. "There."

"Why didn't you tell us any of this earlier?" Kirk demanded to know.

"Because you're looking for facts," their guide answered reluctantly. "Everything I told you is rumor. We haven't found any trace of them. The people spraying these symbols and distributing flyers are just children and deluded followers and worried citizens. They're afraid of a galaxy where everyone is allowed to travel anywhere they wish. That would destroy our culture completely."

Lenissa raised her head. "You truly have no idea about the Federation. We don't destroy cultures. We enjoy them, preserve them, and facilitate exchange so we can all learn from each other. Infinite Diversity in Infinite Combinations is the basis of Vulcan philosophy, and Vulcans were among the founders of our league of worlds."

The Renao sized her up. "Yes, I can tell how much you preserved your cultural heritage, Commander. What nation do you belong to?"

"I'm Andorian."

"And do you wear Andorian jewelry? Is your uniform Andorian? The cut? The fabric? Your weapon maybe?" He had raised his voice considerably, and Grakk stepped closer, growling and ready to keep ak Bahail back if the conversation escalated.

But Lenissa stopped him with a wave of her hand. She was security chief, after all, and very much capable of defending herself.

"I'm wearing a Starfleet uniform," she replied calmly, "just like everyone else in the fleet. During service we're all equal. That doesn't mean that we have forgotten our identities."

"If you say so… I say, you have fallen victim to your expansion madness."

Jenna Kirk put a hand on Lenissa's shoulder. "Come on, Lenissa. This is the wrong time for philosophical arguments. We've got a job to do."

Nodding slowly, Lenissa turned toward her. "Yes, you're right. Some people are simply beyond help."

Snorting quietly, their pilot grabbed his communication device.

Lenissa, Kirk, Mokbar, and Grakk went to the plant's entrance where a guard waited for them. Like pretty much every Renao, he wasn't happy to see the alien investigators. But their permits had been issued and signed by the sphere council, which opened every door for them on Onferin except military facilities.

During their wait for the manager who would guide them through the plant, they pulled out their tricorders, taking initial readings.

Lenissa had barely activated hers when it gave off an alarm. Surprised, her antennae straightened. "I'm detecting large quantities of tekasite." She turned around to face Kirk and the Klingon.

"Interesting," the chief engineer said. "I can't detect any trilithium or protomatter."

A wiry Renao arrived, wearing dark coveralls with bright yellow warning stripes on the sleeves and pant legs. He carried a protective helmet tucked under his arm. He was followed by a man with a box full of additional protective helmets. *So far, business as usual,* thought Lenissa.

"Welcome," the man said. "I'm Foreman ak Partami. And you are the investigators?"

"That's right." Jenna Kirk introduced everyone.

"I'm not particularly happy about you snooping around during working hours but nobody asks my opinion, anyway.

So, put your helmets on and let's get this over with."

"That's very kind of you."

"Before we start, Foreman," Mokbar said, "we have detected large quantities of tekasite in your plant. Why is that?"

"We process it." Ak Partami laughed. "Cemoudan manufactures industrial explosives for mining operations; didn't your investigations reveal that? I thought that's the reason why you're here."

Kirk and Lenissa exchanged knowing glances.

"Obviously, our people neglected to mention that," the chief engineer said.

"It's all completely legal. We have a license, and we work under strict security regulations. You can see for yourself. But please don't touch anything. You never know, it might be highly explosive." He laughed again.

"Where do you get the tekasite from?" Lenissa asked as she carefully placed the helmet on her head, as it hadn't been custom-made for Andorians. It squashed her antennae uncomfortably.

"From various sources," ak Partami said. "Lhoeel, Xhehenem... Tekasite is a fairly common commodity within the Lembatta Cluster. You can find ore veins in numerous rock formations." He grimaced. "Funny enough—we mine tekasite in order to manufacture explosives, which in turn we use to mine more tekasite. Oh well, at least it's not reactive in bound form. It needs to be pure if you want it to blow up when you hit it. Did I mention that you shouldn't touch anything around here?"

Without waiting for an answer he turned and walked off.

Great, Lenissa thought. *At least one of the three substances required for their bombs is readily available for these radicals whenever they take a walk in the mountains.* She had no idea what it took to purify tekasite, but she was hoping it was highly complicated. Otherwise, her search for the needle in the haystack had just taken a turn for the worse.

On certain days, Gilad ak Bahail hated his job. In general, he loved being a member of the Spherekeepers of Auroun. He had chosen this profession because he wanted to protect the weak and keep order. Since he was a child, he had always had a strong sense of order and of the value of harmony. For that reason, he'd always been against the opening of Renao borders to other spacefaring species, and to facilitating an exchange with Federation or the Klingon Empire or anyone else. They were the worst kind of sphere defilers, acting without restraint or good judgment. It didn't matter if their motives to cross sphere after sphere was scientific curiosity or conquest—the end result was the same kick to the face of harmony.

And now, he had to fly these people all over Konuhbi so they could breathe down innocent people's necks to come to a questionable decision as to whether ak Bahail's fellow countrymen were all fanatics or not.

He condemned murder—of course he did. That came with the job as keeper. The attacks on Federation and Klingon facilities were the worst kind of atrocities. But a small part of ak Bahail couldn't help but admire the mad, bold men and women who were behind the attacks. Their fight for the order of the universe had reached a level that he hadn't dared to dream of. They were ready to give their lives for the great cause.

And what did he do? Help outworlders to catch them.

There were days when he really hated his job.

His communicator device whistled quietly. A line of text appeared in the display. *"Are you still there?"*

Squinting, Bahail straightened himself. "Yes," he typed. "Was lost in thought."

"Dreamer," the answer came promptly.

He could have called his elder brother and talked to him directly. But they were both at work—Namoud worked a late shift in the hydroponic gardens of Auroun, while he was playing nanny to Federation and Klingons—so they preferred to communicate silently via text messages. He couldn't get the thought about the extremists out of his head.

"Hey, Namoud," he typed, "have you come across the Purifying Flame yet?"

"These religious warriors?"

"Yes."

"Not personally, no. But I've seen a lot of flyers recently lying around the streets. Why?"

Ak Bahail glanced out of the Kranaal's cockpit window toward the plant grounds. "I'm piloting four of these outworlders around while their ships are in orbit. And they are hunting people from the Purifying Flame."

"And?"

"I'm asking myself whether I'm doing the right thing."

"You're a keeper. Isn't it your duty to hunt extremists?"

"If they hurt the Home Spheres, yes. But these people are fighting for the harmony."

"With questionable methods."

"You have to make sacrifices for the greater cause."

"We can't fight against the entire universe. That's madness. These Klingons will bring us down."

"But they're doing wrong. They're destroying the order."

"You and I see it that way. But billions of outworlders see it differently. What are we supposed to do? They outnumber us, and they're stronger than us."

"It's frustrating."

"If it's any consolation, I don't think these people will get any results on Onferin. The Purifying Flame supposedly comes from the colonies. All that's running around here are flyer distributors and Leppa-soapbox-preachers."

"If you say so."

"Brother, I have to go. The agricultor is coming."

"Alright. See you in a few days."

"Sure. And don't let the Creatress hear what you're thinking about the extremists. She'll kill you."

Ak Bahail couldn't help but smiling. Their Creatress was radical in her own way—she firmly rejected the Harmony of Spheres. She dreamed of the Renao joining the Federation. Fortunately, she belonged to a very small minority.

"I'll be sure to be careful," he typed. "After all, I want to live long enough to watch the sphere defilers crawl back to their Home Spheres."

"Ha, good luck." His brother cut the link, and ak Bahail also switched off his communicator.

Still smiling, he leaned back in his pilot's chair. He had decided to continue to do what the strangers told him to. But he would neither hurry nor make an effort. He wanted fate to decide whether they encountered members of the Purifying Flame or not.

Suddenly, the cockpit door next to him swung open. Confused, ak Bahail looked left. All he could see was a dark figure wearing a mask. Wanting to open his mouth to utter a surprised sound, his hand reached for the shock pistol at his hip. He wasn't able to complete either action.

A shimmering blue beam fired at point blank range hit him.

Darkness enfolded ak Bahail.

When Kirk's away team left the chemical plant an hour later it was dark outside. Nights this close to the equator fell quickly, and their pilot had warned them about that. However, the darkness was not why Lenissa's hand reached for her phaser as they walked out to the landing area, but rather what she didn't see in it.

"Where's Keeper ak Bahail with our Kranaal?" asked Jenna Kirk, speaking Lenissa's thoughts. "They were right over there on that landing pad."

They walked over to the pad and had a good look around. They didn't see their aircraft anywhere, nor did they find any traces of where it or the pilot might have gone.

"He abandoned us," Mokbar snarled, baring his sharp teeth. "He probably thought that we should make our own way home after the argument with Commander zh'Thiin."

"That wasn't an argument," Lenissa said dismissively. "I didn't hit him once."

"I don't think he left us on a whim either," Kirk said. She pulled out the planet-wide communicator device that had been given to her to establish contact with her Sphere Keeper partners on Onferin without having to involve the *Prometheus*. "I'll call his superiors to…"

What she wanted to say remained a mystery because a shimmering blue beam cut through the warm evening air and hit Kirk straight in the chest. She gasped and collapsed.

Lenissa had her phaser in her hand before her brain even registered the fact. She ducked, firing into the direction where the shot had come from. Grakk, beside her, was hit as well. The giant Klingon staggered but he didn't fall. He shook like a dog, reaching for his disruptor that—unlike Lenissa's weapon—was not set for stun. He fired quickly, hitting a parked hovercraft, sending its fragile roof flying in a shower of sparks.

Another two blue beams hit the Klingon. This time, Grakk fell to his knees. He cried out something in Klingon, rolled his eyes, and fell forward, hitting the landing pad's stony ground with a loud thud.

Lenissa's hand slapped her combadge. "Lenissa to..." she began, trying to establish a link, but something hit her in the back.

A wave of liquid fire shot through her body. Twitching uncontrollably, she tried desperately to hang onto her weapon. She felt as if she was falling, and a bright flash of pain shot through the back of her head when she hit the ground. Stunned, she looked up. A dark, faceless figure towered over her, pointing something at Lenissa's chest. The figure uttered several words that Lenissa didn't understand.

A trap, she thought. *The Purifying Flame...*

Blue light engulfed her, and she lost consciousness.

29
NOVEMBER 14, 2385

Achernar II

The city of Heliopolis was large, and yet it seemed parochial. The Ferengi named Glomp laughed derisively as he traversed a street corner in one of the more dubious sections of the spacious urban center. It had been more than two centuries since human colonists had settled down on this rock in the Beta Quadrant, naming it after a famous place in Ancient Greece. In the meantime, representatives from other nations had joined them, taken root, and started families. But these days, not much was left of the idealism and the hope that the founders of this settlement once felt.

This wasn't the city's fault. Was it the colonists' fault that a non-corporeal entity by the name of Redjac paid a visit to Achernar II—or Alpha Eridani II as it was also called in the Federation's star charts—in 2156 committing ten atrocious murders? Was it the colonists' fault that the Romulan Commander Donatra renounced the Romulan Star Empire more than two hundred years later, making the base for her Imperial Romulan State in the Achernar system? Did Heliopolis do anything to justify the reputation that clung to it?

Of course not. And Glomp didn't really care for its political or historical importance. His dislike was based on a much simpler criterion: he found Heliopolis to be just plain ugly. Not just the rundown neighborhood to the south of its center where Glomp had just emerged from a shabby transporter station into the humid summer afternoon air. No, this entire metropolis had disgusted him from the moment he had arrived at the spaceport. It had nauseated him in the high halls of administration, and it certainly didn't enthrall him now that he finally approached his destination.

The warehouse was located on the edge of the neighborhood. It was a dirty gray complex made of perma-concrete with wide doors that had been welded shut. Weeds grew unchecked all over the yard. Glomp stopped after rounding a corner and seeing the building for the first time with his own eyes. At first, he thought that he had the wrong address. But no, this matched the information he had found in Thokal's files, as well as the results of his own clandestine investigations.

There was no movement, and the silence was almost deafening. It was hard to believe that the city center was not far away. Dirt and small stones crunched under Glomp's boots when he entered the yard, walking toward the small door on the warehouse's back wall. The control pad to the right of the door hung tilted out of the wall and had obviously been broken for many years. The door didn't respond to motions either. So Glomp raised his hand and knocked.

Nothing happened. A siren wailed in the distance but it died down again soon. He knocked again, this time noticing a hum. Turning his head, Glomp spotted a small camera above the door in one of the façade's wide cracks. Instinctively he tried to picture his effect on the unknown observer: a lanky Ferengi with ears that were far too small, a gaudily colored jacket, and a forehead where you would need a magnifying glass to find the two bumps that were typical for his species. The image would relay someone who was no kind of threat—more like a bad joke.

Glomp rapped the door for the third time, which prompted a blue light to emit from the lens—a scan that went from head to toe. Soon after he heard footsteps. Someone opened a small wooden hatch on eye-level in the door. Two eyes with an annoyed expression came into view. "Get lost!" a harsh voice snarled.

"*Jolan tru*," Glomp used a Romulan salutation, pronouncing it with a very strong accent. Was it obvious how nervous he felt? Were they able to see how long it had been since he had swapped his extremely hapless career as a secret agent for a job in finance, which suited him much better? He was afraid they would, and that fear increased his nervousness even more. "I'm here for the, uhm, replicator."

The annoyance in the eyes transformed into incredulity. "What?"

Glomp squinted, confused. The person who answered the door should have reacted differently upon hearing the agreed password. Thokal hadn't mentioned snags like that.

"No, a loan isn't necessary," he continued, sticking with his lines he had been given. "I'll be paying cash."

The person on the other side of the door stared for a moment, then closed the hatch. Glomp was at a loss, standing outside the closed door. What now?

He was just about to knock for the fourth time when the door opened to reveal a very large Romulan. He wore dark, loose clothes, had jet-black hair, pointed ears and—much to Glomp's terror—a disruptor in his left hand.

"*You?*" he said, eyeing Glomp. "*You?*"

"My name is…"

The hand with the disruptor twitched. Glomp fell silent.

"Spare us the explanations," the Romulan said. "Facts speak louder than words."

He stepped aside and a second well-muscled Romulan appeared in the doorway and grabbed Glomp by the shoulders, turning him around and shoving him against the perma-concrete wall in order to search his jacket and pants pockets. When he was finished he pulled a hand scanner from underneath his clothing, pointing it at the Ferengi.

"Listen, that really isn't necessary." Glomp's knees were getting weak. He was no longer used to this kind of field work, and even back when he was, he'd made a complete mess of things more often than not. But he knew that he had to stay in character. "Our agreed schedule makes it clear that…"

"The meeting has been scheduled with Mak," the first Romulan interrupted him sharply. His finger tightened around the disruptor's trigger. "Not with you."

That was it. The all-important moment. The one he had been practicing for in front of the mirror for hours. The reason why Thokal had turned to him of all the people he could have put on this mission because he was the only Ferengi.

Glomp turned around. "Damnit, I *am* Mak!"

"You." The Romulan snorted. "You're the famous weapon dealer from Ferenginar? The one everyone's looking for but hardly anyone has ever seen?"

"That's right," Glomp lied again. He raised his hand to reach into his inner jacket pocket.

"Slowly!" The Romulan jerked the disruptor menacingly.

The second Romulan waved his hand dismissively. "He's unarmed. There's absolutely nothing in his pockets."

Not in those that you found, Glomp thought. Slowly, he

ripped open one of the inner lining's seams and pulled out a flat, rectangular datapad.

"Absolutely nothing, eh?" the man with the weapon growled. His companion gawked.

"This is a list of all articles that I intend to purchase." Glomp activated the pad and handed it to the Romulan. "Just like we discussed. So? I'm on time. I've got the latinum. If you keep your side of the deal, we will all walk away happy and satisfied with this encounter."

Silently, the man with the weapon skimmed through the data on the small display. Glomp knew the list by heart, although Thokal had been the one to write it. It consisted of various small military items—from hand weapons to components for the construction of a cloaking device. Hopefully, it would be sufficient as bait.

A few seconds later the Romulan looked up. "You want to buy all that, yes?"

Glomp nodded. This was another moment of truth, and he knew it. If what he and Thokal tried to lure out didn't happen now it...

It happened.

"Why just that?" the Romulan asked. A hint of a smile played around his lips as the Romulan handed Glomp the pad back. "If you are who you claim you are, and you have sufficient financial resources at your disposal, my partner and I can offer you so much more than just disruptors and shield generators."

Glomp relaxed a little. He knew this smile. It was much more familiar to him than the intricacies and pitfalls of an agent's existence. This was the smile of a seller looking at a goldmine; one who might be powerful, but not the sharpest tool in the toolbox. Easy prey.

"I'm listening," the Ferengi said with fake surprise. He returned the datapad to the not-quite-so-secret-anymore inner pocket. Once again he cursed the day when he hadn't paid attention and had neglected the Third Rule of Acquisition: *Never spend more for an acquisition than you have to.* To this day, Glomp still continued to pay off the favor that the cunning Thokal had done him… time and time again.

Ferengi weren't born for danger, but for profit. Glomp had learned that much during his short and inglorious career as an agent. They excelled at bank counters, at the stock exchange, at intergalactic markets, and in smoky back rooms—anywhere where deals were signed and gold-pressed latinum changed hands. Although the best among them were barefaced liars, only very few of them were suited to be secret agents.

The two Romulans from Heliopolis's worst neighborhood had escorted "Mak" to their transport and blindfolded him with a black piece of cloth. They assured him it was for his own safety. He had heard the drive's humming before the transport had lifted off, heading toward a destination that only the Romulans knew, but which allegedly contained everything that an arms dealer could possibly wish for.

Glomp would never have thought that he would swap his desk at the Ferengi Commerce Authority for a seat on a reeking Romulan transport—and his computer console for a blindfold. But life and the Rules of Acquisition had—again—taught him otherwise. What did the Eighth Rule state? *Small print leads to large risk.* How true! Especially if it was small print in a contract with an old Tal Shiar agent.

Thokal's silence had cost Glomp much more dearly than he had originally anticipated. Maybe, he sighed inwardly while trying to peer through the black fabric, it might even cost him his life one day.

"Satisfaction is not guaranteed," he muttered gloomily.

He felt a hand on his shoulder. "What did you say?" Hararis, the second Romulan, asked.

Glomp swallowed and forced himself back into the role of the slightly overextended but professional criminal. "Nothing, nothing. I just quoted a Rule of Acquisition. Are we there yet?" He had lost all sense of time. How long had they been in the air? Half an hour? An hour?

"We are," Hararis said. "You can take off the blindfold, if you wish."

Glomp removed it immediately. Squinting, he looked around and groaned quietly when the lights of the narrow cockpit hit his eyes. The inside of the transport was tiny and dirty. Two of the three consoles lining the cabin seemed broken. Only the center station below the oblong window made from transparent aluminum seemed to be active. Keval, the one with the disruptor, sat there, navigating the ship toward their destination.

Looking out the window, Glomp saw that their destination was located within a volcano crater underneath a black sky. The Ferengi saw deep holes, dry stones, vastness, and void. When the transport descended into the wide crater, the vacuum above it flickered briefly.

An energy field, Glomp realized. He would have to remember that.

"Is this a moon?" he asked. "The dark side of a moon? It's dark enough here…"

The only light sources were two spotlights on the transport's front. Two bright light cones, illuminating the moon's darkness.

"That is none of your business." Hararis's answer was almost friendly. His companion navigated the vessel down and toward an opening in the crater wall.

A cave. In a crater. Underneath an energy field. On a moon.

Glomp sensed that he had hit the jackpot. Thokal's and his efforts were crowned with success. These were definitely the right people. Now all he had to do was to survive.

Several minutes later the three unlikely traveling companions stood inside the cave. Another energy field at the cave entrance ensured atmosphere, oxygen, and artificial gravity inside the cavern, protecting them from the unforgiving void outside. The transport had been able to pass through this wall without any problems.

When he looked around, Glomp was unable to hide his amazement. The cave was bursting with military equipment: ship components, weapons, canisters containing trilithium and other explosive chemicals, shield generators, and much more.

And this is just one cave. How many of these caves had he spotted during their approach? Five? Seven? Did they all contain these kinds of treasures? That stuff must be worth a fortune.

"Did I promise too much?" Keval asked, spreading his arms. "Whatever you need, we can supply you with, Mak. Why aim low when you can reach high? What was on your list again?"

Glomp swallowed hard. He had found what Thokal was looking for, he was sure of it. And yet, this day took a completely different turn than expected.

"Forget the list, Keval," he said, hoping that the real Mak would say the same thing in this situation. "Let's go to your office. I'll write a new one."

Both Romulans laughed, satisfied, and Glomp joined in, although it sent shivers down his spine.

* * *

The on-board computer of the cloaked Ferengi shuttle beeped angrily. Glomp battered it with his fist until it stopped. Promptly, all displays died.

The Ferengi hissed in frustration, but the power outage did not last long, and the consoles sprang back to life again. This time, they finally showed him what he wanted to see. "There we go."

It was the middle of the night in Heliopolis, and Glomp had commenced his second journey of this memorable day. He had left to pay the crater another visit—several hours after his first visit. Owing to a small tracking device that he had planted in the cave without Keval or Hararis noticing, he found the place with ease. Now, his cloaked shuttle floated above Achernar II's moon, only several dozen meters above the same crater he'd visited earlier. Finally, Glomp was where he belonged—behind a console.

He was no longer in the uncomfortable role of agent, but rather an employee of the Ferengi Commerce Authority, who was second to none working on a computer. No matter whether he wanted to calculate interest, monthly installments, or the systems of energy field generators—data columns were data columns. You merely needed to know how to handle them, and they would do anything you wanted; even more so when they had been upgraded to a level that most worlds didn't permit for privately used devices by a retired Tal Shiar analyst.

On his console's monitor, Glomp watched a simulation of what he hoped to achieve. In theory, it all looked good. "Computer, calculate probability of this data manipulation's success."

The value promptly appeared below the animation: 98.8 percent.

Glomp's hands tingled. The result hardly gave any reason for complaints, but he was nervous. What if he made the one point two percent mistake? What if Thokal's supercomputer was wrong?

And besides—what was the old analyst thinking, anyhow? Keval and Hararis were crooks of the lowest order—disillusioned ex-soldiers pining for the past. Therefore, they had decided to make a profit because the Star Empire had become too peace-oriented for their liking. With their supply of military equipment stolen from the Imperial Romulan State in its final days, as well as some new objects, combined with numerous contacts among old, secretive friends in Praetor Kamemor's forces, they had developed a flourishing enterprise. They stole deftly from the Romulan military and sold to anyone who could raise the cash, right under the noses of the Senate. Some of the most infamous aggressors in the quadrant were among their clients.

What did Thokal have to do with these criminals? Why did he care about a few stolen *Scorpion*s?

But Glomp knew that he didn't really want to know the answers to these questions. The old analyst probably intended to put a stop to Keval's and Hararis's game. Put a stop to a prospering enterprise! *No*, Glomp decided, shuddering, *I'd better not think about that.*

The things you do for old friends…

"Computer," he said, "execute program." Then he closed his eyes, dreaming of yields with high interest. Not three seconds later, a noise of confirmation reached his sensitive ears. Glomp opened his eyes again. The safety energy field above the crater had indeed gone. Thokal's supercomputer and his own calculations had sabotaged the Romulan technology successfully—just like the simulation had promised.

Expected restoration in 15... 14... 13..., Glomp watched the countdown on his main display and realized too late that he should have acted already. Gawking wouldn't get him anywhere.

"Computer," he shouted frantically, while the numbers decreased continually, "ahead quarter impulse."

The shuttle lurched forward. It descended into the deep moon crater just in time. Had it been two seconds later, it would have been caught in the restored energy field.

Glomp touched down on the same landing pad that the Romulans had alighted upon earlier. He scanned for security measures on the inside of the cave that might make his life difficult. When he found some, he spent more than half an hour hacking into their systems and deactivating them, before finally climbing out of his shuttle and walking to the rear of the spacious complex, where the offices were located. There, he had sealed a deal with the Romulans as the arms dealer Mak.

The tricorder he had brought from his shuttle had been programmed to emit an interference signal for the deactivation of the office door, which it performed without a hitch.

After breaking in, he stood in front of Keval's console. As expected, the computer was permanently running. Glomp crouched down, removed his little tracking device and placed it in one of the many pockets in his jacket, before beginning with his actual work.

Glomp's knowledge about Romulan data systems was fairly limited but it still didn't take long. Just like he had done with the security systems previously, he programmed a subroutine that would cover his tracks in the system, before deleting itself. He found his way around the central memory system, bringing up the desired information on the monitor.

Lo and behold—there were the *Scorpion* attack fighters that Thokal had been talking about. Four of them had been delivered to the Lembatta Cluster, according to Keval's files. They had been sold to a Renao. Additionally, several tons of trilithium had been delivered—enough to blast entire colonies to smithereens.

Two heartbeats later, he heard the alarm.

Glomp ran. Disruptor beams hit the cave walls next to him, while more and more light sources in the dome-shaped ceiling were being switched on.

How could he have been so foolish? A supercomputer and a few tricks didn't mean that secret weapon stashes weren't guarded at night. He had assumed that he had been able to interrupt the energy field unnoticed—but what if he was wrong, and they *had* noticed it?

He who dives under the table today lives to profit tomorrow— that was the Twentieth Rule. Why had he ignored that wisdom? Why had he put himself in danger?

When Thokal called him next time looking for a fool to do his dirty work, Glomp would definitely *not* accept the call. Let him publish the images. Things could be worse… he could be killed.

Again, a beam missed him by only a few centimeters. Glomp could smell ozone, and he felt stone fragments hitting his sensitive earlobes. Whimpering, he ran on.

His pursuers—there had to be at least two, and he had probably woken them from their sleep—were only several steps and two or three enormous stacks of supplies behind him. His lead was hardly worth mentioning. Glomp tightened his grip around the isolinear rod where he had stored the purloined data and ran as fast as his short legs would carry him.

Finally, he reached his shuttle. The hatch was still open, just as he'd left it. Had the guards gone aboard? He didn't know, and couldn't waste time trying to find out before boarding. The shuttle was his only chance to escape.

Another shot. This time, the beam struck the shuttle's hull. Wincing, Glomp sent a short prayer to the Divine Exchequer, and leaped into the small ship. It was empty.

"Close hatch!" he squealed in panic. "Close hatch!" The computer executed his order immediately. "Activate cloaking device." With shaking hands Glomp pushed himself up from the cabin floor where he had landed and went to the helm. "Initiate escape maneuver. Protocol Glomp 2. Activate shields."

The console acknowledged the orders. A fraction of a second later he heard the drive come to life. The shuttle took off from the cave floor. Again, disruptor beams hit, but they only struck the shields, which they couldn't penetrate.

What if they have stronger weapons on the moon's surface? The thought flashed through Glomp's mind. *What if their sensors find me despite Thokal's cloaking device? What if Keval himself is waiting for me up there to shoot me down from orbit?*

He didn't have any answers to those questions. He only knew that he wanted to get off this rock as quickly as possible.

"Computer, disrupt energy field generator again. Method two." During these panic-filled minutes Glomp just wished that he were back in his office on Ferenginar, looking out from his window onto the capital city that was wet from rain. If he made it back home, he promised the Divine Exchequer that he would never undertake another long journey again. Enough was enough.

Fortunately, the night watch in the hidden complex didn't have any secret weapons on the moon's surface—or if they did, they neglected to use them on his cloaked shuttle. They were probably stunned that their unwelcome guest had managed to deactivate their energy field yet again in order to leave the crater and go to warp.

"One thing is certain," the Ferengi mumbled, settling into his cockpit chair as he left the Achernar system far behind him. "The real Mak just made some powerful enemies today. And he's not even aware of it."

He placed his isolinear rod—his little souvenir for Thokal—on the edge of the console and programmed a course for Romulus.

30
NOVEMBER 15, 2385

U.S.S. *Prometheus*

Richard Adams had barely left the turbolift and entered the bridge for the start of alpha shift when Ensign Winter looked up from his communications console with a look of significant apprehension on his face.

"What's wrong?" Adams asked, stopping dead in his tracks halfway to his command chair.

Commander Roaas rose from the chair and walked toward Adams. "We were just about to inform you, sir. One of the away teams has not reported back as ordered. So far, all attempts to contact them have failed."

"Which team?" Adams asked the tall Caitian.

"Kirk and zh'Thiin's team, sir. They were out in the industrial estates of Konuhbi with Mokbar and Grakk from the *Bortas*. They should have returned to the *Prometheus* at midnight ship's time, which would have been early evening in Konuhbi. But the team hasn't checked in."

Adams looked at Winter, touching his combadge on his uniform. "Adams to Kirk."

Nothing happened.

"We already tried that, sir," Winter said. "Our signal won't reach the recipient. But I can't say whether it's due to the atmosphere, or whether Commander Kirk's combadge has been switched off."

"Find out." Adams touched his combadge again. "*Prometheus* to Commander zh'Thiin. Can you hear me, Commander?"

The silence remained.

"This is the captain, Lenissa. Respond."

Everywhere on the bridge officers turned around or looked up to follow proceedings with growing concern. Adams also had a bad feeling about this.

Winter shook his head. "We're not getting through. I can't reach any of the combadges."

"Sensor scans, Commander Carson," the captain ordered. "Show me my people."

Sarita Carson's fingers danced across the ops console, but she shook her head to let him know that she had already tried that while he had been absent. "Negative, Captain. I can't locate any of their combadges."

"Vital signs?" Roaas asked, stepping behind her to look over her shoulder.

"I'm picking up several humans and Klingons on the planet's surface," Carson answered. "That's about all I can tell you due to the interferences from the atmosphere. However, I can't find any humans or Klingons in Konuhbi—and not a single Andorian anywhere on Onferin."

Roaas and Adams exchanged a silent glance. Adams hadn't had a lot of sleep—the lengthy talks with Onferin's government representatives as well as the stiff diplomatic function last night were taking their toll on him. But his fatigue had completely faded.

"The other teams?" Adams asked quietly.

Roaas nodded. "We were able to get in touch with all other team leaders on Onferin. They have been warned, and they're on the lookout for the missing team. But Onferin is a large planet, and when technology doesn't want to play along…"

Adams ground his teeth in an attempt to keep his frustration at bay. He was only able to help his people if he kept his calm.

"Should I have Councilor ak Mousal contacted?" asked his first officer.

Adams considered and rejected the suggestion. "Not yet. Get me Kromm first, Mr. Winter. Patch him through to my ready room as soon as you get in touch with him. And let Ambassador Spock know that I would appreciate his presence during that conversation."

"Aye, sir," Winter said.

"You've got the bridge, Commander," Adams said.

"Captain." Roaas leaned forward, lowering his voice slightly. "We might also have another problem. Lieutenant ak Namur called the ship last night, asking for reinforcements to arrest two suspected sympathizers of the Purifying Flame. The arresting team was under Klingon command. The Renao never arrived on the *Prometheus*."

Adams frowned. "They could be on the *Bortas*."

Roaas tilted his head. "That's what I'm worried about. You and I know the Klingons. Don't you think it might lead to political complications if citizens from the Home Spheres disappear on Klingon ships?"

The captain's face hardened. "I know what you mean. But we need to save our own people first. Afterward, we can take care of the Renao." With these words, Adams turned and left the bridge.

Within moments, the door to the ready room hissed behind him and he stood at the desk in his ready room, staring at the monitor on his desk's left corner. The flat screen displayed the seal of the United Federation of

Planets above the *Prometheus*'s registry.

One and a half seemingly endless minutes went by. Adams eventually sat at his desk, but nothing changed on the display.

The doorbell chimed. "Come," Adams said.

Ambassador Spock stood outside the doorway that hissed apart. Slowly, he entered the small ready room. The old Vulcan seemed alert and intent. He wore a dark robe, and Adams envied the calm he saw on the ambassador's face. "Captain," Spock said. "Mr. Roaas has briefed me."

In that moment, Winter's voice came from the intercom. *"Bridge to Captain Adams. Sir, I've got Captain Kromm for you. Patching through."*

"Very good, Ensign," Adams replied. He motioned for Spock to take a seat on one of the two visitor chairs in front of his desk.

Captain Kromm's visibly sleep-deprived face came into view on the small screen. The Klingon commander wore the same uniform as on the previous day—and he was in the same foul mood.

"What do you want, Adams?"

Adams described the situation. Kromm's scowl deepened. He looked to one side, barking an order. Shortly after, he received a reply, which he obviously didn't like very much. *"We can't reach our people, either. Something is definitely wrong. You know the way to ak Mousal's office just as well as I do. I suggest you grab a phaser and we meet there."*

Adams shook his head. "Negative, Captain. Let me contact the Councilor and ask him for a statement."

"A statement?" The Klingon laughed incredulously. *"How often do you want him to lie to you before you stop trusting him? Do you think the Renao asked our mine workers on Tika IV-B for*

a statement before they terminated their lives? They are terrorists, Adams. The High Council doesn't negotiate with terrorists!"

"And the Federation doesn't jump to conclusions," Adams retorted. "Give me fifteen minutes, Kromm. I'll get back to you. *Prometheus* out."

Before the Klingon got a chance to protest, Adams cut the link. Then he looked at Spock.

The Vulcan ambassador nodded. "You made the correct decision, Captain. The means of diplomacy outweigh spontaneous overreactions."

Adams snorted quietly. "With all due respect, Ambassador, but there are situations when I couldn't care less about your diplomacy."

Spock raised an eyebrow. Did Adams imagine things or did he detect a faint amused glint in the eyes of the older man?

"What?" Adams asked brusquely.

The corners of Spock's mouth twitched. "You reminded me of someone whom I used to know a long time ago. He also cared little for diplomatic ways when he didn't deem them expedient."

"And what became of him?" Sighing, Adams clenched his fists. He hated feeling helpless like this; standing by idly while the mills of diplomacy and protocol ground slowly.

"He would reach his goal every time."

Both men fell silent for a short while. Then Adams tapped the combadge on his chest. "Adams to Roaas. Commander, I'm ready for ak Mousal now."

"Understood, sir," the Caitian replied. *"We will patch him through as soon as possible."*

The conversation with the highest councilor of Onferin ended as quickly as it had begun. Ak Mousal appeared to be horrified by the news Adams relayed to him. He assured them that he knew nothing about this matter, vouching for his people once again. He also promised to set the law enforcement officers on Onferin onto the case of the missing visitors.

Adams wasn't satisfied when he terminated the conversation. On the contrary, his frustration had risen with every word from ak Mousal. "I'm recalling the away teams. If this is a kidnapping—or worse—the risk is too big."

The Vulcan nodded, pensively. "With your permission, may I put forward a counterproposal?"

"I'm listening," he said.

"Dispatch someone else to the surface," Spock said. "Someone who is already your eyes and ears among the population. Your away teams are more alert than ever. If you call them back now, you will dig trenches to start a war where your intent is simply to protect rather than fight."

Adams tilted his head slightly, weighing his options. "Captain to Lieutenant ak Namur."

The Renao responded immediately. *"Ak Namur here, sir."*

"I need you in my ready room."

Spock nodded approvingly.

"Understood, sir. I'm on my way."

Less than a minute later, the lieutenant arrived. He was a little surprised to find Ambassador Spock with his captain.

"You wanted to see me, sir?" he faced his commander.

Adams briefly described the situation. "Help us, Jassat. We need your insight more than ever. Explain your people to us. Where might our officers and the two Klingons be?"

Ak Namur threw his hands up. Adams had never seen him using this gesture of cluelessness that was typical for his species, and he wasn't sure whether he liked it.

"I'm afraid I can't explain them to you, sir," the young Renao began. "I... I can hardly understand them myself anymore. Least of all this xenophobia that has gripped my people. The Renao are not naturally aggressive, Captain, you know that. They are isolationist. That's how I used to know them, anyway. Kidnapping visitors from other worlds? No, sir. The thought itself would be absurd to me, if not for all the experiences from the previous days."

"Absurd or not," Adams said, "we need to do something. I want you down there, Jassat. The other teams are already looking around, but most of all I need someone inconspicuous. I need you—and I'm willing to place a security detail at your side."

Ak Namur raised his hand defensively. "No, sir. Commander Roaas suggested the same thing when I entered the bridge. If I'm supposed to be inconspicuous, I need to be ordinary. Alone."

"The situation could be dangerous," Spock said.

"I'm aware of that, Ambassador," ak Namur replied firmly. "But being afraid is not a disgrace."

The half-Vulcan nodded. "Indeed."

"And there's a lot at stake here, sir." Ak Namur glanced from him to Adams and back. "This is not just about Kirk and zh'Thiin and the two Klingons, but also about my people. It's about answers to questions that concern me more than you might imagine."

Adams mulled it over before nodding tersely. But the bad feeling in his gut wouldn't go away. "You go, son," he said quietly. "Bring them back."

"Aye, sir," the lieutenant promised, heading for the door.

As soon as he had left the room, Roaas said, "*Captain,*

I've got Councilor ak Mousal for you. And Captain Kromm on another channel."

"Patch them both through, Commander," Adams said, looking at Spock. "Conference call."

"Aye, sir."

The screen on the desk flickered to life again. This time, the screen was split in half; the seemingly impatient Klingon was on the left, while the supreme Renao Onferin's appeared on the right.

"Councilor?" Adams began. "You asked to speak to me."

Ak Mousal nodded. *"Captain, I can already report some investigation results. Our authorities have picked up the Kranaal pilot who was supposed to guide your away team through Konuhbi. Keeper ak Bahail assures us—and I'd like to emphasize, he comes across as very believable—that he has been ambushed on the landing area of a Cemoudan chemical plant by unidentified attackers."*

Captain Kromm laughed, jeeringly.

The Renao ignored the Klingon and continued with his report. *"In his statement to my officials, he claims that they stunned him and dragged him away. Forensics are searching his Kranaal as we speak. When the Keeper came to, he had been abandoned in a desert outside of town with his small transport vessel. He doesn't know anything about the fate of his passengers."*

"And we're supposed to believe that, eh?" the Klingon asked.

"You may question the Keeper yourself if you wish, Captain," ak Mousal replied. *"I'm sure he will answer you just as openly and honestly as he did my officers."*

"The pilot had been removed from the scene," Spock said quietly, "in order to ensure unrestricted access for the perpetrators. They needed to reach the targets of their endeavor—the away team."

Adams nodded. "I agree. They're not after their own

people, but after us strangers." He addressed Kromm and ak Mousal. "Thank you for the information, Councilor. Please let us know immediately, if new details surface."

The Renao promised to do so and terminated the connection.

"*You're making a mistake,*" Kromm said. His image covered the entire screen now. "*You're standing idly by, when you should be laying waste to the whole of Onferin. You mustn't leave a stone standing until our people return!*"

"You underestimate me, Captain Kromm," Adams said, looking at the ambassador.

Spock nodded silently. He also knew that an attack on Onferin wouldn't do anyone any good.

"I'm already one step ahead," Adams continued, facing Kromm. He thought about Lieutenant ak Namur, hoping for a miracle.

31
NOVEMBER 15, 2385

Somewhere on Onferin

Lenissa awoke, surrounded by darkness. Her head hurt, her chest was in pain, her tongue felt swollen and without sensation, and apparently someone had tied her legs together and her arms behind her back. Once she realized that she had been bound, she understood why she couldn't see anything. Someone had pulled a sack over her head. *We have been abducted*, she realized. *It's got to be the fanatics from the Purifying Flame.*

That realization was equally comforting and horrifying. The former because she could have wound up dead. The latter because she might be soon.

Her survival training took over. She had been trained for situations like this by Starfleet Security. First, she needed to find out more about her situation.

She tried to avoid any obvious movements and strained her ears to listen into the darkness. Male voices reached her ears, but they were very quiet, so it stood to reason that her kidnappers weren't nearby. Cautiously, she fumbled about behind her back. The ground felt hard and cold: stone covered with some rubble. Considering the slight echo of the voices and the nature of the ground, she surmised that they were either in the ruins of a very large house or inside a mining tunnel or cave.

She tried to focus on the voices but she couldn't understand a word. This was only partly due to the fact that the men spoke quietly. Lenissa also didn't understand their language. Obviously her combadge had been removed so she couldn't rely on the universal translator. She assumed that they had also taken her tricorder and her phaser. At least she still wore her uniform, which gave her some hope.

She needed to find out whether she was being guarded, and where the others from her away team were. Groaning quietly, she moved a little, as if she had just woken up.

A rough voice answered. Again, she didn't understand a word. But she realized after a while that the voice spoke Klingon. "Mokbar?" she asked.

"Grakk?"

"Mokbar, Commander," someone with a strong accent answered. "Kirk? Zh'Thiin?"

"Zh'Thiin."

"Ah."

Lenissa cursed herself inwardly. Right now she wished she had spent more time at the Academy on voluntary language courses. Her Klingon was limited to a handful of phrases and orders such as, "surrender," or, "drop your weapon." She knew these sentences in about twenty languages—just in case. None of these were particularly helpful in this situation.

She heard a quiet grunt from a woman, and a body next to her shifted. "Kirk?" Lenissa asked.

"Yes, I'm here," the chief engineer answered. She uttered a curse that would have made a Pakled garbage freighter pilot blush. "What is this?"

"We've been abducted," Lenissa said. "Probably by the Purifying Flame. Right now, we don't seem to be guarded though, or our guard would have made himself known by now."

Mokbar said something, and then he growled into his beard.

To Lenissa's surprise, Kirk answered him.

"You speak Klingon?" the Andorian woman asked.

"A little. When I was a child, my parents and I used to live on a space station near the Klingon border. There was a merchant there who had his mind set on teaching all children Klingon culture."

"And? What is Mokbar saying?" Lenissa asked.

"We should try to escape."

"My sentiments exactly." She tried to get to her knees, which wasn't easy with her legs bound. "Let's see if I can pull this hood off my head." The young Andorian woman leaned forward, shaking her head, and she finally managed to get the sack off. When she looked around, she found her assumptions confirmed. Their accommodation looked very much like an old mining tunnel. Dim, reddish light shone from the main tunnel into the small cave where they were being held captive. Lenissa saw her three companions. Kirk and Mokbar were still fighting against their hoods, while Grakk was still unconscious. In addition, the entrance to their chamber was sealed by a shimmering energy field.

Kirk, who was next to her, finally managed to remove her hood. Squinting and with disheveled hair she examined her surroundings. She leaned closer to the wall. "I think this is a tekasite mine. Unpurified tekasite is not reactive, right?"

"That's what the Cemoudàn foreman claimed," said Lenissa. "But who knows whether we can trust him. We were abducted from the landing area in front of his plant, after all. And someone must have informed our kidnappers of our whereabouts."

Mokbar cursed because the sack's seam had caught his hair and wouldn't budge.

"Keep still," Kirk said to him, and repeated the order in Klingon. She tried to help him, and their joint efforts managed to free the *Bortas*'s engineer as well.

"Now we need to get rid of our bonds." Jenna Kirk tugged on hers.

"That won't do any good. The ropes are made from reinforced synthetic fiber. Not even our big warrior over there will be able to tear them apart." Lenissa nodded toward Grakk, who lay motionless on the floor. "But I might have an idea." She shifted toward Kirk, turning until her feet were close to the engineer's hands. "Try to reach into my right boot. I believe the kidnappers have missed the knife I'm carrying in there."

"You're carrying a knife in your boot?" Kirk sounded half incredulous, half amused. "Were you part of a gang on Andor during your childhood?"

The young Andorian woman's antennae bent belligerently forward, but the human woman couldn't see that. "I just don't want to be unarmed, that's all."

They were lucky. The short knife was still stuck in its secret holster in Lenissa's bootleg. Cautiously, Kirk pulled it out and handed it to the security chief who cut through her wrist ropes. Once that was done, it didn't take long to untie the others as well. Kirk headed straight for the entrance to take a closer look at the energy field. The Klingon engineer knelt next to his comrade, trying to wake him. When he pulled the sack off Grakk's head, he growled.

Lenissa went to Mokbar's side. She also saw the reason why

Grakk hadn't moved. His tricipital lobe was broken in several places, and he sported a large bruise on his left temple. He didn't budge when Mokbar spoke to him and shook him. Lenissa searched for his pulse and checked his breathing. With a grim expression, she shook her head. "He's dead," she announced. The Klingon probably had been wounded during the fight— perhaps suffering an unfortunate fall—and their kidnappers had either been unable or unwilling to treat him. Now, he had died from his injury, which might have been treated in sickbay aboard the *Prometheus*. Even the *Bortas* sickbay might have been able to help him. "Barbarians," she hissed quietly.

Mokbar opened the dead man's eyes, looking into them deeply, before throwing his head back and looking up to the ceiling.

"No!" Kirk gasped. She lunged across the room to throw Mokbar down to the ground, silencing him with a hand across his mouth. She hissed something in Klingon.

He snarled something back at her harshly, shaking her off. Pleading, the engineer repeated her words.

The Klingon growled and turned away.

"What was that all about?" Lenissa wanted to know.

"He wanted to perform *Heghtay* for his fallen comrade," Kirk explained, "the Klingon death ritual. That involves shouting a warning to the Black Fleet that a new Klingon warrior is on his way to join them—something we really don't need right now."

"How did you change his mind?"

"By telling him that he can shout as much as he likes, when his shouting doesn't endanger us."

Lenissa's expression was grim. "Do you think our kidnappers intend to kill us?"

"I don't know. But..." Outside in the tunnel, the noise

increased. Kirk fell silent, putting a finger against her lips. She scurried along the rock wall until she stood next to the entrance, so she couldn't be seen from the tunnel. Lenissa joined her. Mokbar stood across the room from both women, facing the entrance.

I really hope they deactivate the energy field before realizing that they can't see us any longer, the young Andorian woman thought. The grip of her right hand tightened around the hilt of her knife.

A prisoner's first duty is the attempt to escape, her instructor had told them at the Academy. *Don't you ever just resign to your fate in the hope that someone will come to rescue you. The probability that you'll be dead by the time your colleagues find you is high.*

Lenissa heard the sound of chairs being shifted and bottles being opened. Apparently, there was some kind of lunch room next door. Her shoulders slumped. It didn't seem as if their kidnappers had any intention of looking in on them any time soon. She noticed that Kirk tilted her head slightly forward as if she was intently listening in. "Do you understand them as well?" the security chief whispered.

Jenna Kirk nodded. "Jassat taught me Renao—and I taught him Federation Standard," she answered quietly. "That was one of our favorite pastimes four years ago before he went to the Academy."

"You're a true linguist, Commander," Lenissa said admiringly.

Kirk shrugged. "Anyone can use universal translators. Now please, be quiet." She gestured at Mokbar that he should keep silent as well. They listened in tense silence. Kirk grimaced. She moved her mouth silently as she tried to comprehend what their kidnappers were saying.

"What are they talking about?" Lenissa whispered. Her

antennae moved restlessly on top of her head, trying to catch as much sensory input as possible. But all she sensed right now was the energy shield's electrical field that locked them in.

"They're discussing what to do with us," Kirk reported under her breath. "One of them suggests using us as leverage. They want to blackmail *Prometheus* and *Bortas* into leaving, by threatening them with our deaths."

"Captain Adams will never go along with that," Lenissa said. "Neither would Kromm. Besides, what good would it do? Even if the ships withdrew, nobody could keep the *Prometheus* or the *Bortas* from returning as soon as we were back aboard." *Or dead*.

"It sounds as if they're trying to bide their time. His comrades are also skeptical, but the man believes they only need a few more days to finish the ships."

"Ships? What kind of ships?"

"No idea, they didn't say."

Lenissa remembered the attacks on both Starbase 91 and the fleet base on Cestus III. Would the extremists modify even more Romulan *Scorpions*, transforming them into suicide bombers? They couldn't let that happen. "That plan won't work," she said. "Captain Adams will never yield to the demands of terrorists."

"That's what one of the guys out there reckons as well." Kirk hesitated and her eyes widened.

"What?" the young Andorian woman prompted. "Keep translating, Jenna. What's he saying?"

Jenna Kirk turned to face her. Her expression showed that she didn't like what she had just heard. "He suggests making an example of us." She swallowed. "He wants to throw us into purifying flames."

32
NOVEMBER 15, 2385

I.K.S. *Bortas*

"Captain?"

Kromm grunted irritably and kept walking. He wasn't in the mood to talk to his underlings. He'd done enough talking during the long and—in his eyes—useless briefing with Adams, the diplomats, and the red-skinned chieftains of Onferin. They were still none the wiser about the fate of his kidnapped crew, further warehouses and industrial plants on the planet had been searched for explosives and stolen Romulan goods to no avail, and worst of all… Qo'noS was still the target of ruthless terrorists. So what exactly should he talk about with his underlings? His anger? About the incompetence of Starfleet and their spineless sympathizers? Their inability to put their foot down and get things sorted? Martok himself had charged him with the mission Lembatta Cluster! It was his chance to gain glory and respect—*deserved* respect, not this pretense of him being the "hero of the *Ning'tao*" when he hadn't even been on board when the Klingon warship achieved her feat.

But the Federation were far too polite to assert themselves. Even when faced with the enemy they refused to clench their fists; instead, they relied on the oh-so-mighty power of diplomacy. No wonder they had stumbled from one existence-threatening crisis into another in recent years. Some time soon, Kromm assumed, someone would pull the floor out from under their feet. When that happened, he vowed as he stomped toward the bridge through the *Bortas*'s corridors, he would watch, raise a large jug of bloodwine, and laugh.

"Captain?"

Kromm stopped. He had clenched his fists without noticing; a gesture of triumph, following his fantasies. Furiously, he punched the corridor wall.

"What?" he barked at the lieutenant who was following him stubbornly.

Klarn was an officer of ambiguous character. Sometimes, his actions were of remarkable unscrupulousness, on other days he was as obnoxious as a *klongat* that was keen to mate. Now that his captain had finally turned around to face him, he visibly winced.

"Sir, I... we... there's something, you should know."

Kromm took one step toward Klarn. He knew that his rage was directed at Adams, Rozhenko, Spock, and the Renao. Klarn was merely the target, not the source. But that didn't make any difference right now. "I don't like to be disturbed while I'm thinking. Furthermore, I don't like it when someone follows me around like a Ferengi would follow a customer with a bursting purse." He had lowered his voice menacingly to no more than a hiss. "But least of all, I dislike being disturbed without receiving any coherent information. *What* exactly should I know, Lieutenant?"

Klarn swallowed hard. His eyes flickered around, and his hands trembled. He leaned forward, also lowering his voice.

"Not here, sir. Let's go down to deck twenty-four."

That was enough. Kromm jerked his *d'k tahg* from its sheath on his belt. Dim light reflected on the broad blade of the warrior weapon as he grabbed Klarn by the scruff of his neck, pressing the weapon against his throat.

"I'm not in the mood to repeat myself, Lieutenant," Kromm said, enjoying his furious heartbeat and the rush of blood in his ears. At last. Finally, he could let off some of the steam that the Federation had caused with their inaction. "And I believe that I have made myself perfectly clear."

Klarn licked his lips nervously. Again, he looked around to all sides, but they were alone in the corridor. No one would help him. And why should they?

"So, are you going to tell me why you believe you should badger me with your unbearable presence, or should my weapon draw blood?" Kromm laughed quietly. "I assure you, it would give me great pleasure. Today more than ever. Officers are replaceable, Klarn."

"Sir, I..." Klarn swallowed again. "I can't tell you out here in the corridor. It's about security!"

"In that case, talk to Rooth," the captain said, not lowering his weapon.

Klarn shook his head tentatively.

"No, sir. The security chief wouldn't be a good choice in this case."

The *d'k tahg* brushed against Klarn's twitching neck.

"Do you doubt the competence of my staff, Lieutenant?" Kromm asked menacingly. "You're part of that staff yourself—a fact that I'm very much regretting right now. Do you think that Rooth is a warrior without honor?" In his heart of heart he wished for that to be true. It would give him another reason to end Klarn's pitiful existence right here, right now. It would only require a decisive move of his wrist. His blade would do the rest. Oh, how he was longing for blood...

"Captain, with all due respect." Klarn's voice almost

broke. "The lieutenant commander would act differently in this matter. He would lack the required decisiveness. Besides, you're the captain. The glory should be yours and yours alone."

Kromm hesitated. "Glory?"

The lieutenant nodded gingerly. The corners of his mouth hinted at a weak smile. "Follow me down to deck twenty-four. I promise you will not regret it."

Kromm gave it some thought. He should just kill this pathetic little worm just to blow off some steam. The glint in his eyes, though... That wasn't fear, Kromm realized. It was the sparkle of someone who felt that victory was at hand.

"Deck twenty-four?" he asked.

Klarn nodded again. "I'll show you."

With a deep sigh the captain let go of Klarn, lowering his blade. "I'm warning you, Lieutenant. If you're wasting my time, then today will have been the last time that you've disturbed a superior officer."

Klarn straightened his uniform, taking a deep breath. "Don't worry, sir," he said with a firm voice and promising smile. "You're going to like it."

Kromm couldn't believe his luck. Speechless, he stood in front of the closed door to a small equipment room on deck twenty-four. His crew didn't frequent this deck very often, and this room was particularly difficult to find among the large freight containers and oily tools. In the door on eye level was a small hatch that could only be opened from the outside. Upon Klarn's advice, Kromm had just opened it to peek inside the equipment room. Since then, he'd been in awe.

"Who knows about this?" he asked when he finally found his voice.

"Just Ruut and me, Captain," Klarn answered. He stood right next to him, his shoulders squared and his eyes straight ahead. The glint in his eyes seemed brighter than the lights in the corridor. Klarn was proud—and highly satisfied.

"We picked them up on the planet's surface only a few hours ago. We had reason to believe that they have been in contact with the Purifying Flame."

"And?" Kromm prompted. In his mind he still pictured the two exhausted, scared, bleeding Renao—a man and a woman—held captive in that equipment room.

Klarn smiled an evil smile. "Ask them yourself, sir. As I said—you're the captain."

Kromm nodded. Indeed he was. And it was about time that he began acting like one. He should take matters into his own hands, instead of complying with Rozhenko, Adams, Spock, and the others. How had Grotek from the High Council put it? Qo'noS was longing for a solution to the Renao problem. One that deserved the term "solution" and didn't base itself on idle talk. Suddenly, Kromm felt as if a huge treasure had landed in his lap. Martok had given him a chance, and now it was up to him to use it.

"So Adams doesn't know that these two Renao are aboard the *Bortas*?" he asked Klarn.

"You just spoke to him, sir." Klarn's grin increased. "Did he ask after them?"

"No."

"There you go. Presumably, the cat commander forgot that he had sent us to catch the couple."

Kromm drew a sharp breath. "What are you talking about? Commander Roaas knows about this?"

"So what if he does?" The lieutenant shook his head dismissively. "They have other concerns on the *Prometheus* than two insignificant Renao."

"Perhaps for the moment—but eventually, they will remember that these two have disappeared. They will quickly determine that the suspects can only be here aboard our ship!" Kromm couldn't believe it. How could one man be so stupid?

Again, Klarn shook his head. "Not if we have answers before then."

Irritably, Kromm stifled a curse. *Answers*, he repeated in his mind. Of course, Klarn was probably right! If these Renao were in the hands of Adams and his pets rather than here aboard the *Bortas*, they would take a lot longer to disclose what they knew, because Starfleet would treat them completely different from the way Klarn had done during the past few hours. And that meant wasting valuable time.

Klarn has done the right thing, Kromm realized. *He brought them here instead of taking them to Starfleet. And to prevent them from using that against me, he had waited to see if they would ask questions of their whereabouts.*

"Are they talking?"

Klarn pointed at the control panel next to the door. "Ask them. Just input the entrance code, and the door will open."

Without taking his eyes off his lieutenant, Kromm pulled the *d'k tahg* from its sheath again. "Oh, I intend to do far more than that," he snarled, grinning. Klarn grinned back.

Captain Kromm opened the door. He had only taken one step into the room when the woman began whining. These noises were music in his ears.

33
NOVEMBER 15, 2385

Konuhbi, Onferin

"*Bortas to Captain Kromm.*"

"What do you want, L'emka?"

"*Sir, where are you? We have a priority message for you from Captain Adams, but the computer says you're no longer aboard the ship. And—*"

Kromm interrupted his first officer with glee. "I don't like your tone of voice, Commander. And it's neither your nor Captain Adams's business where I am. I'm busy."

"*With all due respect, Captain, you can't simply—*"

"What I can or can't do is my decision, Commander! I'm the captain! And I'm telling you that I am busy with an important task." He smiled sardonically. "So you can tell Adams, he can talk to you or to Rozhenko for all I care. That's all he ever does, anyway."

Silence. Two seconds later L'emka's voice came from the communicator on his sleeve.

"*Understood, sir,*" she confirmed. "*May I inquire nonetheless where you are?*"

"Where I should be, Commander," he answered, and a confident growl came from his throat. "Almost there. Kromm out."

As soon as he had closed the channel, he pulled out his disruptor, turning around to face his escort. Klarn, Ruut, and three members of his security team waited a few meters behind him for his orders. Without a word, Kromm walked over to them, looked at Klarn and nodded.

"We're ready, Lieutenant. Let's end this."

"With the utmost pleasure, Captain," Klarn replied. He lifted the disruptor rifle in his hands, aimed at the opening mechanism of the inconspicuous door in front of him and fired.

Then things started to happen very fast. The door looked like all the other doors on this level of the arcology. Its simple structure could not withstand the beam of channeled energy. A few fractions of a second later, its security mechanism had been destroyed, and Ruut advanced with the three soldiers into the small house.

His people hurried from one room in the small Renao flat to the next, but they found nothing. Concerned, he shot Klarn a glance. Were they too late?

Suddenly, he heard Ruut cry out, "Here! Captain, I've got him."

"Leave him alive, Ruut," Kromm shouted back. Grinning, he clapped Klarn on the shoulder. "I'll do the rest."

Klarn and he entered the back room.

Joruul ak Bhedal didn't live very comfortably, Kromm noticed at first glance. He really had imagined a hatemonger's dwelling to be much more interesting. Not that he knew much about Renao interior furnishing—and frankly, he didn't give a *warrigul*'s wet fart about it—but even to him it was more than obvious that the shabby furnishings didn't bear witness to wealth.

Kromm followed his security detail into the back room. There was ak Bhedal flat on his back on a small bed consisting of several cushions and blankets. Ruut prevented him from getting up with a disruptor. The bland bed was next to the perma-concrete wall, on which the Purifying Flame's emblem had been painted.

Ak Bhedal didn't move. He was older than the two suspects Klarn had found. All he wore were wide black pants. Even the traditional facial jewelry was missing. He had raised his hands and he was pursing his lips. The expression of his violet glowing eyes was cold. He glared at Kromm.

"Joruul ak Bhedal?" Kromm asked, as he crouched beside the prone man. He tucked away his disruptor, smiling sardonically, and pulled out his *d'k tahg*. "My name is Kromm. I'm either the captain of the I.K.S. *Bortas*, or the deliverer of terrible pain—it's up to you."

The Renao didn't say anything. They had woken him from his sleep. Only when Kromm brushed the tip of his blade across his chest, slowly moving toward his crotch, the man's lips began to twitch.

"Yes?" Kromm prompted him. "You want to talk? Is that right? So, talk: where are my crewmembers that you have abducted?"

"You won't hear a word from me!" the Renao whispered. Fury flickered in his eyes, and his fingers twitched. "You hear me? Not a single word."

Kromm grinned, looking up to Klarn. "That's interesting. Ak Busal and ak Lavoor said exactly the same thing to start with—and later, they didn't want to stop talking at all."

"And we didn't even have to torture them to death, sir," his lieutenant added.

Kromm's grin became even bigger. "Oh well," he said with carefully rehearsed airiness, "at least not both of them."

Ak Bhedal started to perspire rather profusely. "Who are you speaking of, Klingon? I don't know these names."

"Just as you don't know this, presumably," Kromm said, pulling a crumbled flyer from his uniform pocket. It showed the emblem of the Purifying Flame. "We found this in ak Busal's quarters." He pointed at the symbol on ak Bhedal's wall. "It seems you have something in common with them."

"Not just that, Captain," Lieutenant Kroge spoke up behind Kromm. When Kromm turned around, the security man stood right behind him holding a stack of flyers in his hands. He must have found them in another room. "They all like political pamphlets. But our host here seems to be much closer to their origin than ak Busal, sir. The room next door is full of these things. Propaganda material and inflammatory pamphlets against us, against Romulus, against Earth…"

"That corroborates ak Busal's statement," Klarn said.

Kromm nodded. He looked at the Renao again, moving his blade another two hands' widths further down. "Did you poison the youths' minds, my friend?" he asked quietly. "Did you plant your wicked philosophies into their young heads? Did you tell them about the galactic harmony that people like me allegedly destroy? Did you want them to spread your twisted ideas throughout the world, just like ak Busal and ak Lavoor did out there in Massoa, so they could find more followers for you?"

The Renao stared silently at the ceiling of his sparsely furnished bedroom. Kromm knew this expression. The man knew that he was finished. He just didn't want to give Kromm the satisfaction of admitting it.

"You know something?" Kromm continued quietly in an almost friendly tone, while the tip of his *d'k tahg* gently toyed with ak Bhedal's black waistband. "Do you know what we call people like you on Qo'noS? Oh, the Federation probably has lots of names for the likes of you. They would refer to you as demagogues—radicals who are delusional and dangerous. But in *my* home?" He shook his head. "For us, you're a source of information, my friend. Nothing more."

Ak Bhedal still remained silent. Abruptly, Kromm took a swing with his free hand, hitting him hard in the face with a faint crack. Blood trickled out of the Renao's nose, ran down his cheek and seeped on the pillow. Ak Bhedal didn't even flinch.

"Where does your pathetic group of fanatics hold my officers captive?" Kromm snarled into ak Bhedal's left ear.

"Burn in Aoul's fire!" the Renao cried.

Captain Kromm smiled coldly. "Oh, I will. Without a doubt. But you first." And he stabbed him.

Somewhere on Onferin

When their kidnappers came to take them, they were prepared—at least Lenissa thought they were. Without any equipment, Jenna Kirk wasn't able to shut down the energy field that blocked the entrance to their subterranean prison, so they returned to their positions by the wall, put their ropes carefully back in place and pulled the sacks back over their heads—not before they had carefully cut eye slits into them, using the sharp edges of Grakk's armor. Their hands behind their backs, they waited for the Renao, hoping to attack them when the time was right.

Finally, four Renao came. Lenissa peered through her eye slits. The men were masked with black cloth. She saw one of them shutting down the energy field. They entered and each approached one of the prisoners. None of them had drawn a weapon but they carried pistols of an unknown design in holsters on their belts.

"Who's there?" Kirk asked, pretending to be frightened.

"Be quiet!" said the man who approached her. "Come."

Lenissa's captor grabbed her by her upper arm, hauling her to her feet. As soon as she stood upright, the ropes around her ankles, which were only loosely draped, fell to the ground.

The man made a surprised sound. Lenissa used this brief moment of distraction to bring her hands forward and turn sideways so that his flank was exposed to her. With her right hand, she tore the hood from her head, while she aimed at his throat with her left hand. At the same time, she yanked her leg up, kicking him in the knee from behind. The combined leverage effect made her kidnapper bend his knees while tumbling backward.

Behind her, Lenissa heard a deafening roar when Mokbar attacked his opponent. Beyond that, she didn't pay any attention to the progress of the other fights and concentrated on her opponent. She faced her staggering kidnapper, striking at his throat for the second time. Much to her annoyance, he wore some sort of scarf around his neck, which softened her blow.

The Renao slammed into the wall. His hand jerked to the holster, drawing the pistol. Just when he wanted to lift his arm, Lenissa moved her left hand fast as lightning, grabbing the pistol's barrel and pulling it aside. With her right hand, she hammered against the inside of his wrist, disarming the Renao. She wanted to take two steps back to put some distance between her and her opponent, so she could lift the pistol.

Right at that moment, a body slammed into her and she staggered. Hastily, she fired a shot. The glittering blue beam crackled, but missed and hit the stone wall. Taking advantage of the momentum, Lenissa dropped to the ground, rolling backward. When she came up onto her knees, she raised the pistol again.

Very quickly she assessed the situation. One of the Renao was on the ground, motionless. Mokbar had struck him down with all the might of a furious Klingon. The second Renao still wrestled with the infuriated engineer. Her opponent just pushed himself off the back wall of the room, but he was unarmed. The final kidnapper who had thrown Kirk against Lenissa posed the biggest threat. He held his beam pistol in his hands. Before Lenissa managed to pull the trigger, he fired a shot. The stun beam hissed through the room, hitting Jenna Kirk. Her body convulsed and she collapsed.

Lenissa fired a fraction of a second later, cutting down the Renao. The Renao she had been fighting lunged toward his fallen comrade, trying to seize his weapon. He rolled sideways, took aim and fired at the same time as Lenissa. His shot came too quickly, though, and since it hadn't been properly aimed he missed the Andorian woman by an antennae's length. Her shot, on the other hand, hit him dead center. This was why she practiced her marksmanship every day on the *Prometheus*'s holodeck.

We're going to make it! Lenissa thought.

In the back of the room Mokbar head-butted his opponent who collapsed with a sigh. But at the same time three blue beams hissed into the room from the door, hitting the Klingon in the chest, stomach, and thigh. He howled in agony, threw his arms up in the air and staggered backward before collapsing unconscious.

Three additional Renao stormed into the room, pointing their weapons at Lenissa. "Put weapon down!" one of the men screamed at them in broken Federation Standard. His ruby red eyes glowed like molten lava.

Lenissa glared back at the men. Her antennae jerked forward like daggers as she raised her pistol. *For the Prometheus!* she thought and fired.

One of the men fell. The other two fired back. A terrible pain jolted through Lenissa zh'Thiin's highly strung neural pathways before everything went dark.

She was rudely awakened by a slap in her face. "Wake up!" a man with a rough voice demanded.

Lenissa squinted against the red light of a miner's lamp.

Her head felt as if it was about to explode, and a piercing pain seemed to have settled in her chest. She probably had a few fractured ribs. She attempted to move, but soon realized that her arms and legs had been bound again.

Quickly she tried to find her bearings. They were still inside the mining tunnel, but in a more open area this time. Crates had been stacked in one corner, and the remains of some canned dinner had been left on a simple metal table. Kirk, Mokbar, and Grakk were tied up and lay next to her on the ground. More Renao woke them and pulled them to their knees. Unlike Lenissa, the other three had sacks over their heads again, though why they'd bothered with Grakk was anybody's guess.

One man standing opposite her with a small black box in his hand caught her attention.

Her tormentor, who had masked himself with a cloth again, leaned down to her. "What you did wasn't very smart," he said with a noticeable accent. "One of my comrades is dead. You're going to pay for that, I swear."

"You also killed one of my comrades," Lenissa snapped. "And you kidnapped us. What do you expect? That we apologize for our attempted escape?"

"Defiant shrew!" The man hit her over the head, striking one of her antennae. A terrible pain jolted through Lenissa, and she gasped. The Renao could not have known that antennae were the most sensitive body parts of an Andorian. She tried to hide her agony but wasn't entirely successful, and her opponent noticed it. Surprised, he looked at her. His gaze wandered back to her antennae, and the menacing glow in his eyes intensified. "You're a coward," Lenissa spat at him, hoping to distract him. "Hitting someone who is tied up…"

"Someone who knows how to put up a fight when she's not tied up, as I have noticed," he replied. "But you're not important. Even I am not important. The only thing of importance is the Harmony of the Spheres. And I'm prepared to do *anything* to restore it."

The man grabbed Lenissa's left antenna, squeezing it hard. She drew a sharp breath and doubled over. She felt dizzy, and she almost vomited. Tears of fury and desperation welled in her eyes. The Renao turned to his companion with the black box.

"Start the recording!" he demanded.

34
NOVEMBER 15, 2385

U.S.S. *Prometheus*

Richard Adams clenched his fists. He felt himself trembling with fury. The captain didn't like to lose control, but he couldn't help himself in this situation.

"We repeat again, to make sure you understand perfectly well," said a masked man in the recording that the *Prometheus* and the *Bortas* had received a few minutes ago from an untraceable source. *"If you don't remove your ships from orbit by the eighth hour Auroun local time, and if you don't leave the Lembatta Cluster within two days, these hostages will suffer and die. We are prepared to sacrifice everything and anything for the Harmony of the Spheres—including the lives of your officers."*

The man grabbed Lieutenant Commander zh'Thiin from behind by the collar of her dirty and partially ripped uniform. Just like the others, the young Andorian woman kneeled in front of four heavily armed extremists. Unlike Kirk and the two Klingons she didn't have a hood covering her face. It was obvious that she had been beaten. Blood had dried on her lip, and her left cheek looked dark blue and swollen. One antenna had been badly mangled.

The recording zoomed onto Lenissa's face. The man's face also came into view when he bent down to her. Only two glowing red eyes and a small strip of red skin were visible.

"Look closely. Look at her face. You will not recognize it

when we're done with her. Unless you give up. If not, you will be responsible for everything that will follow. The Purifying Flame will and must bring new order to the galaxy. Nothing will stop us. Nothing."

The image froze. Zh'Thiin's eyes were full of pain, fury and shame; those of the man were full of fanaticism, which sent a shiver down Adams's spine.

"Switch it off," he said.

Lieutenant John Paxon obeyed. The face of zh'Thiin's deputy chief of security, who had been born and raised on Starbase 7 in the Andorian sector, showed barely suppressed rage.

Without a word, Adams sat in his command chair in the center of the bridge. Beta shift had started an hour ago. He had been in his ready room, writing a report for Admiral Akaar when they had received the recording a few minutes ago.

Lieutenant Commander Senok, the Vulcan commander of the Beta shift, stood beside the chair. His hands were clasped behind his back, his face stony. Senok had called the captain to the bridge immediately.

Taking a deep breath, Adams rose, straightening his uniform tunic. "Ensign Harris," he turned to the communications officer on duty. "Summon the entire executive staff to the conference room. Additionally, call Counselor Courmont and Ambassador Spock. And inform the Klingons."

"Yes, Captain," Harris said. Her fingers danced across the console.

"Mr. Paxon." Adams nodded invitingly at the security officer. "You're with me."

"Aye, sir."

Both left the bridge and followed the corridor to the conference room. Adams had an idea. "Computer, is Lieutenant ak Namur back on board yet?"

"Negative."

Adams had half expected that. If Jassat had returned from his mission on Onferin, he would have reported to him immediately. The captain touched the combadge on his chest. "Adams to bridge."

"Bridge here, sir," Senok replied.

"Put me in touch with Lieutenant ak Namur."

"Right away, Captain."

The turbolift reached its destination, and they stepped out into the corridor.

The young Renao's voice sounded over Adams's combadge, dotted with static from atmospheric interference. *"Lieutenant ak Namur here, Captain."*

"Lieutenant, report. Have you found a trace to our kidnappers?"

Ak Namur hesitated briefly. *"I'm... I'm sorry, sir, but no. I really don't know what's going on here. The mood here in Konuhbi is very different from Auroun. It's a mixture of paranoia and religious radicalism. I don't have any explanation for that. I'm finding it very difficult to talk to the locals. Some don't seem to be able to help me; others give me the feeling they don't want to help. Although I'm not wearing a Starfleet uniform, the fact that I'm interested in outworlders seems to make me suspicious."*

"Understood." Adams had been afraid of that when he had sent Jassat on his mission. But he had to grasp that last straw if there was even the slightest glimmer of hope that this might help him to save his people's lives. "Keep trying, Lieutenant. The situation has deteriorated."

"I'm doing my best, sir." Ak Namur's voice was firm, but

there was an underlying hint of desperation. The young Renao really wanted to help; to prove that his people were good, and that the extremists were deluded exceptions to that rule. Failing to do so must have been causing him terrible discomfort, but Adams wasn't able to take away these inner demons. Not now.

"I know you are. Adams out." The captain closed the link. The door opened and Spock walked in.

"Captain. I am glad we both arrived at the same time. I have news from Romulus."

"Good news, I hope," Adams replied glumly.

"Perhaps," Spock said. "The mystery surrounding the *Scorpion* ship used for the attack on Starbase 91 seems to have been solved. My contact on Romulus told me about an illegal black-market network. It would seem they are smuggling Romulan military technology as well as dangerous substances from the Achernar system out of their empire. Evidently, the Renao purchased several *Scorpion* attack fighters that had been previously decommissioned. I would surmise that they have dismantled them in order to re-create them. He has also discovered indications that the Renao acquired trilithium and protomatter."

"How much?"

"The materials they probably still have at their disposal should be sufficient to carry out another twelve attacks of the same magnitude as before. However, they might also have access to other sources."

Adams shook his head, pursing his lips. "That's not good."

"Indeed," Spock agreed.

"And where's the good news?"

"I have contacted the Romulan government and have advised them—including Praetor Kamemor herself—of the illegal activities. I expect that the operations on Achernar will cease before long, and that the instigators will be rendered harmless by the Tal Shiar or the Romulan military. That will only marginally diminish the imminent danger originating from the fanatics—it will, however, limit their resources in future."

The captain glanced at Spock gratefully. "That's better than nothing—and at least a small beacon of hope in these dark times."

The ambassador bowed his head. "May I ask why you called this meeting?"

"You'll find out in a minute," Adams replied.

Again the door opened and Roaas and Mendon came in. Carson, Courmont, Barai, and the deputy chief engineer Tabor Resk—a Bajoran—followed shortly after them.

"What's wrong, Captain?" Courmont asked when all of them had gathered around the table. "Do we have news from the kidnap victims?"

"Yes, and it's not good." Impatiently, Adams looked toward the door. He tapped his combadge. "Adams to bridge."

"Bridge here."

"Where are the Klingons?"

"Captain Kromm said he will be with you soon."

Frowning, Adams listened. He wondered what kept Kromm, but decided that that was the least of his problems. "All right, thank you." The captain glanced at his staff. "I guess we'll begin."

Everyone sat down, and Adams played the recording that he had just watched on the bridge. Roaas's ears twitched, and Mendon blinked hectically. The others watched with grim and horrified expressions.

"All right," Adams said to no one in particular once the recording had finished. "We need to get our people out of there. As soon as possible. Suggestions?"

"I've been trying to lock onto Lieutenant Commander Kirk and Lieutenant Commander zh'Thiin with the *Prometheus*'s biosensors ever since their disappearance," Mendon said. "Lieutenant Commander zh'Thiin should be especially easy to spot because the bioreadings of Andorians and Renao are vastly different. Unfortunately, the planet's dense atmosphere and the radiation from the system's primary star are interfering with sensors."

"We're working on fine-tuning the sensors," added Tabor, "sacrificing range for precision by filtering out currently unwanted data. Unfortunately, this means our search will take more time because we can only lock on a limited surface area."

"We should focus on the region of Konuhbi," Adams said. "We don't have any evidence that the kidnappers took the hostages out of town."

"We also don't have any evidence that they didn't," Roaas pointed out.

"True, but it's the right place to start. The attack was fast and purposeful. That indicates that the Purifying Flame have an operational base within that city or its immediate surroundings. You don't give up a good operational base, least of all when you know that your opponent doesn't have any local knowledge, and that their technology is jammed by environmental circumstances."

"Captain, maybe we could increase the sensors' resolution if we separate the *Prometheus* and work with triangulation," Paxon suggested. "It might have the same effect as a linked sensor grid during a fleet operation."

"Not a bad idea," Adams said.

"Captain, how much of a risk are you prepared to take?" Carson asked.

"What do you mean, Carson?"

"The *Prometheus* is inherently capable of flying in an atmosphere, and of landing," his second officer replied. "Even when she's separated, it's possible to enter into an atmosphere, although that would require an enormous amount of energy for the primary hull. Hypothetically speaking… if we were to put Lieutenant Paxon's plan of triangulation into action, we could enter deep into Onferin's atmosphere to reduce the interfering effect from Aoul. At the same time, we would fly below the strongly reflecting gas levels in the upper atmosphere and avoid them."

Adams mulled over what he had just heard. "Commander, what do you think?" he asked Roaas.

The Caitian nodded. "We should be able to pull that off. If you want…"

He was interrupted by Captain Kromm who stormed into the conference room, escorted by security chief Rooth, another Klingon officer Adams didn't recognize, and Alexander Rozhenko who appeared to be somewhat out of sorts.

"Captain, I've a lead," the Klingon announced without greeting. Pride stood in his eyes—and overt arrogance. "I know where the captives are."

Spock raised an eyebrow.

Adams looked at him skeptically. He didn't dare hope that Kromm spoke the truth. "Where did you get that information?"

"My people investigated, just like yours," Kromm replied.

Adams didn't like the tone of voice Kromm used, but he decided that this problem could wait. "Where are they?"

Kromm bared his teeth. "I thought you'd never ask…"

35
NOVEMBER 15, 2385

Konuhbi, Onferin

The entrance to the tunnel system where the extremists were
hiding was located in a canyon that a river had washed into
the gray-brown rocks of a mountain range. The place twelve
kellicams south of Konuhbi was an excellent hideout. Scattered
ore and mineral deposits in the stone disrupted transporter and
sensor locks from orbit. The canyon was very narrow, so landing
an aircraft required a masterly performance from any pilot.

The only option to approach the hideout was using a
ground vehicle, which gave the defenders ample time to
prepare for any arrivals. But the Renao fanatics had not
reckoned with the Klingon Defense Force and Starfleet.

"Report!" Kromm ordered. He was in command of a
task force of ten people, preparing for their attack. Behind
them was the *Prometheus* shuttle that they had landed on the
sloped summit. Kromm would have preferred to fly down
to Onferin in one of his own heavily armed shuttles, but
even he couldn't deny that Starfleet had more sophisticated
transporter technology, and that was part of their attack plan.
On this world full of jamming sources, reliable technology
was worth more to him than his Klingon pride. Besides, there
was no honor to be gained by transporting their troops from
one place to another. The imminent fight would bring him the
honor he so desperately sought.

"I can see two guards down there. There's also a concealed camera above the entrance," the deputy security chief from the *Prometheus* reported. Paxon lay prone at the edge of the chasm, peering through his phaser rifle's electronic sight.

"Moore, switch on the directional interfering field," Commander Roaas said to a woman with cropped blonde hair. He was the second-in-command to Kromm.

"Aye, sir." She pressed a button on her mobile device, pointing its parabolic antenna toward the canyon. "Visual and radio transmissions interrupted."

The Caitian turned to Paxon. "Mr. Paxon, take out the guards."

"Understood, Commander." The security man took aim and shot twice in short succession. Golden light flashes flared into the canyon. "Targets down," he reported.

Kromm stepped to the edge. He looked down into the ravine and saw two people lying next to the tunnel's entrance between the rocks. "Are they dead?"

"No, sir," answered Paxon. "Commander Roaas ordered to set all weapons to stun."

The Klingon snorted. "Bah." He glanced at the *Prometheus*'s first officer derisively. "Don't expect such mercy from us Klingons."

"Everyone fights in their own way, Captain." The Caitian's reply was grim but calm.

"As long as we can free the hostages, I don't care." Kromm turned to his people.

"Back to the shuttle. We're beaming down."

They materialized in shimmering columns of light at the bottom of the canyon. The guards still lay motionless where they had fallen. In front of them stood the entrance—a dark hole that looked like the black maw of a monster in the twilight between the towering mountainsides. Nothing moved, which indicated that they hadn't been spotted yet.

"Ready weapons," Kromm said.

Lieutenant Klarn and the three *bekks* escorting them raised their disruptors. Klarn as communications officer had no place on this mission, but he had insisted on participating in the rescue operation. Since they owed the trace that had led them here to his initiative, Kromm had agreed. He liked Klarn's way of thinking. Unlike L'emka, he didn't shy away from doing what had to be done to bring honor to the Empire in general and the *Bortas* in particular. *Maybe I should promote him to a post with more responsibilities,* Kromm pondered. *Such as security chief, for example. Rooth isn't getting any younger.* But that was for after the battle.

Beside him, Commander Roaas, Paxon, and the three from the *Prometheus*—Moore, another human called Cenia, and a Tellarite by the name of Gral—took their positions. They activated their belts, bringing up the personal deflector shields, and pointed their phaser rifles at the entrance.

Nodding, Roaas looked at Kromm. "Let's go in, Captain."

The Klingon growled affirmatively and took point. Starfleet captains might send their underlings into battle; Kromm preferred fighting battles himself.

With their weapons at the ready they advanced into the tunnel. When it grew darker, they switched the small spotlights on their rifles on. Rough-hewn stone with veins of glittering mineral deposits surrounded them.

Paxon pulled his tricorder out. "Tekasite, sir," he said. "We probably shouldn't fire with maximum power, else these tunnels might blow up around us."

With an irritable grunt the captain motioned toward his men to adjust their weapons accordingly. It was sufficient to kill their opponents; they didn't need to vaporize them. In the next moment, he frowned. The tunnel turned out to be a blind alley.

"What's this?" Confused, he hit the stone wall with his fist.

Roaas shouldered his rifle. "Lieutenant, give me your tricorder."

Paxton obeyed and the first officer made a few adjustments, before sweeping the area with the device. His whiskers twitched and he smiled. "Thought so."

"What?" Kromm demanded.

"A holographic wall, here on the left." Roaas pointed at the rock.

Kromm tried hitting that point with his gun stock. There was a small discharge, a crackling noise, and the wall flickered. "Where did these fanatics get holowalls from?"

"From the same source as their protomatter and *Scorpions*," the Caitian replied. "The galactic black market. For people detesting transgression of spheres so much, the Renao do an awful lot of interstellar trading."

"They are mad," Kromm said. "Don't waste logic on them." He motioned toward his men. "Switch off the energy barrier."

Klarn and the other three men took aim.

"Wait, sir," Moore asked. "Let me do that. I should be able to short circuit the energy field without them noticing."

Kromm grunted. "Very well, but hurry." He was keen to fight.

The blond took the tricorder from Roaas and inspected the wall. Finally, she kneeled down, pulling out her phaser. She directed the beam at the wall and cut through it with surgical precision. The generator behind the wall packed up with a muffled bang, and the fake wall disintegrated. A long tunnel, lit by reddish miner's lamps came into view. In the distance they heard faint voices.

"Let's go." Kromm again took point and pressed ahead.

A moment later an alarm sounded through the subterranean tunnels.

Lenissa zh'Thiin looked up when the piercing sound of a pit siren started wailing. She couldn't see anything because they had put the sack back over her head, but she heard men shouting and sensed that everyone went into a frenzy. She thought she heard shots being fired in the distance.

"Jenna," she whispered.

"I hear it," the engineer whispered. "It sounds like our people are coming to set us free."

Mokbar growled something in his mother tongue that Lenissa didn't understand.

"Klingons," he added in Federation Standard. "Disruptors."

"He's right," the Andorian woman said. "That's not just phaser fire. I can hear Klingon weapons as well." She began to hope that they might survive this day after all.

Someone grabbed Lenissa's legs and untied them, before clasping her arm. "Get up!" one of her captors demanded.

The security chief didn't make any effort to follow that instruction, but she was hauled to her feet. Finally, the sack was pulled off her head. This time, the Renao wasn't masked. The combined attack from Starfleet and Klingons must have come as a surprise to this cell of extremists. For the first time, Lenissa could see her tormentor's face. He seemed surprisingly young, not a year older than she was. Despite his youth, he had a grim aura and in his violet eyes burnt a flame that would have been regarded as a sign of madness in other species.

"Come with me," the man snapped at her. "If you refuse…" He slapped her antennae which sent a nauseating pain through her skull.

Kirk and Mokbar were also hauled onto their feet next to Lenissa. A few men with outdated-looking guns scurried past them. Two more Renao threw stuff into a crate in the room next door. *They're trying to escape*, Lenissa realized. *So their defense must be faltering.* She had to buy some time… somehow.

The man raised his hand again.

"No!" she shouted. Her shoulders and antennae slumped forward as she feigned capitulation. "I'm coming."

"Let's go then." The man turned to his comrades, issuing orders before they all rushed off.

"They're taking us to some ships," Kirk translated what she heard.

Lenissa was surprised. "They have ships down here?"

"Apparently."

"We need to buy some time."

"Quiet!" her captor demanded, dragging her with him. Lenissa allowed herself to be hauled forward but a few steps later she stumbled at a ledge and fell. The impact was hard because she couldn't soften it with her hands but she accepted that, if her ploy would only work.

The Renao cursed as she almost brought him down with her. He managed to steady himself at the last moment. He grabbed Lenissa's uniform tunic and yanked her to her feet. At the same time he pulled his weapon—an old-fashioned model that shot projectiles—from his belt. Panting, he held the muzzle of the archaic looking killing tool under her nose. "No silly tricks, or you'll regret it."

Lenissa glared at him. "Oh really? If you wanted to kill us, we'd be dead by now. So you obviously need us as insurance."

"Not *all* of you," the man replied. He turned around, pointing his gun at Jenna Kirk.

Horrified, the engineer's eyes widened—as did the eyes of the man clutching her arm. Before one of them had a chance to say anything, the man with the weapon fired a shot at point blank range. The pistol's report was deafening in the narrow corridor, and Kirk winced. She yelped in horror and stared aghast at her right upper arm, where a blood stain expanded slowly.

"Are you going to do what I say now, or should I shoot her in the stomach as well?" the man asked. "You have no idea how painful these bullets are when they hit your body."

Kirk had turned pale, and she was grinding her teeth, while swaying back and forth. She was probably just short of fainting.

Hesitantly, Lenissa gave up her resistance. She was ready to die for the ideals and the protection of Starfleet. But it was also her duty to protect the *Prometheus* crew. Besides, dying in these dimly lit tunnels was pointless. They had to live and continue fighting if they wanted a chance to put a stop to the terrorists' activities.

"You will pay for that," she said quietly.

The Renao shook his head. "No, you will pay—for quite a lot, as it happens."

Kromm leaped behind a metal crate to take cover. Where he had stood a moment before, a blinding energy bolt cut through the tunnel's cold air. The Klingon lifted his disruptor rifle and fired back. One Renao was hit. Screaming, he whirled around before collapsing with a gaping, smoldering hole in his chest.

Kromm growled, satisfied. This mission finally began to take a turn to his liking.

His people's shots hissed through the tunnel next to him. Across the corridor stood Starfleet officers, firing short, precise bursts of fire. The Tellarite Gral was hit on the hip. His personal shield flickered yellow and disintegrated. The fight had been going on for several minutes, and the protective energy fields had increasing difficulties handling the ballistic projectiles that the Renao fired from their outdated weapons. Another shot hit Gral in the arm, and he dropped his weapon.

"Retreat," Roaas ordered the Tellarite. "You can't do much here."

"Negative, Commander," answered Gral. He bent down, picking up his rifle with his left hand. "I still have a second arm."

In front of them another defender fell to the ground. The rest of the Renao took to their heels.

"Charge!" Kromm shouted and ran. The others followed suit.

Suddenly, the tunnel exploded.

A thunderclap echoed through the tunnels. Lenissa felt a strong draft in her back. Dust fell from the ceiling.

Her kidnapper grinned ominously.

"That should keep your friends busy—if they're not dead already. Fools! Did they really think we weren't prepared for an attack?"

Lenissa spat a curse in her mother tongue at him, as she had run out of ideas. She prayed to Uzaveh, the Infinite and Eternal, that none of her friends had been caught in the explosion. The notion that Roaas, Carson, or Geron had died trying to rescue her was unbearable.

The three Renao kept running, dragging Lenissa, Mokbar, and the injured Kirk with them. They rounded a corner into a vast cave with a high ceiling. Lenissa's eyes widened when she spotted almost two dozen small space ships scattered around the cave. Most of them were small transports for freight and passengers, but in one corner were three large, sleek ships with prominent weapons systems.

A frenzy of activity surrounded the vessels. The Renao loaded freight containers and barrels with dangerous goods symbols. *This is larger than I thought,* Lenissa thought. She wondered whether they had been taken to the secret headquarters of the Purifying Flame.

The back of the cave was open, looking out onto a craggy mountain landscape. The young Andorian woman was confused for a moment. Such a big opening in the rock would have been a much better starting point for an attack from the combined Starfleet and Klingon task force. Why did her companions fight their way through the narrow tunnels? But then she spotted a slight flicker in the air before the panoramic view. *A holographic field.* These terrorists never ceased to amaze her. They attacked with *Scorpions*—but they fired projectile weapons. They hid in caves—yet they concealed the entrances behind sophisticated holotechnology.

Their guide ushered her toward one of the shuttles. "Get in there. We're leaving Onferin."

"Where are you taking us?" Kirk enquired, panting. Her uniform sleeve was drenched in blood but she bravely stayed on her feet.

The man glanced at her derisively. "You'll find out, won't you? Get in!"

"No!" With a strong yank, Lenissa managed to break free from the Renao and started running. She had no idea where she should run to, but she knew that she could *not* climb aboard that spacecraft. If the Renao escaped with them aboard that ship, she, Kirk, and Mokbar were as good as dead.

The man shouted something after her that she didn't understand. Two Renao, a man and woman, hauling a container into the cargo hold dropped it and ran toward Lenissa, trying to intercept her. The security chief bent forward, ramming her shoulder into the woman, flinging her aside. She avoided the man who attempted to grab her with a quick sidestep before kicking him between the legs, hoping that he was as delicate in that spot as most humanoid males were. He was.

She heard the report of a shot behind her—not the humming of a stun beam but a shot from the projectile weapons.

Lenissa ducked her head and kept running across the cave in the vague hope that she would buy some time for their rescuers to reach them. A bullet ricocheted off the outer hull of a shuttle. Another one hit the ground in front of her feet. She wanted to take cover behind a stack of crates when she felt a burning sensation on her thigh. A hot streak of pain jolted through her and she lost her footing. Lenissa screamed and staggered. She wanted to limp on but the leg gave way underneath her. Panting she collapsed on the ground.

A few seconds later her tormentor had reached her. He bent down to her, hitting her in the face with a fist. "You…"

Another hit. "… are…" Another hit. "… driving me…" A fourth hit. "…crazy."

Lenissa lost consciousness.

Coughing, Kromm got to his feet. Dust hung in the air in the corridor and small pieces of rock covered the ground. His arms and legs were stinging where tiny stone fragments had hit him. He shook off the pain like a *targ* did unwanted parasites from its fur.

Kromm glanced around. Two members of his task force had been hit hard. One of the warriors—Klarn—was still alive, but his leg had been crushed by a large rock. It was uncertain how long he would last without treatment. One of the Starfleet members lay motionless on the ground—the Tellarite Gral whose personal shield had failed shortly before the blast. His crushed skull didn't leave any doubts as to whether he was still alive or not. All others had been lucky. They'd been thrown to the ground by the blast but their shields seemed to have prevented serious injuries. Groaning, they scrambled to their feet.

The captain bent down to pick up the disruptor that he had dropped. "Bocar," he addressed one of his people. "Take care of Klarn. Get him outside and make sure he's beamed to the shuttle. Then catch up to us."

"Yes, Captain," Bocar confirmed, shouldering the injured man.

Kromm took a few steps forward and found the tunnel blocked. Cursing, he turned around. "We need to find another way."

"There is no other way," Lieutenant Paxon replied. "The first branch was behind the Renao's defense line—and that is buried beneath stone."

"Well, we'll shoot a path through it." Kromm pointed his disruptor at the rocks that were blocking their path.

"Sir, don't forget the tekasite," Moore warned.

Kromm laughed. "The tunnel has just been blown up. If that didn't ignite the tekasite, our shots won't pose much danger, I'd say."

Commander Roaas nodded. "I agree with the captain. In this part of the tunnel there doesn't seem to be any tekasite ore. But you should check again, just to be on the safe side, Paxon."

The deputy security chief pulled his tricorder out again, sweeping the wall. "You're right, sir. The wall is clean."

"In that case, fire," Kromm ordered. "Maximum energy."

Three disruptor blasts and four phaser beams hit the rubble that had fallen from the ceiling, vaporizing it instantly. Several boulders dropped down but they spread out and didn't pose insurmountable obstacles. Kromm ran ahead, the others followed him.

The tunnel forked. Roaas sent Paxon along with Moore and Cenia in the right passageway. The Caitian stayed with Kromm and his remaining two soldiers. As quickly as possible they advanced into the secret hideout of the extremists. They didn't meet any more resistance. The Renao seemed to have taken advantage of the minutes after blowing up the corridor and escaped. The strike team passed hastily abandoned sleeping places and an arsenal that hadn't been completely cleared out. Finally, they came across the body of a Klingon, lying in a small room they had to pass through.

Bekk Morketh knelt beside the dead man. "It's Grakk, Captain. He has been beaten to death—like a wild *Ha'DIbaH*."

Kromm's face distorted with rage.

"They're going to pay for that!" It took him quite some

effort not to intone the death howl.

In the distance they heard a faint hissing noise that multiplied quickly.

"Those are engines," Kromm said. "The cowards are attempting to escape." He ran, abandoning all regard for safety. The fanatics mustn't get away. He wanted to drive a knife into their bodies and taste their blood.

They rounded several corners before reaching a subterranean cave that had been cut into the mountain.

"No!" cried Kromm when he saw the last two of an unknown number of escaping ships take off and disappear through a wide exit. He yanked his disruptor up, firing at them to no avail. Quickly the two transporter ships vanished. Little spots on the red sky showed that even more ships were on their way to orbit.

Roaas stood beside Kromm and touched his combadge.

"Roaas to shuttle *Charles Coryell*. Come in."

"*We hear you, sir,*" a faint voice said through the interference.

"Call the *Prometheus*. The followers of the Purifying Flame have escaped with their hostages. They're fleeing into orbit. They must be stopped at all costs before they can go into warp!"

"*Understood, Commander.*"

Frustrated, Kromm kicked an abandoned barrel. He had been cheated out of his honorable victory. Now it was down to Adams and L'emka to stop their enemies and to save the surviving hostages. He glared at the sky.

"Show us what you've got, Captain."

36
NOVEMBER 15, 2385

U.S.S. *Prometheus*, Onferin

"Red alert!" Adams ordered when he received the away team's warning. Since Roaas and the others had set off to rescue zh'Thiin, Kirk, and the two Klingons, he had been fidgeting in his command chair on the *Prometheus* bridge, waiting for their report.

Now he had received a report—and he needed to act.

"Battle stations!"

Sarita Carson rose from her place at ops immediately and hurried toward the turbolift. She needed to get to the battle bridge of the lower hull section.

Lieutenant Shantherin th'Talias and the officers from the beta shift would gather on the bridge of the upper section. There was no need to staff all three sections of the *Prometheus*, as the tactical computer was capable of controlling the sections when they separated for multivector attacks. But Adams preferred to have his personnel in control. As sophisticated as computers might be, they were not capable of making the decisions that sometimes needed to be made during a battle.

The turbolift door hissed open again, and Ensign Robert Vogel entered the bridge to take over at ops. Next to him at conn, Jassat ak Namur sat up straight. He had been called back when the rescue operation for the hostages had begun. Adams wished his executive officers—Roaas, zh'Thiin or

Paxon—were by his side right now. But all of them were down on Onferin. He had to make do with the men and women who were still aboard. *And they're all extremely well trained Starfleet officers,* he reminded himself. *That's why they're here, assigned to this ship.*

"Battle bridges are ready," Winter announced from the communications station.

"Understood," Adams replied without turning around. His eyes were fixed on the bridge's main screen. "Ensign Vogel, how many escaping ships are we dealing with?"

The stocky man's fingers danced on the console surface. "I'm reading eleven small spacecraft; seven are transport shuttles of various types, three are attack fighters according to their energy signatures. The shuttles are escaping on different vectors. The attack fighters are approaching us and the *Bortas*."

"Find out which of the ships our people are being held on."

"Yes, sir."

"Captain, the *Bortas* is hailing us," Winter interrupted.

"Open frequency, audio only."

"This is Commander L'emka," the *Bortas*'s first officer said. *"We will deal with the attack fighters, Captain. You go and catch those shuttles with our officers."*

Strictly speaking, Adams should have given these orders but he felt that now wasn't the right time to argue over petty details. "Understood." On the main screen he watched the *Vor'cha*-class cruiser pass his ship as the Klingons threw themselves into the fight with ardor.

Adams turned back to ops. "Mr. Vogel, report."

"I'm sorry, Captain. The radiation from the primary star is interfering with our sensors. I can read life forms aboard the shuttles but I can't distinguish whether they are Renao, human, or Andorian."

Adams uttered a curse. He wished he hadn't ordered Lieutenant Tabor not to modify the sensors after Captain Kromm had pointed them in the direction of the hostages. Adams had assumed that it would no longer be necessary to weaken the general sensor performance in order to increase the focus. "Looks like we're doing it the hard way," he mumbled. "Ship by ship." He gazed at Lieutenant Chell at the technical station. "Lieutenant, do your utmost to compensate for the radiation's interferences."

The Bolian nodded dutifully. "Aye, sir."

The turbolift door opened and Ambassador Spock entered the bridge. "Captain, if I can be of any assistance... I have significant experience with precarious situations."

Adams sized him up. On the one hand he was grateful that the famous Starfleet officer offered his services; on the other hand, he had reservations. The half-Vulcan had been a civilian for the better part of a century now.

Spock raised an eyebrow. "If you are concerned that I am not capable of handling the *Prometheus*'s systems, I can dispel your concerns. I have had ample opportunities during these past days to familiarize myself with the ship's controls."

A crooked smile played around Adams's lips. Of course he had. He was Spock, and Spock didn't do things by halves.

"I should have known," replied the captain. "Please, take tactical control."

"Very well, Captain."

The Vulcan went to the spot that Adams's first officer usually occupied. Ensign Gleeson—a ginger-haired, pale Irish woman—got up and changed over to the environmental controls.

"Ambassador Spock, mark all escaping ships," Adams ordered. "Mr. ak Namur, calculate interception course. We eliminate the shuttles one by one and beam their crews aboard when we're close enough."

"Sir," Vogel said, "we won't have enough time to do that. The shuttles are escaping at top speed toward the sun. I'm picking up a large ship there. It's leaving its position, and it's coming closer."

Adams rose from his chair. "You had better believe that we will do this, Mr. Vogel. Full impulse speed ahead. Computer: initiate separating sequence. We're going into multivector assault mode."

"By the Ancient Reds!"

The woman sitting to the left of the pilot in the narrow cockpit section of their escape ship half jumped from her seat.

"What's the matter?" growled her seatmate.

"The ship! It's separating! Look, Ramou, here on the screen. It's separating into three ships. They're hunting our friends."

The man—he was the leader of the small group—uttered a word that Jenna Kirk didn't understand. It was probably a curse.

"These devils always have another technological trick up their sleeves." He half turned in his seat. "Kumaah, we need more speed!"

"I'm doing the best I can," another male voice shouted from the engine room that was located in ship's aft section.

Kirk risked a few furtive glances. They sat in the passenger section in the center of the small transport, squashed between metal crates, mobile computer terminals, and two barrels with conspicuous green danger symbols of Romulan design on their outside. In front of them crouched a fourth fanatic, holding his projectile weapon in his hand. He wasn't devoting all of his attention to the prisoners, as his eyes kept wandering to the cockpit.

Kirk breathed deeply. The gunshot wound on her arm felt as if someone had pierced it with a red-hot poker. One of the kidnappers had ripped a strip of cloth from her uniform, using it as a makeshift pressure bandage for the injury. That wasn't really a professional treatment for her wound, but under the hectic circumstances it was the best her kidnappers could manage. At least she wouldn't bleed to death.

They also hadn't had enough time to bind their prisoners properly. The Renao had tied all of their hands behind their backs, but they had not secured their legs, nor had they put sacks over their heads again. But that didn't make much difference. Zh'Thiin was pale and trembled from the leg wound and the beating to the face she had taken from Ramou. Kirk's right arm was still more or less useless as well. Mokbar was the only one who might be able to put up a noteworthy resistance.

But one man alone—against four armed people? Kirk sighed inwardly. *No way.*

Zh'Thiin closed her eyes. Kirk shifted closer.

"Commander," she whispered, concerned. "Lenissa, stay with us."

"Don't worry," zh'Thiin replied quietly. "An Andorian doesn't die that easily." She opened her eyes again, and suddenly, Kirk saw a determination in there, that she wouldn't have expected given the swollen antenna, the battered face and the blood-stained leg.

The small shuttle shuddered as Kumaah in the engine

room strained the drive to the limit. For a fleeting moment, Kirk was afraid that they might die because their escape ship simply broke apart.

"You're killing us, Ramou!" her guard who seemed to be driven by similar concerns, shouted in the general direction of the cockpit.

"The outworlders will kill us if they catch us," the pilot replied dryly.

Kirk looked back to zh'Thiin and saw her looking furtively at Mokbar who sat doubled over half a meter away on a passenger bench. The Andorian woman turned back to Kirk. "Tell him in Klingon that he should pretend to be completely exhausted. Make him fall over so that his head ends up beside me. And then he can gnaw through my ties with his teeth. I will give him a sign when the guard isn't watching, and when he's alert. Got it?"

"You're crazy," Kirk whispered. "Haven't you had enough for one day?" But there was a hint of admiration in his voice.

"It'll be enough when we're free or when I'm dead," the security chief replied grimly.

Kirk nodded. Lenissa was courageous, without a doubt. *If I hadn't lost my heart already, I might even fall in love with her*, shot through her mind.

The plan seemed desperate but at the same time it had a lot of potential. The Renao had taken the hidden knife away from zh'Thiin, after they had investigated how the "outworlders" had managed to free themselves from their bonds the first time. However, no one had taken Mokbar's sharpened teeth into consideration—including Kirk.

She turned toward the engineer. Her Klingon wasn't perfect but it was sufficient to explain zh'Thiin's intentions to Mokbar.

The woman in the cockpit started wailing. "They have captured ak Manas' ship—and Joruun's. We won't make it. We will all die!"

"Shut up!" Ramou snapped at her. "We have almost reached the *Medibha*."

Grunting, Mokbar rolled his eyes and fell over. Their guard had been paying attention to the cabin and jumped. When he saw what happened, he smiled a sinister smile, lowering his weapon again. He said something in Renao that Kirk didn't understand.

"Even the strongest will fall," he added in broken Federation Standard, taunting the prisoners.

Don't count your chickens too early, you bastard, she thought. *This day isn't over just yet.*

"bortaS blr jablu'DI'reH QaQqu' nay'!" Second Officer Chumarr's grin might have been able to scare even the demons of Gre'thor—the mythical realm to which the dishonorable Klingon dead were condemned—when he looked up from his tactical console. Commander L'emka nodded. Revenge was—according to an old Klingon saying—a dish best served cold, indeed. *And it's very cold in space…*

On the bridge's main screen the remains of the second of three attack fighters spread out. They had dared to confront the Klingon battle cruiser to help their criminal friends escape.

L'emka deeply despised these fanatics and their cowardly attacks during the past few days, but she had to respect the three pilots for their courage. No one sitting in a small one-man fighter attacked a mighty ship such as the *Bortas* if they weren't driven by death-defying courage… or by mind-consuming madness.

"The last fighter is coming round," Chumarr warned. "Incoming on starboard."

"Maneuver the *Bortas* to face him with our upper defense turrets," L'emka ordered the pilot, a man named Toras.

"Commander!" *Bekk* Raspin at the sensor console spun around. The black eyes in the Rantal's white face were widened. "I'm picking up trilithium and tekasite aboard their ship. They're carrying a bomb."

"Fire!" L'emka angrily ordered Chumarr. "Fire with all that we've got."

"Firing disruptors and torpedoes. Close dispersal pattern."

Blinding green streaks cut through the black space and a salvo of four photon torpedoes launched from the bow, heading in a wide curve toward the attack fighter. The pilot was firing relentlessly, and his intention seemed obvious. He intended to plunge into the *Bortas* in a desperate act of self-sacrifice to drag her down with him.

"We won't hit him!" shouted Chumarr.

"Keep firing," L'emka replied. She leaned forward in her command chair. Another Klingon quote came to her mind: *taH pagh taHbe'*—to be or not to be...

The torpedoes found their target, ripping the small attack fighter to pieces, no more than one *kellicam* away from the *Bortas*. An explosion exceeding the normal parameters by far propelled the small Renao ship forward. Inertia drove the flaming, dying projectile into the left starboard deflector shield.

"Hold on!" L'emka shouted when the cruiser shuddered despite its enormous mass. Lighting flickered, and one of the consoles overloaded. It burst into small pieces, sending sparks flying everywhere.

"Starboard deflector down," Chumarr shouted over the chaos.

Another explosion shook the Klingon battle cruiser, and the power on the bridge failed.

"Captain, the *Bortas* has been severely hit," Spock said at the tactical station.

"What happened?" Adams inquired.

"It appears that one of the Renao fighters almost rammed them. Based on the particle and radiation residue, that vessel must have carried a bomb aboard. Just before impact the *Bortas* succeeded in intercepting them, but the cruiser has been badly damaged as well."

The captain looked straight ahead. "On screen."

The image of the small transport following the *Prometheus*'s command section vanished and was replaced by the Klingon ship that floated in high orbit above Onferin. The *Bortas* was listing heavily, and she was losing atmospheric pressure on her starboard side. A cloud of debris floated around her. Minor secondary explosions shook the ship's aft section.

"Mr. Winter, hail the *Bortas*."

"Aye, Captain."

The image changed again, and a dimly lit bridge with emergency lights appeared.

Commander L'emka straightened herself in her command chair. She was visibly shaken, but apparently unharmed.

"*Bortas*, this is the *Prometheus*. Do you require assistance, Commander?"

"*Unnecessary, Captain. The Bortas is a sturdy ship. She won't be beaten that easily. My engineers are already effecting repairs.*" She nodded at Adams with a determined expression. "*We've completed our task, Captain. The fighters have been eliminated. Now all you need to do is capture the fleeing ships so we can get our people back and determine at last who's behind all this."*

"Good luck, Commander. Adams out." When the link had been terminated he clenched his right fist and hit his chair's armrest with grim determination.

"All right. Let's finish this."

37
NOVEMBER 15, 2385

Renao transport, approaching Aoul

Zh'Thiin attacked suddenly and unexpectedly, taking her guard by surprise. With her unharmed leg she vaulted from her bench toward the guard, who had just turned his back on her. The man shouted, but she quickly yanked his head back, hitting against his throat to silence him. Gurgling, he fell to his knees. The female Renao whirled around in the cockpit, while the Andorian woman ducked and pulled a knife from her opponent's belt.

"Mokbar!" she shouted.

He turned around stretching his tied hands toward her. With a swift movement zh'Thiin cut his ties, before facing Kirk.

"The captives!" the Renao woman shouted. "They're getting loose!"

"No time," Ramou said at the helm. "Neutralize them."

Her hand reached behind the back of her seat, pulling out a beam weapon.

Zh'Thiin threw the knife at her. Instinctively, the woman darted back, taking cover. The blade thudded into the plastic casing of her back-rest with a muffled sound.

When the Renao lifted her head again, Mokbar lunged toward her with a scream.

Kumaah appeared in the passageway to the engine sector.

He held a silver tool in his hand that he was using as a club.

"Watch out!" Kirk cried.

Zh'Thiin threw herself to one side when the Renao swung at her, panting, with wide eyes. The bench broke with a sharp crack when he struck it with the heavy tool.

Kirk slid to the floor. Her hand fumbled for her guard's gun, which he had dropped. Her heart hammered as if it wanted to break free from her chest. For a brief moment she didn't even feel the injury to her arm. They needed to take control of the shuttle here and now, or it was all over.

She heard a woman scream from the cockpit, followed by a Klingon's battle cry. The engineer hoped fervently that the Klingon wouldn't damage the ship in his rage.

As if her thought had been a cue, the shuttle suddenly rolled sideways. Kirk had almost reached the Renao's weapon but now it slid out of reach again. Zh'Thiin and her opponent both cried out in surprise when they lost their balance. After a moment, the inertial dampers took over, neutralizing the centrifugal forces that affected the cabin.

There was a thud and a rumble. Kirk turned her head and saw the Renao called Kumaah slumping in between the crates. He had probably slammed into them during the transport's sudden movement. Zh'Thiin leaned heavily on one of the barrels, holding her leg and panting. Her antennae were swaying as if she was about to faint.

"Just a second," she murmured, dropping the tool that she had apparently taken off her opponent to use herself. "I'll be right…"

A deafening howl interrupted her. Both women looked up, alarmed.

"No!" Mokbar roared, hitting the small ship's console with both his fists. "This cannot be!"

"What's wrong?" Kirk asked. She noticed the woman and her tormentor Ramou. Both were dangling in their seats. The woman's forehead sported a gaping wound while Ramou's head hung at an unnatural angle. There was no life in his open eyes. Mokbar had been on a terrible rampage.

"He activated the self-destruct," the Klingon said. "With the last dying breath of his pitiful existence he activated the self-destruct!"

Kirk pushed past the freight. "Get out of the way and let me deal with that."

Mokbar grabbed the two Renao, tossing them unceremoniously out of their seats and onto the deck. Then he made his way into the passenger area, leaving the cockpit to the engineer. Zh'Thiin limped to her side.

Kirk registered everything with a quick glance. Ramou had switched the drive to overload. When the impulse energy discharged, it would tear the ship apart with or without barrels full of dangerous substances aboard. The power level was already way above the red line. She didn't know whether she'd be able to stop it.

"I need to get to the engine room and switch the drive off manually."

"Forget it," zh'Thiin said. "It's too late." She pulled a few levers. "Zh'Thiin to *Prometheus*. Can you hear us? Zh'Thiin to *Prometheus*! Please come in!"

Winter turned excitedly in his seat to face Adams. "Sir! I'm in contact with Commander zh'Thiin."

Adams whirled around. "Status?" he asked.

Winter put his fingers on the receiver in his ear.

"Commander zh'Thiin, this is the *Prometheus*. What's your status?" He listened.

"Audio," Adams ordered.

"... *tion is terrible*," Lenissa zh'Thiin's voice reported from the comm system. *"We have assumed control but the pilot switched the drive to overload. We're about to blow up. Get a lock on us and beam us out of here right now. I repeat: beam all of us out of here immediately!"*

Adams jumped out of his chair. "Mr. Vogel, trace the signal. Mr. ak Namur bring us into transporter range. Full impulse speed."

"Ship located," Vogel replied. "Distance: six hundred thousand kilometers."

"ETA: ten seconds," ak Namur added from conn.

Adams said, "Mr. Winter, tell the transporter room to stand by."

"Yes, sir."

"Hang on, Lenissa." The captain clenched his right fist. "Hang on..."

"They're coming to get us," zh'Thiin shouted. "Gather everyone together." She scrambled out of the pilot seat.

"Wait." Jenna Kirk frantically worked the controls in front of her, while staring at the overload display of the impulse engine. "Maybe I can buy us a little more time. If I vent the plasma feed line and..."

"No time, Jenna! We need to get out of here. Tell Mokbar to bring the woman and this Kumaah guy. I want to know what they know." She whirled around, stumbled when her injured leg gave way and bumped into the frame of the passageway. She cursed under her breath in her mother tongue.

Frustrated, Kirk realized that the security chief was right. Anything she might try now would be a waste of time. She stood up and joined the others. Quickly she relayed zh'Thiin's orders to Mokbar. The big engineer grabbed both incapacitated Renao.

In the back of the ship the whining of the overloading engine increased. The lighting flickered. Something in the aft section banged and crackled.

"Come on, Captain," whispered Kirk. "Don't let us down."

The whining increased to a piercing sound.

"Captain!" Jenna Kirk shouted desperately. "Now would be a good time!"

A veil of shimmering sparks enveloped her.

The Renao transport exploded.

Adams stared at the expanding debris field for two horrifying seconds, before he turned toward his chair, activating the intercom.

"Bridge to transporter room. Chief, tell me that you got them."

"Wilorin here," the voice of the Tiburonian transporter officer answered. *"It's good news. Commander zh'Thiin, Commander Kirk, a Klingon, and two unconscious Renao have arrived aboard safe and sound."*

It felt as if someone had halved the gravity on board. A huge weight was taken from Adams's shoulders. Winter and Vogel cheered, Gleeson clapped her hands, and Spock tilted his head in satisfaction. With a beaming smile, Adams straightened himself. "Very good, Chief. Excellent work. How are our guys?"

"Kirk here, Captain," the chief engineer said. *"Thank you for*

the rescue at the last second. We're battered, but we're alive."

"Glad to hear it, Commander. Report to sickbay. We have everything under control here."

"Understood, Captain." Jenna Kirk closed the channel.

"At least, more or less under control," Adams added quietly.

He looked at the main screen where one last ship darted toward the bulky spacecraft that maintained its course toward them. The small ship seemed to have been significantly modified; its impulse engines were absurdly large for a vessel this size. Like the other small vessels, it wasn't capable of warp speed. But they needed to come up with something if they wanted to catch up with the escapees before they reached their destination. *On the other hand, the mothership will not escape us either,* Adams pondered. *The Renao's technology allows them a maximum speed of warp five, if that. They are no match for the* Prometheus.

"Mr. ak Namur, ETA until interception?"

"Fifty seconds, sir. It will be close."

"Phasers and tractor beam on standby. If we can't catch the small vessel, we will stop the mothership."

"Locking on target," Spock said.

"Commander Carson and Lieutenant th'Talias report successful interception," Paul Winter said. "The hull sections are catching up to us."

"Very good," Adams replied, nodding.

"Thirty seconds," ak Namur said.

Anxious, Adams went down the three steps into the control pit and took position behind his pilot, as if he could grab the escaping ship with both hands if he was two meters closer to the main screen. Mesmerized, he watched how their prey approached its target.

"They're slowing down," Vogel said. Suddenly, the ensign looked up in confusion. Adams also noticed what was happening. The small ship flew above the larger ship and simply continued its course.

"They didn't dock," Vogel exclaimed, surprised.

"I read no life forms aboard," Spock said from the back of the bridge.

Confused, Adams turned around to face him. It took another two seconds before he understood. "They beamed aboard the bigger ship?"

Spock's fingers danced across the console. "Incorrect. According to our sensors, the transport was initiated by the larger ship."

"The Renao shouldn't have any transporter technology at their disposal!"

"Indeed. Presumably another purchase from the black market."

"Five seconds." Ak Namur fidgeted in his seat. "Four. Three."

"Lock phasers on their stern. Tractor beam on standby."

"We're in firing range."

Adams stabbed in the general direction of the main screen with his index finger. "Fire!"

Suddenly, a blinding white flash filled space. The outside sensors reacted instantly, decreasing the brightness, but it was too late. Red dots danced before Adams's eyes when the light vanished a second later. Squinting in confusion, the captain stared at the main screen. Space in front of them was empty.

"What was that?" he asked, facing Spock. "Did we destroy them?"

"Negative, Captain. I detect no debris."

"What did we just witness then?"

"Captain." Vogel's voice sounded just as perplexed as Adams felt. "The computer just registered a fading space-time distortion."

"Fascinating," Spock commented. The Vulcan turned away from tactical controls, raising an eyebrow. "It would seem that we have just witnessed an unknown variety of faster-than-light travel."

"What do you mean? Did the ship jump into warp?"

"No, Captain. Apparently, the Renao are capable of folding spacetime in order to facilitate a jump across an unknown span."

"Long-distance sensors are not able to detect the ship."

Adams turned to look at the empty space again in disbelief. The giant sun Aoul hung in space less than one hundred million kilometers away, providing a slightly curved horizon on the bottom of the screen.

"So they can jump several light-years?"

"Not necessarily, sir," Vogel answered tentatively. "Our sensors are severely incapacitated by the radiation in the cluster. We're barely able to see as far as one light-year."

"That doesn't change the fact that they escaped."

"No, sir."

Turning his back toward the main screen, Adams walked back up to his command chair. Deep in thought, he stood beside it.

Questions upon questions went through his mind. Why hadn't anyone known about this extraordinary drive? The report from Starfleet Intelligence didn't contain any hints about that. Had the Renao developed that technology themselves—and if so, when and how? Or was there yet another unknown entity in this game; someone who'd supplied the extremists with extraordinary high technology?

Well, we've got one answer at least, Adams realized. *We know how the fanatics of the Purifying Flame managed to approach their attack targets without any warp-detection sensors triggering an alert.*

They really needed to chase up the origin of this technology and find out how it worked. They couldn't rule out the fact that the Renao were able to jump halfway across Federation space. In that case, they might appear without warning right above central worlds such as Andor, Vulcan, or Earth. He preferred not to contemplate the destruction they might cause.

"Captain," Spock said, coming over to join him. "I believe the danger we are currently facing is far greater than we have imagined."

Adams looked at the Vulcan ambassador with a grim expression.

"I'm afraid, Mr. Spock, you're absolutely right there. And it's our duty to avert it." He stood upright and straightened his uniform. "So I guess, we had better get started."

EPILOGUE
NOVEMBER 16, 2385

U.S.S. *Prometheus*

Sickbay seemed to be the most important location aboard the ship this evening. Geron Barai hardly found time to drop by the small reception area in his medical center. But whenever he did, he discovered new faces: worried crewmembers who had come to ask after the welfare of their rescued colleagues.

Much to his surprise, he also spotted the captain. "You too, sir?"

Richard Adams smiled briefly, thanked the visibly stressed-out officer at reception and walked over to Barai. His face had worry lines, but his expression showed determination. "What's the situation, Doctor?"

"You could have contacted me via combadge, sir," Barai said, surprised. "If you want information you don't have to come here from the bridge to…"

Adams interrupted him with a wave of his hand. "You don't pay sick bed visits via combadge, Doctor," he said, and the smile returned. "Especially not with *these* patients."

Barai understood and grinned back. "You're not wrong." Shoving his hands into the pockets of his white coat, he accompanied Adams to the treatment and recovery rooms at the back of the ward. They could hear the grumpy voice of Barai's current most important staff member as they walked.

"Oh no, Commander! You will not put weight onto that leg before I have finished your treatment."

"Damnit, Tric," protested Lenissa zh'Thiin's furious voice. "I *can* get up!"

"What you can or cannot do is a decision based on medical grounds," Barai's assistant objected, "and as much as I feel for you, I'm the one making these decisions."

Barai and Adams stood in the doorway of the treatment room. Jenna Kirk lay on a biobed, laughing and holding her stomach with her left hand. Her right hand was being attended to by Ensign T'Sai. The second biobed was occupied by zh'Thiin. The young Andorian woman sat up straight—much to the chagrin of the Emergency Medical Holographic program—and had swung her long legs over the edge of the bed. Frustration showed in her eyes when she looked toward the door.

"Geron, you tell him!"

"You heard the lady, Tric." Barai entered the room. He sighed loudly, winking at the security chief furtively. "You don't get to boss Commander zh'Thiin around. Not even when you're a doctor. Unfortunately."

With his hands on his hips the EMH stared at him, filled with indignation. The computer-created hologram looked like a human male in his late thirties. He had full, chestnut-brown hair, an oblong face, and dimples in his clean-shaven looking chin. He was slender, wearing a black and blue Starfleet uniform. A medical tricorder dangled from his belt. The EMH never appeared without it, so the crew had given him his nickname, Tric.

Holodoctors with the looks and personality of Tric were a thing of the past. Far more modern models were in use these days, and they had been programmed into the *Prometheus*'s databanks. But the crew had gotten attached to Tric and his legendary overzealousness. So Captain Adams didn't find it difficult to stick with the EMH Mark II program. Barai was under orders to update Tric's skills and knowledge, but to leave his looks and his bedside manner untouched. So on the inside Tric had evolved into an EMH Mark XI, but on the outside he was still the same.

"Doctor Barai, I really must protest!" the hologram turned to his superior officer from Betazed, looking for support. "You know as well as I do that medical instructions outweigh those of military personnel. Commander zh'Thiin will be fit for duty when we tell her—not when she decides that she is."

The Andorian woman had completely recovered after a brief treatment. Her antennae bent forward menacingly. Barai knew this reaction all too well: Niss was rapidly losing her patience and was about to explode any time soon.

"How do you feel, Commander?" he asked her.

"Excellent, Doctor," she answered with a strained voice, rolling her eyes. "I'm fit enough to rip holoemitters from walls with my bare hands."

"Hey!" Tric whirled around to her, horrified. The network of holoemitters that had been installed aboard the *Prometheus*—a novelty in Starfleet's latest ship designs—gave the independently thinking and acting program the freedom to move outside of sickbay when the situation demanded it. "I don't see any reason for threats, Commander."

"Oh, Tric," snarled zh'Thiin, and her eyes sparkled ominously. "You think that was a threat? This is just the beginning."

"That's enough," Adams interrupted the banter. The captain smirked but his tone of voice was steady. "Commander, you're staying here for as long as the doctors deem necessary."

Tric nodded, satisfied. "Thank you, Captain."

Adams ignored him. "Commander Kirk. How are you doing?"

"All that's still hurting is my diaphragm, sir," Jenna Kirk answered from her bed. She looked at her arm as T'Sai switched off the tissue regenerator. "I guess I'm almost ready for duty."

"She needs to rest her arm a while longer," Barai explained quickly, trying to distract himself from Niss's furious glances, which were directed at him now. "Other than that, the Lieutenant Commander is as good as new."

"And Mokbar?" the captain asked.

Barai sighed. "I wanted to treat him but the stubborn warrior insisted on being transferred to his own ship. According to my colleagues there, he's recovering reasonably well."

Adams nodded, pleased. "All right," he said, looking around in the treatment room, rubbing his hands. "Get back on your feet, you hear me? And yes, Commander zh'Thiin, that pun was intended."

The Andorian woman silently rubbed her thigh. Her wounds had been tended to in the meantime. The contusions to her antenna forced zh'Thiin to stay in bed; something that she obviously didn't agree with.

Barai knew her silence very well. It was born from defiance.

Slightly concerned—and with a hint of a guilty conscience, despite Tric being right—he studied her. He had been extremely worried for her recovery. *The main thing is that you're back with me.* He liked her. No, it was more than just "like." Even if she didn't want to hear it. She defined what had been happening between them for the past weeks differently. Barai wasn't like her. He couldn't just switch off his gut feeling, or separate his emotions from his desires. He didn't want to either. But if he was to tell her that, their little affair would end instantly—and maybe their friendship as well. You didn't need to be a Betazoid to know that.

Andorians, he thought, half amused, half insecure. *Loyal as Jem'Hadar soldiers, fearless as the Borg… and if they get going, more furious than a bunch of Klingons.*

The captain wasn't a telepath, but even he seemed to read Niss's silence. He smirked.

"We all want your best, Lenissa."

"I know, sir," she replied, and it did sound more approachable than she actually felt right now. "And I'll stay here for as long as the doctor orders." With these words, she looked at Barai with one of her feared "I'll-talk-to-you-later" looks. She had probably forced the Renao to their knees with that look. At least Barai wouldn't be surprised if she had.

"Fantastic." Relieved, Tric looked from Adams to Barai. "That means my work here is done. Doctor Barai, can you take over?"

Barai nodded. "Thank you for your help, Tric—again."

Tric tilted his head slightly. "Anytime, Doctor," he said, audibly pleased. "Anytime." Then he switched his holographic presence off, vanishing into the ship's data storage.

"One more thing, Doctor," Adams said to Barai. "How are our… guests? I don't see the Renao anywhere around here."

Barai's mood darkened. Those fanatics had brought nothing but misery and pain to innocent people; they even had tortured Niss. But as a doctor it was his duty to attend to them just as carefully and meticulously as he did to his other patients. He had always adhered to this duty, and that would never change.

"They are next door, sir. Kumaah is still unconscious, and his female partner has been questioned by zh'Thiin's staff as far as her health permitted, but she's as silent as a grave."

Adams sighed. "I was afraid you might say that."

Barai shook his head. "Ambassador Spock is with them now, Captain," he continued. "He has been for quite a while."

That seemed to cheer Adams up a little. "Do I have your permission to look in on the Renao briefly?"

"Of course, sir." Barai smiled at him ruefully. "But I will give you the same warning that I have given the ambassador: please don't expect too much from this visit."

Adams nodded, but there was a certain truth in his eyes that ran deeper than any worries could ever have done. "Don't underestimate hope, Doctor," he said quietly. "Without it, you and I wouldn't have departed for the stars."

Jassat ak Namur stood in front of the closed door to a patient's room, chiding himself inwardly. Why was he so nervous? Where did this insecurity come from? He just wanted to visit a few fellow countrymen whose behavior was inexplicable to him.

"*Just,*" he thought and snorted without humor. *Good one, "just." I really have to tell Moba that.*

He drew a deep breath, straightened his shoulders and took a step forward.

"Hang on," said the security officer by the door. Ensign Mathieu Curdin was one of zh'Thiin's younger team members. He had short-cropped, ginger hair and freckles. "I might have to live with you standing next to me in the corridor, *Lieutenant.*" The last word sounded almost like an insult. "But that doesn't mean that I have to let you into rooms that I am supposed to guard."

"I'm a Starfleet offi—"

"You're a red-skin," Curdin hissed. "Do you really think that the uniform can hide that fact? You're no different from the two who are in there."

Jassat took another deep breath, keeping his anger at bay. "You should watch your mouth, *Ensign*. Otherwise, you'll be guarding the brig next—from the inside." With these words, he unceremoniously pushed the Frenchman who tried to block his way to one side and opened the door.

The windowless room behind the door was small and empty, save for three biobeds—the one on the left was not in use—medical equipment, and an old half-Vulcan.

"Ambassador," Jassat said, surprised. "Sir, please excuse me. I didn't know that you were…"

Spock stood to the right of one of the biobeds. He had been leaning over the female patient who slept there, but now he stood up, turning around to face ak Namur.

"There's no reason to apologize, Lieutenant," he said. "You're not disturbing me." He looked at Curdin who stood glowering in the doorway with his hand resting on his phaser. "It's alright, Ensign. Mr. ak Namur is quite welcome."

Curdin reluctantly removed his hand from his weapon. Finally, he withdrew to his post in the corridor.

"Are you sure, Ambassador?" The young Renao man had the feeling that he had walked in on something that wasn't any of his business. "Somehow you seemed to be… well, I don't know." He groped for words. "Busy?"

"I was indeed," Spock agreed with him. There was no reproach, no disapproval in his voice. "That doesn't mean, however, that I cannot appreciate your presence. Please, come closer, Lieutenant."

Jassat hesitated and walked into the room. The door closed behind him immediately. He briefly glanced at Kumaah, his unconscious childhood friend on the other biobed. He had heard that he was involved in this matter. But there was a painful difference between knowing something, and actually seeing it. Quickly, he focused on the ambassador again.

Spock raised an eyebrow. "Do you know this man?"

Jassat swallowed. "Yes. No. I don't know. I thought I knew him—but that was many years ago. Now, he's a stranger to me, just like that woman next to you." Sighing, he shook his head.

The ambassador interlaced his fingers. "May I ask you a question, Mr. ak Namur?"

"Certainly."

"Did you have the opportunity to think about the conversation we had several days ago? About my questions regarding your role aboard the *Prometheus*… and your home?"

The previous days had been strenuous—and they had passed a lot faster than Jassat had thought possible. Still, he suddenly felt as if every twist he had lived through and each decision had pushed him closer to the core of that one particular question. It was as if he hadn't been looking for answers so much for Captain Adams but rather for himself.

"Yes, sir, I believe I did."

Spock nodded. "And I assume that you have edged closer to an answer?"

Jassat remembered their encounter in Starboard 8. He recalled the accusing looks of several crewmembers and the angry words from his old friends on Onferin. He thought about Captain Adams's trust, and he visualized the majestic hives of Massoa, Aoul's light reflecting off the arcology's glass façades and that of the Terran sun reflecting off the waters of San Francisco Bay. He pondered wasted chances, parting of ways and the inherent right of all living creatures to a free will.

"I am who I am, sir," he said, and suddenly, the words just came out of his mouth faster than he could think them. "That's my role. It's the only one I'm capable of playing. It's not defined by circumstance or the opinions of others—I define it myself. I'm Renao and a lieutenant in Starfleet. *I* am my own home. I am myself."

Spock remained silent for a while. He seemed pensive and almost a little sad. Finally, he nodded. "Well said, Lieutenant ak Namur. I hope that you will hold on to this insight… and that you will find opportunities to build on this foundation. I say this from one wanderer between worlds to another."

Again, Jassat had the feeling that he only recognized a fraction of the meaning in Spock's words. But he sensed that this fraction would have to be sufficient. At least for now.

"A second question, Lieutenant. As Renao and as a member of Starfleet: does an end justify its means?"

Jassat blinked. "I'm sorry, sir?"

"An end," repeated Spock. "Do you think that a noble end under certain circumstances justifies the means by which you reach it?"

Still, the Renao didn't understand. "A noble end is worth any means, sir." He had learned that lesson in the ethics seminars at the Starfleet Academy over and over. Now, he cited it mainly because he had no other answer.

Spock looked at him, nodding. "Because the needs of the many outweigh the needs of the few. Am I correct?"

"Of… of course," Jassat replied hesitantly. "Personal interests are far less important than those of the community.

The common good always comes first." That was also taught at the Academy, but did Spock—the legendary Spock of all people—want to hear truisms from him?

"Interesting you should say that," the Vulcan muttered. He turned around again. Bending over the sleeping Renao woman on the bed, he spread his fingers.

Jassat was taken aback.

"Sir? What... what are you doing?"

"I am getting my hands dirty, Lieutenant," Spock answered quietly and without looking at him. "I am putting the needs of the many above the need of one person. I believe that the current circumstances demand that."

"I don't understand," Jassat said.

Spock's hands moved closer to the woman's temples. "The spirit of your fellow Renao seems to be in an uproar. When they were brought aboard, they were hardly responsive. Doctor Barai's instruments detected utter chaos in their brainwave patterns. He was unable to offer an explanation for that. Thus it seems that the task at hand—to find the urgently required answers—falls to me. But I can guarantee you, I do not take pleasure in doing so."

As soon as the Vulcan's fingertips touched the Renao woman's temples, she woke. Horror flashed in her dark eyes, but it quickly turned to fury.

"Please forgive me," Spock said quietly, his attention completely focused on the woman. "I deeply regret this, but I sincerely hope that I can help you, if you let me."

The lieutenant's eyes widened. Suddenly, he understood what Spock intended to do, and he was shocked.

"My mind to your mind," Spock mumbled, closing his eyes. "My thoughts to yours."

The Renao woman whined. Her face distorted to a

grotesque mask of fury. Rage burned in her eyes, and her hands that had been secured to the side of the bed convulsed.

"My mind to your mind," Spock repeated quietly, his voice fading. His face showed the terrible exertion required to do this. His fingers held the woman's temples, cheeks and jawbones as if they would never let go again. "My thoughts to yours."

Jassat had never witnessed a Vulcan mind meld, but he knew that Spock's father's species was capable of this telepathic feat. Such a mind meld required concentration, training, and mental discipline from the executing person. Two conscious minds were briefly combined into one during the process. If unskilled people attempted the procedure it could lead to irreversible damage to both involved. For generations, the ethical and moral implications of this intrusion into the private sphere of another sentient being had been fervently discussed at Starfleet Academy.

He realized that that was what Spock had been talking about when he mentioned the ends justifying the means. He had wanted to know whether Jassat agreed with his approach. Spock obviously didn't condone it, but he was equally convinced that they had no other choice in the matter.

Jassat heard a faint whimper in the otherwise quiet room, and gasped when he realized that it came from both Spock's mouth and that of the Renao woman at the same time.

The woman stared at the ceiling; her eyes showed no expression. Spock also seemed to have passed out, but Jassat saw his fingers trembling slightly. He also noticed the strain in his body language and sensed his determination.

Finally, it happened. "The eyes…" whispered the woman, and Spock whispered it with her. "The red eyes in the darkness… The Son of the Ancient Reds…"

Shivers ran down Jassat's spine. Helpless, he observed the terrifying scene, wondering if he should intervene or call someone—a doctor, a security officer, both. But as much as he was unsettled by the events unfolding in front of his eyes, he understood why Spock employed these drastic means. The survivors of the terrorist cell that the *Bortas* and the *Prometheus* had uncovered on Onferin had fled into the unknown, taking most of the mystery with them. Instead of answers, Captain Adams and Captain Kromm were faced with new questions. Jassat was convinced that he wasn't the only one who felt that these questions were even bigger than the previous ones. And the threat that the Purifying Flame posed hadn't decreased at all, despite all the best efforts of both ships' crews.

Something needed to be done. Urgently. And the two ships didn't have too many options to choose from, especially since Ev and Moas had committed suicide, according to Captain Kromm. Commander Roaas had given Jassat the bad news. The young lieutenant was equally tormented, ashamed, and horrified by this information.

"The son," Spock and the Renao whispered again. It sounded extremely important, like a secret from ancient times. "The Son of the Ancient Reds."

A sound behind him made Jassat jump. Afraid and feeling somewhat caught, he whirled around. The door to the room hissed open, and Captain Richard Adams appeared in the doorway.

Perplexed, Adams looked at him. "Lieutenant?"

"Sir, I… we…"

"The situation is much worse than we had anticipated," Spock's voice announced—*only* Spock's voice—behind the stammering lieutenant's back. "Unfortunately, my suspicion was correct."

Jassat looked over his shoulder again. The scene by the bed had changed considerably. Spock had stood up again, and he had removed his hands from the woman's face. The mind meld was finished. The Renao breathed heavily with exhaustion and stared into the distance, while the experienced Vulcan had better control over himself. He looked as if nothing had happened.

Spock nodded a greeting toward Captain Adams, folding his hands in front of his stomach. "The assessments from Starfleet Intelligence were *not* incorrect," he reported. "The Renao are not a threat to us. That is to say, the threat does not originate from the Home Spheres or from their government."

"But from whom?" asked Adams.

Without a word he studied the unconscious Kumaah and the woman who was slowly calming down. Both of them were in physically good condition, at least according to the monitors above their beds.

"Captain, this woman is not acting of her own accord," Spock said. "I could see it in her mind, sense it in her thoughts. She thinks she's acting in accordance with the beliefs of her culture regarding the spheres. But she's barely aware of the fact that her deeds exceed what her people deem appropriate. And that awareness is rapidly fading away completely. Captain, she is under mind control. I cannot tell you for certain who is responsible, but it would seem to be an entity or a group that she calls the Son of the Ancient Reds. It is possible that most of the extremist Renao are under the same influence—perhaps even the entire nation."

"The entire nation?" Adams gasped. "Spock, if that were true…"

The Vulcan nodded. "I know. But it does fit the evidence. My conclusion is only logical."

"But how is that possible? Think of Himad ak Genos and all the other government representatives we encountered these past few days. They may not have been sympathetic toward us, but they weren't openly hostile, either. Where's your mind control there?"

Spock glanced at Kumaah and the Renao woman. "That I cannot tell you, Captain. My knowledge is currently just as limited as yours."

"And what about if you had to speculate, Ambassador?"

Spock took a deep breath. "Perhaps the influence comes in waves. Perhaps it stops at geographical borders. Perhaps certain individuals among the Renao are immune, due to unknown biological reasons, for example..." He shook his head. "Captain, I cannot tell you more than I know. Only one thing is certain: the mind of this poor woman is unhinged. She no longer has control over her life. She believes she is doing the right thing—but she is no longer able to ascertain the difference between right and wrong."

Jassat didn't believe his ears. A strange power, manipulating his people? Was it possible that a strange force manipulated his people and drove the Renao to violence? It would explain why so many of his childhood friends were acting so odd. But he couldn't imagine how something like that could be possible.

Adams frowned. "So we know more than we did—but we're just as helpless as we were before we came to the Lembatta Cluster. The rage and religious madness might have come from the outside and they were probably forced upon the Renao. But that would make matters even worse because we don't know whether this crisis can be solved with diplomacy and reason. We need to unravel this mystery in order to put a stop to this threat."

"Agreed." Spock stood next to him. "But I believe I have learned one thing during the mind meld: We are on the right path. The truth might be greater than we initially anticipated, but it is hidden somewhere in the Lembatta Cluster."

They fell silent, and all three men seemed to dwell on their thoughts.

Finally, Captain Adams said, "All right. Let's go on a wild goose chase." He sighed deeply. "Admiral Akaar will be delighted when he reads my report…"

"I've got good news and bad, Dick."

Richard Adams sat at his desk in his ready room, staring at the computer monitor. It displayed an eyes-only subspace message from Admiral Akaar.

"The bad news first. I have spoken to Starfleet Intelligence and Starfleet Security about your report on the situation on Onferin. We also can't offer an explanation for your discoveries regarding the madness of the Renao and their peculiar propulsion system, and we share your concern. What's going on in that cluster right now is disconcerting. And we're dreading the moment when it will claim more casualties—from us or the Renao."

"I know the feeling," Adams mumbled.

"The good news is that we're giving you the task to unravel this mystery. I assume you didn't expect anything less. Travel deeper into the Lembatta Cluster, Dick. Find the survivors of that terrorist cell that you have flushed out. Find whoever is behind the Purifying Flame. And find this ominous Son of the Ancient Red, if he even exists. Get to the bottom of this, once and for all, for our welfare and that of your hosts. The safety of the galaxy might depend on that."

Adams nodded silently. The Renao wouldn't be too enthusiastic about that but there was too much at stake, and they could ill afford to defer to their sensitivities at this point.

"*We will try to clear the way for you diplomatically as best we can, given the distance,*" the Capellan continued. "*But I'm afraid that the majority of these efforts will remain on your shoulders. The cluster is not too keen on talks with outsiders. Therefore, Ambassadors Spock and Rozhenko will stay to support you. Spock's expertise is unmatched, Dick. Make good use of it.*"

That's something, at least, the captain thought. Suddenly, he felt old. Old and tired. He thought of Karen, of Nanietta Bacco, of the Borg, the Dominion and the Typhon Pact. He wondered when all this would come to an end. *Whether* it would come to an end, or if they would continue to be hamsters in a wheel of violence, slaving away day in and day out without making any progress, because the game they were playing didn't have fair rules.

You mustn't think like that, he admonished himself. *Anyone who thinks like that has already lost. And they've lost more than just their ideals.*

The *Prometheus* was in the Lembatta Cluster to help. It was meant to carry the metaphorical torch into the darkness to bring light. They were supposed to save lives, and to minimize dangers. That was all that mattered. That was their mission, and nothing had changed.

"*Qo'noS has ordered the* Bortas *to stay with you also,*" the fleet admiral continued. "*I've heard that the High Council is pleasantly surprised with Captain Kromm's commitment, and they are hoping for further accomplishments. I dare say that this is the Council speaking and not the chancellor. Martok has remained silent.*"

Adams nodded, knowingly. Kromm's straightforward, ruthless behavior stood in contrast to the chancellor, who sympathized with the Federation. If it was down to Martok, another ship would be out here with the *Prometheus*; a ship with a more agreeable commanding officer than Kromm. And if it were down to the council, the entire fleet would be present in the cluster. The *Bortas* seemed to serve as a compromise.

"Look after yourself, Dick. You're far from home and our protective hand doesn't reach far into the Lembatta Cluster. But I'm afraid you're exactly where we need you—urgently. Good luck, Prometheus. Akaar out."

The monitor went black briefly, replaced by the Federation emblem.

Exactly where we need you. Sighing, Adams rose, switched the monitor off, and left the ready room.

The bridge greeted him with its usual hustle and bustle. Ak Namur sat at conn, Carson at ops. Winter briefly looked up from his communications station, and Roaas left the chair in the center of the bridge, as soon as Adams walked through the doorway.

"Report, Commander."

"Nothing to report, sir," the Caitian announced. "According to your orders we have calculated and set a course for the inner Lembatta Cluster, but we're still waiting for the green light from Fleet Headquarters before we proceed. What did the admiral say?"

Adams looked at the main screen. The bottom half was filled with the northern hemisphere of Onferin. Above it, he saw the strange view of the red nebulas and glowing stars of the Lembatta Cluster.

"Mr. Winter, put me through to the *Bortas*."

"Aye, sir." A few seconds passed before the young German spoke again. "Link established, sir."

"On screen."

Onferin and space vanished and were replaced by the

Bortas's bridge. Adams saw Captain Kromm in his command chair. The Klingon leaned forward, propped his hands on his thighs and displayed a triumphant grin on his face. To his right stood Ambassador Alexander Rozhenko. His almost stoic calmness stood in vast contrast to the captain.

"Adams," Kromm said. *"The ambassador and I have been expecting you. So? What's the news from Earth? The High Council has already given us the order to continue the journey, and to hunt down these cowardly* petaQ *until we're standing before their bleeding corpses. What about you?"*

"Starfleet is far less keen on bloodshed," Adams said dryly. "But their mission for us is just as clearly stated as yours, Captain: We will accompany you into the cluster. For the good of all, this mystery about the Renao needs to be unraveled before there are more casualties to lament."

Kromm threw his head back and laughed. *"That's the way I like you, Adams. So, the prey has been flushed out, our blades are sharp. Are we going on a hunt?"*

Adams settled in his chair, his eyes fixed on the screen. He sensed his crew around him, heard the familiar humming of the engines in Jenna's engine room and the quiet signals of the various bridge stations. And suddenly he knew that Akaar was wrong. He wasn't far away from home. He had his home with him.

"Go ahead, Captain Kromm," said Richard Adams, nodding at his counterpart. "The *Prometheus* is right behind you."

The Klingon battle cruiser and the Federation battleship left Onferin's orbit, gathering speed. Ahead of them in the stellar nebula glowed the red suns of the Lembatta Cluster. Somewhere out there was the answer to the question what was happening to the Renao. Adams had to find it—as soon as possible—or the galaxy would face another war.

ACKNOWLEDGEMENTS

A novel cannot be written in a vacuum—metaphorically or literally. Many people have contributed to this book, and the authors would like to take the opportunity to thank them.

Markus Rohde and Andreas Mergenthaler from Cross Cult shared our dream to write German *Star Trek* novels for the very first time, and they tirelessly worked toward making this dream come true. Julia Courmont from CPLG—Copyright Promotions paved our way to the USA, and John Van Citters from CBS gave our project his blessing. For that, we are very grateful. We would also like to thank Tobias Richter, the digital wizard, who not only created a CGI model of the *Prometheus* for this trilogy but also embedded it into three marvelous cover motifs. We're also grateful to Anika Klüver, our editor, who picked up the small deficiencies that our manuscript contained at first with sharp eyes and pointed them out to us with gentle words.

Furthermore, we deeply appreciate all the creative *Star Trek* minds beyond the Pond for the fantastic stories they created. Naming all those who inspired us would go too far. We would, however, like to mention John Jackson Miller, who took the time to link his *Prey* trilogy with our *Prometheus* trilogy. He did so very subtly, but every reference will help to tie our novels into the *Trek* literary tapestry.

On a personal note, we'd like to express our eternal gratitude to our families for providing a creative environment that kept us full of enthusiasm during our journey through this project. In moments of self-doubts or acute writing blockages, there was always someone around with a comforting word and a cold beer to pick us up and get the warp drive back online. We really appreciate it!

ABOUT THE AUTHORS

Christian Humberg is a freelance author who has written for series including *Star Trek* and *Doctor Who*. His works have so far been translated into five languages and won German-language prizes. He lives in Mainz, Germany.

Bernd Perplies is a German writer, translator and geek journalist. After graduating in Movie Sciences and German Literature he started working at the Film Museum in Frankfurt. In 2008 he made his debut with the well received "Tarean" trilogy. Since then has written numerous novels, most of which have been nominated for prestigious German genre awards. He lives near Stuttgart.

APPENDIX

1. U.S.S. *Prometheus* Personnel

1.1. Alpha Shift

Commanding Officer Captain Richard Adams
First Officer/Tactical Commander Roaas
Conn/Pilot Lieutenant Jassat ak Namur
Second Officer/Ops Lt. Commander Sarita Carson
Communications Ensign Paul Winter
Security Chief/Environmental Lt. Commander Lenissa zh'Thiin

Chief Engineer Lt. Commander Jenna Winona Kirk
Science Officer Lt. Commander Mendon
Chief Medical Officer Doctor Geron Barai

1.2. Additional Crewmembers

Commanding Officer Beta Shift Lt. Commander Senok
Commanding Officer Gamma Shift Lieutenant Shantherin th'Talias
Deputy Chief of Security Lieutenant John Paxon
Deputy Chief Engineer Lieutenant Tabor Resk
Deputy Chief Medical Officer Lt. Commander Maddy Calloway
Transporter Officer Chief Wilorin

Counselor Isabelle Courmont
Barkeeper Moba
EMH-II (EMH-XI) Doctor Tric

2. I.K.S *Bortas* Personnel

Commanding Officer Captain Kromm
First Officer Commander L'emka
Officer/Tactics Commander Chumarr
Conn/Pilot Lieutenant Toras
Ops Bekk Raspin
Communications Lieutenant Klarn
Security Chief Commander Rooth

Chief Engineer Commander Nuk
Science Officer Lieutenant K'mpah
Chief Medical Officer Doctor Drax
Transporter Operator Bekk Brukk

ALSO BY

BERND PERPLIES & CHRISTIAN HUMBERG

STAR TREK
PROMETHEUS

IN THE HEART OF CHAOS

The situation in the Lembatta Cluster is deteriorating rapidly. Fleets from the Federation and Klingon Empire are heading for the borders. The crews of the U.S.S. *Prometheus* and I.K.S. *Bortas* are racing against time to break the cycle of violence that is spreading through the Alpha Quadrant. Adams and Kromm are on the trail of a secret weapons facility, but instead discover an enemy from their pasts who seems utterly unstoppable. Together, they search for the answers to their questions, before the galaxy goes down in flames.

Available November 2018

TITANBOOKS.COM